MILA 2.0
RENEGADE

ALSO BY DEBRA DRIZA:

MILA 2.0

L.A DE 2.0

DEBRA DRIZA

HarperCollins *Children's Books*

First published in the USA in 2014 by Katherine Tegen Books,
an imprint of HarperCollins *Publishers*
First published in Great Britain by
HarperCollins *Children's Books* in 2014
HarperCollins *Children's Books* is a division of HarperCollins*Publishers* Ltd

77-85 Fulham Palace Road, Hammersmith, London, W6 8JB

www.harpercollins.co.uk

1

ISBN 978-0-00-750730-6

Printed and bound in England by Clays Ltd, St Ives plc

MIX
Paper from
responsible sources
FSC™ C007454

FSC™ is a non-profit international organisation established to promote
the responsible management of the world's forests. Products carrying the
FSC label are independently certified to assure consumers that they come
from forests that are managed to meet the social, economic and
ecological needs of present and future generations,
and other controlled sources.

Find out more about HarperCollins and the environment at
www.harpercollins.co.uk/green

MILA
RENEGADE 2.0

ONE

If I could record real-life moments in my head like a DVR, this afternoon would top the list as one of the most replayed. Far fetched? Maybe for a normal girl. But normal wasn't a word that applied to my life anymore. Though, at this precise moment, I was giving it my best shot. Focusing on the now—just me, salt, sand, and the blazing sun baking my skin and reflecting off the dark-haired boy's head like a million tiny sparklers.

White froth lapped at the shore mere inches from my toes—6.15, to be exact—but my focus remained intent on his head, bobbing out past the breaking waves. He dove under them with the fluid ease of a sea creature, and even from here I could catch glimpses of the sheer bliss on his face. Hunter was completely in his element.

Enjoy it while you can, I silently urged him. We wouldn't be staying long.

Or maybe we would. I had decisions to make yet, about my future.

Overhead, a seagull squawked before dive-bombing a leftover morsel on the sand. At the harsh cry, something rippled in the far recesses of my mind, then disappeared.

I shivered, like the sun had dipped beneath a cloud.

Hunter swam with sure strokes in my direction, water curling behind him in a huge arch. I held my breath. Compared to the wave, he looked so small and insignificant. The water swept him up, and in an explosion of white foam, he vanished.

I jumped to my feet, but then he rose from the water like an offering from the sea. My phantom heart returned to its regularly scheduled pumping cycle. I sank back onto my motel towel. Silly. Of course he was fine.

Not that I didn't have reason for major anxiety issues.

He padded toward me, water beading on his bare skin, his shaggy hair clinging to his neck and causing rivulets to rain down his chest.

"Sure you don't want to come in? The water feels great."

"No thanks." Too hard to be on alert when you were in the middle of the ocean. But of course, I hadn't said that. My no-swimsuit excuse was much less of an eyebrow-raiser.

Hunter threw himself onto the sand beside me, flinging

tiny droplets onto my bare arm. I watched them cling to my skin, and Hunter's gaze followed mine.

"It's not because of that, right?" His gaze skimmed my left shoulder, which was covered by the sleeve of my slightly rumpled T-shirt. "Your arm's okay in water?"

"Yeah, it's fine." But his attention made me self-conscious. I folded both arms over my bent knees, making sure the right one ended up on top. Not because I was bashful about my prosthetic limb, like Hunter assumed when he saw wires protruding from it like busted bicycle spokes back in Clearwater, but because my arm wasn't really prosthetic.

Not in the true sense of the word, anyway. Though, technically speaking, I guess you could consider all of me prosthetic. One of the many pitfalls of being an android.

My stomach twisted, making me sigh. Another pitfall? Finding a tactful way to tell the boy you liked the truth about your little issue with nonhumanness.

In my defense—I didn't know him all that well. Not unless you considered a shared truck crash, a late-night interlude involving a barn, and a date gone wrong to be the cornerstones of a profound relationship. Yet from the moment I'd met him, something about him called to me. Maybe because we were both loners. Maybe that was what formed the basis for our instant connection. All I knew was that after my world had imploded two days ago, I'd made a panicked phone call and Hunter had answered and here we were, in Virginia Beach.

He trailed his fingers along the area between my sleeve and elbow. I could feel the individual granules of sand that clung to his skin, but I was more focused on the thrill generated by his touch.

"I can't get over how real it feels," he said. "I had no idea they'd come so far in prosthetics."

"It's a prototype." I looked into his eyes. "Experimental. Seems to be working okay."

He shook his head. "I'm not sure I'd have the courage to be a test subject."

Test subject, ha. That was one way to describe it. Not that I'd really had a choice in the matter. "The risks were low."

"Still, you're like on the frontier of science."

If only he knew . . .

"Do you realize how many people will benefit because you were willing to take a chance?"

"Don't make me sound like a hero. I'm not."

He grinned. "Modest, too."

I flicked some sand at him, hoping to get us off this subject. His eyes narrowed. Then, he leaned over and shook his mass of dark hair. Water drops flew everywhere, catching me in the face. I threw up my hands and squealed.

"I'm sorry, did I get you wet?" he said, all false innocence and fluttering lashes.

"Fiend," I said, but my smile faded after a few moments.

Silence hung between us, filled with the repetitive roar of waves, voices of the scattered tourists enjoying the early October sun, and the expectant hush of things left unsaid. I'd yet to explain to Hunter the reasons behind the panic-struck phone call that had summoned him to my side.

He hadn't pressured me, but it was only a matter of time. I couldn't expect someone to drive across five states at the drop of a hat without rewarding him with some kind of feasible explanation. The problem was—in my case, the truth sounded less feasible than the most fantastical lie.

"Are you sure your parents are okay with this?" I swept my arms wide to indicate him, me, us, Virginia Beach. All of it.

I saw his broad shoulders stiffen, watched his toes shovel into the sand. He averted his gaze. So apparently I wasn't the only one hiding something. That probably shouldn't have made me feel better, but in a perverse way, it did. "Do they not know you're here?"

A shadow passed over his expression, but it was chased away an instant later by his smile. "Oh, they know. They told me that I should come help you. As a matter of fact—and don't take this wrong—but when I told Mom about the first time I saw you at Dairy Queen, she encouraged me to get to know you, make new friends." His smile eased into a wide, off-center grin. "Not that I needed any encouragement."

Warmth blossomed beneath my ribs. I remembered that day when he'd walked into the Dairy Queen while I'd been there with some other girls. Something about his easygoing demeanor and searching gaze had pulled me in instantly, but I'd never realized he'd felt the same.

I stood and skipped a few feet forward to where the sea lapped at the shore. Stooping down, I cupped my hands and scooped up a handful of frigid water, careful to keep my back to Hunter so he couldn't spot my growing grin. The next instant, I whirled.

"Catch!" I said, flinging the water at Hunter.

He sputtered when the water unexpectedly hit his face, and the sight of his shock—open mouth, wide eyes—was so comical, I giggled. I backed up, skipping and dancing away.

"Oh, you're in for it now," he mock-growled, jumping to his feet with that same lithe grace I remembered. With his low-slung board shorts and his wet hair glistening in waves around his neck, he looked like a beach bum. My gaze skimmed his bare chest and I swallowed. Make that god. Beach god.

I backed away down the shore and he raced toward me, kicking up water at my legs. We exchanged splashes, laughing like toddlers, and then he grabbed my hand and pretended to drag me toward the oncoming waves. He stopped before we went too deep, and we stood there together, allowing the foamy white ocean to swirl over our ankles.

The water, the sun beating down, the drag of the tide. All of it flitted through my mind, reminding me of . . . something. Before I knew what I was doing, I was spinning in a circle, twirling with my arms outstretched. Feeling the wet sand squish between my toes.

Twirling, in the sand. Another niggle. A pinch, in a corner of my mind.

I remembered this joy, this gladness.

The next instant, it was gone.

I felt a tug at my hair, and opened my eyes. Hunter's face was only a few inches away. I inhaled salt and sweat, sandalwood and a hint of sunscreen. "Don't worry about looking too cool or anything," he teased. But his wink suggested approval of my beach antics.

He stepped closer, until our toes touched beneath a tiny hill of sand. The instant shock of awareness intensified when he bent forward, his breath tickling my ear, triggering my heart to pound harder. A slow, steady warmth traveled through my body, from my head to my arms, all the way down to my tingling toes. I yearned for his nearness in a way that I longed for nothing else. Maybe that was the reason I'd called him. Grief and fear had nearly dragged me under, and in the past, Hunter had been one of my only sources of comfort.

"Sorry," I said, struggling to keep my tone light.

"Don't be. You're just . . . you."

I turned my head, gazing off into the distance. Just me? And who might that be?

In a stroke of irony that thankfully only I could see, red words blinked to life in my head, accompanied by an all-too-familiar digitized voice. My voice.

Apparently the universe's way of reminding me of exactly who—no, *what*—I was.

Threat detected: 4.52 mi.

I froze. Four and a half miles? What the—

Two jets, due west.

I whirled, searching the air for a sign of them.

"What are you looking at?" Hunter asked, cupping a hand to his forehead to shield his eyes from the sun.

There.

"Jets."

"There's a huge naval base in Virginia Beach, isn't there? Cool."

Not cool. Not cool at all. My hands tightened as images from the past deluged me, with crystal-clear precision. Suburbans, men with guns. An airplane filled with soldiers, transporting Mom and me to a secret compound. Tiny, barren holding cells. The salt-and-pepper hair of General Holland, and the smug satisfaction that oozed from him when he issued the order to have me terminated.

Mom. Bleeding out after being shot on Holland's command. By one of Holland's men.

The gasp-clench of loss wrenched my chest and almost doubled me over, reminding me that Mom was gone. Dead. Murdered by a madman under the guise of defending his country.

I'd never see her smile at me again. Never hear her voice. Never tell her that I loved her.

"I wonder what kind they are?" he said, snapping me out of the dark place.

I didn't answer, because just then, something moved within my eyes. I actually felt my pupils contract. A thin layer slid open, accompanied by a subtle clicking that only I could hear.

Zoom: Activated.

Another click, and the planes enlarged to fill my field of vision, like I'd fired up a pair of high-tech binoculars. The images grew and grew in size, until I could capture enough detail to place them.

F/A-18 military jets.

A 3-D schematic of the jets burst to life before me, rotating to show me all sides.

Red letters blinked behind my eyes:

Presently unarmed–drill mode likely

"Not sure," I murmured, turning away in relief. But as the weight drained from my limbs, a heavy certainty filled my heart. The planes served as a forceful reminder that this carefree beach time with Hunter was coming to an end. No matter how hard I tried to push reality away, it kept sweeping back over me, as surely as the tide rolled in.

And like the rhythmic cycle of the tide, two names repeated themselves, over and over again.

Richard Grady. Sarah. Names that had slipped from Mom's lips not long before she'd died. I was most confused by Sarah.

"You always were so brave, Sarah. So brave," she'd said. But she'd been talking to me, looking at me. Why would she mistake me for this unknown Sarah?

Abruptly, I started in the direction of our motel. "Let's go."

I could tell Hunter was confused by my sudden urge to leave, but at the moment, I wasn't up to explaining everything. I needed to get away, to return to the relative safety of the motel room.

As we walked, we passed an amusement park across the street, a motionless Ferris wheel towering in the sky. As if mocking me with all the normalcy I would never have. Hunter had once taken me to a carnival. In those brief moments, I'd caught a glimpse of a *real life*. What it might feel like to actually be human.

Maybe that was another reason why I'd called him. He always made me feel as though I was more than just some fancy gadget created in a lab.

After one last longing glance, I looked away. I couldn't

live in the past, but I also couldn't have a future until I learned everything I needed to know about my past.

Richard Grady. This Sarah person. The other Milas.

Maybe once I knew everything, I would finally be free to create a real life. Maybe even one that included Hunter.

We continued down the boardwalk, though I could sense Hunter's concern in the way he kept sneaking quick glances at my profile. To the east, the waves rumbled toward the sand, mingling with the excited squeals of the few scattered children. From Hunter's brief conversation with the woman selling ice cream earlier, we knew the crowds had dwindled considerably since summer. But there were still plenty of tourists and locals out sightseeing and soaking up the sun.

My gaze caught on two men up ahead. I quickly dismissed them. Not fit enough. No weapons.

Too many people here for comfort. But at least we didn't look conspicuous amid a sea of other pedestrians. Plus, Virginia Beach had seemed like the perfect spot—I had such great memories of this place.

Even if those memories were programmed rather than real.

"So, is everything okay? You seem pretty tense."

"I'm fine. Just a little headache," I said with a carefree wave of my hand, even though carefree had long ago fled my capabilities. A shriek jerked my head to the right, before

I realized it was just a young girl, fleeing an older boy and his two handfuls of wet sand.

My hand closed around my emerald pendant while something flashed in the back of my head. A man, and a woman, dancing along the shoreline. Gulls shrieking overhead, the roar-crash of waves—

Memory banks compromised, defragment.

Image recall.

The flicker of memory, gone. No—more like, stolen.

I shuddered, and Hunter was there in a flash. He put his arm around my shoulders and pulled me close. "Maybe we should go back to the room—it's going to be dark soon anyway. And we still need to talk."

Talk. Right. I couldn't tell you how much I was looking forward to that.

I mean, how did that conversation go, exactly? Thanks so much for coming and oh, by the way—I'm an android.

I must have stiffened, because Hunter sighed. "I'm here for you, okay? You have to know that."

I allowed the unnecessary air to exit my nonhuman lungs in a huge exhalation. I peeked up at him, afraid of what I might find in his faded-denim eyes, but they were soft. Warm. Inviting.

Like he was just waiting for me to open up and let him in.

"Thank you."

He lifted my hand and traced my knuckles with his thumb. Then he shrugged, a loose-limbed movement of his shoulders, and I was transported back to homeroom, where I'd seen him perform that motion for the first time.

Homeroom. I'd been in homeroom less than two weeks ago. Now, classrooms and blackboards and high school cafeterias seemed impossibly out of reach. Funny how torture and death could do that to you.

We rounded the final corner, to where the Sea Breeze Motel sat about half a block down. The lobby was tiny. Shabby, too, with faded green upholstered chairs and scarred wood floors. Rooms at the Sea Breeze came cheap for a reason—nothing looked to have been upgraded in decades. But at least it was clean.

The pulse of anxiety in my ears throbbed louder and louder the closer we came to the motel. Once we got to our room, I was supposed to magically conjure up a way to tell Hunter the truth. Right.

Why wasn't there an android program to facilitate the important stuff?

The motel room mirror was still fogged with steam from my shower. I rubbed a small, blurry opening in the cloudy white and my face stared back at me. I lifted my hand, turned it this way and that, then traced my knuckles with my thumb. The way Hunter had earlier. I rubbed a bigger circle, my skin glistening under the harsh light. I looked up and down my figure, trying to see myself through Hunter's eyes. I looked real enough—skin, muscle, curves—but would I feel real to him?

That thought made my face grow hot. My gaze floated upward and I was surprised to see a hint of pink blooming in my cheeks. We'd never even kissed. Why was I thinking of him touching me?

As I shoved the mortifying thoughts from my head and lifted the brush to my short, platinum blond hair—which I'd dyed from black just after Hunter arrived—my hand trembled. Another motel room, another mirror. My long, brown hair floating to the floor, while Mom stood behind me, her blue eyes worried.

I turned away and finished drying off with the skimpy motel towel. I slipped into a pair of navy sweatpants with a big "I ♥ Virginia Beach" on the butt—classy—and a plain white tank. Even less couture than my cozy flannel jammies from home, but hey, what could you expect for $8 on the clearance rack? I couldn't afford to squander the money Lucas had given me on fancy clothes.

Lucas. I winced, like I did every time my thoughts turned to the guy who'd been injured helping me escape from General Holland's secret SMART Ops compound. Lucas, the nerdy proctor of my insane tests—the budding scientist with a heart of gold. Thanks to him, I not only had my life, such as it is, but I also didn't have to strut around in an outfit I'd bought off a homeless woman in D.C. *That* shirt had been covered in stains that refused to yield—at least not to the tiny packets of detergent provided by the coin dispenser downstairs.

I caught another glimpse of myself in the mirror and grimaced. Procrastination, thy name is Mila. After sticking out my tongue at my bedraggled reflection, I reached for the door and opened it with what I hoped was a confident smile. Time to face Hunter and his questions. Time to face the truth. I had this.

Or not. I barreled forward, only to feel my resolve fizzle when I caught sight of his lanky form, sprawled across the bed by the window.

"Ahem."

He bolted upright, as if the state of Virginia had just broadcasted that motel-room reclining was illegal. He snagged the remote from between folds of the crumpled comforter and turned down the volume, then scooted to the edge of the bed. Very proper, with his feet on the ground and hands in his lap.

O-kay. I sat opposite him, combing my fingers through my wet hair to give myself something to do. The quiet thickened, so I distracted myself by counting red circles on the curtains—fifty-two.

He looked at me before quickly averting his eyes. "I

forgot to tell you, I like your new haircut," he finally blurted to the remote in his hands.

"Thanks." No need to tell him I was on version two already since the last time we'd met.

At least not yet.

The bed creaked like an old floorboard when he shifted his weight. His gaze skimmed me again, taking in my bare shoulders, dampened from where my hair dripped down, and then his eyes dropped to his lap again. He cleared his throat and that tiny "ahem" crackled between us.

I crossed my arms, his unease making me all too aware of the fact that I was in a motel room with a boy, not a chaperone or parent in sight, and oh by the way, we were going to spend the night together.

For the second time in under two minutes, heat crawled up my cheeks. Not *spend the night*, spend the night. But still. When I'd called Hunter and begged him to come help me, the potential for extreme awkwardness hadn't really been front and center in my mind. I'd been consumed with grief and panic. Thoughts of Hunter had gotten me through some of the darkest moments—before my mother died in my arms. Then thoughts weren't enough. I needed someone I could trust. Even though we'd only known each other for a few weeks, the way Hunter looked at me as though I were important, as though I mattered . . . it made me feel safe. There was no one else I could call.

Hunter started tapping a drumbeat on his thigh—a nervous habit I'd noticed when I'd first met him—and even though his nearness made my artificial nerve endings fire and my synthetic heartbeat quicken, I felt the tension between us like a concrete wall.

Oh, wow. This was going so well.

"Is it just me, or is this cohabitating thing kind of weird?"

"Not just you," I replied in a rush. So fast that his lips lifted into that familiar, quirky smile. Something sizzled down my spine, once more making me want things that could never be mine. Things I could have if I were more than a bundle of circuits and transmitters. Things like a normal life.

Things I could maybe have if I chose not to follow through on Mom's dying words.

We faced each other across the short gap between the beds, our knees close to touching.

"How about we make a pledge?" he asked. "I'll start. I, Hunter Lowe, solemnly swear to stay in my own bed, except in case of emergencies. Or if you're snoring really loud—then I can come over and elbow you. Or, you know, if you invite me over—just to watch TV or something," he tacked on hastily, when my eyes widened. "Wow, I never realized that you had a gutter mind. Tsk." He shook his head.

"Whatever." I grinned back, then remembered my exact

thoughts in the bathroom and tried not to cringe in embarrassment. "And I pledge to stay in my own bed, unless you make more terrible jokes like that. In which case I'm going to clobber you with your own pillow."

"You drive a hard bargain, but deal. And now that the horribly awkward moment is over, are you ready to tell me what's going on?"

His smile didn't waver, but that was because he was totally clueless. The truth was sure to slap that smile right off his face. I'd had a difficult time believing it. I still hadn't accepted it. How could I expect him to?

I bunched my hands into the comforter, rough from multiple washings, and squeezed. I could do this. I could do this. I could—

The words congealed in my throat. I swallowed hard.

"I promise not to judge," he said.

So many things about him got to me: The softness of his voice. The way he leaned toward me, as if his life hung on my every word. The slowness of his hand sliding down my hair. The way he twirled several errant strands around his finger.

My eyes fluttered shut. There was something about his sincerity, and how it mingled with the sparks his touch ignited, that filled a tiny bit of the void inside me. I couldn't lose that, and being honest with him might lead to him walking out the door without ever looking back.

I know this is going to sound crazy . . .

What would I do without him to remind me that a part of me, at least, was alive?

You see, the thing is . . .

And what if he left and told someone what I really was?

The secret I've been hiding all along . . .

I opened my mouth to tell him the truth, but my backup story came pouring out instead. "Mom and I got in a huge argument . . . ," I started, then faltered.

Was I really doing this? Lying, to the one person I had left in the world?

"Because you were moving to Germany, right?"

The attentive tilt of his head encouraged me to continue, but I was momentarily blindsided. I remembered the frantic phone call I'd made to Hunter from the airport in Canada, before Mom and I were snagged by Holland's men. I'd told him I was leaving Clearwater, and that was probably the last time I'd told him the truth.

I willed myself again to set things right with him, but failed.

"No, she . . . she told me I was adopted."

It was selfish of me to lie. Utterly, unforgivably selfish. I couldn't deny that.

But then I thought of the day Mom handed me that iPod. The day a power-hungry general's drawl changed my life forever and ripped away my very identity. Simply by telling me the truth, he'd erased my entire life, stolen my parents, and blasted my hope. *Truth*—was it really that great? Because in my experience, it was a taker. It took away all that was good, leaving behind pain and fear and an endless funnel of betrayal.

"She just dropped that on you, out of nowhere? So the guy who you thought was your father, the one who just died . . . ?"

"Not my real dad."

"Wow. That's . . . wow."

I bit my lip and averted my gaze, my stomach clenching, revolting against my betrayal of Mom's memory. Yes, she'd programmed me with false memories of a father who didn't exist, but as a way of protecting me. And it had worked. While I'd known sadness before that day in the barn, I hadn't really known despair.

So perhaps keeping Hunter in the dark right now was actually less cruel?

"I'm sorry, Mila. That must be really tough."

Even though I was trying to convince myself that I was somehow doing Hunter a favor, his sympathy was just too much. I rose and strode over to the window—there was no way I could look him in the eye right now. I stared outside while my fingers curled around the worn wooden sill.

Crunch.

Crap, too hard. I eased up immediately, but not before

new jagged lines branched out into the already faded white paint. Hopefully Hunter wouldn't notice.

"So, what now? Did she tell you anything about them?"

When I didn't answer right away, he added, "We don't have to talk about it if you don't want to."

I felt like such a fraud, even when I was silent. Justifications for lying kept filing through my mind, like someone shuffling a deck of cards. For instance, if Hunter was going to stay with me, then I had to have a valid reason for hunting down Richard Grady. And him knowing the truth about me could possibly put us both in danger—if he remained unaware of the situation, I could have more control.

But the guilt building inside me made me doubt I could keep up this charade for more than a day.

I just needed to work my way up to breaking the news.

Tomorrow. I'd tell him tomorrow.

"No, it's fine. That's what this trip is all about. She gave me a name, Richard Grady. But that's it. She's refusing to help me find him, or give me any other clues whatsoever. She got incredibly pissed when I told her I'd look for him all on my own."

"When you called, you said your mom was . . . gone."

I nodded jerkily, like something was suddenly wrong with one of my mechanisms. "I know. I meant she . . . she left me behind."

Mom's broken body appeared behind my eyes. I saw

her sinking into the depths of the Potomac, and her voice echoed in my ears.

Find Richard Grady . . . he knows . . .

Her last words, right before one of Holland's bullets killed her.

Holland. Just the name ignited a fiery, churning hatred within my core.

My fingertips had been sliding down the smooth glass, but now they pushed harder, full of pent-up frustration. The window creaked in protest, and I hastily yanked my hand away.

"So does this Grady guy live in Virginia?" Hunter asked. "Is that why you're here?"

"I thought he was. I'd found some information, but it turned out to be a dead end."

Please don't ask me any more questions. I don't know how many more lies I can tell you.

My back still to him, I said, "Anyway, thank you so much for coming. The thought of continuing to do this on my own . . . it just . . . thank you."

I heard the bed creak, heard his soft footfalls. I spun around to face Hunter. His soulful eyes, filled with compassion and understanding, nearly had me confessing everything. In this moment, I wanted to believe he could accept what I was, but in the likelihood that he couldn't, the dangers to me would increase. Again I tried to reassure myself that my lies offered him a shield of protection as well. He couldn't reveal what he didn't know.

"Any time," he said gently. "I could tell when you called that something bad had happened. I can't believe she went to Germany without you. Who does that?"

"Well, I can meet her there, if I want to, but I'm not sure if I do," I said, hoping to salvage some sliver of Hunter's respect for my mom. "I know being adopted isn't the end of the world, but I have a right to meet my real father, and she just didn't see it that way."

"I don't blame you for wanting to find him. It sucks that your mom never told you the truth." Then he cocked his head, like he was noticing something strange.

"What?" I demanded, inwardly panicking. Had he seen me crack the windowsill?

"Nothing. It's just—don't be mad, but based on how jumpy you've been, I was sort of expecting something a little crazier. Like your mom was abducted by aliens."

I stared at him incredulously for a moment, before losing it. "I can't even—" I gasped, trying to talk through the laughter and failing.

"What can I say? I had a crush on Scully from *The X-Files* growing up."

The ball of tension that hadn't left my gut since I'd been on the run was beginning to disintegrate. "You hide it well, Hunter Lowe, but you are a total nerd."

His eyes suddenly filled with shock, and he glanced toward the window. I was on instant alert again. "What?" I said, listening intently, pulse starting to pound in my ears.

No human threat detected.

A car, a group of kids in the distance, the faint rumble of the ocean. Nothing of concern.

"Shhh, be careful how loud you say that. I don't want my secret getting out."

I groaned. "Hate to tell you, but it's too late for that."

"Those are fighting words." With a mischievous smile, he grabbed my wrists and pulled me toward him, whirling me around at the last second until my back was pressed firmly against his chest. One of his arms wrapped loosely around my neck, the other around my waist.

I stiffened at first—hello, there was a cute boy pressed against me—but then the sensation of belonging coursed through me, too potent to resist. I closed my eyes, savoring the solid feel of his body. This . . . this was exactly what I needed. Hunter was exactly what I needed.

"Don't worry. I promise I won't leave you behind. I'll be with you every step of the way, if you let me."

Hearing him say that, I didn't think I could ever feel so amazing and awful at the same time.

"We should probably get some sleep, since we'll be on the road tomorrow," I said.

I slipped under the covers of my bed and despite

everything, I was completely conscious that he was climbing into the next bed over. Heat fanned itself through my arms and legs, a feeling that I was pretty sure had nothing to do with the slight weight of the frayed blue comforter.

"Good night, Mila."

"Good night."

I clicked off the light and willed my body to relax in the darkened room.

Night vision: Activated.

With the help of one of my android functions, everything blazed back into view. Ugh, so not helping. Meanwhile, Hunter's breathing turned rhythmic and slow and for the first time I could remember, I envied him.

I squeezed my eyes shut. Take that, stupid night vision. But the blackness only sent my tension skyrocketing. Because instead of seeing our motel room, now I was remembering a different one. The last time I'd stayed in a motel, Mom and I had been woken in the middle of the night by scouts from the Vita Obscura, an organization that wanted to gut me like a fish to see how I worked—and then sell my technology to the highest bidder. We escaped, but who was to say it couldn't happen again?

A perfect image burst into my head. Mom tackling one of the men, binding his hands with a zip tie. Mom, back at Clearwater Ranch, her long blond hair pulled back into a practical ponytail as she headed to the barn.

Mom, staring at me as the light in her blue eyes faded.

A sob unfurled and I put a hand to my mouth, trying to stifle it. No good. The other bed creaked. I heard Hunter's bare feet pad onto the carpet, and then a moment later his arms surrounded me.

I went rigid at first—I'd never been in bed with a boy or been held this tightly before—but as he whispered, "Shhhh, it's going to be okay," I gradually snuggled against him.

My back fit against his chest so perfectly, and oh god, he was so warm. I could feel his breath ruffling my hair. Suddenly, I wanted nothing more than to turn over and be face-to-face, to feel his lips graze mine.

I lay silently for a moment, summoning up the courage to do just that. Minutes passed and after a while, his body felt heavy against mine. Had he fallen asleep again?

A whirring in my brain, and then the red lights flashed:

Pulse: 48 bpm.

Breathing rate: 8 bpm.

Sleep state: Likely.

Leave it to my android functions to remind me that really, truly *being* with Hunter was something that would never be possible.

After ten minutes of lying there, motionless, I eased myself out from under his right arm, my body freezing when his breathing altered. But it evened out again, so I slipped to my feet, feeling his fingertips slide against my arm before falling away, the loss of physical contact both freeing and terrifying at the same time. A sharp pang almost made me climb back in and nestle up against him.

But the strange room, the noises, even Hunter's presence—everything was foreign and the ghost of the past still hung over me. Sadness, anger, fear . . . a whirlwind of emotions threatened to consume me, and a giant android self-implosion was about the last thing I wanted to foist onto Hunter right now.

Grabbing the key from the bureau, I put on my shoes and crept to the door.

Sometimes, when my feelings overwhelmed me, I wondered if I shouldn't try to emulate Three, just a little. My android twin never struggled with terror—or fear—or the heartbreaking pain that made your phantom heart feel like it might crumble to pieces.

Sometimes, when the agony of Mom's loss felt like someone had picked up a saw and excised the most important part of me, I wondered if maybe Three was onto something.

Then I pictured Hunter's sleeping face and the thought slowly disappeared.

TWO

"Where are you going?"

My hand was on the doorknob when I heard Hunter's voice, a little roughened by the bit of rest he'd had. A part of me wanted to stay here with him, but everything was closing in on me. I needed to get out of this motel room.

"I couldn't sleep. I thought I'd take a walk, tire myself out."

"I'll go with you."

"You don't have to."

"Mila, it's late. I'm not letting you go out there by yourself."

His protectiveness touched something deep inside me. If there were any dangers out there, I was better equipped to handle them, but he didn't know that.

"Besides," he added, "you still owe me a date."

I couldn't stop myself from smiling. Our little trip to the carnival a few weeks ago had been met with continual interruptions, including horrific memories of a past I didn't know existed. As much as I wanted to be alone, I also hoped maybe this time our date would be normal.

I heard him tying his shoes, tugging at the laces hard, and then his soft footfalls as he approached. I opened the door and stepped out.

I gulped down huge breaths of salty humid air—useless, since my lungs weren't really lungs, though I seemed to have a hard time remembering that. Not many pedestrians were out at this hour. Weeknight, off-season.

Hunter shut the door behind us and tested to make sure it was locked. Then he stepped up beside me and threaded his fingers through mine. "Let's head down to the board-walk."

As we walked along, a little orange dot blinked on a map before me, showing my trajectory and every street option nearby. I was thankful that my internal GPS system had finally kicked in again after conking out for a while post-escape. Not that I needed the GPS right now. Hunter was guiding me.

We reached the boardwalk. The fragrance of the salt air seemed heavier, and a cool breeze surged off the ocean, whipping my hair in periodic bursts. An almost-full moon dominated the sky, lighting patches of inky water with a soft, silvery glow.

"Thank you for coming out here with me."

Turning his head slightly, he met my gaze. "That's why I'm here."

As if summoned by his sincerity, the truth bubbled up in my throat. Right here, right now. I could end the subterfuge. I wanted to. Desperately.

I glanced back out at the ocean, at the secrets churning underwater, and the moment passed.

"What about school?" I asked.

He tipped his head to the side. "Fall break. We have a week before we have to be back. Not a lot of time to find your dad, but enough maybe."

Maybe, and if not, I couldn't ask him to flunk out because of me. But the thought of moving forward with no one to turn to—

"Hey, you're shivering," he said.

"Little cooler than I expected it to be out here." Another lie.

In a gesture as natural as breathing, he slipped his arm around my shoulders, brought me in against his side. I put one arm around his back.

Suddenly, everything seemed so very . . . effortless.

We continued on down the boardwalk, the planks

reverberating and echoing our footsteps. I could see the stationary Ferris wheel again.

"Shame the amusement park is closed," he said.

"I don't know. Our last date at the carnival didn't turn out so good." It had been going well—up until I recalled torture inflicted at General Holland's hands.

A devious grin crawled across his face. All of a sudden, he removed his arm from around my shoulder, closed his hand tightly around mine, and started jogging down the boardwalk toward the amusement park. I was able to keep up easily, could have outraced him, but all I wanted was to stay near him.

It seemed there were even fewer people now than when we first stepped out of the hotel. Only an occasional straggler. Hunter slowed down, glanced around, then walked past the entrance and continued on down the street, taking a turn down a dark path that seemed meant for special personnel.

"What are we doing?" I asked.

"Finishing our date from before."

We stopped. I shifted my weight from foot to foot. "I'm not sure this is a good idea."

"Just hold on." He released his hold on me and began examining the wire fence in front of us. "Here," he finally said. "I think we can get in here."

"We're going to break in?"

He shrugged.

"It's illegal."

"What's the worst thing that could happen? They'll kick us out. It's not like we're stealing, or damaging property."

True. At least, that was the worst thing that could happen to *him*. He didn't have my baggage with the law.

I chewed my lip. Even so, he had a point. If we were caught, surely they wouldn't haul us in. But I didn't know how far of a reach General Holland might have right now. Had he alerted authorities? Or had he hired some sketchy PI to track me down?

This seemed too risky. Until my sensors proved otherwise.

Search radius: 100 yards.

Human targets: Zero.

No threat detected.

Even so, I felt nervous.

"Look, if someone comes, you can tell them I coerced you." Hunter bent down and intertwined his hands, providing me with a stepping place so he could vault me over the fence.

Never mind that I could most likely rip a hole through the fence with my bare hands.

"Brawk, brawk," he teased. I let out easygoing laugh, but I could feel pinches of worry hitting me at the base of my neck. Still, I had to put my trust and faith in what my scans

were telling me. Hunter and I were alone; no one would see us. With all the rides turned off, all we could do was walk around.

I owed him this silly and sweet romantic gesture.

More than that, I wanted it. For me.

I placed my foot on his hands, and he hoisted me up. I grabbed the fence and vaulted over, landing firmly on my feet. Then I watched in amazement as he scaled the taut web of metal and wires in the blink of an eye.

"Impressive," I said.

"Used to go rock climbing with my dad." He took my hand and began leading the way.

"Are you and your dad close?" I asked.

"Not so much anymore. But let's not talk about him. This is a date. We're supposed to talk about you. What's your favorite ride?"

He was probably not going to believe that I had no idea because I'd never been on any rides, but as we passed the carousel, an image flashed through my mind—a wooden horse that was going up and down, small hands clutching the pole. The world spinning by, faster and faster.

Another errant pseudo memory. I was sure of it.

Only this time, recalling these thoughts caused the faux skin near my temples to burn and my vision to blur. When I tried to take a step forward, I stumbled and caught myself by latching on to Hunter.

Weird.

"You okay?" he asked.

"Yeah, sorry, just missed my step in the dark."

He studied me for a moment. "You sure? We could head back if you wanted."

I gazed into Hunter's eyes and thought of how close we had been to kissing on our first date; how I had pulled away from him when those disturbing images of the first MILA being tortured had suddenly flashed before me.

How from there my life had crumbled to pieces.

But if I could just forget everything for a few hours—forget the reality of who I was and how I got here and what I'd lost along the way—maybe he and I would have a chance to make something out of whatever was happening between us. Even if it only lasted for a little while.

"Are you kidding me? We're *so* doing this."

"Yes! I knew you had it in you," Hunter said, full of unabashed glee.

I smiled and took his hand, my sensors immediately recognizing his racing pulse. It seemed all too clear he was more excited about this adventure than I was.

"So you never answered my question," he said, leading the way for us.

"Hmmm?"

"Your favorite ride."

"Oh, right," I said. "The carousel, I guess."

Hunter gave me a funny look. "Seriously?"

"What's wrong with that?"

He tapped his chin in faux concentration. "What *isn't* wrong with it?"

My mouth fell open in mock dismay. "Take that back. The carousel is a classic."

"Classic? How old are you? Forty?" he replied.

Um, more like a few months old. If we were using created-on dates. "You're just jealous of my excellent taste in rides."

"No. It's just that I picture you on the front of a roller coaster, screaming your head off and laughing with your arms in the air."

Something guarded inside of me gave way. I could see the image clearly, and I wanted it. I wanted to be that girl. Happy and free; excited about the unexpected. I wanted to see myself through Hunter's eyes

Acting on a whim, I leaned forward and wrapped my arms around him. His chin rested on my head, my cheek against his chest.

Subject's heart rate: 92 bpm.

Inspiration levels: Elevated.

Hyperventilation unlikely.

"What was that for?" he whispered.

I glanced up at him, whispering the words in my head I wasn't brave enough to voice. *Because you make me feel alive.*

But ultimately, "Just because" was all I said aloud. His lips grazed my forehead. The contact was brief, but the warmth inside me lingered. "So, are you going to prove me right?"

"About what?"

He tipped his head in the direction of a gigantic roller coaster named the Blazing Inferno. The ten-foot sign for the ride was engulfed in flame-like streamers and the winding track was painted bright red.

"I would, but I don't think we can run the roller coaster by ourselves," I said.

"You happen to be looking at a trained professional."

I raised a skeptical eyebrow. "You're kidding me, right?"

"Nope. Back in California, I spent a whole summer working as a carnie."

"You never mentioned that before."

He took my hand and began pulling me along, his smile broadening. "So I have a few secrets."

As we closed in on the ride, prickles of concern traveled up my arms. Starting up the roller coaster was going too far, wasn't it? Were there silent alarms on these things? What if some security guard showed up and found us here trespassing? We'd be brought somewhere for questioning—and questions about who I was and where I came from were pretty unanswerable at this point.

"Hunter, this is crazy," I said the moment we arrived at the Inferno's entrance.

"We're not going to get caught. Trust me."

"It's not that," I lied.

God, I was getting so freakishly good at it.

He squinted at me curiously. "Would you rather go on another ride? The Ferris wheel would be easy. All I'd have to do is throw one lever, and we'd be up so high, we could see for miles."

I had to admit, that sounded wonderful. So wonderful I was finding it hard to say no.

"Come on, it'll be fun," he pleaded.

I closed my eyes for a minute as my android brain performed another scan. This time to make sure there weren't any cameras or secret security systems hidden in the shadows. This amusement park seemed rather antiquated, so maybe the owners didn't have the right technology in place. We did hop their fence, after all.

Advanced perimeter scan.

Video capture capabilities: Zero.

Alarm triggers: None.

I opened my eyes to Hunter biting his lip with anticipation. Resistance was futile.

"All right. One lap on the wheel."

"You won't regret it," he said.

That was the problem. I didn't regret any of the time I spent with him. Not even when it wasn't in his best interests.

We jogged over to the entrance gate of the ride, our fingers loosely intertwined. I climbed onto the bench seat while Hunter got behind a few of the controls, his brow furrowing together as he tried to familiarize himself with them.

"You okay over there?" I asked, my legs swinging back and forth, the tips of my shoes skimming the ground below.

Hunter glanced up and winked. "Piece of cake."

He flipped a switch and the frame of the ride lit up with hundreds of tiny white lights. My stomach plummeted and we weren't even moving.

Wattage: 10,000 watts.

Visibility: High.

A voice inside my head said I should put a stop to this. All of it—this date; this relationship or whatever it was. Especially when a giddy-looking Hunter dashed over, slid next to me on the seat, his eyes beaming.

What was I doing? Every second I spent with him was putting him in danger. I just had to accept that, no matter how much it scared me. No matter how lonely I'd be without him.

Without anyone.

"I have it on autopilot. Prepare to be dazzled," he said, locking the bar into place. It reverberated with a metallic clang and suddenly I felt trapped—like I was being held in that coffin-like device within Holland's nightmarish compound.

"I'm not sure I can do this," I mumbled.

"Are you afraid of heights?" Hunter asked, and I heard the skepticism in his voice.

I shrugged, even though that so wasn't the case.

"We don't have to, if you don't want to," he said softly. "I can go stop it now."

The disappointed slump of his shoulders sealed it for me. "No, it's fine."

With a slight jerk, the huge wheel began turning and we were slowly lifted toward the sky, our feet dangling beneath us.

"I have a confession," I said quietly.

These words came out and I hadn't meant them to.

"Yeah?" He looked at me intently.

More silence. Even though I was trying desperately to eke out the truth. Then I realized I could just simply break things off with him. Tell him we have to go our separate ways after this. I didn't even need to give him a real reason. I could just say what boys in Clearwater would tell my ex-friend Kaylee when they were done with her: It was for the best.

But eventually, the truth won out.

Well, not exactly.

"I've never ridden a Ferris wheel."

Hunter looked at me, stunned, before his lips twitched up. "You see? This is what happens when you like the carousel. You go all soft."

I rolled my eyes and laughed. Hunter joined in.

He wanted to be here with me. Why was still a bit of a mystery, but I knew that sending him away—whether I told him who I was or not—was going to hurt him. Not physically, of course. But there was no way he'd understand. Calling him across the country to see me one minute, sending him away the next. He'd think I was playing some kind of cruel joke.

I turned my head and looked out toward the edge of the park, watching as the world below grew smaller. I started telling myself I could spare him that hurt. I could protect him, better than I protected Mom. Together we could make it.

Together was for the best.

"Not bad, huh," Hunter said, gesturing at the view.

Scattered lamp posts lit the boardwalk, the moon reflected off the ocean. It was all so beautiful, peaceful. The salty breeze wafted over us. Hunter's fingers lightly squeezed my hand, and I realized he was doing it without thought.

Like we were a couple.

As we reached the top, I wanted to stay here forever, just Hunter and me above the fray, away from all the troubles that plagued me. I found myself wondering if finding Richard Grady was something I needed to do right now. Hunter only had a week with me—maybe the search could wait. We'd still have to go on the road, though. There were too many people trying to track me.

Actually, capture and dismantle me was more like it. If Hunter was with me when I was found by Holland or the VO, I didn't even want to think about what they might do to him.

"I have a confession, too," he said, his voice snapping me out of my thoughts.

I turned to face him as the wind ruffled his hair. "Should I be scared?"

"No," he replied. "Well, maybe a little bit."

"Okay, go ahead."

He blew out a nervous breath. "Mila, I really like you."

An embarrassingly goofy grin started forming on my lips so I quickly tried to cover my mouth with my hand.

"Wait, did you already know?" he said, smiling.

"I had a feeling," I said.

Too many feelings, in fact.

Always.

"Well, I don't just say that to every girl I meet," he said as the Ferris wheel embarked on its second revolution. He paused a beat, and then added, "Only every third one or so."

I poked him in the ribs, and he fake winced before pulling me closer. "I'm joking. I only say that to girls I travel cross-country for. Which, to date, has only been you," he whispered, his mouth close to my ear.

I closed my eyes, forgetting how many times we circled,

forgetting everything but how close Hunter was. Tonight was special, a memory that was real and that I could call my own. No one would be able to take this moment away from me. Ever.

Another reason why I wasn't sure I could let him go.

He made me want to live a life I wanted to remember.

THREE

My sleep cycle ended at precisely 8 a.m. the next morning. I opened my eyes to Hunter sprawled across his mattress, one hand flung out to the side, the other curled up on the pillow. The blue comforter had long ago been kicked to the floor, and the sheet was bunched up over his chest. He had earbuds in his ears, totally unaware that we needed to remain vigilant and alert to any strange sounds. Unaware that I was a moving target.

Unaware that I wasn't worthy of his Ferris wheel confession.

He looked so innocent, with his long eyelashes resting on his cheeks. And so very kissable, with his lips softly parted.

The mattress squeaked as I climbed out of my bed, but Hunter still didn't move. Carefully, I sifted my fingers through his hair, relishing the silken feel of the strands. He breathed deeply, but thankfully didn't stir.

I knew I shouldn't be touching him. No, I didn't *deserve* to touch him. What I should do was send him home, where he would be safe. My hand wavered hesitantly, before I gave in and traced the curve of his cheek, the rasp of five-o'clock shadow on his jaw.

His eyes flew open, and his hand shot up.

Threat detected: Feint back.

My body started following the android command and then I remembered—this was Hunter. With effort, I forced myself to relax and let him tug my hand over until my palm covered his mouth and I felt his lips press a soft, feather-light kiss to its center.

My other hand braced me, flat against his chest, and beneath it, I felt his heart race. As if momentarily hypnotized, I lowered my head to his, slowly, like the invisible line that connected us together was shortening and I had no choice but to obey its pull. I didn't know how long I'd been imagining this kiss, and even though I knew deep down doing this was woefully inappropriate of me, I wasn't able to reel myself in.

He turned his head to the side at the exact same moment the red words flared.

Human threat detected.

A muffled clang of metal came from outside the window.

I stiffened, yanked away, and straightened just as something rapped at our door.

"Housekeeping."

"Come back later," I hollered, my face flushing. Even the arrival of the worker couldn't mask the fact that I'd just been rejected. I walked over to my bag and started packing it, keeping my back to Hunter. I couldn't meet his eyes. Not now.

"Mila?"

I moved a few things around in my bag, making sure my hands stayed busy. "Mmm-hmm?"

"Turn around and look at me."

I stopped, hands buried. Then, steeling myself, I turned to face him. "Yes?"

He pushed himself up until he sat on the bed. "Don't feel weird. I just—you're clearly going through some things right now. I don't want to feel like I'm taking advantage of you."

While I stood there, absorbing his words, he smiled. "There's no reason to rush into this. We're cohabitating, you know."

A wave of relief swept through me—he wasn't rejecting me, he was just being a gentleman—but I still felt pretty humiliated and ashamed.

Because I was totally taking advantage of him.

"I'm going to run to that internet café and grab us some

coffee," I said, my voice wavering a little.

"Sounds good. I'll hit the shower while you're gone."

Hunter pushed back the covers and stretched his arms overhead, the hem of his shirt lifting and revealing a thin sliver of perfectly cut abs. I felt a surge of heat rush up my neck and averted my gaze, cursing myself inwardly for acting like such a dork. For goodness' sake—I was an android, not some real teen girl raised in a convent. And they were just muscles. Rectus abdominis, transverse abdominis, obliques—see, I could even name them all, and knew their functions. Everyone had them—no big deal.

I swallowed hard. Yeah, right. Tell that to my stupid traitorous imagination.

Hunter rose and grabbed his duffel from where he'd stashed it under the bed, and carried it toward the bathroom. Then he paused, surrounding me with the sweet-musky scent of sandalwood and soap. "Good morning, by the way."

"Good morning," I said, holding back a dopey, breathless sigh.

He turned to enter the bathroom, whistling a little, when I realized I had something important to ask him.

"How do you take your coffee?"

"Surprise me," he said over his shoulder.

Oh, yeah, I could do that.

When I stepped outside, another beautiful Virginia Beach morning greeted me. The sun blazed low over the ocean like a golden ball, spreading sparkling reflections off the water and looking almost close enough to caress the distant waves.

Nine minutes later, I ducked into the internet café. It was long and narrow, with rows of computers at individual desks arranged neatly along walls painted with graffiti-style art. The bitter aroma of coffee wafted from behind the circular counter in the middle.

I should get the coffee and head straight back to the room, but the computers were calling to me. No matter what was going on with Hunter, Holland was out there, and I needed to know what details he'd leaked to the public, if any. The one thing that had kept me from all-out panicking so far was the fact that the general had a giant ego. Creating a true APB for me would involve admitting to his superiors that he'd allowed their top-secret, billion-dollar experiment to escape. Again. I was willing to bet he'd keep that information locked away for as long as possible, and send his men to find me in a clandestine operation.

But I needed to know for sure.

I settled into a brightly upholstered chair on the far left side of the desk housing the computer and performed a quick scan of the café's occupants.

A group of three high school boys, laughing and nudging one another as one of them pointed at the monitor. A middle-aged man, dressed in sagging jeans and a Hawaiian shirt, being nagged by a similarly middle-aged woman on his right. A young girl, alone in the back corner. And the twentysomething guy behind the counter.

Weapons scan: No guns found.

None of them looked remotely interested in me.

As I reached for the keyboard, an odd eagerness pulsed through my fingers. Behind my eyes, a red light blinked to life.

Open ports?

My body tensed as I remembered. In order to get Mom out of Holland's secure underground compound, I'd had to communicate directly with the computer that held me captive. Machine to machine.

The code, glimmering into being—an endless stream of numbers, symbols, letters.

A roar that slithered into me, a presence all around me, one I could reach out and touch without ever moving my hands.

The portal, bursting open under my command.

Open ports, I thought with more conviction.

A roar of energy as a connection was formed, and just like that, a door in my mind flew open. Like a vacuum sucking in air, colors and information burst inside. As if the information had been lying in wait this whole time, hoping for an opportunity.

A spark ignited, deep in my chest. A tiny thrill of excitement.

This time, all of it so, so simple. Like my body, my

brain, had been born for this, had been craving this very thing without me even knowing it. Strands of code rushed through my head in glimmering streams, without any of the terror from before. Instead, I practically buzzed with an awakening power.

With ease, I separated the strands, searching for a name.

Mila Daily.

No news reports, nothing that looked ominous. I didn't even see a record of my enrollment in Clearwater High—how had Mom managed that?

On to the next name, then, the one on my phony passport: *Stephanie Prescott.*

Nothing.

Nicole Daily.

Nothing.

Feeling my shoulders lighten with each nonproductive search, I decided to search one more name.

Lucas Webb.

My proctor-turned helper back at the compound. I never would have escaped without him, and how had I repaid him? By getting him shot in the leg and smashing up his classic Camaro, which Mom and I had "stolen" with his help for our getaway.

Lucas. Whose parting words to me had been, "I think you make an excellent human."

I angled my head away. Surely Lucas was okay. We'd

been careful to cover our tracks, to pretend that he was a hostage.

He was fine, he had to be. The alternative was too awful to even consider.

I cross-referenced with MIT, and found him almost immediately. I felt a jolt of recognition in my chest, a flicker of warmth, when I pulled up his college photo. His disheveled hair had actually been tamed, but the shirt was a little rumpled. No smile, just an intense stare into the camera.

His bio flashed before me, and I zeroed in on his mother's name:

Joanna Holland Webb.

Holland. So, Lucas really was General Holland's nephew. And even though I'd guessed, back at the compound, shock still held me captive. If anything, the confirmation only made Holland more of a monster. What kind of man designed an elaborate test that revolved around his nephew being tortured?

I shivered, the memory of the wrench in my hand all too vivid. Not a pathway I ever wanted to explore again.

I searched for anything postdated from the time I'd escaped the compound, hoping for some shred of evidence that he was okay. Anything to stem the guilt twisting me into knots.

And I found it. A single tweet, short and vague. *I met an excellent human.*

An inadvertent smile tugged at my lips, and my lungs

collapsed with relief. A signal—the same words he'd told me, back at the compound.

Lucas was okay.

I slumped into the chair, my lips moving in a silent *thank you.*

Straightening, I searched *Washington, D.C.*, and the date of Mom's death, pushing away the feeling of anguish that suddenly stabbed at my core.

A headline shimmered into view.

Woman Found Murdered in Downtown D.C.—Witnesses Questioned.

As I sat bolted to my chair, I processed the rest of the article:

> *An unidentified woman's body was pulled from the Potomac early this morning. Preliminary reports indicate the woman was in her mid-to-late thirties, Caucasian, and suffered from multiple gunshot wounds. Several locals near the area where the body was recovered claimed they saw a young girl, with short dark hair and between the ages of fifteen and eighteen, leaving the area under suspicious circumstances, wearing a blood-splattered shirt. Authorities are trying to track down more information.*

A sketch materialized. A drawing of a face. My fingers pressed hard on the keyboard. A drawing of *my* face. And a surprisingly good one, at that. Apparently the transient I'd traded clothes with in the wee hours of the morning near the Potomac had a good eye for detail.

The wide deep-set eyes, the strong curve of the jaw . . . even the smattering of freckles. For anyone who knew me, that sketch was easily recognizable. The words accompanying it were even more ominous. I was the lead suspect in Mom's murder. That was outrageous. Of all the—

A heaviness pushed against my ribs, filled my chest like hardening cement. Because while I might not have been holding the gun that shot Mom, there was no doubt she was dead because of me.

Holland might not have released that sketch, but I felt his peppermint breath burning down my neck all the same. And now that the police had this much, what if someone recognized me and reported in? What if it got back to someone in the military other than Holland—someone in the military who knew what I looked like, outside of his lackeys? Well, not the military, exactly—but SMART Ops. The clandestine unit that dealt in artificial intelligence and cutting-edge research. The secretive military group headed up by a man who was more than willing to sacrifice lives in pursuit of his twisted agenda.

I braced myself against the hatred that burned in my heart, waited until my skin no longer felt like it would split down the seams. One thing was for sure—the investigation had started. Mom's body had been recovered, which meant a medical examiner, fingerprints . . . Sooner or later, they were going to uncover her real identity. And when they did—

Any fleeting thoughts of flying under the radar with Hunter for a day or two flew out the window. I had to find Richard Grady. Now.

In less than a second, I'd discarded thousands of Gradys through an advanced search. None of them relevant. I wasn't sure exactly what I was looking for, but the facts sped through my head at lightning speed.

Gradys, from all over the country. The world. I sifted through facts, searched for holes in stories—Gradys missing big chunks of their lives, which might suggest involvement in a clandestine organization. Gradys from military families. Nothing was ringing a bell, and although only a few seconds had passed, I knew I was operating on limited time.

Finally, I found three possible candidates.

One was a buff blond man who looked vaguely Scandinavian, had worked in Homeland Security, and now lived in Denver.

The next was retired military, a thin man with a receding hairline and puffy eyes who'd gone through an ugly divorce where, in an article, his former wife had blasted him for spending too much time on covert ops and not enough on his kids. Interesting.

But the one who made my heart pound with excitement had been named in a tell-all book by a former government operative as a CIA data analyst, even though according to his online persona, he'd worked for a military supplies company. There were no photos online, either—not a one. In this day and age, an oddity, for sure—and one that most likely wasn't coincidental. But the thing that really made me sit upright was his grandmother's birthplace.

Clearwater, Minnesota.

If that was a coincidence, it was one I was willing to gamble on.

His current residence was listed as Knoxville, Tennessee.

I began recording all the details.

"Hey, anyone else having a Wi-Fi issue?" Somewhere to my left, I heard an irritated male voice.

"Yeah, I just got booted," returned a younger voice to my right. Out of the corner of my eye, I saw the teen boys scowling at their monitor, fingers pounding on the keys.

Crap. Maybe my supersecret android method of using the internet wasn't so supersecret after all. Was I jacking up the Wi-Fi for everyone else? Hogging it, somehow?

Just as that thought materialized, somewhere, in a dim cavern in my mind, I felt a tiny pinprick of awareness. A needle-sized hole, worming its way into existence. I hadn't opened any new ports, or issued any new commands. I'd never felt that spot before.

So what was it?

Around me, the disgruntled voices were growing louder as the Wi-Fi refused to cooperate.

Close ports.

In a flash, my mind cleared. The wormhole disappeared. And a loud "Yes!" sounded from the scraggly-haired boy on my right, accompanied by a fist pump.

Apparently, Wi-Fi was back.

"What are you doing?"

I whipped around and faced Hunter.

He dropped his hand on my shoulder. "Sorry, didn't mean to startle you. It's just that I got a little worried when you weren't back in the room when I got out of the shower."

His jaw was freshly shaved, his hair damp and curling at the ends. He looked amazing, but I couldn't just put off my search for Grady on the basis of cute hair and smooth cheeks. I had to ensure that Mom hadn't died in vain, which meant that I needed to survive. The only way to do that was to keep moving and stay vigilant.

And the more I stared at him, the harder it was to fit him into the equation.

"I was doing a little more research. On my dad."

"Did you have any luck?"

I nodded. "I think I may have found him this time."

Hunter looked surprised, not that I could blame him. "Really? That's great. Where is he?"

"Knoxville."

"Tennessee?"

At my nod, he plucked his phone from his pocket. "So we should try to call him, right?"

I shook my head. "There was no phone number listed." Considering his previous occupation, I doubted that he had a traceable phone at all.

"Then I take it we're driving out there?" Hunter asked.

I sort of half shrugged, like, *Who wouldn't want to drive across the country in search of a total complete stranger?*

As we stood there, in the middle of the café, I noticed one of the teens elbow his friend and nod at us. Fear twined icy tendrils through my body. Why were they staring? Had they recognized me, from the drawing?

I yanked on Hunter's arm and started for the counter. "Why don't we grab that coffee I was supposed to get and map out a plan?"

As we stood in line, I knew it may be the stupidest move ever, but I had to know if they were still looking, so I peeked over my shoulder. They were. And when they caught me staring, the middle one's grin widened and he elbowed his friend again. Then, he proceeded to make obnoxiously loud kissing motions on his arm.

Turning back to study the menu mounted on the wall, I wasn't sure whether I should laugh or roll my eyes. I did neither. I just allowed the relief to wash away my fear. Still, even though they hadn't seen anything suspicious, that didn't mean my concern had just gone away. There was a picture of my face, circulating out there on the net.

Now more than ever, I had to try to be someone else.

Or flat-out disappear.

Fifteen minutes later, Hunter and I sat on the back of a wooden bench, our feet on the seat, our elbows on our thighs. As we sipped our coffees, I watched the waves roll in and thought about how carefree he'd appeared yester day as he'd swum in them. Then in the distance, one of the military jets zoomed across the sky, and I hunched my shoulders, my mind reeling back to all the suffering Lucas had gone through because he'd befriended me. Even though he was okay now, the consequences he'd experienced were more than anyone should endure.

I crossed a line inside of myself and made a choice. I couldn't put Hunter in danger any longer, and now that a police sketch of me was being broadcast online, we were in much too deep.

"So . . ." Staring hard at the horizon, gathering my resolve, I cleared my throat. "I figure you can just drop me off at the bus station."

Out of the corner of my eye, I saw him snap his head around, his brow furrowed. "What?"

I forced myself to look at him, to keep my voice and

gaze steady. "Look, I don't know anything about this man or how he might react to me showing up on his doorstep. He could be really pissed that I tracked him down. Besides, there's no point in you giving up your fall break for what might turn out to be another wild goose chase."

"Yeah, you're right."

I was relieved by his acceptance, but disappointed at the same time.

"It'd be way more fun sitting in my room playing video games." Then I heard it, the sarcasm in his voice. "Come on, Mila. I don't have anything better to do. And if this guy does turn out to be a jerk, you don't want to be by yourself."

I shook my head. "I can't ask this of you. I can't be that selfish."

"Why do I get the feeling that there's more to it than that? Are you upset about this morning, about the kiss that didn't happen?"

"No, that's not it."

"Then what is it?"

I finished off my coffee and looked at a nearby trash can. Calculations of distance, angle, velocity, and wind speed flashed through my mind before I tossed my empty coffee cup—perfect shot, no rim.

"Is there something you're not telling me?"

Talk about a loaded question. I fiddled with my hands in my lap, with the fraying fabric of my jeans. Waiting for the words to come. "Look, Hunter, I . . ."

My throat tightened, trapping the rest of the sentence inside. I pictured the horrified look on his face when I answered him honestly. Him backing away in disgust.

I coughed and tried again. "Here's the thing . . ."

I closed my mouth without finishing my thought and Hunter's eyes glazed over, like his mind was suddenly someplace else. The bench creaked as he vaulted off it, tossing his cup into the trash can at the same time. He headed toward the waves.

I guess he was fed up with me.

"Hunter," I whispered into the stillness, but of course he couldn't hear me.

The space inside my chest shrank, or at least it seemed that way. Because all of a sudden, this enormous pressure smashed and shoved at my synthetic heart, my stomach, everything, until it felt like they were flattened, distorted into much smaller shapes. *Should I go talk to him?* I wondered, as I watched him pace back and forth at the water's edge, kicking up sand with his steps. Or should I just leave, make my way to the bus station on my own? Or maybe—and here was a timely thought—maybe I should never have called him in the first place.

The cramp in my chest intensified as I slid off the bench and my shoes sank into the warm sand. I walked over to where Hunter now stood with his arms at his sides, just staring into the dark blue water beyond. I reached for his closest hand, and laced my fingers with his. But even though we were touching, I felt his distance. It was like a Grand Canyon of distrust was forming between us, and it was all my fault.

"I'm sorry," I said softly. "It's not that I don't want you to come with me."

That was the truth.

"Then why won't you let me?" he muttered.

One manufactured heartbeat. Two. By the time I got to three, I hoped I could give him an explanation, anything that might make this easier—for the both of us.

"I . . . if I told you, I don't think you'd understand."

Hunter had traveled across multiple states at the drop of a hat to help me, and yet this was all I could bring myself to say.

When he didn't reply, I started to pull my hand away, but then I felt him curl his fingers more tightly around mine and the panicky stomach-plunging-to-my-feet sensation that had taken over me a minute ago subsided.

I just didn't want him to hate me.

A ragged sigh erupted from Hunter, and like we were somehow connected, the easing of his tension flowed into me, through our linked hands. He turned and he drank in my features like he could absorb every tiny line and curve. Read every lie.

His voice was barely audible over the sound of the ocean surf. "My dad walked out when I was nine. My mom got remarried when I was eleven."

He dropped my hand and stuffed his own into his pockets, kicking at the sand beneath his feet. "You know how when some dads walk out, the mom makes up a story about why? Something nicer than what really happened?"

"Mm-hmm."

"Not my mom. She and my stepdad don't believe in sugarcoating. So when she thought I was old enough, she told me all about him. How he had a drug problem, got arrested. Went to jail and repeated the same mistakes again and again after he was paroled. Finally, he realized having a son cramped his style, so he stole her spare cash, her jewelry she'd inherited from her grandmother. Stole her wedding ring, which she took off every night to clean. Then he bailed."

Oh my god. "Hunter, I'm so sorry. I had no id—"

But he held up his hand. "Let me finish. I'm not telling you this to make you feel sorry for me. I'm telling you because—you'd think because of her being so honest, I wouldn't want to find him, right? Wouldn't want to get to know him? I mean, what kind of kid would want an asshole like that in his life? But I do. I feel like something is missing—like, how can I know myself if I don't know my dad? Even if he's a total douchebag."

He gazed off into the distance again. His next words were so soft, even my superior auditory functions had to work overtime so I could hear. "Sometimes, I think I would have been better off if she'd lied. Because now all I can wonder is—what if I turn out like him? What if there's something wrong with me?"

A fierce protective instinct flooded my nonheart. I wanted to assure him that there was nothing wrong with him, not even close. That he would never turn out like his deadbeat father. But I held my tongue while he continued to talk.

"My point is, I *do* understand. I know what it's like to want to find someone, your family. There's this part of me that hopes maybe my mom got it wrong. Maybe, I don't know, maybe he had to leave us for the good of mankind or something, just pretend to be bad. That's what always happens in comic books, anyway."

He rubbed one hand down the back of his neck and exhaled. "It's just . . . I get it. I know what it's like to be searching for your family. I want to help you. You have the courage to do what I've only ever thought about doing. I know it's scary, but what I don't understand is you calling me to come here, just to push me away."

"I promise it has nothing to do with you," I told him. "It's all me."

Groaning, he looked up at the sky. "I can't believe you

said that." Then he dropped his head and skewered me with his gaze. "Look, if you're not into me, just say so."

I barked out a strangled laugh. "Actually, the problem is I like you way too much."

Hunter tried to hide a smile, but wasn't able to squash it before I could notice. "And how is that a problem exactly?"

I could stand here all day, ticking off the reasons. And I'd spent the last twenty-four hours batting them away like a persistent swarm of mosquitoes. But I'd made a decision. Being together wasn't for the best. As much as I wanted to protect him, I couldn't guarantee that I would be able to. Hunter's safety mattered above everything.

Even the truth.

"It just is," I said.

"Can't you give me *one* day?" Hunter asked. "I need one day to show you that having me around is a good thing."

"Hunter, I—"

"If you want me to go after that, I swear I won't argue with you," he went on.

I was so touched by how hard he was trying to persuade me that my throat locked up, refused to work for a minute.

One day. Hunter thought it was enough time, but I knew otherwise. Life could go from beautiful to ugly in a fraction of a second.

"Also, Tennessee is on my bucket list! You can't deny a man the chance to check off something on his bucket list," he added, his eyes wide and pleading, like he was scrambling for more excuses to give me.

There it was again. Laughter. Coming out of my synthetic belly, traveling out of my fake lungs, and then carrying on the wind. The corners of my lips turned up into a smile, and I was happy.

Legitimately, authentically happy.

How is that a problem exactly? Lately, happiness—even just a shred of it—had me buying into the lies I'd told. Not only to Hunter, but also to myself.

One more day. Everything will be fine.

"Okay, but I think you might need to revise that list," I said, finally giving in. "It sounds kind of lame."

Hunter smiled—the quirky, lopsided grin that hooked me back in Clearwater—and slipped an arm around me.

"I can't think of anyone better to help me with it than you."

FOUR

I should have been panicked, or ready to attack at the slightest provocation. The way I'd felt when Mom and I were on the run. Today was no different from the day we tried to cross the border into Canada, or get on a plane to secretly fly out of the country.

But on the first leg of what Hunter dubbed "The Bio Daddy Road Trip," all I could feel was relaxed. Ridiculously relaxed, given the circumstances.

Hunter insisted on taking the first turn at the wheel, and as he steered, we talked. Or rather, he talked, clearly a not-so-subtle but considerate attempt to keep my mind off my traumatic personal life. He talked about his manga collection, San Diego, the friends he'd left behind, more manga. How much he missed the ocean but not the traffic. How he hoped that he could take me with him to visit someday.

"You'd love it there. We could go to the beach, stay late, and have a bonfire. Then the next morning, we could drive up to the mountains and go for a hike. My friend's dad has a cabin in Big Bear, so we could stay for free. It would be amazing," he said with a sigh.

"Especially if we could read some manga while we were there," I teased. "Seriously, though, it *sounds* amazing."

And it did. Once I found Grady and put together the broken pieces of my past, then I had . . . nothing. No plans, no family, no idea of what my future would be like—only that I'd be constantly looking over my shoulder for the rest of my life. Even so, the fact that Hunter liked me enough to include me in his visions of the future . . . it meant everything to me.

I leaned over and pressed a kiss to his cheek before sliding back into my seat.

"Just because?" Hunter asked. With a sudden boyish grin, his fingers traced over the spot. So endearing that I was tempted to kiss him again.

"Just because," I said.

Over the next few hours, I still kept a careful eye on the cars around us, and performed quick scans whenever we stopped. But that never seemed to prevent me from enjoying myself. Like when we pulled over for an impromptu Slurpee—

Me: "Why is there a tiny shovel on the end of the straw?"

Hunter: "What, they don't have Slurpees in Philly? There's always a tiny shovel on the end of the straw."

Me: "So you don't know either."

Hunter: "Just drink your Slurpee."

—or flicked water at each other while Hunter washed the bugs off the Jeep's windshield. Times like these, I could almost forget the reason we were on the trip in the first place.

To pass the time, we played a game where we took turns naming animals in alphabetical order. As it turned out, Hunter liked to take a little creative license.

"Hare," I said.

"Icky bird."

I folded my arms. "You're making that up."

He shrugged, his face a picture of innocence. "Am not. They're indigenous to Tibet, and they were named for the sound they make during mating rituals. *Icky, icky, icky.*"

"You've got to be kidding."

"Oh, no. I don't kid about icky birds."

"You could have just said 'iguana,' you know."

"But then the icky bird would have felt slighted."

"Okay, fine. I'll let that one slide. We wouldn't want to offend such a prestigious Tibetan avian species."

He turned to grin at me. "Now you're getting it."

By the end of the game, we'd both done more laughing

and fabricating than anything else.

"Wow, I haven't played that since I was a kid," Hunter said, once we'd finally settled down.

"Did your parents teach you?"

A pause. "No, my friends' parents did on the way to soccer meets." A lengthier pause, and then, "do you ever wish you had a brother? Or a sister?"

I stole a glance at his profile while he drove, but his eyes remained intent on the road.

Images flashed in my head. My face, only not mine, staring me down right before we had to race through an obstacle course designed by a madman. Her quizzical expression when I tried to talk about Mom. Her insistence that we were sisters of sorts. Sisters who competed to see if one would have her entire existence erased, with the push of a few buttons.

A chill wrapped around me like a night breeze. "No," I said. "Not really. Why? Do you?"

A tiny muscle twitched in his jaw, a stiffness echoed in the way his shoulders squared against the seat back and the curl of his fingers on the wheel. He waited a tick, then deflated. "Yeah, I do. Mainly just to have someone to talk to at home. My parents come and go a lot, and they're . . . well, let's just say they're all over the place with their attention. One minute they're all in my business like I'm ten or something, but the other fifty-nine, they act like

I'm forty and don't need anything from them. Sometimes I pretend that I have a brother, and we make fun of how weird they are while we hole up in my room and watch really shitty TV."

The tiny lump that had started forming in my throat grew in thickness, but I swallowed it away. I'd give anything to have Hunter's dysfunctional little family.

At least he knew them. At least they were alive.

"Do you ever feel like that? Like you just wish you could rewrite history, somehow, to make it play out more in your favor?"

I reached across the seat and rested my hand lightly on his cheek. He leaned into my palm, and my heart swelled. "Every day," I whispered. "I wish I could change the past, every single day."

His eyes met mine, and something flared between us. My heart catapulted in my chest, while suddenly I became aware of how close his thigh was to mine, and of his scent, and the thrum of his pulse beneath my fingers, speeding up its pace.

I let my hand fall away, coughed to clear my confusion. Car. Driving. Not crashing, really important. "None of us gets to decide where we come from, but we can choose where we go from there."

I wasn't sure where the words had originated, but once I uttered them, they felt right. I couldn't allow the circumstances of my creation to drag me down. Nothing could change that. But that didn't mean my entire life was predetermined. I had choices, beyond what Holland envisioned for me.

And I'd be damned if I let him steal my life from me, like he had Mom's.

"You think so?" he said, his lower lip caught between his teeth.

"I do. I also think that your parents suck, if they don't realize what an amazing person you are." He didn't say anything, but the right side of his mouth turned up. "And, for the record—I'm always available to watch bad TV. In fact, hold that thought . . ."

I rummaged through my bag, pulling out the pen and paper I'd taken from the motel. I scribbled on the top sheet, tore it off, and handed it over. "Here you go."

He unfolded it on the steering wheel and read, his smile turning into a full-fledged chuckle.

> *I owe you one entire day of room holing-up and all the shitty-TV watching your alphabet-game-cheating brain can handle.*
> *Mila*

"So I might get another day with you, huh?"

I stared at the stretch of road ahead through the windshield and beyond, avoiding the traveled road in the rearview mirror. "I'm thinking about it."

Later, we switched positions. I could tell Hunter was getting tired as the sun lowered in the sky, because he talked less and instead zoned out to whatever song was playing on the radio, his eyelids slowly lowering. Finally, the steady hum of the tires must have lulled him, because his eyes closed and his face turned soft with sleep.

As I stared at the long, monotonous road ahead, I quickly realized that I didn't like it when Hunter slept. It left me with too much time alone with my thoughts.

Way too much time. Enough time for me to replay images from the past that I'd happily erase from my memory for good.

Android parts, everywhere. Me, wading through piles of discarded arms and legs and other bits of machinery masquerading as human, their skin dry and lifeless under my hands. Flames, roaring in my ears, red-orange waves licking the floor by Mom's bound feet—and the impact my shoulder made when I hit the glass separating us. Lucas's body, crumpling when I struck him in the kidney with my fist—even though it was the last thing I'd wanted to do.

All part of Holland's sick, sadistic tests. All for nothing when he ordered me terminated anyway.

Remembered terror tore through my body—the horror

of not knowing what was happening to Mom while I was locked away in the tiny, barren cell in Holland's compound . . . and the never-ending heart stab of realizing that now, she was gone. Was that pain ever—*ever*—going to go away?

Mom had told me I was brave, only she had called me Sarah. A part of me was so determined to figure out who this mystery girl was, and the other part didn't want to know. What I knew now was horrifying enough.

As the tires rolled on and Hunter slept, I played our escape scene, over and over again. What could I have done differently? If I'd taken a different route through D.C.? Not made that desperate, wrong-way turn on the Kutz Bridge?

The road blurred before me and I took a vicious swipe at my eyes.

If you want to help me, you know what you can do? Live.

Mom's voice, already losing strength then but filled with a surprising ferocity.

Live.

I straightened in the seat, pushed my shoulders back. Everything Mom had done had been for me. To give me a chance to really live—in whatever capacity that meant.

I wasn't about to let her down.

I pushed the button on the door, and the window whirred. The fresh air whipped me in the face, full of damp earth and, yes, some smoky car exhaust, but mostly the slightly sweet decay of leaves falling from trees. Crisp—chillier than I'd expected.

Ambient temperature: 49.5 degrees F.

Instead of refreshing me, though, my body stiffened as Holland's wrinkled, smug face swam in my mind, accompanied by the scream of bullets. The explosive shatter of glass.

In my head, I saw flames licking high, but this time he was the one bound to a chair. His sun-weathered face glistened as the heat drew closer, panic lightening his steel-gray eyes. His fear was a palpable thing, every bit as alive as the artery pulsing in his throat, and a strange sweetness swept through me.

The rage nestled away in a dim corner of my mind roared its approval. I'd give him fire. I'd give him everything he deserved, everything—

"Mila, look out!"

Hunter's shout startled me, and I just reacted. I slammed on the brakes, which resisted, then gave with a sudden jerk—at the same time Hunter threw his hand out, trying to grab the steering wheel. The Jeep careened wildly to the left.

Car approaching, 12 ft.: Collision possible.

Adjust right.

I yanked the wheel to the right, overcorrecting in my

panic, straight for a line of orange pylons. Construction zone. The Jeep's front right wheel smacked one of them, and the crunch reverberated through the interior. The steering wheel jerked under my hands as the tires crunched across the debris scattered over the restricted shoulder.

I hit the brakes. No resistance at all.

Another pylon kicked up and cracked against the hood before it went flying, and in desperation, I swerved back to the left. Which plunged us directly toward a parked construction vehicle.

My heart plummeted to the floorboard at the same time my android instincts took over.

Obstacle, 3 ft.: Veer 5 degrees to the right.

Straighten.

Veer 10 degrees to the left.

Pump brakes.

I hit the brake pedal repeatedly. Nothing. The brakes wouldn't catch, wouldn't stop the car. Meanwhile, the Jeep kept rocketing forward. From my peripheral vision, I caught a glimpse of Hunter's pale face. His arm was extended across my chest in a vain effort to protect me.

Collision imminent, 11 ft.

I tapped the brakes again. Again, no sign of resistance.

8 ft.

The Jeep bucked as an explosion like a shotgun blast was emitted from under the passenger side. Blowout.

In desperation, I pumped the brakes once more. The car jerked, then jolted to a stop. I stared at the back door of the massive truck on the other side of the windshield, the two bumpers so close they could have been kissing.

Obstacle, 3 in. ahead.

Three inches. We'd missed crashing by three freaking inches.

I let my head fall forward onto the steering wheel while Hunter drew in a deep, shuddering breath. "That was . . ." He trailed off.

"Yeah."

Then I shot upright and turned to him, anger suddenly short-circuiting the relief. "What were you thinking, yelling at me like that?"

His jaw hung open, reflecting the dazed expression in his eyes. "The lights . . . ," he finally blurted. "You were driving without the headlights on."

No lights. My night vision had initiated, and I hadn't even noticed. The lines behind my human self and the machine were blurring, faster than I could have ever imagined. I guess the truth wouldn't be denied.

My hands trembled, while at the same time, a steady stream of power burned through my limbs. Power that had once felt like a burden, but was starting to feel like an absolute necessity.

Holland's face flashed again, but this time the fire licked

at his toes. I could almost smell the acrid char of smoke, feel the heat singe my own skin, and the sensation sent a shiver through me.

Overhead, clouds cloaked the moon like a shroud, and in the distance, a solitary star glittered, barely lighting the dark night canvas. The rolling green hills on either side of us were devoid of businesses, of houses. Of streetlights.

I could only imagine how dark it looked without the lights on. Impossibly dark.

I kept my mouth shut and shifted uncomfortably in my seat. Waiting.

Hunter peered out the windshield, forehead all furrowed in puzzlement. He muttered under his breath. "How the hell . . ." Then, with an angry shake of his head, his voice grew louder. "You could have killed us."

No, I couldn't have. But that wasn't something I could share. *No, really, we were never in any danger, because I've got this great night vision built into my head.*

"But I didn't," I said. Because I felt like I had to say something. I hoped he'd leave it at that. I also hoped he couldn't hear the thump-thump-thump pounding in my ears.

He rubbed the back of his neck, shook his head. "That's the thing. How? How did you not kill us?"

It was a good question, really. One that deserved an equally good answer.

Under the unrelenting weight of his stare, my hands

tightened on the wheel. The interior of the car suddenly felt way too small.

Unfortunately, I didn't have a good answer to give him. But as the clouds eased away from the moon, providing a little bit of illumination, I gave it my best shot. "I have really good vision, and my eyes must have adjusted as the darkness crept in."

What an understatement.

"I might buy that if you were some sort of supernatural being, but there are no streetlights out here. None at all."

"There's the moon and stars . . . and it's just not all that dark. I was distracted, thinking about meeting my father. I'm sorry. I didn't mean to give you a heart attack."

"I'm not looking for an apology." He opened the door, got out, and trudged around to my door. When he tried to open it, he discovered it was locked.

Considering the tension undulating off him in waves, I hesitated, which was a totally human reaction. It was like I was scared we were about to have our first real fight. But I opened the door anyway. He reached in, closed a hand firmly around my wrist, and pulled me up. Then his arms were around me and I was pressed to his solid chest. I could feel the tiniest of trembles, the fading adrenaline rush.

"When the car started careening," he began, his voice raspy, "I was so afraid you were going to get hurt . . . or worse."

Holding him close, I sank against him. "We're okay. And I won't let myself get distracted again."

More promises I wasn't sure I could keep.

"No, it was my fault. I guess I didn't realize how upset you are. I should've sucked it up and driven a few more hours." He drew back and held my gaze. "You know, no matter what you learn about him, it doesn't change a thing about who you are."

I wanted to believe him, but knowing my history, it was probably going to change everything—on so many different levels.

"Hopefully the next town has a place to grab a real tire," he said, as he left our embrace and walked to the trunk of the car. As he pulled out some emergency flares and a spare, he said, "Let's try to keep the lights on from here on out, okay?"

"I'm never going to live this down, am I?"

"Nope," he said, smirking. "Can you do me a favor and find something good on the radio? This is going to take a while."

"Sure," I said, getting back into the driver's seat of the Jeep. "Any requests?"

"Yeah, something with a lot of drums and no Auto-Tune."

"You got it." I reached over and started scanning through channels, finding nothing but static. Then, without any command from me, my mind opened, and the red words blinked.

Searching clear frequencies.

As bits and pieces of audio began ripping through my brain, I started trying to pinpoint a local classic rock station. But instead another fragmented image floated before my eyes. Guitar chords accompanying a woman singing; the smell of oatmeal cookies in the air. Small feet standing upon two men's tennis shoes; legs swaying back and forth, back and forth.

Within a few seconds, the song sped up in my mind, the pitch reaching such high levels, I instinctually covered my ears. But that did nothing to stop the music, which was now just an insanely loud screeching sound that was splitting my head in two.

Internal malfunction.

Audio capability compromised.

Reconfiguring . . . please wait.

As the vision faded, I sat there in the car, unable to hear anything but this awful, excruciating noise. My hands began to tremble, so badly that I feared the shuddering would overtake my entire body. Then suddenly I couldn't move an inch—legs, arms, neck. Nothing was moving. Luckily, Hunter was still rummaging around in the trunk and noticed nothing. Whatever this was had better wear off or I would find myself having to explain to Hunter why I was paralyzed.

If it wasn't so alarming, it actually might have been funny. All this time, I'd been worried about the threats in the outside world. Holland. The V.O. Three. The cops. But it wasn't until now that I let this realization sink in.

There was something strange happening inside me that I didn't understand and couldn't control.

What could be a bigger threat than that?

FIVE

We arrived in Knoxville well into the early evening. Hunter couldn't push the Jeep over forty-five miles per hour due to the spare, so it took a little longer than expected. I was quiet for a good part of the drive. I spent an hour or two with my eyes closed, pretending to be asleep while my internal clock counted down the minutes of this one day I had promised him, and praying that these increasingly debilitating false flashbacks would stop.

But when we finally found this Richard Grady's house, I blocked everything out and focused, instructing Hunter to park across the street. House was a pretty tame word, though, given the size of the place. From where we sat in the car, I had a slightly obstructed view of graceful arched columns and beautiful brick construction, broken up by the bars of a fancy, wrought iron gate that led to the horseshoe driveway. Pristine green lawn peeked through, and with the window cracked, I caught a mix of sweet grass smell, chemicals, and the perfume of roses.

Video surveillance detected.

I froze.

Zoom activated.

I heard the clicking near my eyes, felt them narrow. Then my visual field changed, nearby objects racing past while the tree flanking the gate grew larger.

There. A tiny black video camera, nestled in branches that flanked the front gate. Just what I didn't need—someone with CIA ties getting a good shot of my face for posterity.

I blinked, and with an almost inaudible whir, my visual field returned to normal. Only seven cars visible on the street—it was a weekday, after all—all of them newer, pricey foreign models, with the exception of one slightly older but impeccably washed Honda Accord, five houses down on the left at 15432. Five with Tennessee plates, one with Oklahoma, and one Georgia. No rentals.

Access DMV database?

The prompt tempted me, but no. Doubtful anyone knew we were here, and if they did—well, they'd know to cover their tracks.

"We don't have to do this," Hunter said, drumming his

fingers on his jeans while he stared toward the gate. Even though I was acting like I'd rather be anywhere but here, I was surprised he could read me so well.

The problem was, my emotions tugged me in two opposing directions. One part was all tingly with excitement over the idea that, at long last, here was someone who might be able to answer the five thousand and one questions I'd been left with when Mom died. Someone who might allow me to finally let her rest in peace. But the other part writhed with nerves. What if this was the wrong Grady, and we'd traveled all this way for nothing? Or the right Grady, but he refused to talk?

Or worse—this guy was ex-CIA. What if I said or did something that landed Hunter and me back into Holland's hands?

A virtual avalanche of bad outcomes, just waiting to topple down on our heads.

I scanned the sprawling yard beyond the gate and the quiet, tree-lined street in a panoramic sweep, taking in every tiny detail.

Four weapons detected.

But the guns were scattered among the houses. Surely not Holland's men, who'd be armed to the teeth?

Yet what about the V.O.? With all that technology at their disposal, maybe they had weapons that were undetectable.

Human threat detected: 76 ft.

Just a couple of early morning joggers, clad in well-worn, appropriate-looking athletic attire, chatting as their sneakers hit the pavement. Nothing suspicious.

"Let's do it," I finally answered. No point in further delaying the inevitable.

"Remember, I've got your back," he said, creaking open the passenger door. "Like Batman and Robin. Tarzan and Jane. Michael Knight and Kit."

I paused with one hand on the handle. "Who?"

He laughed. "Never mind. Just this stupid old show about a guy and his car. They play reruns on TNT."

I climbed out and put my hands on my hips. "And who's the car in this scenario?" Though tension still plucked my android nerves like harp strings, I was thankful for Hunter's interjection. The way he made me laugh was one of the many reasons why the thought of setting him free was tearing me apart inside. But I had to do it, and I would. Tonight. Once we were back on the road and our day together was officially over.

He loped around to my side of the car and stood in front of me, gently easing a loose strand of hair back behind my ear. "Wouldn't you like to know?" he teased. "Seriously, though, I'm here for you."

My smile wobbled, and I averted my eyes. He was here for me, but only because I'd been hiding things. Holding him close might feel like a dream come true, but in reality, I was exposing him to a nightmare.

The perfumed scent grew stronger as we approached the gate, and just inside, there was a burst of color in reds, peaches, and yellows blooming along the wall—wild and beautiful. Rosebushes, all full of flowers—well, except for that one bush nearest the street—it looked a little picked over compared to the rest.

At five steps out, I realized the gate was electronic. Grady probably had a remote button he could push from inside the house. Troublesome, because I didn't want to give him the opportunity to turn us away before we'd even had a chance to meet.

As I stepped forward, I opened my mind to the networks buzzing all around us. I was intentionally seeking out a thread of communication with the system I knew must be lurking out there, the one that controlled the gate. I found the gleaming silvery strand right away.

Signal detected: Override lock?

Yes.

The briefest of pauses, followed by a tiny burst of power. And then—

Override commencing . . . 3, 2, 1 . . .

Under my command, the gate whirred to life, hissing open with a slow glide to reveal the path to the house. So simple. Barely more trouble than walking. For a tiny, ecstatic moment, I felt like I could accomplish anything.

"Wow, guess someone knew we were coming, huh?" Hunter said.

I watched the gate slide across the track with a small smile, that same thrill of power tingling beneath my skin. Yes, someone did know. Me.

The thrill dimmed when I noted the camera again, watching us from up in the tree like a giant eye. I tilted my head away. When we passed directly under it, I lifted my left hand and pretended to scratch my forehead, using it as a shield. Twenty more steps, then fifteen.

Motion detected.

Human threat detected.

My legs tensed under me and my head whipped toward the door. The elaborate wooden structure swung inward with a heavy groan, making Hunter stop short and me jump back, curbing the urge to shift into a defensive stance.

Target: Visualized.

Engage?

What? No! I ignored the glowing red query as a middle-aged man whirled into the doorway like a ninja, sun glinting off an object in his right hand.

Gun? My human mind formed the thought, at the same time my android brain responded:

No weapons detected.

With a warrior-like yell and the slip-smack of slippers

hitting concrete, the man leaped onto the porch. "Caught you!" And despite the android reassurance, I reared back, my hand shooting out to block Hunter from harm. A split second later, I realized two things: the object in his hand was a water gun, and there was no way he would pass for my biological father. Besides being short and scrawny-thin, and having a receding hairline and a few days' worth of stubble, this Richard Grady was black.

As I digested all of this and felt Hunter grab my hand in sympathy, water streamed from the gun and splashed Hunter in the face.

"H-Hey!" Hunter sputtered, flinging up his hands and ducking.

The man's nose wrinkled. "Now, wait a second. You're not that little fiend from down the street!"

He had a thick drawl—Southern—and the sound sent ice prickling across my skin. The effect might be soothing and inviting for some people, but I didn't trust the friendly cadence.

Holland had taught me that.

Grady's gaze shifted from Hunter to me. His gun hand jerked. But if that was a reaction to my appearance, he recovered quickly. No trace of recognition showed on his craggy face. Almost like he was *trying* to look unfazed.

Hunter swiped water from his eyes while drops dribbled down his chin. To his credit, he managed a smile—albeit a slightly damp one. “Uh, no.”

The man’s eyes slid from Hunter to me. “Did the fiend send you? To sneak up and pick more of my flowers? Damned kid, climbing my fence all the time, nabbing my prize roses, all for that hair-flipping girlfriend of his.” He hoisted the water pistol again and took aim.

I held my hands palms-out in front of my face, in case he got trigger-happy again. “No, I promise! We’re not, uh, flower thieves.”

Hunter snorted and made a noise deep in his throat, one that sounded suspiciously like a laugh. I shot him an evil look, but in reality, I was groping for a way to make this work, since direct questions were out. It wasn’t like Hunter was ever going to buy that this guy was my biological father.

I stared at his unfamiliar face, at the water gun he held aloft. His antics weren’t doing anything to keep my wariness at bay. If anything, his unpredictable behavior made him a wild card. I didn’t trust it, or him.

“We’re not even from around here,” Hunter added.

“That so? You just happen to stumble across my house? Well, I don’t need any solicitors, if that’s what you’re thinking.”

“No, we’re not selling anything,” Hunter said hastily. “We tracked you down on purpose.”

I winced, and watched as Grady zeroed in on that notion. Such a tiny bit of information, but still, more than

I wanted this man to know. Yet. I'd hoped to feel him out a little more first.

He crossed his arms and scowled, all pretenses of playfulness falling away. "And why the hell would you do that?"

I focused on his face to catch even the most minute change in expression. "I was trying to track down a . . . relative of mine."

Grady gave an incredulous snort. "What, you need glasses or something? Because if this here is some kind of joke, it sure ain't funny."

Hunter shook his head and shot me an encouraging look, raising a brow as if to say, *tell him, already.* I sighed. "No, no joke. My mom told me to look for a man with the last name of Grady, so that's why we're here."

Silence. His left eyelid twitched, almost imperceptibly, but for five long seconds, he scratched his chin. "What'd you say your mom's name was?"

I hadn't, and I had a feeling he knew that as well as I did. I hesitated a beat, then said, "Daily." No way could I use Laurent in front of Hunter. Anyway, if this were the right Grady, he would know Mom's pseudonym.

Right?

I watched Grady watch me, my stomach fluttering with a growing collection of worries. Worries that he did know my mom and therefore, knew what I was. Worries that he didn't know either of us. Worries that he'd somehow seen the wanted sketch of me floating around the internet and was, at this precise moment, plotting to turn us in.

When Hunter finally started scuffing his foot on the walkway, Grady grunted, but didn't deign to respond. "Don't know her," he finally said.

"Sorry we bothered you. We'll be on our way," I said.

"Wait." As he scratched his salt-and-pepper stubbled chin, he dissected our rumpled, less-than-daisy-fresh clothing, and the way Hunter was bouncing up and down, trying to keep warm in the gathering night air. Grady hesitated, chewing his cheek. Obviously debating something. From inside, I heard a noise.

Motion detected.

Human threat detected.

He turned at the same time I shifted to the side, trying to get a better view. Then, a head popped through the doorway.

"Grandpa, who is it?"

For a moment, Grady's scowl disappeared. "Nothing I can't handle, Ashleigh. I thought you were getting dinner started." With emphatic hand gestures, he tried to usher her back into the house, but she ducked away to smile at us.

She must have been a year or so older than me, with beautiful glowing skin and shiny dark hair bunched on top of her head. Her left ear sported two tiny silver hoops, her right, a ruby stud—one that matched the one in her nose exactly. Her slim figure was wispy-thin, encased in shredded skinny jeans, a simple blue Star Trek tee, and black boots that laced up the front. Super put together and tidy, in an edgy, so-not-Clearwater sort of way. Except for the splashes of color on her fingers. Red and olive green and a hint of turquoise, dried and creasing in spots where it pulled away from her skin.

"Don't mind him," she said, ignoring his disgruntled snort. "He's always this grumpy. Did I hear that you two aren't from around here?"

I nodded without providing any additional details, but Hunter had no reason to be suspicious so he was a fountain of information. "No, we're from Minnesota . . . but we drove over from Virginia Beach."

My jaw tightened. The dangers of not being totally honest with him were coming back to bite me, and I only had myself to blame.

Ashleigh's lips parted into a round *oh*. "Wow, that's a long way. I'm sure Grandpa would love for you to come in and eat with us—wouldn't you, Gramps?" she said. When he just stared at us, she nudged his bare ankle with her toe. She had an easy, graceful way about her. The carefree, confident air of someone comfortable in her own skin.

What must that be like?

Grady studied us with that inscrutable stare, then grunted. "I suppose they could stay for dinner. That is, if they're hungry."

"Dinner sounds great. Don't you think, Mila?"

Uneasiness had me rocking onto my heels. No, I didn't think. This man watched me a little too closely for comfort, and if he wasn't the right Grady—or worse, was the Grady who Mom had referenced but had somehow had a change of heart—then getting out of here ASAP was the safest course of action. But I had no choice. I had to try to pry more information out of him, get him to open up. Because the reality was, this grumpy, hippo-slippered man with a water gun might be the one person who could give me whatever information Mom had thought I needed. This was my chance to fulfill one of her dying wishes and learn something about my past, and I couldn't just bail on that now.

"Sure, sounds great," I said, putting some conviction in my voice.

"Well, then—come on in, I guess," Grady said, turning and stomping inside. "But don't expect me to clean up for you."

Ashleigh mouthed a silent "*sorry*" behind his back and a tiny *c'est la vie* lift of her shapely shoulders, then motioned us to follow. Before she closed the door, though, I noticed that Grady took a swift glance behind him. Scanning the grounds outside as if searching for something . . . or someone. Then the door clicked shut, and I couldn't decide how I felt. Relieved, to have one more layer of protection between us and the outside world? Or worried that we were now locked inside with a man who seemed far too astute for comfort?

A man who had the potential to lead us right into the enemy's hands.

From the outside, the house looked a lot like its neighbors—colonial style, white pillars. Elegant. However, I was pretty sure the inside was nothing like the other houses on the block.

The bright aqua paint slathered on the walls grabbed my attention the instant I entered the foyer. Adding even more color to that in the living room was a ton of drawings and paintings, each painstakingly framed and hung near eye level.

"Wow," Hunter murmured, as my gaze traveled the wall. Some of the art, on the farthest wall, appeared quite skilled—a three-legged Doberman pinscher, catching a Frisbee, and a little girl digging in the sand. A trio of colorful cartoonish-looking characters, with wild hair and clothes and . . . swords?

"Cool manga characters," Hunter said, nodding at the piece, while I continued my inspection to what appeared to be earlier works from the same artist. Still the bold lines, but these weren't quite up to par: lopsided stars, haphazard hearts, rainbows in only two colors—pink and purple. Ashleigh's painted knuckles suddenly made a lot of sense.

And then, in the middle of the room, what looked to be part of an old convertible sports car—red and shiny. The roof and windows were missing, and what was left had apparently been converted into a table.

The man caught my interest and said, "Found her rotting in a junkyard. Bastards—who treats a classic like that?" When neither Hunter nor I responded, he grumbled, "What, never seen a car as a coffee table before?" then walked into the next room.

Hunter coughed to hide his laugh while Ashleigh whispered, "Weird, right? But cool. That pretty much describes Gramps to a tee, actually."

"I heard that," Grady grumbled from the next room and Ashleigh just shook her head, walking up behind him to drape her arms around his shoulders. For a kook, he was pretty observant—undoubtedly courtesy of his CIA training.

"You love it, and you know it," she said, pressing a quick kiss to his rough cheek. She tilted her head toward us and winked.

"This way," Grady barked, and Hunter and I scurried through the arched doorway that led into an open kitchen, full of stainless appliances, a glass and wrought iron table, and a long, burgundy-speckled granite counter. My gaze zeroed in on the butcher block, which magnified in the side of my visual field. Information flashed.

Potential weapons: Chicago Cutlery, butcher knife, 6 in. blade.

Um, good to know, I guess.

The floor was wooden, with black-and-white stripes. A nod to the kitschiness of the rest of the house.

Networks detected.

The red words flashed. Blink. Blink. Blink.

GradyHome Network: Accessible.

GrSecureNet: Access blocked.

I frowned. So this was much weirder and more intriguing than the decor. Grady had two networks, one of which was so guarded, even I couldn't obtain access? Unusual enough that my fingers curled and released, to help deflect some of my growing unease.

Grady motioned to the table, toward two of the red-cushioned chairs. "Sit down. I don't like it when people hover."

Hunter pulled out a chair for me, then sat in the one beside it. I followed suit more slowly. I didn't like having commands barked at me. It reminded me way too much of Holland.

"What did you say your names were?" Grady asked.

I went still, my palms pressing down into my thighs. We hadn't actually, and I'd prefer to keep it that way. But Hunter had no such reservations.

"I'm Hunter, and this is Mila."

I pretended to pick at a hangnail while I watched Grady for even the slightest change in expression. Nothing. Not so much as a twitch when Hunter said my name. But his stare drilled right through me.

"You one of those girls who slinks around and never talks?" he said with a scowl.

My head flew up, startled. Then I shrugged, deciding to go with it. Me, passing as a sullen teenager? I should probably be flattered. I doubted Three would ever be accused of that.

Ashleigh padded over to straddle an empty chair at the table. Completely unself-conscious, she draped her forearms over the chair back and rested her chin on top. "So, what brings you guys to this less-than-thrilling part of town?"

Grady frowned at her. "They're looking for Mila's relatives—the O'Dailys."

Did it mean something, that he'd gotten the name wrong? Or was he feigning ignorance?

Hunter shifted position in his chair so that he could once again rest a hand on my shoulder. "Just Daily," he corrected.

Grady's gaze slid back and forth between Hunter and me, before he grunted. "Hope you kids like steak, because that's what we're having. I threw some on the grill right before you came, and I always cook a few extras. Or, if you're one of those vegetarian people like that one," he said, nodding at Ashleigh, "we've got some healthy crap—grilled eggplant."

Ashleigh grinned. "Do you really want to get into another debate of factory farming practices in America?"

Grady held up his hands as if deflecting a punch and backed away. "I didn't say anything." But he winked at her, brown eyes shining. I bit my lip and had to look away, my heart aching. These two shared the kind of bond I'd never have again. Not with Mom gone.

"I'll take steak, thank you," Hunter said.

"Me too," I murmured, having lost what little fake appetite I'd possessed.

Grady grunted a reply, then opened the dark oak cabinet doors and rummaged around, before pulling out an oversized platter. He headed toward the sliding glass doors that led to the backyard, opened them, and walked outside, to where a built-in grill was the centerpiece of a brick-lined patio. A huge yard, at least an acre.

A harsh ring came from somewhere down the hall. Grady appeared in the doorway. "Ashleigh, keep an eye on those steaks for a second—I'll be right back."

As I watched him depart, Ashleigh laughed. "Gramps doesn't believe in cell phones—he thinks they're too risky. Old folks."

I shifted uneasily in my chair. She'd cemented my observation that Grady was the suspicious type. Speaking of which, who was calling him, and did we have any reason to be concerned?

I stared in the direction Grady had gone, then pushed to my feet. "Where's the bathroom?" I asked.

Ashleigh pointed. "Around the corner and down the hall." I saw her pull a black and maroon smartphone out of her pocket as I sped out of the room. "I don't know how he survives without one of these. I mean, seriously, how do you keep in touch with your friends without one?"

I started down the hall, then paused outside of a closed door. From the other side, I could hear the low murmur of Grady's voice, but still couldn't catch what he was saying. I bit my lip in frustration. Surely there should be some kind of way to hear?

Voice amplification requested?

The new prompt just appeared, popping into my head out of nowhere like an uninvited guest. But not unwelcome.

Yes.

A pulse in response. And then:

Tap left ear three times to activate.

Hurriedly, I lifted my index finger. Tap. Tap. Tap.

Voice amplification activated.

Choose voice to apply?

A blue circle appeared, and then separated into three distinct smaller circles. Grady, Hunter, and Ashleigh? I guessed. I focused on the one on the left.

Suddenly, every other noise fell away, until all that was left was Grady's drawl. I'd chosen correctly. The sound was merely a faint whisper at first, growing and growing in volume in time to the numbers that flashed before me.

2x

Tiny concentric rings pulsed outward from the circle, in sync with the increasing volume.

3x

5x

Each time, the rings pulsed, and the volume rose, until finally, Grady's voice filled my head, loud enough to distinguish his every word with crisp, clear definition.

"I'll be at the course next week, don't you worry, John. I'm gonna kick your behind on the back nine holes."

I couldn't hear the voice on the other end of the phone, but I did hear an odd tapping.

GrSecureNet in use.

The update notified me with a single power surge, and I realized Grady was typing on the secure network. My gut tightened. Coincidence? Maybe. Maybe not. Either way, I needed to find out.

"Thanks for calling me back so quickly. Yeah, I'll keep you posted . . . that's right. Three-six-three-seven."

I took a hasty step back, my manufactured pulse pounding a crazed rhythm in my ears. That number, 3637. Too many coincidences now. I knew that number, and it was one that no one but Mom should know. That was the number in our street address from Philly. Our fictitious address, the one that only existed in my programmed memories.

Or so I'd thought. Was it a real address, and I'd somehow just alerted Grady to check it out? Or was it a code, one that Mom had shared with Grady?

I knew now that Grady was involved somehow, but I still couldn't tell if he was friend or foe.

By the end of the night, I would find out. By whatever means necessary. But I had to be very, very cautious.

"Talk to you soon."

I heard a click, and I scrambled away from the door, turning toward the bathroom. Meanwhile, the blue circle representing Grady quit pulsing and shrank in size. I backed out of the Grady circle in my mind and in doing so, inadvertently swept over the other two, activating them.

"I'm glad you guys decided to stay. Gramps is great, but he's so overprotective. He wouldn't dream of letting me live on campus, and it gets a little dull not having anyone my age around to talk to, you know? I want to travel so bad, and of course he won't hear of it."

"Why's that?" Hunter's voice this time, loud and clear.

I reached the bathroom doorway, ready to dart inside the second Grady's door opened. Now, I just needed to figure out how to turn this sucker off.

Deactivate volume amplification?

Yes.

Tap left ear three times to deactivate.

"Not safe, too many crazies, blah blah blah. It's so

awesome that you get to travel with your girlfriend! She seems pretty cool."

My fingers froze in midair. Girlfriend? I didn't want to hear Hunter shoot that down . . . but I couldn't seem to make my hand move.

"Yeah. She is. And we are lucky to travel together—it's been great."

With fingers that were suddenly less steady, I tapped a third time, then entered the bathroom and just stood there in a trance. She'd called me his girlfriend, and Hunter hadn't argued. That was insane. Ridiculous. And utterly, completely amazing.

My phantom pulse pounded; my almost heart swelled in my chest. For that one, fractured moment, I let myself forget everything, and just feel all the giddy elation of being a real girl. I allowed myself a few moments of fantasy life—me, Hunter, a romantic road trip with nothing more to do than explore foreign places and hold hands while the sun set. Then, I forced my mind to return to reality, and my grin fell away. If Hunter really was my boyfriend, we were about to have the shortest relationship ever.

Because nothing had changed. I had to figure out exactly what Grady knew.

And then I had to tell Hunter good-bye.

SIX

We settled in to dinner, but if I was hoping for a silent meal, I was quickly dissuaded of that notion.

Grady surveyed me over his plate as he stabbed a piece of meat. "So, tell me where you're from again?" he said, in a bland manner.

Too bland? I wondered, a whisper of unease threading through me.

"I'm originally from San Diego, and Mila's from Philly, but we met in Clearwater, Minnesota," Hunter said.

"That right?" Grady's fork paused a beat. Then, he shoved a bit of steak into his mouth and started to chew.

I waited for him to mention his connection to Clearwater, but he let it pass without comment. While I supposed it was possible he didn't know where his grandmother was from, I didn't find it likely.

"Your folks okay with the two of you taking off like this?" Grady said after swallowing.

Hunter shrugged and I said, "Yeah," with as much conviction as I could muster.

"Grandpa, let them eat already," Ashleigh said with a roll of her eyes.

"Now, now, don't you shush me. Just making some small talk with our guests, that's all." Grady quelled Ashleigh with a stern look. She immediately focused on cutting her eggplant into tiny, even bites.

Grady took a swig of water before turning back to me. "So, you're searching for your . . . family member? Something wrong with your parents, they can't give you more information than a name and the help of this young man?"

My fist balled in my lap. Too many questions, especially when clearly he knew more than he was letting on. Or was he just on a fishing expedition, trying to reel me in? Either way, this interrogation was doing nothing to ease my misgivings.

If only I had a way of knowing if he was on my side.

"Well?" Grady barked, when I hesitated too long.

Hunter glanced at me before frowning at Grady. "Mila's adoptive dad recently died, so she's having a rough time."

Some transient expression flew across Grady's face.

Surprise? Sorrow? Disdain? It was impossible to tell. The next moment his lids lowered, and when he lifted them again, his eyes were shuttered. "I'm very sorry to hear that," he said, and if I didn't know better, I'd believe he was telling the truth. "Heart attack?"

"Fire," Hunter said.

Grady cleared his throat while Ashleigh gasped, pressing one colorful hand to her mouth. "Oh, Mila, that's terrible—I'm so sorry."

Her sympathy, at least, was real. I felt a twinge of guilt, even as sorrow over my loss swept through me. Though my dad was a figment of Mom's fertile imagination, somehow that knowledge didn't completely erase my feelings.

When Hunter's hand reached under the table for mine, I grabbed it, taking strength in his strong, comforting grip.

Several minutes later, Hunter pushed his almost clean plate away. "That was delicious—thank you, sir."

Grady dragged a napkin across his mouth and tossed it onto the table. "Welcome." Since Hunter's explanation about the fire his shoulders had lost some of their rigidity, and though he still exuded an air of caution, at least now I wasn't afraid he would jump up and forcibly evict me from the house at any minute.

"So, are you retired from the government?" Hunter filled the silence with small talk, and I realized my mistake immediately. I should never have told Hunter my suspicions about Grady's true occupation. They'd wonder how we knew.

Ashleigh's cup rattled the table when she plunked it down. "Government? You must be confused. Gramps was an IT guy for a military supplies company, but he didn't technically work for the government. Right, Grandpa?"

"That's right," he said mildly. Not at all the hostile reaction I'd expected. Maybe I'd gotten it wrong, after all.

He leaned back in his chair, folded his arms. "But even working outside the military, we learned a few things about self-protection, too. Ain't no one getting into my house without me knowing about it—got video surveillance and an alert any time that damned gate opens."

Those details slipped past Hunter, but not me. He was letting me know that he'd seen us before he'd ever opened the door—which meant that whole water gun thing had been a ruse.

My stomach lurched, and I straightened in my chair.

"And if they try to take something of mine? Well, they'd have a fight on their hands, that's for sure. But I've always found it's the people you know who are the most dangerous. You know the statistics—more violent acts are committed by people you know than strangers. That's why I'm a big fan of the saying: keep your friends close, and your enemies closer."

He stood abruptly, grabbing his plate off the table and

heading for the sink. And on that ominous note, dinner was over.

I digested everything that had just happened, and uneasiness rolled through my stomach. This man was too volatile to question outright, and I didn't trust him any more now than I had when we'd first pulled up.

Hunter grabbed my plate and his and followed Grady to the sink, while I sat there and waffled. One thing I had learned was that Grady knew something. More than likely, he was the Grady who Mom had sent me to find. But that didn't mean he was reliable.

Still, I had to find out what he knew. Which meant I had to get him away from Hunter and Ashleigh. If only for a brief time.

I saw my opportunity when Ashleigh rose and headed for the hall. "I'll be right back, Gramps—got to check on a homework assignment."

One down. "Hey Hunter, would you mind grabbing my sweatshirt from the car? I'm getting a little chilly." I wrapped my arms around myself for emphasis.

"Sure." He stretched, then pulled the keys out of his pocket.

"Let me get the gate," Grady said as he walked from the kitchen. He returned a moment later. "Good to go."

I watched Hunter leave the room and listened to Ashleigh's footsteps thumping up the stairs, but I waited until I heard the front door close before turning to Grady, grappling with how to approach this. He moved in on me before I could say a word.

I tensed when he grabbed my arm.

Engage?

My muscles tensed, ready to pounce.

"We've only got a few seconds, so I'm going to make this quick. I know who you are, and I'm trying to grab what was left for you, but it's proving a little more challenging than I anticipated. Did anyone follow you here?"

"No," I whispered, barely able to speak over the giddy rush sweeping up my throat.

"Good." We both heard a thump overhead. Ashleigh, heading for the stairs. "When they get back, just follow my lead. Real quick—Nicole, is she . . . ?"

His eyes asked the question that he couldn't utter, and I bowed my head, feeling the burn in the corners of my eyes.

I heard a gruff sound, like Grady had something stuck in his throat. "She told me to assume as much, if you came knocking."

A pause. And then, "That boy—you vetted him, right?"

"Vetted?"

He scowled. "Check out his fingerprints, search his name? I guess not, based on your reaction. I'd hop on that, if I were you."

Hop on a fingerprint search? How exactly was I supposed to do that?

His gaze dropped to my throat. To Mom's pendant. He shook his head. "Damn. I don't know how she did it," he said, under his breath.

"Did what?" I whispered at the same time we heard Ashleigh around the corner. He shook his head and stepped back.

"Nothing. It's nothing. Look, I'm trying to get the files she left for you, but I need a little time—"

Footsteps pounded down the stairs and he stepped away. I wanted to reach out, grab his shirt, and yank him back, demand that he finish what he'd started. But Ashleigh was almost back, and then the front door creaked open, and the opportunity was lost.

"So, good news," Grady said when they both reentered the kitchen. "Mila and Hunter are going to spend the night. We wouldn't want to send them back out this late."

Ashleigh's mouth fell open a little, and her shocked eyes darted from Grady to me. Meanwhile, Hunter handed me my sweatshirt without saying a word.

"Is it okay with you? You seemed so tired on the way out," I hastily filled in, and he shrugged.

"Sure, sounds great. Thank you," he added, for Grady's benefit.

Grady waved him off. "Glad to help," he said gruffly. "I'll leave the gate open for now so you can gather your stuff. Now, Ashleigh, can you show them to the guest room? Good thing we've got two twin beds. I'll check back in in the morning." He raised his cup at us, as if in salute, but his brown eyes caught mine in a meaningful glance, before he turned and headed out.

Ashleigh watched him leave, her expression thoughtful. "Well, you two certainly worked some kind of voodoo. Gramps is a good guy, but he's not what I'd call hospitable." With a tiny wave of her hand, she motioned us to follow her to the staircase. "Why don't you go grab your things, and I'll wait here."

I followed Hunter to the front door, waiting inside while he trotted out to the car and returned shortly with our bags. I made a move to rejoin Ashleigh but his hand on my elbow made me pause. "I'm sorry you didn't find what you were looking for," he whispered, his eyes a little bloodshot from lack of sleep.

"It's okay," I said, taking his hand in mine.

"There's always tomorrow, right?"

I wasn't prepared for the sudden stab of pain in my chest, right in the vicinity of my pseudo heart. The last day or two, I'd been swept up in the way Hunter made me laugh or how he looked at me. But it was his hopefulness that kept me going. When I sent him away, he'd take tomorrow with him . . . and honestly, I was afraid of what would be left behind.

★ ★ ★

We followed Ashleigh upstairs, to a narrow berth that branched in two directions. She led us to the last doorway on the right.

"So, here's the guest room," she said, pushing open a door in the upstairs hall. Inside were two twin beds, decorated with mismatched quilts in a riot of colors. A stripped pine chest of drawers and nightstand were the only other furniture, and a big square window was the only thing on the wall. Hunter and I dumped our meager belongings onto the floor.

"Bathroom is the next door over—feel free to help yourself to toothpaste, shampoo, the works. Towels are under the sink."

After we thanked her, she paused with one hand on the doorjamb, for the first time looking a little uncertain. "If you guys aren't tired yet, you should come hang out in my room for a while."

I didn't really want to—my time with Hunter was so limited as it was—but I wasn't sure how to say no. Especially when I remembered how she'd said it got lonely around here, with just the two of them. Hunter obviously felt the same because he nodded. "Sure, why not?"

She led us past the bathroom, to the door we'd passed when we'd first reached the top of the stairs. As soon as he saw what was inside, Hunter stepped forward and spun in a slow circle, the hiss of his indrawn breath filling the space around us. From ceiling to floor, the walls were practically wallpapered in posters and original drawings. Reds and blues, blacks and grays—faces with big eyes and crazy hair peered back at us. Manga.

An easel with a purple tarp underneath took up one corner of the room, but Hunter was already striding toward a massive bookshelf that was against the far wall. "Unbelievable," he breathed, his fingers reverently tracing some of the spines. "You've got so much amazing stuff."

"I know, right?" Ashleigh said, following him over. "I started getting into it when I was ten, and Grandpa just keeps buying them for me. What about you, Mila—do you like manga?"

I shifted my feet. "I've never read it."

"But we're going to remedy that soon," Hunter said, though he was too enthralled to bother to turn back and look at me.

They launched into an animated discussion of titles and characters with foreign-sounding names that I didn't recognize. Forgotten for the moment, I moved around the room, taking in the rest of her belongings. A fancy-looking bed with a black fabric headboard, brightened by splatters of paint here and there. A desk with the newest laptop and a huge laser printer and boxes and boxes of what appeared to be colorful art supplies stashed underneath, the chemical perfume of paint drifting throughout the rest of the room.

I walked closer to a corkboard, where different-colored fliers and pictures overlapped, competing for space. Painting classes, babysitting jobs, and—

"You compete in martial arts?" I asked, reading the announcement.

"Huh? Oh, yeah, once in a while—Gramps insists," she said, before turning back to Hunter.

My gaze skimmed over to some shelves, and there, on the middle one, I saw a black belt, neatly folded. More than once in a while, from the looks of it.

I glanced over my shoulder. Their dark heads were bent over the books together, almost like a couple, and I couldn't help a pang of jealousy. I had no right, though. Ashleigh was exactly the kind of girl Hunter deserved to be with. The kind of girl who not only shared his interests, but didn't have to lie at every turn.

The kind of girl he might end up with, once I turned him away.

I hated the imaginary females that paraded through my head, unbidden, so I turned away in search of a distraction. Anything to ease the sudden weight in my chest. I latched on to the bookshelf and walked over to the far edge. My fingers dragged across several cracked and worn spines, before pausing on one slim volume with a burst of recognition.

Ghost in the Shell.

I knew this title. It was the same one I'd seen Hunter reading back in the courtyard in Clearwater.

Curious, I wiggled the copy out from between the other books. I opened the cover and when my finger touched the first page, a prompt blinked to life.

Scan images?

This was a new one, but . . . why not? After glancing over to make sure Hunter and Ashleigh were still distracted, I allowed my android abilities to take over.

Yes.

Estimated number of pages: 276.

Approximate scan time: 92 seconds.

Almost three pages per second, I registered, and as I touched the page again, my fingertip vibrated. I felt a flash of heat, and then letters and pictures converted to an information stream, traveling from the page through my skin and exploding up my arm. The pictures reappeared inside my head. I could barely flip the pages fast enough to keep up.

My body tingled with a newfound energy. I had always enjoyed reading. Now I had the ability to learn a limitless number of stories. I could catalog and house entire collections. Experience them all.

About a quarter of the way in, though, the excitement dissipated. My hand started trembling, just the tiniest bit. Halfway in, the tremble turned into a shake. And then I just stopped and stared. Stared in disbelief while my body went cold, cold, so cold. I lowered the book and swallowed at the huge brick in my throat. Gazed at the back of Hunter's head while his hands flew in wild gestures, in what I gathered was a reenactment of some crucial manga fight scene. I desperately tried to will away the terror threatening to squeeze me with iron fists, tried to subdue the mad thump-thump-thump of the faux pulse pounding in my ears. Grady's voice, questioning me.

"That boy—you vetted him, right?"

Out of my memory banks came an image from the past. Hunter, sitting on that bench in the courtyard back at Clearwater High, reading this exact book. His first day at school, yet somehow, he'd found his way to my favorite spot—the one where I went to be alone, where no other students bothered me.

I hadn't questioned it then, that or the way he'd shown up as the new kid at school shortly after I did, because why should I? Back then, I hadn't even known what I was. But maybe I should have.

Because that book that Hunter had been reading, back in Minnesota?

That book was about a girl. A girl who was an android.

Beneath the growing stranglehold of fear, of doubt, of disbelief and anguish and denial, a thought was so frantic, it felt like a beating, throbbing pulse of its own, slapping against my skull. That one thought consumed me.

How well did I really know Hunter? How well?

As quietly as possible, I closed the book and eased it back into the vacant slot, not wanting to draw any attention to what I'd read. It was just a precaution, I told myself. A total coincidence, nothing more.

Except—how many coincidences could you have, before a chain of events could no longer reasonably be construed as random? The events in question flashed through my head with perfect precision. Hunter, showing up that day at the Dairy Queen—when I just so happened to be there. Hunter, in the courtyard—the one place where I could always count on being alone. Hunter, transferring to my English class.

I took one unsteady step away from the bookcase, then two, as the timeline replayed, faster and faster.

Hunter, consoling me in the barn, and asking me out on a date. So accepting of my "prosthetic" arm after a joyride got me tossed from a truck and my circuits were revealed. So willing to travel across the country in an instant when I'd called him.

Across the country to help me, on the strength of one date and an almost-kiss.

My fists clenched, tighter and tighter, and I had to turn away. None of that made any sense, though. I mean, if he'd really been stalking me, why had he let me see the book in the first place? It would have been so easy to have been reading, I don't know, *Huckleberry Finn*, or whatever boys liked to read these days. Though he clearly had a genuine interest in manga, based on the discussion he was still having with Ashleigh.

I stared at his tall form and my breath caught around a desperate mix of uncertainty and terror and hope. I found myself shaking my head. No.

Not this kind, sensitive, magnetic boy who'd always been there for me. There was no way, *no way* he could be teamed up with Holland. Right? His hair was the opposite of military-approved, and besides, he was too young. Unless he'd lied about his age?

I bit my lip and studied his profile. Okay, so maybe he could be seventeen, eighteen max. But doubtful he was older, right?

Then again, Lucas hadn't been much older, either.

And the military wasn't the only group after me. I also had the Vita Obscura to worry about.

The Vita Obscura. Who had, coincidentally, shown up not long after Hunter came to town. In fact—and now I was feeling dizzy—hadn't they attacked our house while Hunter had me out on a secret date?

My mind couldn't even reconcile that notion. Was I being paranoid? Hunter, part of the group who wanted to dismantle me, piece by piece, and make a fortune off my technology? No. It was unfathomable. I mean, beyond not believing that Hunter could be part of such a terrible plot, surely a member of the V.O. wouldn't actually go so far as to try and kiss the girl they knew was an android . . . would he?

A hand flew to my mouth. But we hadn't kissed yet—not really.

"I don't want to take advantage."

That's what he'd said, back in the motel room. But what about all the other times we'd been close? Was he feigning interest to lead me on? I had no way of knowing his true motives. Hunter had said it himself at the amusement park.

"So I have a few secrets."

The uncertainty, the back and forth, bubbled up inside me, until I worried that I might explode at the slightest provocation. Like I was a hand grenade primed and ready to be thrown. The room was too small, too crowded. Too full of horrifying possibilities.

"I'm going to use the bathroom and get ready for bed," I said abruptly. "Good night."

Hunter stopped midsentence and straightened, his smile fading. "I'm sorry, Mila. I didn't realize—"

"No! I mean, I'm fine." I continued backing toward the door. I needed distance. Distance to clear my mind, to prove to myself that these thoughts were crazy. Hunter couldn't be part of this whole conspiracy. If he was . . .

No. I shook off the thought. It was too terrible to contemplate.

I forced my lips into a smile. "You two finish your book talk."

"You're sure?" Hunter wavered, taking one step toward me but then looking back over his shoulder. I waved him off and whirled for the door.

A second later I was inside the bathroom, door locked, pacing the floor and trying to curb the rising dread that made my head too heavy to function.

Stop it, I told myself. Suck it up and *think*.

It was times like these when I almost envied my updated, improved "sister"—MILA 3.0. She never had to worry about emotions interfering with her logic.

With one more deep breath, I stepped away from the door and toward the oval mirror hanging over the sink. Ever since I'd escaped from Holland's compound, I'd had this constant niggle, this worry that after everything that happened, the tests they'd subjected me to, and the things I'd done, that one day I'd look in the mirror and see a completely different girl staring back at me. At the very least, I expected Mom's death to leave some kind of mark, like a faint haze of sadness that aged my otherwise youthful face.

But no. My face looked exactly the same as always. Same bright leaf-green eyes, same exact skin tone, same oversized lower lip. I looked in the mirror and what I saw made me tremble. The hair, it was different, but the face . . . I still looked exactly like Three.

As I stared at my reflection, I felt some of the terror, the anxiety, fade, leaving behind a calmness, a steadily growing sense that controlling my emotions equaled controlling my future.

Three was the kind of person—machine—who could torture people without remorse. Who wouldn't care if someone—say, a boy—had betrayed her. To her, emotions were just masks—responses programmed into her so she could pass as a human. Three wouldn't feel pain if a human died. She wouldn't agonize over lies. She would just . . . exist.

Something that sounded like a nice option at the moment.

The logic soothed me, wrapped around the frantic feelings and smothered out their harsh edges. But a tiny voice shrieked its protest. My human voice. Of course, Three would also do General Holland's bidding without a second thought, no matter who got hurt along the way. Three was the perfect weapon.

But if Three was the perfect weapon, then one thing was damned certain. I could learn how to become one, too. On my own terms.

I averted my eyes and splashed cold water on my face, took care of my simulated biological functions, as Holland had so kindly put it, then retreated to the spare bedroom. Thankfully, Hunter was still with Ashleigh, which gave me time to slip into my sleep clothes. As I changed, my gaze fell on his duffel bag, which sat on the floor against the wall.

The thing had been in our old motel room, and right there in the backseat for the entire car ride out here. Yet not once had I thought to check the contents.

I approached the bag, forcing one foot to step in front of the other.

I'd performed a weapons scan outside, and none had shown up in the vicinity of Hunter's Jeep. But that didn't mean he wasn't hiding other things in there. Or the V.O., with their sophisticated gadgets. Maybe they'd come up with something undetectable.

I unzipped it with trembling fingers, pushing clothing aside. Pausing to clear the hitch in my throat when the room filled with his distinctive scent. I rummaged through every inch, including his toiletry bag. Unless the V.O. had designed toothbrushes that doubled as Tasers, there was nothing to find.

No gadgets, no weapons. But if he were V.O., wouldn't there be evidence on his cell?

I pulled out his smartphone, tapping the screen with hesitant fingertips. If I were wrong, this was unforgivable. Delving into his private information like I was entitled.

Acting just like a spy.

Nothing incriminating there, either. A gathering relief rose in my chest, small at first, but growing to an epic size. There was nothing here to indicate that he was anything other than the boy I thought he was. If he were with Holland or the V.O., surely I would have found something. A weapon. One of those interference gadgets the men who'd attacked Mom and me at the motel had had.

There was only one place left to check now, and then I would put this out of my head for good.

The Jeep.

After rearranging Hunter's bag the way I had found it, I headed for the hall, hanging back a second to give my sensors a chance to update.

No human threat detected.

I crept down the stairs without incident and was out the front door in record time. Darkness had fallen, and my vision kicked in, illuminated the night with that slight red cast.

Night vision: Activated.

I raced down the walkway to the edge of Grady's property, on swift and quiet feet. I reached the gate.

Signal detected: Override lock?

I debated an instant before declaring it too risky. Not with Grady monitoring when the gate opened and closed.

This time, I would have to climb.

I studied the giant post that housed one side of the gate,

then bent my knees and prepared myself to launch. With a forceful jump, I propelled myself toward the layered stone at full speed. My left foot hit first, high off the ground, and without losing momentum I immediately vaulted upward and off, twisting to the right. I surged toward the top, my fingers catching the end of a metal spike, and I hauled my body upward. A moment later I straddled the gate, before dropping to the pavement on the other side.

I landed easily in a crouch, holding my pose when a car pulled into a garage at the far end of the street.

When no one else stirred, I jogged over to Hunter's Jeep and hunkered down on the sidewalk side, pressing against the vehicle, trying to be as invisible as possible. I needed to know if there were any weapons or spy tech around.

Initiate scan.

No weapons detected.

Good, that was good.

Tracking device detected: Back driver's side wheel well.

My phantom heart kicked in my chest. Let me be wrong. Let it be something else.

I dropped to the ground and pushed myself under the Jeep, scraping my neck on loose gravel. My nostrils filled with the pungent combo of asphalt and oil. I scanned the back driver's wheel well—flash of red.

Tucked away, almost buried by the tire.

My fingers didn't want to function but I forced them. I grabbed for the object, carefully pinching it by the sides. The texture wasn't firm like I'd expected, but yielded a little. Squishy. The object resisted my first two gentle tugs to remove it, but finally pulled free, with resistance.

I shifted the tiny square until it dangled in front of my face. A cube of metal, with a blinking red light. Encased in a silicon-like substance.

The very same GPS device used by the V.O. to track us before. I looked closer, and it got even worse. Inside the device was a tiny microphone.

I lay there for at least thirty seconds, dazed. I cursed myself for not scanning the car before and my heart buckled and twisted, as if trying to escape the proof in my hands.

Then, I replaced the device in the wheel well and scooted out from under the Jeep. When I went to stand, my legs went leaden. My stomach surged into my throat. I squeezed my eyes shut, as if that could blot out reality. I couldn't move. Couldn't breathe. Couldn't think. The pain was staggering, enough to double me over.

A pile of coincidences, finally toppled by the last, most damning one.

Hunter was with the V.O. He had been all along.

That ever-widening hole, deep in my pseudo heart? That was the feeling of hope dying. I couldn't lie. Up until that moment, a tiny reserve of hope had still slumbered deep in my chest. Dormant but alive. But as I stared at the GPS, the reserve evaporated, leaving a dried-up, cracking riverbed in its wake.

A few streets over, a car engine turned over with a hiccupy grind, reminding me that I couldn't stay here forever. I had to get out of the street and back into the guest room, before anyone noticed my absence.

On autopilot, I reclimbed the gate and crept back to the house, my mind festering with a toxic blend. Disbelief. Acceptance. Betrayal. A sense of loss so staggering, I thought my legs might yield. And finally, unanswered questions, assaulting me with a sharp bite. How could Hunter betray me like this? He'd known the truth about me all along, and he hadn't revealed a thing. I'd felt guilty about not telling him everything, but he'd been deceiving me. I saw everything in a different light. Why he avoided kissing me. Why he insisted upon coming with me. Was the story about his lowlife dad even true?

And if he was V.O., why hadn't they made their move? What could they possibly be after? The same knowledge I was seeking? Or something else?

And, ultimately: *what the hell did I do now?* I couldn't run, not without the information I'd come for. In fact, I couldn't do anything that would give away that I knew the truth about Hunter. Until I came up with a plan, I had to play along.

I consulted my sensors before easing the front door open and creeping into the house. I paused to listen before heading to the stairs. Safe, until I stepped into the hallway, when I heard Hunter's voice from around the corner, bidding Ashleigh good night.

Traitor.

My insides contorted in anguish while I whirled, racing for the bed. Hunter's footsteps padded down the hall. I couldn't face him. Not until I'd had time to process.

Target distance: 10 ft.

Target distance: 5 ft.

With no time to spare, I tossed back the quilt and slid underneath. My eyelids shut right when the door opened.

"Mila?" he whispered, his footfalls soft as he edged closer to my bed.

I kept my face relaxed and my eyes shut, breathing slowly and deeply, while under the covers, my fingers dug into the sheets and a cyclone whirled in my head, tearing away at every certainty and shredding it to pieces.

The irony crashed down like a falling plane, landing right smack-dab in the center of my chest. Here I'd been planning on leaving him to save his life . . . and the whole time, he'd been planning to betray me. And for what?

That was a mystery I needed to uncover. And fast.

Head turned to the side, I waited, the crush of betrayal never relinquishing its grip. I waited while he rustled in his duffel bag. Waited while he left the room for the bathroom and returned. Waited while he crawled into bed, whispered, "Good night," and rolled onto his other side, earbuds in his ears and music faintly seeping through.

Waited until the bitter tears stopped slipping beneath my lashes and dampening the pillow.

When his breathing had quieted for long enough, I waited some more, considering and discarding plan after plan.

Run? No. Now, more than ever, I needed the information Mom had sent me after.

Subdue Hunter and demand answers? Not yet. I couldn't risk that he'd alert the V.O. somehow. The last thing I wanted was for them to know *I* knew they were monitoring my every move.

Tell Grady? Uh-uh. That would only potentially put him and Ashleigh in more danger. Besides, how did I know Grady wasn't double-crossing me right this very moment? If this had taught me one thing, it was that the command Mom had given me before we reached Holland's compound still stood.

"Don't trust anyone."

As it turned out, her advice was excellent. If only I'd heeded it a little sooner.

I needed a course of action, though. Something to do. I would not sit around, waiting on a man who might or might not be an ally, in a bed less than three feet away from a known enemy. I couldn't.

No, I would hunt down the information myself.

After reassuring myself that Hunter still faced the wall and wasn't stirring, I crept out of bed and into the hall. I hovered in the doorway, listening for any signs of activity.

Faint tapping, from the direction of Ashleigh's room. Nothing from Grady's.

I dried my tears, tucked my pain into a compartment somewhere deep inside, and turned the key. Then I eased my way down the stairs. I had to reassess everything now, and I couldn't do that without information. I needed a new plan of action.

Grady had asked if I'd vetted Hunter. Now was as good a time as any to rectify my oversight.

SEVEN

The hall was clear, as my enhanced hearing had insisted it would be. My bare feet made little sound as I padded down the stairs, pausing outside the doorway on the left. Grady's study.

The door was barely ajar, so I eased it open, slowly, just in case. Darkness greeted me.

Night vision activated.

The office illuminated with a reddish-hued glow, and I took everything in with a quick sweep. A framed family photograph on the wall next to another of Ashleigh's drawings (this one of a dragon, probably recent, based on the advanced technique), shelves with assorted nonfiction books and espionage thrillers, heavy wooden desk with old laptop and wireless printer. Gray carpet, with faint marks in four spots on the far side of the room, indicating the furniture had been moved recently. Odd end table constructed by flipping a car wheel onto its side and attaching a circle of glass to the top. A faintly floral smell, which I attributed to air freshener, since it was too far for the roses to permeate and neither Grady nor Ashleigh were wearing perfume. No other access to the room except the door I was standing in.

I crossed the floor to the swivel chair, careful not to make it squeak as I scooted it toward the desk. I touched the closed laptop—which was adorned with a large sticker featuring a stick man that said "Life is good"—and realized that he hadn't turned it off. It was just in sleep mode. I opened it and bright blue flashed as the laptop fired up. Not especially stealthy.

Then, the icons popped up and I rested my fingers on the keys, and as I did, the hum vibrated inside me, starting in my core and working its way up to my head. Like before, I sensed two separate networks—one accessible, one blocked.

We'd have to see about that. I'd start by running a simple search. Using my hands to anchor myself, I issued the command.

Open ports.

At the same time, I heard a creak.

The sound stopped me, and the glowing data ceased its humming whirl. My eyes slowly lifted upward, to where I'd heard the noise overhead.

It had come from Grady's room.

I waited, unnecessary breath caught in pseudo lungs, while the creaking continued in a rhythmic pattern. Creak. Creak. Creak.

He was out of bed . . . and walking.

I waited. I couldn't be caught in here, going through his things. No way he'd swallow any story I concocted.

I heard more creaking, only . . . not in the direction of his door. Instead, he headed to the left. Silence loomed for a few moments while I stood, undecided, not sure whether I should abort the mission or not. And then a whir of water. Flushing.

A few louder squeaks of the bed, until finally, everything was quiet again.

Open ports.

The data whooshed inside this time, with the electrical burn accompanying it up my arms. My entire head tingled, crackled with the seductive gleam of information, the strands glistening and twirling as if performing a free-form dance. It was like I could feel them slide between my fingers, sleek and sinuous. The knowledge poured into my mind like water from a pitcher, lit with an iridescent glow.

I embraced the power, the knowledge, the reality that I could acquire any information I wanted.

Within the strands, I searched for one name.

Hunter Lowe.

Of course thousands of possibilities flew through my head, so I backtracked, seeking information linking any of them to the military or other suspicious activity. Nothing. So I sorted results until I found my Hunter.

Only, he wasn't mine anymore.

The internet confirmed that he'd attended a San Diego high school, before coming to Clearwater.

Nothing remarkable in his family history, either. His stepfather ran his own software company, and his mom taught for an online university. I studied their faces—his mom, pretty with high cheekbones and wide-set eyes, a darker blue than Hunter's. Her dishwater blond hair cut in a short, carefree style. His stepdad, with a broad forehead, emphasized even more by a receding hairline, brown eyes smiling slightly at the camera. Nothing especially remarkable about either of them. Did they have any idea what their son had gotten involved in?

I searched further, but didn't find much. A reference to a childhood soccer game here, a listing under National Honor Society there. But no red flags. Nothing that jumped out and shrieked, "V.O.!"

Whatever the answers were, I wasn't going to find them here. I considered waiting for Grady to provide more information, but I hadn't vetted him. And after what I'd discovered at the Jeep, I was finding it difficult to believe anyone was truly a friend. Who had Grady been talking to on the phone earlier? Why had he insisted we stay the night instead of just giving me the information so we could go? Was he as dishonest and conniving as Hunter?

I had little doubt that the answers I sought would be hiding in the secure network, GrSecureNet.

Once again, I opened myself to the energy shimmering around me, and felt for the slippery, less solid pathway that led to the hidden network.

There. Found it, and slam! Hit up against a mental door.

Access denied, the network communicated. *Verify user?*

Oh, no you don't.

The command slid from me with ease:

Override lock.

That familiar roar. Muffled at first, then growing in volume; like a wave crashing toward shore. A surge in current. Then, the barrier holding me out yielded, a door swung open.

GrSecureNet: Access granted.

An exhilarating rush surged beneath my skin. Grady couldn't keep me out. No one could.

I traced his pathways, like tracing dangling threads back to their spools. The threads led to little green boxes, hovering in midair.

Files.

I shifted their positions, trying to get an idea of which would be the best place to start.

Recently Downloaded—Confidential.

That seemed like as good a place as any.

Open file.

Access restricted: Protected data.

Even before I tried the usual command, I knew that something about this door felt different. More secure.

Override lock?

Intruder suspected. Enter password or system lockdown will commence in 5, 4—

Crap! Password? I didn't have the password. Given enough time, I could probably hack one, but not in—

3—

Three seconds!

In desperation, I tried one more time.

Override lock! Admit user!

Illegal command. System lockdown commencing now.

It was like a dimmer switch had been turned on, inside my head. The shimmering green faded, and in the next instant, vanished. In its wake was a hollow echo—a void where mere moments ago, there had been life.

Damn.

A rapid-fire blinking filled the void a moment later, the lights rearranging themselves into words.

Nice try but no dice. Don't worry—I have the files you need upstairs.

Grady. Shock shot me to my feet, and I stumbled back from the desk. What . . . ? How . . . ?

Are you coming?

I only hesitated for a split second.

Yes.

Creak. My head whipped toward the door. I'd been so involved in the search, so engrossed in unlocking levels, that I hadn't monitored my external environment.

"Grandpa? Grandpa, I have to show you something—"

Ashleigh appeared in the doorway, still in her shredded jeans and T-shirt from earlier, clutching her phone in her hand. She froze when she saw me heading her way.

"Where's Gramps?" Her arm shot out to block my path and I stopped short to avoid a collision. No smile now; her mouth was a grim line as she studied my face. "Pretty good, but they got the chin wrong. Still, I knew it was you."

I drew in a steadying breath. "I don't know what you're talking about," I said, keeping my voice even while creasing my brow into an expression of confusion. "What chin?"

"I ran a search when you let it slip you knew Gramps worked for the government. Took a photo with my phone and uploaded it, and hit on the police sketch. If that's not you, then you can explain why it looks exactly like you to the cops."

I stepped forward. "Look, it's not what you think," I said urgently. "I didn't do anything. I swear, I'm not planning on hurting anyone. Just let me leave and we'll be out of here. We won't bother you again. Ask your Grandpa—he knew my mom!" I said.

"Yeah, right."

I ducked to cross under her arm, but her foot whipped out, catching me in the stomach. I tumbled onto my butt, the gray carpet masking any sounds of my fall.

"You aren't going anywhere. The cops are on their way—they'll be here soon."

Cops.

Pushing hard on the palms of my hands, I launched to my feet in one smooth, effortless motion. Ashleigh still blocked the doorway, her body lowered into a defensive stance, but all I saw was an obstacle to my escape.

I would not let the police find me. No matter what.

Human threat detected.

Engage?

Yes.

I feinted left, followed her motion that way, then darted right at the last second, when she was still midlunge. She recovered her balance in time to shoot out her right hand, but I saw it coming a mile away.

Block target's attack with left arm.

Spin toward target, initiate choke hold.

I spun to face her back and reached out to wrap my arm around her neck, but hesitated. She wasn't a bad guy—just a girl trying to protect her grandfather.

Initiate choke hold.

Block–

Too late. Her elbow smashed into my face. I hit the edge of the doorjamb before stumbling out into the hall. While I regained my balance, all the while cursing my hesitation, she picked up the chair and swung.

Obstacle, 8 in. from impact. Block.

This time, I was ready.

As the chair back flew for my face, I grabbed it with my right hand, stopping the motion with ease as anger flared.

I watched Ashleigh's eyes widen, heard her gasp. Felt the wood crumble beneath my fingers as my hand clenched harder and harder. Pieces fell to the floor like so much sawdust, and she scrabbled backward like a crab.

"What are you?" she whispered, gaze glued to the ruined chair.

Her horror-stricken expression said it all.

Freak.

That triggered an answering fear inside me, but I shoved it away, allowing the anger to take its place. So when her foot shot out, I grabbed it. I wrenched her ankle to the side. Her body followed, twisting into the air before slamming the wooden floor with a loud thud.

Target: Down.

In the far-off distance, a siren wailed.

No more time for games.

I allowed her to push to her knees, wincing, but her tense shoulders and narrowed eyes told me she was still full of fight. This time, I didn't hesitate. When she stumbled to her feet, I grabbed her arm, whirling her around. As I wrapped one arm around her neck and used the other as a brace, pushing her head down until I started to feel her body weaken, I whispered, "I'm sorry."

And when her body slipped to the floor, and the red light flashed—

Target: Immobilized.

—I tried to take comfort in the knowledge that the effects were only temporary. When she regained consciousness, she would be fine. Now, I had to get upstairs, get my files from Grady, and grab Hunter—before the police arrived.

Here I'd been preparing myself to let Hunter go, and as it turned out, the circumstances behind having to take him with me hurt a thousand times worse. I could possibly use him for leverage. At the very least I needed to find out what he knew.

Thumps sounded from overhead. "Ashleigh?" Grady yelled from his bedroom. "Everything okay?"

Out of time. I leaped over her body and raced up the stairs, when Grady burst from his room. His thin hair was disheveled, his striped pajamas rumpled. He held a gun.

"What the hell is going on? Where's Ashleigh?"

He pointed the gun straight at me, but that wasn't what held the oxygen captive in my chest. It was the rectangular piece of plastic in his left hand.

I zeroed in on the object. A SIM card.

The siren in the distance was still far away—too far for Grady to catch with his normal human ears—but I knew they were drawing closer.

"Is that for me?" I said, nodding at the card.

He cocked his head, brows hunched over grim eyes. He lowered the gun. "Tripped something when I pulled it off the computer. Some kind of alarm that shouldn't have been there."

"Why would they—"

"Files are encrypted. Does them no good without a decoder."

Who knew about the files, had set the alarm? The V.O.? Or Holland? At this point, I didn't know if it mattered. All I knew was that I had to get out of here.

"Here, take it," Grady said. "I can't break into the files, but I know you can." *I know you can.*

Slowly, I raised my eyes from the tiny scrap of plastic and metal up to his face, in time to see him give one curt nod. He knew. He knew what I was. He was afraid, but he was helping anyway.

"Before I forget, Nicole wanted me to tell you that the

answer is always close to your heart."

Before I could process that, a faint moan rose from downstairs. I stepped closer to Grady. Close enough to catch a faint whiff of his cinnamon toothpaste, and the sudden flare of his nostrils. There was no time to explain. My hand snaked out and closed on the drive before he could snatch it away while he scooted to the side to peer down the stairs.

"Ashleigh?" he whispered. Then, his eyes narrowed and the gun lifted.

"You know that can't hurt me," I said, then cursed my impulsive tongue. He put two and two together almost as fast as I did, and lunged for the guest room door.

For an instant, my feet stayed planted, a logical voice insisting that this might solve one of my problems. If Hunter were dead, he couldn't talk.

No.

My emotions rejected the voice, overpowering it with a single surge, freeing my feet to lunge after him. I grabbed the collar of his pajama top at the same time he reached for the door handle. He turned while I yanked him backward, the door smacking against the frame.

He contorted against me, surprisingly strong. His gun hand whipped in my direction.

I thrust my hand out, pushing his hand up, up, toward the ceiling. A shot rang out and echoed.

Twist gun hand to break grip.

Left knee to groin.

This time, there was no hesitation. I disarmed him, and sent him crashing to the floor, doubled over in pain an instant later. Guilt swelled in my chest like a balloon full of dirty air, but I pushed past it and darted into my room.

Hunter was still lying on the bed, headphones in place. He hadn't heard a freaking thing.

When I saw his motionless figure, a sliver of doubt poked a hole in my certainty. Would a V.O. operative really check out at a time like this?

Then I remembered the other coincidences and my certainty resealed. No time for this now, not with the alarm Grady had triggered. Right now, we had to go.

I tucked the gun into my waistband—who knew when I might need it?—and jerked the earbuds from his ears. "Get up!" I shouted as I raced over to grab our bags. "We're leaving! Life or death," I added, when he looked like he was going to take his time.

"What? Are you—?" But the expression on my face cut him off. He shot to his feet. Barefoot—his shoes were in the duffel bag—he stumbled after me. "I thought we were spending the night?"

"Change of plans. I'll explain later but right now, we need to go."

I wanted to believe it was testimony to his trust in me, but it was more likely proof of his guilt that he followed without question. At least, until we got to the top of the stairs, where Grady was still doubled over on the floor.

"Jesus, Mila, what's going—?"

"I'm so sorry, Mr. Grady," I shouted over him, hurrying past. "I promise—Ashleigh will be fine. Just a choke hold. Hunter, he'll be fine, and I can't wait for you," I added, giving Hunter's arm a harsh yank when he stooped over to check on Grady. "The car. Now."

Looking like he'd just been blindsided by a semi, Hunter turned away from Grady and stumbled after me. I was sure to a normal guy, this would look like a total train wreck. Grady down upstairs, Ashleigh slowly crawling to her feet downstairs. Being yanked out of bed and shoved out the door in the middle of the night, without warning. But Hunter wasn't a normal guy.

He was just an incredibly skilled liar.

I made swift work of the stairs, passing a worse-for-the-wear-looking Ashleigh at the bottom. "Your grandfather needs your help."

Hunter followed, but in his silence, I swear I felt the sting of his accusatory stare drilling into the back of my neck. We burst out the front door, and all of a sudden, the siren's screech was magnified. They were close.

"Are we running from the police?" Hunter finally gasped, as he tried to keep up with me. We raced across the brick-lined path, onto the concrete drive, the night wind cold and biting as it whipped our faces. Unlike last night, the dark sky tonight was backlit with what looked like a thousand stars, their sparkle gleefully illuminating us for anyone who cared to watch.

"I'm not taking another step until you answer me," he shouted. I craned my neck, and sure enough, he'd stopped, hands on his thighs, gasping for breath.

Suddenly furious at his subterfuge, I whirled, ready to unload the full brunt of my rage. He was vermin. Lower than low. Worse than Holland, who at least hadn't whispered sweet nothings to me when he tried to stab me in the heart. No, Holland would stare straight into my eyes, and let me see the blade coming. Whereas Hunter . . . Hunter would slip it between my shoulder blades with one hand, while the other pretended to hold me tight.

But I couldn't just unleash on him. I had to act the same as before. Like I had no idea he was V.O. I had to best him at his own game.

I grappled for an excuse.

Think, Mila! What would you have said to get him to go before you knew his real identity?

Simple. Prebetrayal Mila would have stuck as close to the truth as possible. And now, there was even less reason to stray. He already knew everything.

"Look, you're going to have to trust me on this. They made a mistake—they think I'm someone else. A girl wanted by the police. I could explain it to the cops, but we're underage, traveling without guardians . . . I had to defend myself. Do you want to be taken in to the station?"

"Do I want . . . ?" He trailed off, lips parted in disbelief, eyes sweeping over my face like he was trying to place a stranger.

From the south, I heard a new siren, its wail joining the other. I couldn't wait—but I couldn't leave Hunter, either. He had to come with me. Even if I had to drag him.

I'd taken one step toward him, to do just that, when he picked up his feet and kicked into a run. "Once we get in the car, I want to know exactly what the hell is going on here."

Yeah, so do I. I want to know who you really are and why you're truly with me.

I commanded the gate to open when we were still many strides away. We slipped through the widening gap and sprinted for the Jeep.

The sirens were so close now.

I jumped into the driver's seat and flung the bags into the back. I didn't even wait for Hunter to close his door before I peeled away from the curb. I was sure the closest siren was coming from the north, so I whipped the car in a one-eighty and headed the opposite way. Terror pounded a rapid rhythm in my heart. If we passed them going the other way, and they bothered to get a good look inside . . .

I couldn't allow that to happen.

And all the time, I was acutely aware of the GPS device. Blinking away like an armed bomb beneath my feet. Reminding me that as long as I had Hunter with me, the V.O. would follow my every move.

I floored the gas and after a brief hesitation, the car lunged forward. Hunter didn't speak, but his hand was gripping the handle on the ceiling, so tightly his knuckles whitened. I made it two blocks before I heard the siren around the corner. I shut off the lights and whipped into an empty driveway on my right.

I turned off the engine and scooted down in the seat. "Duck," I hissed, and Hunter followed suit.

Through the window, blue and red lights flashed, moving quickly. When they disappeared, I peeked out the window, to see the taillights fading. I restarted the car and a moment later, we were hauling butt toward the freeway.

Meanwhile, the flash drive pressed into my thigh through the material of my jeans. A reminder, I guess, that no good deed went unpunished. I curled my hand around it. Hopefully whatever was on here would give us a new lead on what to do next, because if it didn't . . . I was lost. Alone in a world with no purpose.

Hunter shifted positions, slouching away from me and brushing at his wayward lock of hair, and my android heart rang hollow. Alone in a world where, no matter how hard I tried to sustain it, hope bled out all around me.

I patted my pocket one more time. And if the files were some kind of trap? Well, then . . . then I was as good as dead.

Even though some would argue that I was never alive to begin with.

EIGHT

I steered the Jeep away from Grady's house, on high alert. Every car we passed was a potential threat; every pedestrian, a potential soldier—coming to take us back. The night sky loomed overhead, much too festive with its parade of stars. At least this time, I'd remembered to use the lights.

Hunter remained silent, watching the flashing scenery as if slightly catatonic. Feigning shock—a wise choice. What kind of person wouldn't succumb to it after being hauled out of bed by his girlfriend to run from the cops?

The kind who worked for a secret espionage group. I snuck a sideways glance at his tall form, slumped against the passenger seat with his mussed hair spilling across the window. He didn't look like a fraud. He looked like a normal—gorgeous but normal—boy.

Then again, I looked like a normal girl, so that proved exactly nothing.

He remained motionless, except for his left hand, clenching and unclenching in his lap. The silence drew out between us, making the interior heavy with tension.

After a few more tenths of a mile, he turned to face me. No quirky smile now. Not a hint of that tenderness I'd caught in his eyes earlier. Just incredible strain, attacking his forehead with lines, pulling his lips downward. Making his hands ball into fists.

I wasn't sure what type of lies to expect next, so I braced myself.

"You've knocked out an old man who fed us and gave us beds. We're running from the cops—possibly wanted for some kind of crime? What *the hell* is going on?"

His posture, his tone—he had the I'm-the-injured-party thing down to an art. The doubt rose again, but anger rose higher, smothering it with a hot black haze. Liar. Beautiful, deceitful, heartbreaking liar.

I swallowed once, twice, and wrestled my anger into submission. "I told you. Ashleigh thought she saw my picture on a news report and called the police."

"And was it?" he demanded, his volume rising like a crescendo.

"Was it what?"

His jaw dropped, his eyes widened incredulously. "Jesus,

Mila, are you kidding me? The picture she saw. Was it you?"

I flinched at his tone. If he was acting, he was damned good at it. He'd pegged the reactions of a normal boy thrust into this situation perfectly. Freaked out and angry and, yes, scared, all rolled into one.

Of course he had. But why? What were they after? Why the elaborate ruse?

I could only think of two viable reasons. One, they wanted me to lead them to whatever information was in my pocket. Or two, they were conducting an elaborate, up-close-and-personal study. Trusting Hunter to figure out what made me tick, how I reacted, exactly what my android functions were. Basically, a variation of one of Holland's experiments. Test the android's capacity for human emotions, before exploiting her for their own twisted purposes.

"We look very similar," I hedged, the words forced through clenched teeth.

"So it wasn't you." He leaned toward me, and I was assaulted with dual reactions. Recoil from his nearness, battling out the urge to lean in and meet him halfway. I sat still, ignoring them both. "If it wasn't you, why did you run?" he asked.

I gave what I hoped was a helpless shrug. "I ran because I'm scared, Hunter! There's a picture out there of a girl who looks like me, who's wanted for a crime. Do you think the cops would believe anything I had to say? I'm sixteen—as far as they're concerned, I'm a runaway! If they pick me up, it'd be a huge mess—no one to bail me out, and forget about finding my dad," I said, my words tumbling out faster and faster.

He wasn't the only one who could act.

I inhaled an exaggerated breath, then said, "I know, I probably chose wrong, but I panicked. I'm sorry that you got caught in the middle. I was afraid if you stayed behind, they'd arrest you." I forced myself to reach out and touch his arm, prepared to combat disgust at the contact. Instead, tingling spread across my skin like wildfire. Even now.

If only this could be an act, too.

"Okay," he said slowly, rubbing two fingers over his temple. "But what about Grady, and Ashleigh? How did you take them down?"

God. Would he ever stop with the questions? "My mom thought it was important that I learn self-defense—just in case. And they jumped me first."

I didn't add that I'd actually protected him from Grady, because even now, I couldn't produce a single logical reason why. The thought of a bullet entering Hunter's heart made my own feel like it was breaking again. *Stupid*, I admonished. *He doesn't care about you at all.*

As it turned out, apparently that didn't matter. Despite the blistering rage that I barely had a handle on, despite the stab of pain every time I pictured the GPS tucked safely away under the wheel, my heart refused to yield.

But at least I knew better than to trust it now. This was all on me for not realizing that I wasn't the only one who could lie.

His brows shot up. "They jumped you first."

"Yeah."

I saw him shake his head and move his lips wordlessly, like he still had a difficult time comprehending.

"Okay," he finally said. "I thought something was off with that old guy. I mean, really, who defends their flowers. But Ashleigh—"

"She thought she'd get a huge reward."

"So their friendliness, their interest in us was just a lie—to get something from us."

"Exactly."

"I wish you'd yelled or something so I could have come to help you."

He was buying my lies, wanting to support me. Why did I feel guilty? He was lying, too, pretending he didn't know what was going on.

"It all happened too fast," I told him.

Threat detected: 2.8 mi.

My hands clenched the wheel.

Military helicopter: UH-1N, headed southeast.

The 3-D visual overtook my visual field, rotating a large

white vehicle with red, white, and blue stripes across the side.

Armed.

Holland, it had to be. Headed directly toward Grady's house.

I pressed the gas a little harder, praying that I'd put enough road between us and Grady's house to avoid detection, and that Holland was still keeping the details of my escape somewhat guarded, to save his own hide.

But I needed the information Grady had given me, and I needed it fast. Pretty soon, I'd be surrounded by enemies, and without Mom's help I was floundering in the dark.

A ball settled in my throat, strangling my airway until swallowing felt like a monumental task. Mom. I missed her now more than ever.

Hunter's yawn snagged my attention. He wiggled and repositioned his feet to get comfortable. "Maybe we should just find a place to stay for the night—you've got to be tired, too."

Suspicion bloomed, filling my head like a toxic cloud. "I'm fine." No way I was stopping on his count and walking into a trap.

I kept the speed just under the limit, obeyed all the traffic laws, and shoved the hat I'd stashed under the seat low on my head. The scenery had lost all of its appeal. Any sense of wonder, of expectation—gone. It was duty that drove me onward. The sooner I solved that puzzle, the sooner I could disappear. Leave Holland, the V.O., and Hunter behind me.

When another hour had passed without a return of the helicopter or a sighting of a cop, I pulled the car onto a stretch of grass by the road, just in front of a copse of trees. There'd been nothing around for miles, but it wasn't like I could just pop the hardware into my wrist with Hunter there.

For a second, I pictured his face filled with horror, the same horror I'd experienced the first time Mom had shown me the deviant nature of my wrist. Then I shook off the ridiculous thought. More like greed. He'd want to know every little bit he could about my functions, so he could report back.

"Why are we stopping?" These were the first words Hunter had uttered in the last thirty minutes. Ever since our last talk, his mood had been distant.

"I have to . . . you know," I said, waving a few crumpled-up napkins in my hand. Despite everything, my cheeks burned. But I needed a way to ensure my privacy, and this was all I had.

"Ah," he said, his tense expression finally easing when his lips twitched. "Watch out for poison ivy."

"Please."

Cheeks burning even brighter now—seriously, manufactured embarrassment? Get over yourself—I jumped out of the Jeep and darted around back, heading for the trees.

My legs crunched through vines and ivy while I kept plowing a path away from the road. Finally satisfied that I was well out of view of the car, I ducked behind the biggest tree I could find. Through the branches, I could still make out the car, but this was the best cover I could muster. It would have to do.

Night vision: Activated.

The trees illuminated with that familiar reddish glow, making it easy for me to see. Hunter wouldn't have the same advantage. Combined with the fact that I could see if he tried to follow, I should be safe enough here.

I groped in my pocket and extracted the card, closing my eyes for a brief moment while clutching it tightly in my fist. Nerves and excitement battled in my stomach, waging a war that resulted in a weird, jittery sensation, like I could barely stand still. This was it. Here, in my hand, was potentially the only avenue left open to discovering the truth. If this didn't pan out, that road might be blocked in a permanent dead end. Unless I wanted to risk my luck sneaking back into Holland's compound to see what secrets I could find.

A shudder passed over me, and then I opened my eyes, willed myself to take the plunge. I pulled apart the skin on the inside of my wrist, revealing the thin slot. A perfect rectangle, just waiting for someone to insert a card like this one. I waited for the old slithery twist of revulsion to sweep over me. Feet planted, spine rigid, I braced myself. But there was nothing beyond a slight twinge. More of a wistfulness than anything, for realities come and gone and no longer within my grasp. Instead, my body tingled with a kind of heady excitement, and my wrist actually throbbed with a desperate urge. As if encouraging me to insert the card. *Now.*

No more deluding myself that I could will myself into a real human girl. That time was over.

I willed my hand to steady, this time, refusing to avert my eyes from the dark recess into my arm that shouldn't exist. With pinched fingers, I fed the card into the waiting chasm, hope building that finally, whatever truths Mom had hidden from me would start to unfold. Anticipation tingled through my waiting wrist as I watched the card slide in.

Heat first. Then, the familiar buzz of electricity crackled up, up, up my arm.

I put my other palm against the tree, bracing for the overwhelming slam of information that I'd experienced before, which had almost brought me to my knees. But it never came. This time, my mind was prepared for the energy that rushed into my head, opening wide to receive the streams. Not only that, but the more information that entered, the more my entire body felt energized. Almost like my cells were feeding off the data as a source of power.

I threw my head back and outstretched my arms, catching sight of glittering stars that suddenly didn't feel quite as distant as they once had.

I embraced the exhilaration, anticipating when the illegible nonsense would transform into recognizable language. Like the power of alchemizing metal into gold.

Virus scan complete.

Copying data.

Scanning metadata.

A whoosh of information, like a flash flood roaring through a dry riverbed. And then—files. Lots and lots of files.

I latched on to the nearest one, the blinking square a beacon in a sea of chaos.

Open file.

Symbols burst out from the square and I paused, waiting for the frenetic activity to slow, for the gibberish to vanish as the symbols realigned. They pulsed, wavering and merging, like glittering hieroglyphics. Flickering into new rows, assuming new shapes.

Every single one of them, utterly unreadable.

I frowned, waiting for them to move again. But they didn't. The information refused to budge, sticking firmly to its illegible formation.

Why would my mom go to all this trouble to lead me to a file full of complete nonsense?

Encryption override: Rejected.

The words blinked in my head, answering my question. Encrypted. That's right. The files Mom had left were encrypted.

The sinking pit in my stomach vanished. If Mom had encrypted the files, then it meant I possessed the ability to open them. I just had to figure out how.

I focused on the first file. I'd broken codes before—surely I could do it again.

Override encryption.

I waited and . . . nothing.

My fingers curled into rough tree bark as I took a deep breath and tried again.

It was no use. Not even a faint blip, or the slightest sense of unraveling. The data strands moved around, only to form a new nonsensical pattern.

Encryption pattern: Unrecognized.

What did that mean? Why would Mom give me files that I couldn't decode? Had she messed up somehow? Had she used an encryption system that was too new for me to break?

I pictured Mom, her capable, long fingers, her grace under pressure, and the answer was clear. She wouldn't. Somehow, someway, I possessed the ability to open the file. I had to keep trying.

Anxiety uprooted somewhere in my gut, but I didn't

allow it to build. I had to approach this logically. Maybe I was just starting in the wrong place.

I shoved the first file aside and grabbed at another flashing beacon. But every time I tried to get a firm grip, it changed shape, morphing into something insubstantial, before popping back up in another part of my head.

Encryption code: Unrecognized.

Each attempt met the same result. The moment I thought I caught the code within my grip, it wriggled away, too slippery to hold down for long. My hands clenched harder, and I felt the bark crumble beneath my fingers like dried leaves. All this way, just to hit a dead end. Now what did I do?

Methodically, I went through the process, over and over again, a growing numbness deadening my last bit of hope. Nothing. Nothing. Nothing.

I slumped forward. What was I missing? Why was this so difficult? And if Mom had wanted me to open these, why hadn't she left me a clue?

A clue.

Suddenly, Grady's voice rang through my head. "Nicole wanted me to tell you that the answer is always close to your heart."

Could that be my clue? If so, what did it mean? Did it allude to some knowledge I possessed, deep inside, knowledge I kept close to my heart? Like what? The knowledge that I was human? That Mom had loved me? I pondered those ideas briefly before discarding them. That all seemed a little too touchy-feely for her.

I straightened when another idea occurred. Maybe she'd mean literally, like I had another secret slot or drive, somewhere near my heart? My fingers flew under my shirt, prodding and poking over my skin, my ribcage, anywhere remotely in the vicinity. They fell away in defeat a few moments later.

I banged my head against the tree. "Damn it!"

Something had to be there. I'd given up too quickly.

My hands returned to search more thoroughly, brushing the pendant necklace away in annoyance.

The pendant swung and I went still. My fingers found the emerald again, pressed it into my palm. The necklace Mom used to wear. The one that she'd fiercely protected while she was alive. The one she'd handed to me, before the life drained from her eyes.

". . . close to your heart . . ."

I raised the gemstone, rotating it carefully as I inspected it with both my eyes and fingers, scrutinizing every facet for even the tiniest hint that the necklace was more than simple jewelry.

Intact, intact—wait. On one end, I felt the tiniest hint of an imperfection. A tiny crevice, so thin I'd almost missed it.

I tried to tame my rising excitement. It could be nothing. Just a flaw. But, as if a puppeteer pulled my strings, my hand lifted and without hesitation forced my index nail into the groove.

The bottom of the gem slid open, exposing a thin strip of metal. As I stared, something clicked in a dim corner of my mind.

A key. The pendant wasn't just a necklace, but a key.

Letting my instincts guide me, I rotated the pendant until the metal part faced my skin, then pushed it down, hard. Right into the crease of my elbow, and immediately upstream from the flowing data.

The instant the cool metal touched my skin, my entire body jerked. The strands suddenly pulsed brighter, hotter. They grew thicker and thicker and started flashing: huge, forceful flashes that I felt all the way from my head to my toes.

I held perfectly still—terrified that any movement would send the data spiraling beyond my reach again, possibly for good—and pushed through all the chaos to zero in on the file.

Come on. Come on.

The symbols flickered and disappeared. No. Not again.

But then something extraordinary happened. The glittery strands exploded back into existence, sending all the incomprehensible gibberish flying in every direction. Like a firework sending off millions of sparks.

The next moment, the sparks flew back together, but this

time, they rearranged themselves into something readable.

Encryption: Decoded.

And just like that, I was in.

The first file title pulsed into view.

FDP Witness Protection Program

Under that ominous listing, there was a single entry.

Birth name: Daniel Lusk.
Alias: Steven John Jensen.
Last known residence: 2310 Forest Ln, Denver, CO.
Location of new residence (as of August 2012): 2849 S. Highwater, Glen Ellyn, IL 60137

That was it. The extent of the information in that particular file. Which I guess made the next part of my search a no-brainer. Looked like I was heading to Illinois.

All that subterfuge, just to lead me to another name. I rolled them both around in my head, feeling for any familiarity. At the name Daniel Lusk, something sparked in my memory. It vanished too quickly to grasp. Nothing at all at Steven Jensen.

I couldn't help but think it was overkill, somehow. But Mom had to have known what she was doing. Clearly, the guy she wanted me to find was in hiding, and it was imperative he not be found.

Feeling a little deflated, I shifted over to the next glowing box.

Open file.

This file burst open in a kaleidoscope of colors, all of them scattering throughout my mind like dust before the pieces flew back together, rearranging themselves into pixels. A photo this time.

And then the pieces formed the whole, and I could barely think at all. Because I recognized the face of the man in the photo. The brown hair. The eyes that squinted a little when he smiled. The Phillies shirt.

My entire body went frigid, and my hand shot out toward the tree, to support my suddenly shaky legs.

This man, I knew. Even though I'd been told he never existed. I'd mourned his death before I'd discovered the darkest of truths and had all my pretenses of normality ripped away. That he wasn't really my father at all, but an implant. A phony memory installed by my mom to protect me from Holland.

Now I had no idea where the truth resided. Because clearly the man from my memories was, indeed, real.

Why, Mom? I questioned silently. Only the whisper of the wind through the trees answered.

Had she programmed him into my head to make him

easier to find, in case something like this happened? Who was he? Another scientist? A friend? Ex-CIA, like Grady? Who?

I let my mind wrap around the photo, absorb every nuance of his features, while at the same time, the memory of his programmed scent filled me. Musky with hints of pine, and familiar. Was that also another truth in hiding? Would I ever know for sure? Because apparently Mom had done such a good job weaving the truth with lies, I might never unravel their complicated web.

In the background of my mind, the third file square gleamed, waiting to be opened. I reached for it tentatively, a little afraid now of what I might find. But hiding in the dark was no longer an option.

Open file.

Motion. Symbols, dancing through my mind on phantom legs. The information began to assemble, sluggishly, but before it could form discernible language, something crackled through my head, and just like that, everything vanished. Well, everything except one word. Or rather, another name.

Sarah.

My head filled with Mom's weak rasp. *Sarah.*

The sound of my harsh breathing surrounded me. I plunged into the file, sifting through a hollow channel, searching for any kernel of information I might have missed.

But it was like tunneling through a vacuum. Not a speck of data anywhere.

Why? Why would Mom give me an empty file?

And then, the red words blinked into my head, answering my question.

Sarah file: Erased.

Defeat gripped me with cold, heavy fists. The file was gone. Erased by Mom for some reason I would probably never know.

I scraped my fingers against the rough bark. There had to be a way to get that data, surely. Maybe I should try one more time?

With a deep breath, I relaxed my hands, my mind, and submerged back into the empty void where the Sarah file used to exist. Surely a trace of the code was in here, and if I could find that, I could track it back to the original material.

All I felt was emptiness, a stark, sleek void barren of the colorful life that pulsed within the usual data strands.

Nothing, not even a blip. Except, wait.

A flash, followed by a tremor . . . which fizzled into nothing, like waves suddenly disappearing into a flat, placid pond. I concentrated all of my energy, dove in again. This time, I felt something give. This was it! I was going to unlock—

A pulse of sheer white light, so strong I stumbled back.

A sharp, angry sizzle. A shock, brief, but powerful, zapping its way from my head to my hand. Then a burning rush in my wrist and my own robotic voice sounding in my head, without my permission.

All data: Erased.

A firm pinch, replacing the burn.

Eject.

"Mila?"

Hunter's voice sounded behind me at the same time the tiny rectangle pushed up through the drive in my wrist. My other hand flew to cover it, while I felt the weight of his hand drop onto my shoulder.

"You were gone so long that I got worried. I called, but you didn't answer. Everything okay?"

I whisked the card into my left hand and curled my fist around it. The entire thing was hot to the touch. With my other hand, I quickly snapped the pendant shut.

Leaves crackled under my feet as I whirled and slipped the card into my pocket at the same time. I searched his face for any signs of recognition or greed, or even horror, but all I noticed was the confused tilt of his head.

That, and his pupils—dilated as they tried to make use of the tiny amount of light available.

My fingers eased their way out of my pocket while my nonheart steadied. Of course. The light from the open car door only diffused the darkness so far . . . just enough to make out my figure, but most likely not enough for him to see the tiny plastic and metal square that had punched its way through my skin.

No, I was the only one who could see clearly into the darkness and shadows. If only I could erase the dark thought that lingered, unseen, inside me, like a cancer eating away at my last shred of hope.

Don't let the V.O. see what you're capable of.

"Everything's fine."

He gave a funny twist of his mouth before turning. "We should probably get back on the road then."

I followed as he clumsily navigated his way back toward the car, stumbling a few times over branches he couldn't see. One time, I thought he was actually going to fall, so I swooped up and caught him by the arm.

"Thanks." He paused, then his eyes flashed with humor. "Unless you touched poison ivy with that hand."

"Whatever. There's no poison ivy out here," I said, lifting my hand to swat him playfully. I stopped before I could deliver the blow, brushing my hair behind my ears instead. I knew I had to keep up the charade of a flirtation, but that didn't mean I had to believe it myself. Wanting something badly enough didn't make it true. I should know that by now.

Try as I might, I couldn't lie to myself, though. I couldn't change the fact that my first reaction, when he'd walked up, had been happiness. I'd been excited to blurt my news to him, to share that I knew exactly where we were going. Then, reality had crashed down, pulverizing my eagerness until nothing but dust remained.

"If you say so," he teased.

"Come on, we've got a long way to go before we get to Saint Louis." I crunched my way back toward the car, not bothering to pause when I heard his startled inhalation behind me. I'd broken the news like this on purpose, so he couldn't get a good look at my face when I lied about our travel plans. A location not on the far side of the world, but enough out of the way to keep my ultimate destination a secret. I needed to buy myself time to figure out where to unload him and his GPS device. And more importantly, how to unload him.

Despite not being susceptible to the cold, I wrapped my arms around myself and had to force away a shiver.

"Saint Louis? Since when?"

I walked over to the driver's side, busied myself with opening the door. "Since the first Grady was obviously the wrong one. One of my mom's old friends lives there. I figure he'll know something to help me zero in on the right Grady."

A pause while Hunter scrunched his long body into the passenger seat. I fidgeted with the rearview mirror positioning while his eyes searched my face. "Can't we just call him?"

I shrugged like it was no big deal and shoved the key into the ignition, while between us, suspicion hovered like an invisible wall. The corresponding catch of the engine gave me another moment to compose myself. "It'll be harder for him to blow me off if he's staring me in the face."

For an extra-long three, five, ten seconds, all I heard was the engine's hum, the whir of tires on asphalt, and Hunter's even breaths. "Huh" was all he said. But that one noise held a wealth of distrust. He checked the cell phone he'd pulled from his pocket, tapping it a few times and frowning before turning and stashing it back in his duffel. Then, he stared off into the distance, his teeth chewing at the inside of his cheek.

Meanwhile, suspicion pressed against my throat like a boot. What had he been reading on his phone, and how stupid could I be? I should have disabled it when I had the chance. Doubts—they were tormenters, vicious things that picked away at me, piece by piece by piece. Ever since I'd discovered the GPS, I hadn't been able to shake the poisonous burn in the pit of my stomach, like acid eating away at the lining. Even now, the thought of it, blinking away our location to a group of strangers who wanted to rip me apart for money, made the burn intensify.

And beneath it all, deep down, lurked a truth that I wished I could hide from myself. Deep inside, I knew I still cared about him.

But that couldn't change anything.

Bitterness raced across my chest, surrounded my heart, and hardened the pump into the inanimate object it really was.

He sighed and then rolled to face me, bracing his chin on one palm. "I'll go to Saint Louis with you, but after that, I'm done. And I want you to be prepared. In case things don't go the way you hope they do."

The pressure on my neck pinched a little tighter. Hope? What hope? Hours ago, he had been my *only* hope, but now . . .

My mouth twisted. Hunter needn't worry. I already knew nothing would turn out the way I'd hoped. But one thing was for sure.

I would definitely be prepared.

NINE

I checked the rearview for another glance at Hunter's duffel bag. Something I'd been doing far too regularly ever since I'd watched him stash his phone inside. Worry nagged, and once again I cursed my shortsightedness. I should have incapacitated his phone back at Grady's. Now, the uneasy feeling churning in the dark recesses of my body served as a constant reminder of my error.

I guess having overactive emotions isn't my only android flaw.

Rectifying this mistake meant I needed to put his phone out of commission. One by one, I would thwart Hunter's tools, until the V.O. no longer had a way to track me down. Then, I would do whatever was necessary to ensure Hunter couldn't track me down, either.

I needed to buy myself time to get to Chicago and find Steven Jensen. And a plan was slowly formulating. In order to do that, I needed to send Hunter and his GPS in the opposite direction. That way, by the time the V.O. discovered I'd eluded them, it'd be too late to find me again. I'd be long gone.

We'd passed a number of semis during our trip, which helped spark the idea. I just needed a few supplies. Duct tape, zip ties, that ought to do it. That was all I needed to break into a truck, stash a bound and gagged Hunter and the GPS inside, then send them on their way across the country, and out of my life for good.

Another vicious stab under my rib cage, a single flicker of doubt. If somehow, someway, I were wrong about this . . .

No. Those kinds of thoughts would only make what had to be done hurt more. Think like Three, I reminded myself. Force the emotions away.

"You okay to drive still?" Hunter asked.

"Fine."

While I'd been programmed to feel fatigue at regular intervals, it was just that—a feeling. Lack of sleep would never dull my reflexes—because androids didn't need rest.

He stretched his arms overhead. "I'll try to stay up with you this time. So you don't fall asleep at the wheel."

"Honestly, I'll be okay. No sense in both of us being tired."

"Hey." He rested his hand on my shoulder, and my entire body alerted to his touch, signals going haywire as a riot of emotions swept me.

Stop.

"I'm sorry I snapped at you earlier. I'm just tired and confused. Let's talk about this once we've both rested up, see if we can't figure things out. If running from the cops together isn't a bonding experience, well . . ." The soft teasing note in his voice made me swallow, hard. All traces of his smile vanished when he said, "I was wrong before. We're in this together, got that?" The abrupt turnaround made the knot in my throat grow.

His blue eyes stared into mine for several long seconds, and oh, how I wanted to believe in him. I needed something to believe in—something other than Holland and lies and death. "Besides, the radio has been begging me to save it from your substandard deejaying effort," he finished, sounding more like the old Hunter.

While he tapped at buttons to find a more acceptable station, my forced smile faded as my thoughts returned to the duffel bag on the seat behind me.

Target distance: 38 in.

Detection risk: High.

Acquire?

The tightness in my throat returned, traveled downward to my chest. I might have hated lying to Hunter, but it paled in comparison to not trusting him.

More than anything, I wished I could have my hope back.

We sped down the road while he fiddled. "Here we go. Now this is music," he said, sinking back into his seat with an exaggerated sigh while a high-pitched male voice belted out words to accompany furiously paced guitar. As I watched his strong fingers tap an enthusiastic rhythm on his knee, I almost wished that I hadn't found the GPS. Then I could at least enjoy this part of the journey. Live in the moment.

Hunter patted his pockets and pulled out a pack of gum, popping a white square out of the foil and into his mouth. He extended the package to me. "Want one?"

The peppermint smell filled the car, and suddenly, I was transported back. To another man, one who reeked of peppermint and disinfectant, a combination of smells that set my skin on edge. Holland. Trapping Mom in a room full of fire to push me into performing an obstacle course from hell. Holland, chaining Lucas like a dog so that I would torture him—all in the name of "science."

Holland, warning me in his toxic drawl that the V.O. made him look like a saint.

I waved away his hand before settling my fingers on my churning stomach.

"You okay? Looking a little serious there."

I relaxed my grip and shot Hunter a manufactured smile. "I'm just . . . zoning."

I allowed my gaze to linger on his faded blue eyes for an extra heartbeat before refocusing on the road. I wanted to feel human, I really did.

The problem was . . . my need for survival was stronger.

True to his word, Hunter was still awake a few hours later when a digitized voice announced:

Gas level: forty-eight miles remaining.

My hands jerked on the wheel. "What the . . . ?"

"Hey, that's weird. I don't remember switching that on."

Hunter's voice cut through my confusion and I felt a wave of embarrassment wash over me. That had been the car talking, not me. For a moment there, I'd been afraid a new computer had somehow wormed its way inside me.

After all, it had happened before.

"One of us must have hit the button by mistake. Probably for the best—running out of gas isn't my idea of a good time," I said, trying to keep my voice light.

"I saw a sign a few miles back. There's a town a couple exits away."

I knew that. I'd been planning to stop, regardless. This town would be the perfect spot. Grab my supplies and dispose of Hunter. Hide the Jeep, somewhere so that it wouldn't be noticed as abandoned for a few days, perhaps even longer.

"Perfect timing, too. I didn't get a trip to the forest like you did."

"Right." I could feel my cheeks flushing. An android—embarrassed over bodily functions she didn't really need to perform. Another thing I was sure Holland had never programmed.

A high, melodic note distracted me. I heard Hunter squirm in his seat, and finally looked over to see him pulling his cell phone out of the bag. "Sorry," he said. "I turned the sound back on in case my parents tried to call."

He caught my sideways glance and hastily angled the phone away. Then he hit the button on top to make the screen go blank and tossed it to the floorboard. "Parents?" I asked, keeping my tone casual.

"No, no . . . it's nothing."

The note sounded once more, and Hunter reached for the phone again. But before he did, he shot me a quick look—so quick, I wasn't even sure he realized he was doing it.

This time, he angled his body toward the passenger window as he typed on the keypad. The way you would if you wanted to hide whatever message you were sending. My suspicion climbed when, a few clicks later, he chucked the phone by his feet again. "There, turned off the ringer."

"Anything important?" I asked, all the while monitoring his body language out of the corner of my eye. So I noticed when he froze for an instant, before starting up with his nervous finger drumming on his thighs.

"Nah. Just an old buddy wondering when I'll be coming back to SoCal for a visit."

Which sounded perfectly plausible, except for the way he stared out the window, refusing to look me in the eye. Something people tended to do whenever they lied.

In the distance, signs of life sprouted on either side of the highway. Houses, businesses, a few lonely billboards, all mixed in with grass and foliage. A green sign appeared on the right side of the road. GAS/FOOD, NEXT EXIT.

There was a black-and-white squad car pulled up at the first gas station. Hands tense, I kept my foot steady on the gas, passing that station and continuing on. After a half block and several glances in the rearview to make sure no one was following us, I turned into the truck stop across the street, one with a store and restaurant attached. The station had four lines of pumps with only one taken, given the time of night. With a jerk of my hands, I turned the car sharply, so that we were at an outside pump, the farthest from the attached market. I pulled into the middle position, making sure the backseat of the car was shielded by the credit card payment center and pumps.

Less chance of being seen from the store, by curious passengers and workers. Less chance of being seen by Hunter.

Before he could say anything, I popped open the fuel

tank and dug some cash out of my pocket. "I'd better stay out here and pump while you go in and pay," I said, looking back over my shoulder in the direction of the other station. The cop car was still there, lurking.

Threat detected.

Yes, I knew.

My face was out there, somewhere. Just waiting to be recognized.

Hunter waved away my hand. "I've got it. You want anything?"

Snacks. I was discussing snacks with one of the people who wanted to disassemble me. When had everything gone so crazy? "Candy," I said anyway, remembering the unexpected sweetness of the Starbursts that we'd shared, back in Minnesota.

Back when Hunter had still represented a chance at life. Now, he represented the opposite.

"Okay. Be back in a minute."

He reached down toward the floorboard, and for a second, I thought he was going to take his phone with him. But all he did was tie his shoe before unfolding his tall body out of the car. I watched his lean form walk away. Then my gaze roamed over to the semis, lined up on the far side of the lot. As soon as Hunter returned, I'd run inside the store and search for the restraints.

The second Hunter reached for the door to the market, I

swooped down and grabbed his phone. I searched the icons until I found text messages. I went to press the text icon when the phone flashed red.

Low Battery.

I needed to hurry.

A list of phone numbers popped up, so I clicked on the top one. The text bubbles appeared and I scanned:

Where are u?

Hurry up—getting tired of waiting.

I looked to see who the sender was, but all that was listed was a phone number, not a name.

Powering off . . .

"Damn," I breathed, watching helplessly as the screen went black. Now what?

I tried to make some sense out of the texts, but there just wasn't enough to go on. Although the last one sounded odd for a friend to send. Not so odd if the friend was a member of the V.O. waiting for a special delivery.

I stared at his phone, with the gray-and-white-checkered case, sorrow burrowing under my ribs and piercing my synthetic heart. I'd begun this journey brimming with hope, and now . . .

For an instant, I debated plugging the SIM card into my wrist, but after the close call last night, I decided the risk of getting caught was too high. Plus, what if the V.O. had it booby-trapped somehow? No, the safest bet was putting the thing out of commission. Nothing too obvious, as I couldn't risk revealing my hand to Hunter too soon.

I fidgeted with his phone, thinking.

The red light blinked to life in my head.

Disable cell device?

Yes.

Model?

I answered, and instantly, a schematic of the phone emerged before me, a 3-D grid showing me every chip, battery, and wire. A tiny red, pulsing arrow pointed at one spot.

Excessive pressure on power switch will result in device failure.

With my finger, I pushed hard on the circle indicated, increasing the pressure until I felt something inside the phone give.

That ought to do it.

I replaced the phone on the floorboard, in the exact position I'd found it. Now, Hunter had no contact with the outside world.

My gaze returned to the rows of semis. Enough of them for me to trick Hunter over there, then knock him out, without anyone seeing? I thought so. I glanced up, saw that Hunter was at the register, paying, and plotted the rest. I should be able to break into the back of the truck, no problem, but I'd want gloves.

I looked down at my fingers, studying the tips. At least,

I assumed I'd need gloves. Did my biologically grown skin hold fingerprints? I held my fingers aloft and saw the distinctive whorls patterning the tips. It appeared so.

Fingerprints. Grady's reminder chided me. If only I'd been as smart as him, and researched Hunter at the very beginning. He'd told me to get on that—though how he'd expected me to just jump right up and check out Hunter's prints, I had no clue. It wasn't like I carried a forensic kit on me at all times.

Fingerprint analysis requested?

The prompt made my eyes widen. Or maybe I did.

But where? Only one way to find out. I answered in the affirmative.

Yes.

And as though my response had unlocked a hidden door, I knew. Even before the prompt flashed.

To begin analysis, press rounded surface of fingers carefully against print.

That sounded simple enough. I started to look around the car for an item Hunter had touched before realizing: there was nothing in here I hadn't touched, too. Our fingerprints would be commingled everywhere, probably smudged.

The GPS, though. I'd been careful to grab it by the sides. And I needed to get it anyway. Now. Before Hunter returned.

Settling the baseball cap on my head, I stepped out of the

car. A TV was playing just above the pumps. Ignoring it, I pretended to drop something, then practically dove under the Jeep. I zeroed in on the tiny mass with unerring aim. I slid out and pushed to my feet with the tiny object carefully pinched between my fingers. I glanced toward the store and saw that the cashier had handed Hunter change, and told myself to hurry. Meanwhile, the TV screen continued its newscast over the pumps.

"The temperature will take a steep drop tomorrow across the eastern half of the country, so make sure to pack your coats. Now, for your regional news."

I glanced up to see a man had replaced the entirely too chipper woman, then turned my attention back to Hunter. Did I have time to try the fingerprint thing now?

"A fire broke out in Knoxville earlier, burning down a gated estate and taking the two homes on either side with it before firefighters could contain it. A local resident who was out for a late-night jog claims to have spotted a military helicopter in the vicinity, and several nearby residents report hearing a loud, unexplained boom just before the fire broke out. No confirmation yet as to whether this might be related to suspected terrorist activity or not."

I forgot the GPS device in my hand and stared at the screen in mounting horror. There, in the background, were the charred remains of a house, still emitting a noxious cloud of black smoke.

From the cameraman's perspective, an iron gate was clearly visible.

The same gate I'd climbed earlier today.

My free hand flew to my mouth, which had gone suddenly dry. Grady's house, destroyed. And it had to be because of me.

I tuned out the TV, tuned out the station, just focused on staying upright, despite the guilt trying to eviscerate me with deadly claws. I'd never thought, never believed Grady might be in danger. But that was only because I hadn't considered them much at all. And I should have. Mom should have taught me that much.

Hunter emerged from the store and I came to, realizing I still hadn't filled the tank. Hunter flashed me a thumbs-up from the sidewalk outside the door. With unsteady hands, I carefully placed the GPS in my pocket.

"Go ahead and pump," he hollered. "I'll be right back."

I watched as he turned the corner, toward the sign marked MEN'S ROOM.

As I was putting the gas nozzle in place, mind spinning, a minivan pulled into the open spot ahead of me, and moments later, a young boy bounded out of the back door. His mom yanked open the passenger door. "Tommy, you need to wait! It's not safe to just jump out of the car like that."

"Okay—sorry!" But Tommy didn't sound sorry at all as

he scooted around the car to grab his mom's hand. "Can we get M&M's, please? I'll be super quiet in the car this time!"

"Wouldn't that be a change?" the mom muttered, as she and her husband exchanged a wry look over the top of the van. But from the way she smiled down at the boy and ruffled his hair, she obviously wasn't too bothered by Tommy's abundant energy.

A normal family, taking a normal family vacation. Something I would never have, no matter how much I wanted it.

Hunter emerged from the bathroom, flicking his hands like maybe the paper towel dispenser had been empty. He caught my eye and smiled, walking with that loose-limbed, lithe movement that I'd first noticed back in the halls of Clearwater High.

At the sight of him, my breath caught a little in my chest. Just like it had back then.

The image was ruined when, still watching me, he misjudged the curb and stumbled a little, before regaining his balance.

But that stumble conjured another image. A boy with a permanently lopsided walk. A boy who'd worked for Holland. A boy who'd risked everything to save me.

A boy I desperately hoped wasn't in danger, because of me.

Lucas.

So far, everyone who'd ever helped me had had terrible

things happen to them. What if Lucas was next?

An engine rumbled to life, and the family pulled out in their van, leaving us as the only customers. But as Hunter approached the car, the market door opened. A worker emerged, his head ducked as he inspected something on his cell phone. But he kept walking as he looked . . . and he was headed right at us.

I yanked the baseball hat lower on my head and, my neck tingling, stepped around the back of our car to meet Hunter halfway.

He shook the plastic bag on his arm. "Hey, got us a couple of iced coffees and some chocolate—figured we could use the caffeine and sugar."

I nodded. "Perfect." The worker was closer now—only a few strides away. He snapped the phone shut, still frowning.

My entire body tensed. His approach made no sense. Unless . . . the phone. What if he'd seen something on the internet that made him want to detain us? Like my photo?

Or worse . . . could he be V.O. in disguise? One of Hunter's accomplices, posing as a worker? Coming to make their move now? Along with Holland, who could be anywhere? Had he found whatever he was searching for at Grady's? Had he found a copy of Mom's encrypted files?

Target: 15.1 ft.

Weapons scan: No weapons detected.

On the heels of that, another contradictory prompt:

Threat detected.

Weapons scan: Beretta.

The worker's head jerked up, and his lips parted. "Hey, you," he said. At the same time, his free hand dove into his pocket.

Engage?

I lunged before he could extract it.

My hand shot out, grabbing his wrist and twisting it as he attempted to retrieve his weapon. The gun I'd taken from Grady was under the front seat, and I would only use it as a last resort. His weapon flew free of his grasp while I continued with my forward momentum, retaining my hold on his forearm and slipping behind him. I exerted steadily increasing force on his arm, bending it back, while my other hand curled around his throat, squeezing until his voice cut off right along with his oxygen.

"What do you want?" He didn't answer and both my hands tightened in response. As I forced his arm farther behind his back, I felt him jerk against me, as something in his shoulder started to give. I didn't let go. I couldn't. I wanted this man to hurt. It was past time someone had to pay.

"Mila, stop! Let him go!"

Hunter's frantic voice snapped me out of the haze, and I immediately slacked my grip. The man slid free and collapsed to the ground, while my eyes sought whatever he'd dropped. I spotted the object at the exact same moment I saw the police car cruise by.

Threat detected: 42 ft.

The threat had been coming from the police, not the worker. Which made sense, given that the item he'd dropped was a wallet.

Hunter's wallet.

I staggered back, my mind a growing mass of horror. The man hadn't been V.O., or even trying to report me. He'd been a Good Samaritan. And now he was crumpled in a heap on the oil-sticky ground of a gas station as a reward.

"Dude, are you okay?" Hunter was ignoring me now, dropping to his knees beside the worker. No. That didn't make sense. He should know that we had to get out of here, before the cops made another pass. Before one of the truckers emerged and noticed.

What was he doing?

I swooped down and grabbed his wallet, catching Hunter's arm at the same time. "Come on, we've got to go."

Hunter actively resisted me, so I pulled harder, forcing him to his feet. He stared at me, the stun of shock changing the planes of his face. "What the hell is wrong with you? Are you crazy? We need to call nine-one-one, make sure this guy's all right—"

As if on cue, the worker moaned. I took advantage of the distraction to pull Hunter toward the Jeep. All the while, a terrible suspicion formed in my gut.

I steered Hunter toward the car, opened the passenger door, and none-too-gently urged him inside. He climbed in, as if on autopilot, his eyes still glued to the worker. I raced for the driver's seat as the worker tried to push to his knees, his one arm cradled against his chest. He bowed his head in obvious agony.

Hunter shook his head, and like that had woken him from a long sleep, reached for his door handle. I hit the gas, and we shot out of the station before he could finish the action.

We had to get out of here, before the guy recovered enough to get a license plate number.

"Let me out," Hunter said, and when I didn't answer, he repeated himself. Louder. "Did you hear me? I want out."

"No."

His face contorted, and then he fumbled on the floorboard.

"What are you doing?"

"Calling an ambulance. You're insane, and that guy needs help."

Keeping a lookout for the cop car, I found the highway on-ramp and accelerated the Jeep. Nothing was making sense. Either Hunter was putting on an amazing act, or . . .

My fingers traced the outline of the GPS. No. No *ors*. It was an act. It had to be.

His curse filled the car a moment later. "I can't believe this. My phone is dead."

He chucked the phone at the backseat, where it bounced off and hit the floor. His frustration was evident in every tight, jerky motion. He reached to open the glove box, and even though I'd checked the car out earlier, instinct kicked in.

"Keep your hands where I can see them," I said.

He froze for five seconds, his fingers still on the latch. Then, he turned to me. Slowly, with the precise, careful motion of someone fighting to contain their rage. An incredulous expression distorted his face, rendering his mouth almost unrecognizable.

"Have you lost your goddamn mind?"

TEN

Silence ticked off for several moments while I pondered his question, as the Jeep sped down the highway. Was insanity even possible in an android? Didn't that require a human brain? At this point, I couldn't answer definitively. Not with everything that had happened over the last few hours.

Hunter's expression was taut: cheeks sucked in, mouth a grim line, eyes stony. I couldn't ever remember him looking even a quarter of this pissed before.

Uncertainty flickered. If he was the V.O., what possible reason would he have to draw attention to my abilities? Wouldn't it be easier to just brush them off, to avoid questions?

Or . . . maybe he was toying with me. Trying to provoke

different emotions, and see what happened.

"What are you, some kind of jujitsu expert? And even then—I've never seen anyone move so fast," he said incredulously, like he still couldn't believe it.

The uncertainty flared again, strengthened into doubt. But no. This had to be a ploy.

His cheeks had taken on a hint of red, and the muscles in his jaw contracted. "Look, I think I deserve some answers here!"

As though his aggression unleashed my own, anger seared its way up my throat, burned into my mouth. "You want the truth? Fine, here it is." I twisted around, ignoring his stony, unrelenting expression, and the rekindled flicker of doubt it inspired. "That story I told you about my dad was a total lie, and my mom? We're not fighting . . . She's *dead*."

Dead. The word ripped through the car, louder than I'd expected. The images flared to life in my head.

Mom's body, bleeding out in Lucas's car. Me, carrying her to the Potomac, and tossing her in, her hair waving around her like a mass of seaweed as she sank.

A sob cut off the rest of what I'd been about to tell him. I swallowed hard, even though in my case that knot in my throat was purely an emotional memory, and batted at the tears.

"What? How could that—my god, why didn't you say something?"

"My mom wasn't a vet," I continued. "She was a government agent, just like me."

Hunter's hand had been reaching toward me, but it fell back to his side. "Agent?"

It was the most I could make myself say. I chanced a look at his face. His usually intense eyes looked sightless, and his face had paled.

Because he's innocent, that tiny, mutinous part of my heart whispered.

No, no, no. An act, it was just a really good act.

"Spies. We were on assignment, and Mom was killed trying to save me. Now those same people are after me, and Richard Grady is the guy she told me to look up to get help."

"I can't—" Hunter broke off, leaving the silence between us to thicken. His hands covered his face, and I heard the in-out rhythm of his forceful breathing batting against his palms.

Lies. His act, his posturing—all lies.

But slowly and surely, my certainty ripped away, leaving long, gaping holes of doubts. Meanwhile, my traitorous heart thudded with new hope.

He finally lifted his head. "If that's true—and it sounds too unbelievably crazy to be a lie—then how could you do this to me? How could you put me in this situation without filling me in on the details? Jesus, Mila. Don't I have a right to know if my goddamn life is in jeopardy?"

Truth? Or lie? "I was going to tell you—"

"When?" he shouted, banging one fist on the dashboard. "When were you going to tell me? Tonight? Tomorrow? *Never?*"

My heart pounded, harder and harder. This wasn't a lie, it couldn't be. Because Hunter's anger was unmistakable.

And then, if possible, he blanched even more. "Oh my god—the picture, that Ashleigh thought she saw? That was really you, wasn't it?"

I swallowed. No sense in denying it now. "Yes. But I didn't kill my mom. The investigation—it's under wraps. The police really think they're looking for me."

He bowed his head and stared into his lap. I saw when his hands began to tremble. "Why weren't you just honest with me?"

In desperation, I mounted a counterattack. "Me, honest? What about you?" I gunned the gas, shifting lanes to swerve around a slow-moving semi. "Were you being honest when you told me an old buddy was leaving those messages earlier?"

He gave a startled laugh. "Messages? You mean, the ones from my ex-girlfriend, who's trying to get back together with me? Excuse me for thinking that might be a little awkward, given the present circumstances."

In desperation, I pulled the GPS bug out of my pocket.

"If you're not a member of the V.O. then why do you have this?" I asked, waving it near his face.

His hand snaked out to grab my wrist, and while my first reaction was to break his hold, I remained still. He bent his head to get a closer look. His eyes didn't hold a single trace of recognition.

"I have absolutely no idea—should I? And what the hell is a V.O.?"

He was looking at me like I'd lost my mind.

And maybe I had. Because I was starting to believe him.

Driving with one hand, I placed my finger over the top of the GPS, maneuvering it around until my fingertip tingled, and the prompt flashed in my head.

Retrieve fingerprint?

Yes.

"Are you going to answer me?" Hunter said, but I tuned him out. Because just then, the tingling in my finger turned into a slight stinging sensation. In front of me, a pattern appeared, a set of whorls and grooves.

A fingerprint. Well, part of one.

Move 1 mm. to the right. Rotate 3 degrees, counterclockwise.

I watched the print shift, until an almost-full one emerged.

Copy print and search most recent database?

Yes.

At the same time my finger surged with heat, the picture flashed red.

Data uploading . . .

"I can't believe this," Hunter muttered. And then the results burst to life.

Fingerprint match: 99.5% certainty.

George McDevitt. Served time: Hacking bank accounts, internet fraud.

Age: 45.

The photo appeared, and I recognized the man instantly.

Not Hunter. Not even close. No, this was one of the two men from the motel—one of the men Mom and I had tied up and run from.

Out of nowhere, a wave of relief slammed me, banishing doubt's viselike grip on my chest and allowing a giggle to burst free. Hunter hadn't planted the device.

Reality sank in a moment later, bursting the elated bubbles inside me all at once. The GPS slipped from my hand while the implications sank in. While the realization that, maybe, just maybe, I'd made a gargantuan, life-altering mistake started to wrap around my neck and squeeze.

Oh, no. "Hunter, I'm so sorry. I thought . . . I was . . . the V.O. is an espionage group. They were tracking us with GPS."

He looked at the device for a moment, before his eyelids sank shut. "And you thought I was part of them." He bowed his head, shoving both hands into his hair. His breathing turned ragged. "Stop the car and pull over. *Now,*" he emphasized when I made no move to follow his command, the word laced with a quiet fury, and something else. Something that sounded an awful lot like pain.

I steered the car to the shoulder. The moment we stopped, his door flew open. He was wrenching open my door a moment later, breathing hard. "Get out. I'm driving."

I wanted to argue, but one look at his tense face, his stiff posture, warned me to give him some space. He waited on the road until I climbed over the center console, as if the thought of touching me inadvertently was repugnant. And, despite everything, my heart bottomed out at the thought.

I sat quietly while he pulled back onto the highway, his hands white-knuckled on the wheel. When I thought enough time had passed for him to gather some control, I said, "Hunter—"

His head jerked sharply to the side. "No. No talking. I can't . . . I can barely look at you."

I clasped my hands together in my lap, replaying the last few minutes over in my head. Not an ounce of suspicion left, but so much shame. Had I really just blurted out that my mom was dead? Suggested he was an accomplished techno-terrorist? Nearly choked a man to death in front of him, when all he'd been trying to do was return Hunter's wallet?

The shame poured through my gut, sickening in its heaviness. Hunter wasn't an Oscar-worthy actor. He'd never been hiding anything.

That role fell to me, and me alone.

I didn't pay attention when he tapped a few buttons on the Jeep's GPS. Maybe I should have—at least then I would have had some kind of warning, when he pulled off at an exit about ten minutes later. I tensed in the seat, inspected our surroundings with critical eyes, assessing every person, every car, for potential threat.

Even now, a tiny trace of suspicion lingered. Where was he taking me?

It wasn't until he pulled up to a bus terminal that I realized my mistake.

He pulled the car to the curb and shifted into park. When he turned to look at me, the anger hadn't completely faded from his face, but his shoulders were slumped, and more than anything, with his disheveled hair and wrinkled shirt, he looked exhausted.

"I don't know you. I don't know you at all. I thought something was developing between us, but you don't trust me, and you . . . suspect me of being the enemy? I'm going home."

As our gazes connected, I felt the burn of tears once again. Everything had failed me—my emotions, my logic. And now the one person I could count on was leaving for good. Walking out of my life.

The thought of him despising me was more than I could bear. So I attempted, miserably, to explain. He needed to know that I hadn't intended to hurt him.

"I tried to tell you, so many times. But when I couldn't, I asked you to let me go my own way back in Virginia, remember?"

"Yeah, I wish I had listened to you," he snapped.

"I don't," I said. "Without you, I . . . I don't know if I could have made it this far."

Hunter rolled his eyes, like he thought I was talking down to him. That wasn't my intention, but I didn't dare say anything more.

"I'm sure you would have been just fine. So just . . . go, okay?" he muttered.

As I fumbled for the door handle, tears burned my eyes, and I looked away before the first one could fall. When it came down to it, Hunter was right. I shouldn't have dragged him into this, any of this, without telling him the truth. And even now, I hadn't told him everything. It wasn't safe, and if I cared for him at all, I'd let him go. Let him drive out of my life for good.

So many things—feelings, thoughts, words—tumbled through my head, my chest, begging me to share them. To tell him, in this final moment, exactly how much he meant to me. Pour everything out, and be happy in knowing that, at least once, I told the truth. The whole, unvarnished version. And surely there was some peace in that?

But I didn't have the right. I'd squandered it, the moment I'd first stopped believing in him. Instead, I whispered, "It might not be safe for you, on your own. If the people after me come after you—"

"I'll just tell them I don't know anything. Which, fortunately for me, would be the truth."

Would that be enough to keep him safe? I hoped so. Especially if I offloaded the GPS and put the V.O. on another trail that would take them far away from him.

"Now would you please go?" Hunter asked again, sounding more sad than angry.

"Can you unlock the back door?" I said, proud of the way my voice didn't waver. I walked around so I could retrieve my meager belongings. Yet as my hand closed around my bag, I realized I couldn't leave it like that. The things I'd said, the way I'd treated him? And worse, so much worse—the things I'd thought and never uttered? Was this the kind of life I had to look forward to? Searching for the truth, yet not knowing when it slapped me in the face?

I had to apologize. Not that an "I'm sorry" would change anything, but he deserved to hear it. I shut the door, pulled a pen and paper out of my bag. After I scrawled my brief note, I waited a moment while my pseudo heart cracked and shattered, and then threw back my shoulders and walked over to knock on his window. He pressed the button, then closed his eyes, tightly, like he was fighting his own inner battle while the window whirred down.

I forced myself to watch every bit of pain that flitted across his face. I'd been the one who'd inflicted this on him. Me, no one else. All the proof I needed that he was better off without me. I leaned inside and pressed a gentle kiss to his cheek.

"I'm so sorry . . . for everything. The truth is in here . . ." My fist tensed around the note, and I started to crumple it. So stupid. Too little, too late. Then, before I could chicken out, I dropped the square into his lap. "A part of it, at least. And . . . there's a gun underneath your seat, in case you're followed or anything."

"Are you kidding me?" he asked, completely dumbfounded.

I shook my head no. I couldn't be any more serious.

"You're in that much danger?"

"Yes."

Suddenly, his eyes began to glisten, and a part of me prayed that I wasn't imagining it. He took the note in his hand, gripping it so tightly it could tear. I pulled away and hoisted my bag over my shoulder, turning before either one of us could speak. I couldn't bear to hear the anger and disappointment I knew waited in his voice. Not again. Without a backward glance, I headed for the bus terminal, counting my footfalls on the cracked concrete as I went.

One, five, ten steps away from the one person who truly made me feel alive.

And finally, finally, I heard the rumble of a familiar engine. Then the grind of tires on asphalt as Hunter drove out of the lot. And then I stopped in my tracks, sinking to my knees on the sidewalk, while the car sounds faded away. I buried my head in my hands, allowing myself to finally acknowledge the black hole in my chest. I choked back a sob and doubled over, my hands gripping my thighs like I could push reality away by sheer force. I swiped my eyes and wrestled with my composure. When I finally straightened, I pressed my shoulders back and swallowed hard. The rest of this journey, I'd have to make alone. And maybe that had been the right way, all along.

I rehoisted the bag over my shoulder and, after offloading the GPS onto a bus bound for Hunter's home state of California, continued on my path toward the ticket counter. Each step accentuated the empty ache inside me, but I kept on walking. I had to.

There was nothing else left for me now.

ELEVEN

The sky was darkening when the bus finally pulled up to the Chicago terminal. It was hard to believe that just this morning, I'd left Hunter behind. My fellow thirty-eight passengers and I had been on the road for seven hours—without air conditioning for the last two. All of us were thrilled to be getting off, but I doubt anyone was more relieved than me. With each stop along the bus route, there had been more chances for me to be recognized. More opportunities for someone to stop this quest of mine in its tracks. Thankfully, though, I was finally nearing the end of my journey. One more transfer, and I'd be in the right town.

When the bus parked, people jumped up into the walkway of the coach. I waited while they stood, their voices rising in conversation, stretching and shifting from foot to foot. As they shuffled forward in a single-file line of tired humanity, my thoughts drifted back to Hunter. In fact, I couldn't stop picturing his rage-filled eyes since the minute he'd left me. There had been moments on this trip where I literally couldn't take my gaze away from the window, afraid that someone might catch a glimpse, see me crying and want to talk to me. Even now I kept my head averted, waiting until the last person in line had passed my row before rising.

From here on out, making any kind of personal connections was absolutely forbidden. I couldn't afford to take the risk.

Once off the bus, I pushed Hunter out of my mind and collected my bag, then headed toward the schedules to see when my final bus would depart. But as I edged through the crowd at the terminal, I caught a man staring. He'd been scrolling through something on a tablet, and he looked up at my approach. His attention locked on me for a hair too long, before he dropped his head to check out the tablet. When he lifted his chin, it was obvious that his focus zeroed in on my face.

I hunched my shoulders and whirled, walking in the other direction with carefully measured steps while my breath came in short spurts. Once I blended in with the mass of people, he'd forget about me. But not too fast. I didn't want him to think I was running.

When I was about twenty feet away, I paused and sank into an empty chair. He'd seen something, but what? That same article from before, or something new? There was only one sure way to find out.

Open ports.

The information was sluggish in arriving this time, stopping and starting on its journey into my head. As usual, there were tingling strands of code, everywhere. But when I attempted to sift through with my usual precision, the data wouldn't budge. I pushed, harder, but nothing happened. What the hell?

Connection failed. Attempt to reconnect?

I realized then that the Wi-Fi here must be nonexistent or spotty. Maybe there wasn't any in the terminal, and I was trying to glom on to a connection via an independent device. I still needed to try.

Yes.

This time, the information kept flowing.

I searched for Nicole Laurent, and my heart stuttered at the magnitude of hits.

Dead D.C. woman identified as Nicole Laurent, former military scientist . . .

It was like being hit in the chest with a hammer. Not only was Mom identified in the report, the story was also headlining news.

Accompanying all the articles was a photo of Mom, from before I'd known her. Smiling into the camera, her pale blond hair pulled back into a neat ponytail, blue eyes catching the light behind a pair of square-framed glasses. She looked happy. Hopeful.

Things I'd never seen in her during our short time together.

I slumped into the chair, but the horror wasn't over, not yet. Because next up was a photo of me—a new one, this time. One featuring the jagged black hair I had back at the compound.

Girl wanted for questioning in murder . . .

Even though I'd known this moment was inevitable, I still felt the impact like a kick to the gut. My fist flew to my mouth. Holland had finally pulled out all the stops. The bastard; he knew exactly how to rub salt in an already festering wound. I bet my reaction would thrill him.

No matter. I'd never let him win.

Just then, a warning flashed in my head.

Human threat detected.

My legs tensed, the red alert filling me with undeniable purpose. I craned my head to look over my shoulder. The man with the tablet was standing and heading my way.

"Hey!" he shouted, pointing at me. Curious heads followed.

Engage?

My hands clenched into fists. I could. It would be so easy—one quick punch, or one choke hold later, and he'd be out. But too many people. Too public. And my face was out there.

Damage control: Minimize exposure risk.

Discredit enemy.

And on the heels of that:

Threat detected: 10 ft.

Weapons scan: Glock.

I pivoted, just in time to see a blue uniform bearing down on me. I scrunched my shoulders and dropped my head, trying to look less noticeable. Unfortunately, the man with the tablet spotted the policeman, too.

"Hey, over here!" he yelled, waving. "That girl, she's—"

"Officer!" I screamed, trying to drown him out. "Please. That man tried to steal my bag!"

It wasn't going to help much—just a split second of extra time. But that was all I needed. As the policeman glanced away from me to frown his confusion at the man with the tablet, I slipped to the side. Then, I turned and fled.

"Hey—"

Fear pumped through my legs as I shoved past a couple, knocking the man's laptop bag from his shoulder. I didn't know what was happening behind me, but I could guess. The cops were reaching the man. He was showing them the picture, explaining that I was wanted. And then—

"Stop! Police!" The shout rang out from behind, loud in the crisp night air. Ahead of me, the crowd parted like magic, eyes widening in shock, two mothers swinging their toddlers into their arms and clenching them to their chests. Like I was someone to be scared of. Like I was dangerous.

Human threat detected: 36 ft.

Engage?

On second thought—I guess I was.

I tore past a crowd of Japanese tourists, found myself running headlong toward a row of chairs, where passengers still clustered. The one in front of me was wearing headphones and typing away at his laptop. No time to veer, so I leaped onto the empty seat next to him and vaulted over. My foot caught his cord, and the headphones pulled free, tangling on my leg and flapping behind me, slapping the floor. I shook them off and continued running. Over the gathering roar of excited voices, I could hear the policeman yell into his radio. "In pursuit of murder suspect at city bus terminal. Request backup, repeat, request backup. Suspect northbound, on foot."

Engage target?

I tried to ignore the red question flashing in my head, but something about the continual onslaught felt . . . demanding. Like my android self was miffed that I wasn't hell-bent on taking on the city's finest.

I veered for the far exit. Closer, closer. If I could just

get outside, I might be okay.

In the distance, a siren wailed, and I shivered. Well, so long as I had enough of a head start.

I burst outside, the cold air splashing my face with renewed hope. Night had fallen, and though the air was brisk, the exterior was swarming with people. Plenty of streetlights, but also plenty of opportunities to hide. They would be looking for a girl in a green T-shirt and jeans, no coat. I needed to remedy that—now.

Around the station, clusters of people laughed and chatted their way toward local restaurants and shops, oblivious that a wanted murder suspect was on the loose. I glanced over my shoulder, saw the door to the terminal start to burst open. Where could I hide? Or at least disguise myself? I needed new clothes—a hat, a coat. Anything.

As if the thought had commanded them, my eyes started scanning, doing a split-second semicircle sweep of the people ahead of me. Like the computer part of me had taken over my head and was moving it for me. Past a couple holding hands, a group of businessmen, and a cluster of fifteen thirtysomething women, just leaving a bar and grill that vibrated with live music.

The women's feet were strapped into high heels and even higher boots, and their voices were unnaturally loud. One of them was wearing a tiara that said "bachelorette" on her head, with a veil flowing behind her. They all glowed with twinkling LED lights. Some men just inside the interior catcalled as they hung their coats.

"Marianne, do you hear that? Remember, you aren't married yet," one of the women shouted, and the rest cackled their appreciation.

Human threat detected: 52 ft.

Aware of a sudden ruckus back by the exit of the terminal, I darted into the door behind the men. The receptionist looked up, but I said, "Forgot my jacket—got to catch up," with a general wave in the bachelorette's direction. I grabbed the closest women's coat—a long, olive-green one with shiny black buttons, probably five inches too long for me—and a black ski cap, and bolted. I slipped my arms into the sleeves, stuffed the hat on my head, and then hurried to catch the group of women. Luckily, their haphazard weaving meant they hadn't made it far.

I slipped up to the petite redhead bringing up the rear. Her walking was exceptionally bad. "Hey, Marianne said I could borrow your lights for a little bit," I said, matching my pace to her.

She squinted at me. "Do I know you?" she slurred.

I rolled my eyes, trying not to look over my shoulder when I heard the thud of running feet. "We just met in the bar, remember? Marianne invited me to join you?"

As I spoke, my fake heartbeat thundered in my ears. The runner was closing in.

Human threat detected: 22 ft.

"Oh." Shrugging, she handed me one of her lights, which I draped around my neck. I shoved my hands into the coat, turned up the collar.

The footsteps came closer, and I tensed, ready to make a run for it. But at the last second, they veered to the left.

"This way," the policeman shouted. I peeked over my shoulder and watched as he ran toward a compact female figure on the other side of the street.

Now I had a chance. But I still had to get out of here, and the bus was no longer an option.

GPS.

The map glowed to life in front of me, illuminating a crisscross grid of the surrounding city blocks. Every nearby street, every back alley; I saw it all.

I zoomed in on the area immediately surrounding the little blinking dot that represented me, looking for the nearest escape routes. There, just ahead—a narrow side street. When the women descended on another bar, I darted to the right, onto the side street, making sure to walk near a couple so as not to look alone. According to my map, this street continued for another half mile, before connecting to another main drag. I just had to get to that one, and then I'd hopefully be a safe distance away.

I was almost there when behind me, I sensed a presence. I'd started to turn when a hand clamped on to my shoulder and yanked me backward. Hard.

I stumbled through an open doorway, my toe catching on the corner and throwing me off balance. One of my knees slammed the ground before I regained my feet, ready to pounce.

How had someone snuck up on me without my sensors going off?

"Hello, sister." The words stopped me cold, and something scuttled across my skin. That voice. Clear and slightly more baritone than the typical female. Young.

My voice.

Three.

Turning around was a slow process, because my legs were so heavy with dread. I knew exactly what I would find, and there she was, in all her terrible glory. Three-point-oh, wearing my face. My smile. My eyes, though hers were now a dark brown rather than green. Her hair had been altered, too, from long brown waves to a short auburn bob. The slight changes made no real difference, though. To anyone looking closely she was still, in essence, my twin.

The newer version of me. The weapon with fewer pesky emotions.

The android who had helped Holland murder my mom.

Before I could move, think, breathe, she shook the object she held nestled in her palm. A Taser.

"Hopefully, you've discerned your options by now, and

have realized that the only logical one is to stay in place. I don't want to shock you, but I will if you try to run." Her voice, as usual, was a slightly less animated version of mine. Exact same tone, but somehow . . . different.

I kept my chin up, scanning my surroundings, hoping for a way out. We appeared to be inside a women's clothing store. Luckily, it was dark and seemed to be closed. Dresses in a variety of lengths and colors hung against the far wall, while up front, shelves held shirts and sweaters. A row on the other side was filled with shoes, most of them with rhinestones or fancy prints. The shop was on the small side—

Dimensions: 15 ft. by 30 ft.

—and dark. There were two doors near the back, behind the sales counter, but they were only dressing rooms.

Nowhere to run, except back out the front door—which Three was physically blocking. Trapped.

Icy fingers of terror dug into my spine.

She frowned. "Your fear is like a walking advertisement." I guess I made some kind of muffled noise in my throat at that, because she paused, then said, "Oh, you like that? I've been working on my similes and metaphors. After visiting with you, General Holland thought they might be useful in the field."

I couldn't help it; I laughed. "Visiting?" I said, my pitch rising at the end to reflect my growing hysteria. "That's what you call locking me in the compound and forcing me to undergo those insane tests? That's quite a euphemism."

Her forehead scrunched in concentration, like she was trying to make sense of what I'd said. "As for what I was saying—is your fear manufactured, or are you really afraid?"

"We don't all have your control," I said, through gritted teeth.

"What a pity."

"How did you find me?"

A pause; then, that unflappable smile of hers widened. "You still have no idea, do you? How connected we are?"

There might not be blood in my face, but I felt it drain all the same. The idea that she—that we—shared some kind of bond. It was ludicrous. And disturbing, on so many levels. "There's no connection, none. We're not the same at all."

"It's fascinating, the way you try to deceive yourself. Are you shunning your android abilities completely then?"

Her voice remained even, but I saw her lips curl up even more. Like she knew something that I didn't.

I clenched my jaw, refused to answer, to give her any more ammo. Hoped she would drop this whole line of conversation. Instead, she laughed, and what's more, she actually sounded amused. She stepped back, her heavy boots clanking on the wooden floor. With her free hand, she reached out and stroked a green cashmere sweater.

"You see? You can't argue. I'm glad. Fighting your true

nature is just a waste of resources. You were built for specific purposes, and those must be fulfilled."

"And what exactly are those?"

"You'll see."

I looked away. That was the thing I was afraid of. "What happens now? You try to take me back to Holland?"

No way. I'd rather have her shock me now than be dragged back to that sterile compound under lock and key, so he could perform more of his warped experiments.

If I returned, it would be on my terms. I could almost feel the rough skin of his neck beneath my hands, hear the satisfying snap of cervical vertebrae under my fingers. My fists clenched in anticipation and I had to force them to relax.

Terrible, maybe. But no less than he deserved.

"Perhaps."

I couldn't help it—my eyes widened, my mouth drooped in shock. Once again she shook her head. "So many emotions, real ones—what must that be like? No wonder you keep deluding yourself into thinking you can live a human life."

"Then why are you here?" I asked. Not really believing her.

"Someone called the hotline back in Saint Louis—they said they spotted you getting on a bus bound for Chicago. We get a lot of calls, but this person was able to describe you very well. So, General Holland sent me here to check out the lead. Though I did suggest that this lead was probably valid."

That didn't make any sense. "Why did you think that?"

She tapped one finger against her forehead. "Like I said, we're connected, you and I."

My legs suddenly felt weak. Could that be true? No, she had to be lying. Holland had probably told her to say and do this; I could picture his smug grin now. He'd know how much it would mess with me.

Calm, I needed to be calm. Melting down was not the way to escape Three. In desperation, my hand went to Mom's pendant. As I stroked the cool gem, calmness descended, like I'd hoped.

Three followed my hand. The barest glimmer of wonder flickered across her face, but it was fleeting. And then, in the first real show of emotion I'd seen from her—an unintentional show, not purposeful—her lips tightened.

"No matter what you think, nothing can make you what you're not. No artifacts, no sentimental tokens—you were made in a lab. Just like me. We are the same—more than you even know."

"If that's what gets you through the day," I said, refusing to allow her to suck me down that path again.

At first, I thought I'd gotten through to her. Her eyes narrowed, and her nostrils flared. But then she blinked, once, twice, and with those tiny gestures, her expression smoothed back into the one I was so used to. Bland and pleasant. "I see what you're doing, but it won't work. I won't be dragged to your level. I have no intention of becoming obsolete. Now, General Holland has a message for you."

A message?

I braced myself while Three fiddled with something on the end of her middle finger. Keeping her eyes on me and a firm grasp on the Taser. Holland's voice—this would be the first time I'd heard his smooth drawl since I'd fled the compound with Mom.

My breathing rate quickened, making Three pause. "You know that isn't necessary, right? Your cells barely need any oxygen, and they acquire it well enough without increasing how often you use your pump."

I tightened my lips and refused to respond, so she shrugged and continued.

"Here we go." To my surprise, she extended her hand, like she was pointing at the nearest wall.

A blue light, like a laser, shot out from her finger. Then, before my incredulous eyes, the light broadened, widened, contorting and stretching until it formed the hazy shape of a man.

Not just any man. Holland.

I took an inadvertent step back. The illusion looked so real, down to the silvery hair and the menacing smile. I almost expected the scent of peppermint and astringent to assault me at any moment.

Then I caught Three tracking my every reaction, and I stopped short. No showing weakness to the enemy. I needed to remain in control.

"Don't worry," she said, picking up on my agitation anyway. "You don't have this capability." Her tiny smile suggested she was pleased by that discrepancy.

I opened my mouth to make a sarcastic comment, but was cut off when the hologram started talking.

"Hello, Two. If you're listening to this, it means that Three has once again proven why she's the superior specimen. Not that I ever had any doubts on that front."

That voice. I suppressed a shiver, all too conscious of Three's analytical eyes, but the drawl still managed to crawl its way down my back.

Hologram Holland stood perfectly upright, chest out, shoulders back. Just like the real thing. The image was so close, only three feet away. Though I knew it was impossible, I couldn't quite quell the feeling that he could reach out and touch me with his wrinkled hands. And though he could have no idea where I'd be standing, I swore that his pale gray eyes zeroed in on my face.

"Let's keep this brief. You need to come back home. We all know that now that Nicole is gone, there's nothing left for you out there."

Until that moment, I hadn't thought anything Holland said could hurt me anymore. But it was like he'd seen into the very heart of my fears and known right where to stab. And he called the compound home.

Home.

I curled my lip. He was wrong, though. So very wrong. I had one thing left to keep me going.

Him.

Those gray eyes still seemed to track my every move, and when I stepped to the left, they followed. "Well? Aren't you going to answer me?" he said, in that silky drawl, and knots formed in my stomach. Please tell me this was some kind of elaborate ruse.

And then his hand lifted and reached out, and before I could react, it landed on my shoulder.

I gasped and spun away from his ghostly hand. Even though the touch had been all condensation and mist versus his meaty fist, it was like I could feel him grow more present in the room. I didn't ever want him touching me again, in any form.

His soft laugh echoed through the room and curled its way into every corner of my mind, filling the recesses like an insidious poison. "Why so jumpy? Surely even you realize I can't hurt you. Come in with Three and we'll find a use for you, I promise."

His promises were about as valuable as Monopoly money.

Did he really think that would work? That I'd tag along without a fight, right into his lair?

As if he read my mind, the image sneered. "As much as I'd like to get rid of you, the military has other ideas. They think you're too expensive to discard. It'd be best if you didn't fight. Too many shocks in too short a timeframe could result in permanent damage."

His voice had taken on a hint of petulance, and the hologram started to pace the floor. I gave it a wide berth and read between the lines. Someone higher up had gotten wind of Holland's old plan to essentially decommission me, and hadn't been pleased. But that wasn't my problem.

This whole thing was ridiculous. Did he really think I'd listen to him?

He folded his arms across his chest with that familiar smugness and bared his teeth in a feral grin. Once again, I felt trapped. Somehow, this incarnation of him could see me, interact with me. I didn't understand the technology, and I didn't want to. I just wanted him to go away. This was far too close to seeing him in the flesh, a thought that made my stomach sour with simulated bile.

"Oh, I know what you're thinking: *Why should I care what he wants?* Simple. Because I've got something that you care about. Well, someone." His voice lowered to a malignant whisper. "Did you really think I wouldn't figure out who helped you escape? If you'd like to keep your friend alive and healthy, you'll come back with Three. If you don't cooperate, well . . ."

Hologram Holland paused and reached for something outside the field of light. When his hand reemerged, it was holding a wrench. He tapped it into his empty palm, his smile broadening while my entire body went rigid.

My friend. The wrench.

Lucas.

He stepped toward me. "I was sent a notification as soon as this communication started, so I'll notice any delays. Running is futile. We'll never stop tracking you down—your . . . technology is simply too valuable."

Before I could question the slight hesitation over "technology," he continued. "And remember, other lives depend on you."

With those last drawled words still lingering in the air, the hologram vanished. Just me and Three, alone once more. But even though the lights had disappeared, Holland's threat hovered.

Three lowered her arm. "It's time to go. Walk." She jerked her head toward the door.

I turned, forcing one foot in front of the other, my thoughts spinning wildly. Holland had to have meant Lucas, right? I mean, the wrench . . . that was the tool he'd tried to get me to use on Lucas, during that second test. It had to be significant. But why hadn't he just said his name?

I opened the door, the bell overhead ringing merrily as I exited out onto the street. Across the way, a video camera was a silent sentinel.

Three shook her head. "It's disabled."

In the short amount of time we'd been inside, the crowds had dispersed. Now, only a few scattered couples remained. I didn't dare scream, though. I knew what Three was capable of, and I wouldn't endanger anyone else. But a silent scream was building inside me.

Holland had won. Again. He'd found my emotional weak spot and was exploiting it like crazy.

I wanted to run, but the image of the Taser Three held was burned into my head. That, and Lucas. Though Holland's wording still niggled at me . . .

"Left," she said, walking behind me and slightly to my right. Our footsteps seemed louder than normal in the night, which was quiet now except for the hushed conversations coming from the two couples within earshot, who huddled together against the biting wind.

"Where are we going?"

"You'll know soon enough." A few more steps in silence, and then, "Where were you going, when you escaped the compound?"

I kept walking, pretending the question didn't faze me. But the casual way she'd asked made me instantly suspicious. Had Holland told her to ask? And if so, why did he care what my plans were? Was he looking for Jensen?

"Right."

I followed her directions, and found myself back on the street that led to the bus terminal. Here the crowds still ran thick, though not as many people as before braved the frigid night air.

Scanning: 42 humans within a 1000-ft. radius.

I kept my head up, in case an escape route appeared. The map beckoned, displaying every potential right or left turn. Streets where I could try to break free. Reality drew me up short. Lucas. Could I really gamble with his life?

The farther we walked, the more desperation laced my every thought. Soon, we'd reach whatever mode of transportation awaited to take me back to the compound, and I could kiss my freedom good-bye. I knew that from experience. Making a run for it had to happen soon, while I still had the crowd to use as cover.

But when I tried to prepare myself, a wave of disgust held me back. Lucas had helped me escape, and this was how I repaid him?

I swerved to avoid a spilled drink on the sidewalk. When I did, I caught a glimpse of the Taser in Three's hand. She still held the weapon, but her grip was loose, her fingers nowhere near the trigger. That didn't make sense. Why would Three take such a risk?

Holland's words replayed in my head. The military

thought I was too valuable to discard. And too many shocks in too short a time could damage me. Then it hit me. Holland was worried. He was worried that if he brought me back nonfunctional, whoever he reported to would be pissed. To be sure, I zeroed in on Three's hand and accessed the signal in my brain.

Weapons scan: Taser.

Wattage: 50 volts.

Fifty volts. Barely enough to make me miss a step.

As I'd suspected, the Taser was a dupe. But before I could capitalize on that knowledge, the close-up visual on Three's grip made all my muscles cramp and stiffen. In my mind, I was immediately transported back to that carousel. The two small hands, gripping the pole. The world spinning in circles so fast, everything became a dark, grainy blur. When I stopped cold, Three stopped too and stood there, preparing to whip me into submission.

"If you're thinking about testing me, I'd strongly advise against it," she said.

But I couldn't respond. I was trapped inside my own body.

Memory malfunction.

Full circuitry overload: Likely.

Reconfiguring . . .

"I have my orders. Unlike you, I have no problem following them," Three said, pointing out the obvious.

As I stood there, motionless, I tried everything I could think of to break out of this strange fairy-tale-like spell. But I couldn't access any of my systems, no matter what I tried. Three became suspicious and began to circle me, carefully examining me like prize cattle. Then all of a sudden she started talking.

To herself.

"The MILA 2.0 is having some kind of technical difficulties," she said, to no one in particular. After a beat, she carried on, like having a conversation with herself was typical android protocol. "No, I don't think so. She just froze up without any preindicators. If you lock on to my location, could you somehow tap into her core diagnostics?"

It was the question that made everything crystal clear. Three wasn't talking to herself. She was chatting with someone back at the SMART Ops compound.

Someone who knew us better than anyone. Someone who could literally get inside our minds. Someone who Holland threatened to hurt if I didn't comply with his demands.

"Affirmative. Stand by for transmission," Three said.

Seconds later, red letters appeared, and I'd never been happier to see them.

Remote access granted.

Rerouting program running.

System reboot commencing.

Then out of nowhere, a staticky, almost incoherent voice

crackled through my ears.

Mi—buzz—*la?*

Lucas. He was okay. Holland must have been bluffing. There was no way Lucas would still be allowed to communicate with Three otherwise. And I doubted Three realized I was still observing her this whole time and that she'd just given up a huge piece of information here. Which gave me a considerable advantage.

I'm sa—buzz—*don't be*—buzz—*you shou*—buzz.

I felt some activity in my fingers first. Then my toes. But I still couldn't make out Lucas's message. Apparently some of my audio functions were still down. Meanwhile Three canvassed the surrounding area with her eyes, always on the alert, while slowly my arms and legs came back to life.

No one—buzz-buzz—*you have*—buzz—*I can't*—buzz.

What was he was trying to say? I desperately needed to know.

My eyes were the next thing to regain motion. They flicked over to Three, whose stare had just landed back on me. She watched with satisfaction and curiosity as my joints relaxed and my posture returned to normal.

Reroute complete.

Full function: Restored.

Memory errors: Temporarily repaired.

Then, the bursts of static softened, so I could hear Lucas say one distinct word.

Run.

This was one order I was going to follow. No questions asked.

I pushed myself onto the balls of my feet. Preparing to dart into the middle of the crowd. That's when I saw them. Two uniformed officers, emerging from a nearby bar. I went through our appearances in my head. Me, wearing a long coat and black knit hat, LED lights still flashing. Three, wearing boots, jeans, and a long, dark tee.

Her hair was all wrong, but so was mine. And her face—and clothing—were right.

I took a deep breath and grabbed her firmly by the arms, swinging her in a semicircle. When I let go, I watched her crash into the group of people in front of us, amid screams. She and two other women toppled to the ground. The two cops saw the commotion and broke into a run. A big group of partiers on our left slowed to look behind them, curious as to what all the hoopla was about. It was now or never.

While the cops closed in on Three, I ran.

I heard a commotion behind me—threats, blows. A gun discharging. Screams. I winced, but figured Three wouldn't injure any bystanders. Holland wouldn't have authorized that—another scandal was the last thing he needed. No, I figured that Three had just as much motive to run as I did. On a cursory glance she might avoid recognition, but her new hair and eyes would only get her so far, and Holland would not be pleased to have to explain to authorities why there were two of us.

If Three escaped, he could pin this whole thing on me.

I shivered. It wasn't ideal, but I couldn't help that now. By putting Three on the defensive, I might just have enough time to escape. More shrieks, getting closer to me. Then, the pounding of feet.

Threat detected: 30 ft.

I looked over my shoulder, and my stomach dropped like a boulder. Both cops were on the ground, one rolling on his back, the other cupping her nose. A loose semicircle of gaping bystanders formed around them, and from the middle emerged Three. Unscathed and now headed my way, at a dead run. I glanced wildly around for an escape plan. The city grid glowed before me, but that was no help.

Three saw the same thing, and she was too close to lose on foot.

A car. Where could I find a car? I didn't have time to break in, not without her catching me first.

Then, outside another bar, I saw them. A row of motorcycles. Hope sparked. Was it possible that one of them started by remote, like some cars?

Threat detected: 25 ft.

I sprinted.

As I ran, I opened my mind, searching for a signal that went with one of the bikes. Nothing, nothing, nothing.

Threat detected: 20 ft.

I was starting to despair, when I felt it. A thin beam of electricity, boring into my head. Connecting me to the silver and black BMW, third bike down.

Remote access requested?

Relief swelled. *Yes.* I was going to make it.

Override control. Allow access, I commanded.

Access granted. Start engine?

Yes.

Just like that, the engine roared to life.

I was only five steps away, preparing to vault into the seat, when the connection wavered, then sputtered. Before it blinked out completely, I felt another presence, heard another command.

Cut engine.

The engine silenced at Three's command, just as I grabbed for the handlebars. Damn it.

I reached for the connection again, but knew I was going to be too late.

Threat detected: 5 ft.

Duck.

I dropped to the ground, and Three's fist whizzed over my head.

Now I was stuck, sandwiched between a motorcycle on one side and an android with a mission on the other.

Block kick.

I turned, but being so low to the ground made me slow.

The kick connected with my cheek and pushed me back, slamming my skull into metal as I made a desperate grab for Three's foot. The bike wobbled while my fingers just barely skimmed her shoe. It was enough.

I grabbed hold and twisted, pulling her off balance. She rotated sideways and hit the ground. Meanwhile, I located the signal emanating from the motorcycle. I leaped into the padded seat and in my desperation, felt a rush of power burst through me. One forceful command roared out.

Start engine.

The engine revved to life while I pulled my feet up, hands on the handlebars. I squeezed the gas, tensing my thighs when the motorcycle lurched forward. I saw Three jump to her feet and only had an instant to think, *I'm going to make it.* Then the bike jerked to a forceful stop.

Block, left arm.

Trusting my android sensors, I let go of the handlebar and threw up my arm, smacking away Three's grab.

Kick, left leg.

I tapped into that roar of power within me, channeling everything I had into that one kick. Sirens wailed in the background, and behind us, shouts grew louder. I had one shot.

My foot swung out awkwardly from the side position. But I powered through with brute force. Three was grabbing for my arm again, so close that I caught her right in the midsection. Hard. She flew back, her fingers clutching my sleeve, and for an instant, I thought both the bike and I were going with her. Then I twisted and yanked, the sleeve tearing. I hit the gas, and the motorcycle burst forward. I leaned in and barreled down the avenue toward a red light. At the intersection, I saw a semi, getting ready to lumber across.

I made it, I thought.

Threat detected.

Too late, because just then, an arm reached from behind me and latched on to my waist.

I swerved, almost sideswiping a parked car. A frantic glance at the rearview confirmed Three hanging on, her legs flying behind us.

Shit.

I zigzagged the bike, hoping to throw her off her precarious grip. Her fingers slipped, and I bucked my torso, but she wouldn't let go. I swerved again, this time purposely grazing the driver's side of an oversized van. The van's side mirror popped off with a loud snap, but Three hung on.

Wind bit into my face, blew my hair into my eyes, and we were rapidly approaching the intersection. The semi had just pulled out. Cars around us honked their horns, drawing far too much attention. I had to get out of here. Now.

I released my clutch hand and used it to try to pry her fingers from my body. But I was too late. Her other arm snaked around my neck. I twisted, trying to drive and fight her off at the same time.

Ahead of me, the semi loomed, completely blocking the intersection, like a giant metal whale.

Collision imminent: 20 ft. Veer left.

Three slowly arched my head backward, backward. Wind tore at my skin. The handgrips started slipping out of reach. If I was going to do anything crazy to get away, the time was now.

Collision imminent: 15 ft. Veer left.

With a desperate surge of strength, I drove my head forward, loosening her grip for just a second. That was all the time I needed. With a silent prayer, I gunned the bike straight for the semi, feeling Three's startled jerk behind me.

"What are you—"

Collision imminent: 7 ft. Veer right.

But I stopped listening. I hit the foot brake at the same time that I leaned to the left, sending the motorcycle into a skid. Our combined weight pulled the motorcycle down, until we were falling toward the road, the tires screaming on asphalt. The bike started to spin. Three slackened her grip, undoubtedly readying herself to jump ship. But I was prepared.

I got my left foot on the seat. The next instant, I was shoving her down with the bike, while I vaulted off the seat, launching myself up toward the semi's metal carriage. Meanwhile, Three flew with the motorcycle toward the churning tires.

The impact was hard and fast. I smashed into the side,

rebounded, and flew a few feet before landing on the ground with a brutal smack.

At the same time, a horrible metal-on-metal screech filled the air. An explosion lit the sky with tiny orange flames. Parts bounced like shrapnel, brakes shrieked. The semi swayed, skittering and winding to a stop as its back end burned. I lifted my head. The driver leaped from the cab. Three and the bike had disappeared under the truck's massive wheels.

Internal damage assessment:

No. Not now. I had to move.

Get up. Get. Up.

A hesitation, long enough that I wondered if I'd permanently damaged something in the collision. Then, my legs responded. I bounded to my feet. Around me, cars were pulling over, people slamming doors and shouting, running our way.

I stared at the burning wreckage for a moment and my hands flew to my throat. Oh, god. The smashed-up remains of Three's body, slowly melting in the furnace surrounding her. Her brown eyes still wide open. Once the fire died, there would be nothing left of her.

The smell of smoke threatened to unlock memories inside of me, and I feared what kind of response that might trigger. So I raced my way through back streets, cold night air rushing against my face. Along the way, I found an unchained bike and nabbed it. I pedaled along, listening to the sirens in the distance and hoping they wouldn't come for me. All the while, two thoughts spun through my head on an endless repeat cycle.

Three was dead.

And I'd killed her.

The emotions that rose up were conflicting, confusing. Relief, satisfaction, horror, and sorrow, all battling to reign supreme. But one feeling fought hard and rose above the rest. A strange smile twitched on my face, because I was unable to hide my swelling burst of pride.

Holland had sent his best, and I'd come out on top. I'd taken Three down. Me, the "problem child" he'd wanted to terminate. After this, there was no way to deny that he'd greatly underestimated me.

This wasn't the time to gloat, however. I had a job to do. Find Steven Jensen. Fill in the missing blanks about Sarah. But I wasn't going to delude myself. Once the dust died down from this massive disaster, Holland would regroup. As would the V.O. and the police. At some point, they'd be coming for me.

All of them.

TWELVE

Two hours later, I'd ditched the bike in a back alley where hopefully no one would question its presence for at least a few days. After cutting through backyards on street after street, sticking to the abandoned areas and listening intently for the sound of a chase behind me, I finally let the stiffness in my shoulders uncoil a little. I'd ditched the LED lights long ago, and traded the coat for an old brown sweatshirt I found in the unlocked backseat of a car.

I prayed those tiny changes would be enough.

A car raced up the street behind me, but I remained calm and tucked my chin to my chest. Just an ordinary pedestrian out for a walk. The green map unfurled before I could even think, *GPS.*

Thankfully, the blinking orange dot that represented my

position wasn't too far away from my final destination.

4.23 mi.

Apart from a few barking dogs and occasional lights inside houses, there was no sign of life on the streets ahead. But as I walked, the trees grew more plentiful, the houses bigger. The scent of rain, grass, and pine filled the air.

The yards grew bigger as well, with sprawling grass lots and few fences. Long driveways led up to two- and three-car garages. I passed one home, then two. Suddenly, I was at the end of a long, curving driveway. One freshly painted, detached garage sat about twenty feet down, then the driveway curved to the left and ended at another two-car garage, which was attached to a house.

A forest-green SUV waited outside.

This was it. This was Steven Jensen's address.

Initiate scan.

Details autofocused in front of me, enlarging without any prodding. My eyes swept over the first object, then moved on to the next. In under one second, I'd processed all the visual information before me and stored it for safekeeping in my memory.

Green Mercury Mountaineer, license plate DVU234. Trilevel home, eight front-facing windows, one front door, one garage door accessible from front yard. Three pine trees, one blocking full view of front door, two planters, filled with assorted perennials.

So I was here. Now what?

As I chewed on my lip and studied the house, a soft click broke the still night air. My head whipped up toward the sound. A lone car was parked across the street, six houses down. I'd been so caught up in studying Jensen's house, I hadn't thought much of it.

The click had been the driver's-side door opening.

On instant alert, I watched. Ready to pounce. Until the make of the car and the identity of the tall, lean figure emerging from it hit me at the same time.

Jeep. *Hunter.*

An initial burst of joy, immediately chased by uncertainty. Logic cemented my feet to the ground. We'd been apart less than twenty-four hours and yet it felt like years. Three, Holland—look at everything that had happened in that short span of time. Everything I'd accomplished. Solo. Could I have done any of that with him by my side? I knew all too well that the responsibility of keeping him safe was a terrifying burden.

And then all of that concern fell away when my emotions kicked in, a heartbeat later, in an explosion that obliterated everything else.

He'd read the note, which was how he'd followed me here. In my letter of apology, I'd given him my real destination, telling him that there was no one else I'd trust with that secret information.

Telling him that I would never doubt him as long as I lived.

This had to mean that he still cared about me, right? And if that were true—if he could forgive me for what I'd done—couldn't I trust him with the rest of my story?

Hunter turned and closed the door. I imagined him running toward me with ground-covering steps, his face lighting up. But he walked toward me slowly, his face totally apprehensive, like he doubted his decision to come here. The rush of fullness in my chest that began the moment I saw him deflated almost instantaneously.

When he finally stood a few feet away from me, I noticed dark circles forming under his eyes, which were red at the corners. His hands were buried in his pockets, his shoulders hunched forward.

I was worried that I'd completely broken him, but then I saw his lopsided half smile appear on his lips and I sighed a little in relief.

"Hey," he said simply.

"Hi," I croaked.

"Hope you don't mind me showing up unannounced. I just . . . I figured superspies still need friends, you know."

A knife sliced through my chest like it was made of paper. I was so thankful that Hunter didn't hate me and had driven all this way, but hearing that word—*friends*—was more devastating than I could have possibly imagined. He was drawing a line with me, because I'd crossed a line with him. I didn't blame him for that, but god, acknowledging it was unbearable.

When I didn't respond, Hunter's posture stiffened. Cold air swirled between us as he took a step back.

"Was I wrong about that?" he asked.

Actually, he was. I didn't really deserve him, as a friend or anything more. He probably knew it, too, but he was here anyway, sticking by me even though I'd hurt him.

Hunter being here was very wrong. But as this next step in my journey loomed in front of me, and I had virtually no understanding of where it might lead, I couldn't help but take him up on his generous offer. As efficient as I was on my own, and despite my newfound resolve to avoid connecting with anyone, I had a feeling I'd need someone to lean on after meeting Jensen. Now that Three was gone and I was currently out of Holland's reach, the odds were slim I'd ever hear from Lucas again.

There was no one else.

"No, you're not," I said.

Relief showered over me when I saw his half smile branch out into a full-blown grin. Then he rummaged around in his pocket and withdrew a crumpled piece of paper. "I've also come to collect."

I stared at the paper in wonder, recognition dawning as I read the motel's name across the top of the page. The IOU

I'd written him, back in Virginia Beach. I actually laugh-sobbed, unable to believe my eyes. "Wow, you must really like bad TV."

"Yeah, I guess I'm addicted," he said, with an uncomfortable snicker.

I did everything in my power not to read into that.

He gave his head a slight shake. "So, you're a secret agent. No idea how that's possible, but I've seen enough to know not to argue."

A cloud of wariness began to form around me. With Hunter here, I'd need to go back to feigning more humanity than I possessed, hide the side of me that had helped me get this far. Not only that, I wasn't sure how aware he was about the consequences of being my friend.

"Hunter, I should warn you—"

"Don't," he said, holding up his hands. "I know what I'm getting myself into. I just didn't want to abandon you before you found your father. That is, if you're really looking for your dad?"

Jensen's face swam before me, triggering that emotional connection to my programmed past. Technically speaking, I was looking for a man who I'd once thought was my father. But that distinction would make no sense to Hunter, so I decided to keep it simple.

"In a way, yes. His name is actually Steven Jensen."

Hunter crossed his arms in front of his chest. "Okay."

I glanced back at the house, at the SUV in the driveway. "Before we talk to him, we need to make sure it's safe. So I'll want to wait until he leaves and then check out the house for weapons."

He looked at the house again before shrugging. "Just tell me how to help."

Startled, I shook my head. "Maybe you should wait in the car, and then I'll let you know when it's clear. Speaking of cars, we should both get inside yours for now, instead of standing out here on the asphalt."

Street scan: Activated.

No human threat detected.

With my vision heightened, I zoomed in on the windows of the surrounding houses. All clear. No signs of life outside, not yet.

Hunter's car would make do for cover, at least until people were on the move.

Hunter's lips flattened, and his hands shoved into his pockets. "You don't—"

I gestured at his Jeep. "Wait until we're inside," I whispered, then started for the passenger door at a brisk walk.

Once the doors closed, I turned to him, steeling myself for another fight.

Sure enough, Hunter's fingers beat a sharp rhythm on the dashboard. "You don't really think I'm going to sit in the car while you search the house on your own, do you?"

"Yes, I do. Hunter, I'm specially trained for this"—not that I remembered undergoing any of that training, but still—"and you're not. I promise, I'll signal you as soon as I've cleared the perimeter."

"No way. I'm not waiting in here for you while god-knows-what could happen inside that house," he said, nodding toward Jensen's front door. "You told me that your mom is dead, Mila—*dead!* How do you think I'd feel if something terrible happened to you and here I was, twiddling my thumbs in the car?"

I could see from the slight red flush crawling up his neck that he was really getting agitated, and honestly, it seemed like the reaction of someone who had feelings that ran much deeper than friendship.

"Look, Mila, you owe me this," he started, in a much calmer voice. "You have to let me in, so we can . . . you just have to trust me."

"Okay," I said, wanting so much to make everything up to him. "You can come. But just know people die around me."

At that, I pressed a balled fist to my mouth. Too late to take back the words. Hunter leaned forward and gently reached over to squeeze my hand.

"I'm not going to die," he whispered.

And even though I knew it was a stupid, completely meaningless gesture, the human part of me couldn't help but ask, "Promise?"

"Promise," he agreed. And somehow, someway, that made me feel better.

"So, now that we've got that covered . . . now what?"

I looked back at the silent house—still no sign of life from within. "Now? We wait."

As we waited for morning to lead Jensen away from the house, we curled up on our sides, facing each other, our hands lightly grazing.

Just friends, I reminded myself sternly. But my android heart refused to believe.

THIRTEEN

A couple of hours and false alarms later, I saw the glowing red warning.

Motion detected.

I sat up and sure enough, a figure emerged from the house, carrying a box. He wore a bulky black jacket, a black ski cap, and heavy boots. I shifted down in my seat, so I could watch without being seen.

A man. Based on the clothing, it was a man.

Excitement surged like a sudden wind, but it was tempered by the weight of anxiety. Was this Jensen? The man from my memories? Seeing him, in the now . . . my brain bucked at the idea, confounded by its own version of the truth. I craned my neck, but his features were hidden behind the box. He headed straight for the driver's side of his SUV.

As he turned and opened the door, I sighted the back of his head. Dark brown hair, thick with a slight wave. Tall, and well built without being too bulky. Fair-skinned.

My mind retrieved an image, and I leaned up against the glass, my breath forming a white cloud.

It could be him.

He leaned across the driver's seat to shove the box into the passenger side, then hopped in. I caught a glimpse of sunglasses, but with the way his collar was turned up against the cold, not much more of his face. The cloud on the window grew, in time with my shallow breathing.

Height: 6.05 ft.

Approximate weight range: 205–217 lbs.

Distinguishing features: 2.75-in. scar on right hand, extending from 3rd metacarpal head toward carpal joint.

I leaned back. Scar? I didn't remember a scar.

The SUV grumbled to life and within moments started reversing down the first stretch of driveway. I waited for it to turn at the bend and face forward, but no—he angled the car expertly and continued to reverse his way down the second long stretch.

"Is that him? Are we going in soon?"

"Shhh," I whispered, but despite the nerves fluttering to life in my stomach, I couldn't help but smile a little at Hunter's enthusiasm. When the SUV's rear tires hit the street, I waited with growing anticipation to see which way it would turn. If it came our way, I'd get a look at the driver, but then again, he might get a look at us.

"Get ready to duck," I murmured to Hunter.

So it was a mix of disappointment and relief that swept me when the man turned in the opposite direction. A few seconds later, the SUV disappeared as it made a right turn onto another street.

"It's time. Quietly," I said, before easing my door open.

Hunter was a quick study. He mimicked my actions, making a minimum of noise. Maybe this would work out to my benefit, after all. Checking out the house would go much faster with two of us.

The street remained quiet, so we started a leisurely walk across. I hadn't seen anyone, but this way if they came upon us, they'd assume we were out for some exercise. On the other hand, if we ran at Jensen's house like linebackers . . . yeah, that'd be a little more challenging to explain.

"We need to act casual; we don't want to stick out around here," I advised.

"Got it," he said.

He fell into step beside me very naturally.

Like we were good friends.

As we drew closer to the house, I continued to scan the neighboring houses, especially the one right across the street, since it had an excellent view of the front door and garage. We reached the driveway and, without faltering, I steered us onto it.

Hunter leaned over and whispered into my ear. "Shouldn't we be ducking behind those bushes?" he said, motioning to a green plant with rows of bulbous leaves framing the yard between the drive and the house.

I gave a tiny shake of my head. "Too suspicious. This way, if anyone stops us, we say we're looking for a lost cat or something. Actually we better come up with a description too, just in case. What about a two-year-old Siamese named Lucy? She could be adopted from the local ASPCA or something."

He blinked a few times before saying softly under his breath, "You're really good at that."

"What?"

"Making people believe everything you say."

I swallowed hard, wishing that circumstances didn't force me to be good at this kind of thing. Knowing that the truth of who I was wouldn't sound the least bit believable to him.

"Come on, let's keep moving," I replied.

Two more steps. Then four. Suddenly, we were on the bend in the driveway, and turning. This was going to be easier than I'd expected. No one was out, and nothing stirred—

The high-pitched, rapid barks jerked us both to a stop. And then the sound of a heavy body slamming the fence to our right. At the top, a pair of pointed ears jackknifed over the posts, followed by a pair of dark brown eyes.

A dog. A Doberman.

I recoiled. Dogs—what was it about me and dogs? Please, please tell me this wasn't going to be a repeat of the Toronto airport, when dogs had chased down Mom and me? As that thought raced through my head, I realized Hunter was walking toward the fence.

"Hunter, get back here!" I hissed, throwing a hasty look over my shoulder. Still quiet across the street, but that wasn't enough to make me feel safe. Surely the neighbors to our right would be awake now, and if not them, then at least the dog's owners?

"Hey buddy, it's okay. You're a good boy, right? Here's a treat. Cookie?" Hunter said, using an odd, singsongy voice.

This was nutty. We needed to get out—

But then I heard it. Silence. As Hunter withdrew something from his pocket—was that . . . jerky?—the dog pogoed upward again, his shining eyes glued to Hunter's treat-laden hand.

"You want this? You have to be a good boy. Quiet, okay? No barking."

Then, Hunter reached the fence. The next time the dog sprung up, Hunter extended the jerky and, POOF! The dog snatched it and both the jerky and dog disappeared like magic.

"Is that really going to work?" I asked, stunned.

Hunter turned away and shrugged. "We'll see. Just don't make any sudden moves or eye contact, okay? But I think he was just barking for attention. He wasn't growling, and the fur on his ruff wasn't standing up. And did you hear his barks? Don't think he meant business—a serious guard dog probably would have been too suspicious to take the food."

All I'd ever wanted to know about dogs, and more. "What, did you used to train dogs or something?"

He shook his head. "Nope. But my mom watched a lot of Cesar Milan." He gave me a sideways look and at my blank stare, continued. "You know—the Dog Whisperer?"

"The Dog Whisperer," I repeated. "You approached a huge, barking dog on the basis of some guy who calls himself the Dog Whisperer?"

Hunter elbowed me in the ribs and I grinned, but it faded when I looked at the house. We still had to get in without being seen—and since we had no idea where Jensen had gone, we could have hours or only minutes to accomplish our task.

"I'm going to check out that back door and see if it's unlocked—you take the front?" he said, pointing to a door on the nonstreet side of the house that appeared to lead into a room beyond the garage.

"Okay."

Quietly, I walked along the front of the garage, to where

the driveway turned into a brick walkway that led to the front door.

Alarm system detected.

Hurriedly, I took in the surroundings—yellow, pink, and white flowering plants filled a brick-lined planter to my left, and to my right, a pine tree in a cedar-chip enclosure towered overhead. A tiny white sign poking out of the grass.

THIS HOUSE PROTECTED BY EMV ALARMS.

Crap.

I looked up at the moldings around the door, then the windows, and the gleam of wires said it all. The house was rigged with an alarm system. When Jensen had left, had he activated it?

Alarm system armed—override?

"Hunter," I breathed, backing away from the door and turning to run. "Hunter," I tried again, a little louder this time. But before I could hit a sprint, I heard it. A noise where there'd been silence before.

A steady, pulsing beep. Which meant . . .

"Door's locked." Hunter's voice floated around the corner.

I whirled back to the front door, horror-struck. Which meant—Hunter had tried the door, and while it hadn't unlocked, the motion had done something far more disturbing.

He'd triggered the alarm.

While the beep continued its monotonous countdown, I shook off the shock and went to work. Around the corner, I heard the steady clap-clap of Hunter's sneakers on asphalt. I opened my mind, searching for a signal from the alarm I knew resided just on the other side of that door. Completely conscious that we were running out of time with every single beep.

Beep. Beep.

Beep.

Maybe I should have panicked. Instead, my senses thrilled to the challenge. I had this. I'd been made for it.

I heard Hunter hesitate while at the same time I felt the click of a connection. The spark of awareness when my mind interlocked with the humming machine just inside the house. So simple—as smooth as the gentle slick of a currycomb over Maisey's haunches back at the stables in Clearwater—and yet forceful. A heady rush that only came from bending power to my will.

Request permissions.

Permissions granted, the alarm responded.

I strode toward the door, even as the alarm continued to beep. The sinewy tendril of code was within my grasp. All I had to do was trace the tendril back to deactivate the alarm.

I toyed with the code as I approached the door. So simple, it was barely even fun. If I timed it just right . . .

Beep. Beep. Beep.

The alarm beeped, while the countdown played in my head.

Three seconds.

I was two steps away from the door.

Two seconds.

One step.

One second.

I reached for the door handle, at the same time I sent the final command.

Alarm: Deactivate.

At first I didn't feel the other computer acquiesce, and my confidence slipped. Had I waited a moment too long?

But then I realized the beeping had stopped.

The response slid into my mind:

Alarm: Deactivated. Reactivate now?

Cake. Just like I'd thought.

A heady power soared through me, and I turned the knob, reveling as the lock yielded beneath my hand.

Hunter reemerged around the corner.

"I picked the lock." That was one way to put it.

"One of your agent skills, huh?" he said, skepticism lacing his voice.

I looked over my shoulder and saw him take in the alarm sign. But there was no time to reassure him or offer any explanations.

"I watched a news report once, and less than half of the people who have alarm signs actually have activated alarms," I said, opening the door and walking into a faux-wood entryway, stifling a laugh. Oh, Jensen was definitely in the half who paid for guard services.

I gestured at Hunter to hurry, and inspected our surroundings as he rushed inside and closed the door behind us. The house was large—we'd entered into a central landing. Straight ahead was a kitchen, with a living area to our right. Branching out from the kitchen to the left was a set of stairs leading into some kind of basement, and another set of stairs led left and up from the foyer to what I assumed were bedrooms.

Minimal furniture, few decorations. Almost zero knick-knacks. The house didn't look especially lived-in.

I walked into the kitchen, where a long counter made an L around stainless steel appliances. A simple black-and-white Mr. Coffee coffeemaker, a shiny toaster. Takeout menus to Gino's Pizza, The Greek Café, and Mr. Chung Chinese Food, neatly stacked near the sink.

One lone photo, on the refrigerator.

Oh my god . . .

FOURTEEN

I took a disbelieving step forward, at the same time I heard Hunter gasp. He walked straight toward the refrigerator, reaching around the side to pluck a photo away from a silver magnet shaped like a horse. All of my newfound confidence evaporated.

The photo was of three people. Mom, Jensen . . . and me.

In my anxiety over human threats and weapons, I'd never given a single thought to worrying about simple, inanimate objects. But I should have. Because as Hunter extended the picture toward me, my heart—whatever, my pump—felt like it screeched to a stop inside my chest. Then, it burst back to life, pounding out a harsh, frantic beat. Evidence of my mother's lies staring me directly in the face. I gaped at the photo, words failing me completely.

Not so for Hunter. "I don't understand—if you've never met your real dad, how does he have a photo of you, him, and your mom? One that looks really recent?"

Good question. If only I had an answer.

"I mean, that is him, right?"

Another bull's-eye. With a trembling hand, I reached for the photo, wishing I had an answer for him. Or that someone had an answer for me. Lots of answers. Because I had no idea how I'd gotten into that picture—and Hunter was right—I looked exactly the same as I had back in Clearwater. And Jensen? He looked exactly the same as he did in my memory. Before my mother had told me those images were totally fabricated.

"Mila?" Hunter prompted.

I shook my head, my hand refusing to stop trembling, despite my urgent commands. "I don't . . ." My voice trailed off when I noticed more details, all at once. The man's—my fictitious father's—arm was draped around my mom's shoulders, while both of them beamed at the camera. Waves in the background, and sand—we were at a beach. Obviously this photo was taken during a happy time. His other hand rested casually, comfortably, on my shoulder.

And me? I was smiling too. Only . . . it was me, and yet it wasn't.

Apart from my mutilated hair, the happy girl in the photo looked identical to me in every single way, save one. While my eyes were a bright, almost too vibrant shade of green, that girl's eyes were brown. It was like the stun of meeting Three for the first time, all over again.

Wait. Could . . . could that girl be Three? Or One, even—the version who'd existed before me?

Then, I remembered the third, empty file Mom had left for me. Her voice, whispering in my ear.

Maybe I'd finally found the mysterious Sarah.

Maybe I had yet another "sister."

The photo slipped from my grasp as a sea of unanswered questions tossed through me, but the image remained implanted in my head. The memory from Virginia Beach teased at the back of my mind. The ocean, the seagulls, the roar of the waves. Wet sand, squishing between my toes. Then came the one from the carousel. *Spinning, spinning, spinning.* However, instead of becoming paralyzed, the images created a strange warmth in my heart, a feeling that I . . . belonged.

The fragmented images flickered. Then, they were gone.

Hunter bent over to retrieve the photo. He must have stared at the faces for ten seconds before he returned it to the refrigerator. I realized I still owed him a response, but what could I possibly say? Hello, sorry, but I have no clue how I could possibly be in a photo with that man. Oh, and there's a chance that girl probably isn't even me. I seem to have more than my fair share of imposters running around out there—crazy, right?

Hunter turned to me, his arms crossing over his chest. "Tell me what's going on."

I held up my hands. "I swear, I don't know anything about that picture. Nothing."

"But you're not that young there—how could you forget? That could only be, what, a couple of years ago, max? Unless you have a twin," he scoffed.

I coughed to cover my reaction. As an excuse, it really was the only plausible explanation, with the exception of the truth. Actually, strike that. This lie was probably way more plausible.

"Maybe I do have a twin. I'm adopted, remember?"

"But . . . doesn't that mean she's not your real mom?" he said, gesturing to Nicole.

"I don't know," I said, pacing in my agitation. "How could I possibly know?"

He must have sensed the honesty of my reaction, because though his frown deepened, he nodded. "I'm sorry, I didn't mean—it just doesn't make any sense."

No, it really didn't. But we had work to do. "Look, we can talk later. But Jensen could be back at any moment."

Hunter opened his mouth like he might argue, but only sighed. "So what should we do?"

Guilt made me avert my eyes, but that didn't stop the swell of relief. After everything we'd been through, I knew this looked bad. Like I'd gone right back to my old tricks of half-truths and lies. But honestly, at this point, the truth was more nuisance than help. It would steal too much time—time we didn't have.

"Split up. You take downstairs, I'll take upstairs, and we'll meet back in the kitchen."

An emphatic head shake this time. "I think we should stick together, just in case—"

"No, splitting up will make things go faster. We have no idea when Jensen is coming back, so the sooner we do this, the better."

Nothing. And then finally, one curt nod. "I guess you know what you're doing. Just to confirm, I'm looking for . . . ?"

"Weapons, which you should grab, and basically anything that looks suspicious." Which was intentionally vague. I couldn't add that I was also looking for info on the MILA projects, or information as to why Jensen was in witness protection. I figured that time would come soon enough, and besides, if he saw my name on something official-looking, undoubtedly he'd be on instant alert anyway.

That was actually part of the reason I wanted to split up. Not just for convenience—but that way, if I found something referring to my androidness, I could peruse it without fear of being caught.

"Okay," he said, but his words fell on my back, since I

was already halfway up the stairs.

The landing was small, and clean, and opened into a narrow hallway with four doors. One led to a bathroom, one room was completely bare—once upon a time, a bedroom, perhaps—and another was the master. That room was sparsely furnished, to the point that it scarcely looked lived-in. No pictures or art hung on the glaring white walls, and the queen-sized bed lacked a headboard. The comforter was plain navy blue—no throw pillows, no decoration of any kind. No knickknacks cluttered the simple dark-wood dresser, though it was devoid of dust. No desk of any kind in here, either, and all the nightstand held was a digital alarm clock. I hit Alarm and saw it read *12:00*—probably still on its default setting.

Weapons scan: No weapons detected.

I scoffed. No weapons? Seemed highly unlikely. Unless Jensen took them with him?

I pulled out drawers and scanned contents. Socks, plain gray boxers, a few T-shirts and shorts. All neatly folded, and not much of any one item.

The small walk-in closet yielded about the same results. A few neatly hung collared shirts, four sweatshirts, and two pairs of jeans, folded on the top shelf. Only three pairs of shoes total, lined up against the far wall. An odd wave of familiarity cascaded over me as I searched pockets, under jeans, and inside shoes for any hidden papers or weapons. Nothing, and no secret panels as far as I could tell.

I stepped back and did one more quick inspection, and the reason for the familiarity hit me. The closet, the barren room, were familiar because they reminded me of Clearwater. How Mom and I had lived, back at the ranch's guesthouse. It made sense. Back then, I'd thought we'd had so few possessions because we'd lost everything in a fire.

In reality, it'd been because we were on the run—hiding from the government. Just like Jensen was in hiding.

Jensen. The fire. Another wave crashed over me, this one full of remembered emotion, of the searing pain and sorrow that had ripped my chest when I'd thought I'd lost my dad. I'd eventually come to terms with the memories once Mom had told me they were all imaginary—a virtual reality she'd programmed me with to hide my past.

The photo on the refrigerator flashed through my mind and my throat seized. Except, it wasn't all imaginary, because the Dad from those memories actually existed. So how could I possibly know what was real and what wasn't anymore?

Shaking my head, I whirled and did a quick sweep of the master bath. Similarly tidy and with just the simple necessities in terms of toiletries—toothbrush, deodorant, shampoo, lotion—nothing at all to indicate Jensen was anything other than a very neat minimalist. I swept back the brown fabric curtain to reveal the tub—nothing.

A familiar scent teased my nose, making me spin back around to the toiletries. I scanned them again and locked in on a tiny bottle of lotion. I should have noticed it right away—the slight pink color didn't really fit in with the rest of the greens and blues.

With trepidation, I lifted the bottle until I could see the lettering clearly.

Rosemary.

My fingers unscrewed the lid and before I could stop myself, I bent over and inhaled. The sweet herbal scent engulfed me, sweeping me away in a sea of memories. Mom, showing me how to brush Maisey. Mom, sitting behind me while clumps of my hair fell to the floor. Mom, trying to protect me with her very last breath. Her skin still thick with this same exact scent.

I closed my eyes, allowed myself a few desperate moments to sink into the past. To live once again in a world where Mom was alive. Then, with effort, I tore myself free of the fiction and replaced the bottle where I'd found it. Regretfully, I turned away, mind whirling.

He kept her scent with him. Their relationship hadn't been confined to just business.

Who was this man?

Master bedroom—finished. Time to get to the other rooms. I could only hope—and fear—that Hunter fared better in his search.

When I returned to the landing I heard the distant rumble of an engine and froze.

Was it the SUV?

Below me, I could hear the click of wood against wood—Hunter, closing a cabinet?—while the car noise grew louder and louder. Doubtful that Hunter could hear it yet, though. I rushed into the empty guestroom, over to the blinds-covered window that faced the street. Where the blinds met the edge there was a thin slit of visibility, and I peered through.

My faux heart hammered when I spotted an SUV, headed toward the house—a green one, just like Jensen's.

Human threat detected.

Incoming: Ford Escape, license plate LAT916.

A Ford, not a Mercury. And then the car cruised past, allowing my pulse to return to a normal rate.

I reentered the hallway. The study was tempting, with its desktop computer and antique wooden armoire, which probably didn't hold clothes. But above my head, the outline of a square beckoned. An attic.

"Mila?" Hunter whispered harshly.

I rushed over to the stairs. He was standing there looking up.

"It's been a while. Just wanted to make sure you're okay," he said.

"I'm fine. Just a little more to explore. How about you? Any luck?"

"Not so far. It's kinda creepy that the guy has so little here."

"I know, but keep looking."

He gave a brusque nod before heading off to the right.

I hurried back down the hallway where I'd spotted the attic door. I sprung up from my toes and grabbed the thin string that dangled about a quarter of the way from the ceiling, and the square slid away to reveal a hole.

Soundlessly, without any of the groaning or creaking you might expect from a rusty or unused hinge. Which meant someone kept it well oiled.

Of course, the hole was probably at least eight feet overhead—

Distance: 7.90 ft.

I scowled—was that really necessary?

—and there was no ladder in sight.

Glancing quickly down the stairs, to make sure Hunter wasn't watching, I dropped into a crouch. Then I pushed hard off my feet and sprang up, clearing the distance with ease. My fingers curled around the edge of the ceiling, and I hoisted myself up and over.

I was inside the attic.

I'd expected a musty, moldy scent, but instead, caught a hint of cinnamon spice. The area was warmer than the rest of the house, though, for sure—much warmer.

Ambient temperature: 78.2 degrees F.

I'd barely noted the dimness when—

Night vision activated.

Immediately, I saw the source of the cinnamon—two air fresheners, shaped like cones, sitting against the closest wooden slat. Next to it? A flashlight. My fingers twitched with excitement. Oh, someone had definitely been up here recently—multiple times, from the looks of it. Now, to find out *why*.

The first room, if you could call it that, was empty—just wooden slats, thankfully devoid of spiderwebs—and a puffy mass of insulation. Beyond the insulation, a narrow rectangular space beckoned, so I hurried over to the doorway. I pushed into the tiny square of a room, and . . . empty.

I returned to the main part of the attic, turning around to catch what I might have missed. Air fresheners, flashlight. Boards. Insulation.

Wait.

I zeroed in on the insulation. There, at the bottom near the corner, was a barely noticeable slit. I walked over to it, eased it apart . . . and there they were.

Boxes, six of them. The smallish kind with lids—the ones I'd seen teachers in my classrooms use to store papers.

I whipped through the first two in record time—all old paperwork on houses, cars, bills, etc.—all made out to Daniel Lusk. A chill snaked through my gut when I saw where he used to live—Philadelphia. The same place I'd supposedly moved from.

The same place where my dad—Lusk, Jensen—whoever—had supposedly died in a fire.

I shook off the eerie tingle and thrust the papers back into the box, replacing the lid. Interesting, but not relevant, not right now.

The following box was similarly devoid of useful info, and disappointment started to tug at me. But when I pulled the lid off the next box, my hands stilled and I just stared.

A laptop. I lifted it out of the box and opened the black lid. I punched the start button and nothing happened.

Dead. Of course. I rifled through the box for the power cord, but none surfaced. Now what?

Charge battery?

Of course. Who needed a cord, when I was a portable power source, all on my own?

Yes.

Universal adapter: Ejecting.

Before I could register that part of my body housed a universal adapter, I felt something beneath the skin of my right thumb catch. With a springlike motion, a small metal tube ejected from the very tip.

Whoa.

Insert into device.

I traced the metal rod with my index finger, entranced by its smoothness, waiting for that gut-stab of otherness to attack me. The self-hate that had traditionally accompanied such discoveries in the past. It never came. Instead, I inspected the tip with a sort of dazed wonder, all the while, a steady feed of energy blooming in my core.

I had the power to charge things. In a way, I was bringing inanimate objects to life.

Awestruck, I located the hole on the laptop, held it level with my finger, and fitted the tube inside. I expected a jolt, or a huge rush, streaming away from my head. Instead, all I felt was a gentle, steady suction. Pleasant, relaxing. Like I was feeding the machine.

It only needed a small charge to boot up. I just hoped it wouldn't take very long—

Charge complete. Adapter retracted.

The suction cut off, and my thumb detached from the laptop. Okay, I had to admit—that was trippy. Setting the computer back on the ground, I pushed the power button and waited. Within moments, the blue welcome screen greeted me.

I reached out with my mind and issued the familiar set of commands and smashed right into a brick wall.

The rejection felt physical, so much so that I swayed on my feet.

Password?

Of course. Someone like Jensen would keep his files protected.

But I didn't really have time to hack my way in. Luckily

I didn't think I'd have to.

I issued the command, and the adaptor ejected out of my thumb, and I shoved it back inside the machine.

The connection was instant, complete. Now I could sense every bit of the computer, all around me. I could feel it shimmer in the air, sensing my every movement, my every breath. Bending to my will as the sole provider of its energy.

Password override.

The brick wall disintegrated like it'd never even existed, and a moment later, thumb back to normal, I was in. Rows of squares shimmered before me, green and chest-high. Files. They were illuminated with the usual ethereal glow, but appeared more translucent than normal, less substantial. Tiny little boxes that I could almost see through. Something about them bothered me, but I couldn't put my finger on it.

I went ahead and scrolled through them, moving them with my mind. Nothing. Nothing. Nothing. A brief glance at the files yielded the same disappointing results. Only seven, and they felt . . . intentional. Like they were placed there to look pretty and tempting in order to serve as a distraction.

I mean, this last one? A child's essay on the African cheetah.

Totally worthless.

Even as I expressed the thought, a strange flash of recognition pulsed through me as I skimmed the text. Before I scrolled to the next page, I knew what I'd see. A crude crayon drawing of a mother cheetah and her cub.

I stared at the picture as more questions pulsed through my head. How had I known? How could I have possibly seen this report before? I wondered if maybe somehow my computer brain had skimmed ahead and seen the picture before my eyes had.

But no. I didn't believe that. And the déjà vu might be gone, but the feeling left behind an echo, a residue, an eerie, visceral clench that I had experienced that report before, someway, somehow. But . . . could androids really experience déjà vu? And if so, how?

I continued to search, to no avail, and was just about to give up when I noticed letters, floating in the bottom right corner of my field of vision.

M Drop.

M Drop, M Drop . . . what could that mean?

Probably nothing, but I checked just in case.

Store file remotely?

I frowned. Remotely. As in, files were being held at another location?

This was new and different. But then I felt the whoosh of warmth, of energy, that always preceded my connection to another machine or digital entity. The android part of me, taking over again. Before I knew it, I was leaning forward, urging the information into my head. My mind felt open, ready. Eager.

Request permission: Enter M Data cloud?

Permission into M Data cloud: Granted

A moment later, the attic disappeared, to be replaced by shimmering red.

I blinked, entranced with spinning spheres of crimson. Like before, they encased me from all directions, but not in a square. This time, it was as if I stood in the center of a vortex, and they formed the circling tornado around me. The spheres rotated midair, moving in a chaotic pattern, from waist-high up to eye-level. This time, I could see thin, wispy multicolored threads extending away from the files, veering off in multiple directions. No, not threads. Data strings. Indicating which user had added each particular file.

I shut my eyes, momentarily disoriented by all the movement. Just when I thought I'd gotten one of my android functions under control, they had to go and change things on me. But I was mastering the other abilities. I could do this, too.

Stop.

The spheres—files—obeyed instantly, freezing in space as if their batteries had suddenly run out. But I could sense the desire for motion beneath that stillness. Almost like tiny hearts pulsed under each one. I forced the command out with way more power than normal, to keep them from returning to their spinning state.

Open file.

I opened the first file, scanned the contents, and discarded it as irrelevant before moving on to the next.

Open.

Open.

Open.

Faster and faster, the files rotated before me, each discarded one moving to the left as a new one filled its position from the right. They were beautiful, in their continuous dance. Graceful. And in some primal way, disconcerting and slightly sinister.

This process was starting to drain me, and a foreign chill seeped under my skin.

But the next file left me shivering, in a whole new way.

MWPP, Case number 50435

Re: Daniel Lusk

In exchange for services rendered, Daniel Lusk, previously of Philadelphia, PA, shall be granted entry into the military-funded witness protection program (MWPP).

As a condition of gaining admission to MWPP, Mr. Lusk will be required to provide information on the organization of interest, Vita Obscura. As a former member of this organization, Mr. Lusk is in a unique position to provide the U.S. Military with details that could save us millions of dollars in espionage and also prevent weapons from falling into terrorists' hands.

Mr. Lusk's alias will not be provided in this document, as to prevent security breaches that might endanger him.

Any information Mr. Lusk provides on the Vita Obscura will also be documented separately.

That was it, the file in its entirety. But it was enough to send me reeling back. As I moved, the red spheres followed me, and for an instant, I braced myself for an attack.

Clutching to my remaining sanity, I focused on forcing my breathing back to a slower, more sustainable rate. Daniel Lusk. Steve Jensen. The man in the photo. My fictitious dad.

All of them, one and the same.

All of them, former members of the one group that possibly made even life with Holland sound good.

The Vita Obscura.

Why on earth had Mom sent me to this man?

Confusion pounded through me, and betrayal. I tried to push them both away, to make sense of what I'd just learned. I went to rub my forehead. My arms were heavy, cumbersome. Not only had the contents sent me reeling—the act of reading the file itself had been draining.

I fought to remain calm and give myself time to recover, spinning through possibilities. There was only one reason

Mom would have sent me to Jensen—he had to be good now. Obviously he'd left the V.O. if the military was courting him for information, if they needed to hide him to keep him safe. Although my experience with the military thus far had been less than stellar, I knew that most of our soldiers—outside of SMART—weren't like Holland, sadistic and power-hungry.

As I pondered this and more, I realized that the spheres had begun pulsing in a furious manner: harder, brighter. Then, like someone had wrenched the volume up to full blast, a noxious screech pierced my ears—high-pitched and deafening. I gritted my teeth, and that's when realization struck. My ears. They actually *hurt*. Burned, with a searing pain that felt like my flesh was being stripped from my bone.

As I tried to process that, I noticed words, hovering before my eyes. Not a prompt. Not coming from me.

Alarm. Unauthorized user.

I doubled over with my palms on my ears, fighting off the overwhelming noise. Through the chaos, I managed to issue a single command.

Stop.

No response.

The crescendo rose, and the spheres grew larger, brighter, more sinister-looking. Then, in a shattering explosion of light, they disappeared. I remained hunched over for an indefinite amount of time, my ears registering a low, staticky buzz as they adjusted to the abrupt cessation of sound.

But wait. Not a cessation of sound.

Because within the quiet, I heard noises. A man's voice. A grunt. The scuffle of shoes against a wood floor. Followed by a yell.

Hunter's.

I went to burst into a run and—nothing. I couldn't budge. The noise had vanished, but once again I had no ability to move. However, unlike my previous blips of paralysis, this felt different. I wasn't void of energy and life: it was the exact opposite, like someone had tapped into my power source and created some kind of electrical surge that was rendering me immobile.

Every piece of me began to feel this kinetic burning sensation, as if I were a matchbook that had been dropped into a pool of gasoline. Petrified of what was happening downstairs, I struggled to break free. Hunter needed me. But nothing happened. Nothing.

Another crash downstairs, a man's voice. Older, gruff. Familiar, yet not. Hunter's voice, low and quick. I could only catch a few words.

"No, don't move. Stay back—let me talk—wait—"

A gunshot. The sound of glass breaking. Then a cry. And then . . . silence.

Panic urged me to drink in quick, labored breaths, but

I couldn't even do that. I couldn't even pretend to breathe, and although I didn't need to, the inability only fed the terror more.

No, no, no. Calm down. I forced myself to push away the growing whirlwind that clouded my head. This surge had to be linked to the M Cloud, to being discovered as unauthorized. Some kind of electrical current, a trap, overwhelming my power source.

My power source.

I groped inside my head, feeling my way through the darkness, through pathways, through images and visions of the past, stored data, until I found it. But what now? I felt my way around it, the tiny orange cell. Blinking faintly, like the surge had blown it out. I surrounded the cell with every bit of strength I had left, issued the command with force.

Recalibration process: Initiated.

Recharging . . .

The cell blink, blink, blinked, like it had all the time in the world. Maybe it did, but Hunter didn't.

Hurry, I urged.

The little entity gave one big pulse, as if to acknowledge my request. Then, the orange began to brighten at a dizzying rate.

20%

30%

50%

80%

100%

Orange exploded into brightness and I rose, stamping out the inertia that had held me hostage. I spun, raced for the opening, dropping out of the attic into a crouch. I flew down the stairs like Holland himself was on my heels, as a loud thud emitted from the kitchen—the sound a body would make, hitting the tile floor.

Less than a second later I was lunging into the room, taking everything in with a single glance.

Lusk/Jensen, still upright. Standing in the middle of the kitchen, staring down while wielding a bloody knife. A hole in the window above the sink, glass fragments on the countertop.

And on the floor, oh god—Hunter. Slumped on his back, eyes closed. While, over his right shoulder, a lake of vibrant red lapped away at his white shirt. A lake that grew steadily larger.

And Grady's gun, lying near Hunter's hand. He must have run back to his Jeep and gotten it when I was upstairs in the attic, prying information out of Jensen's computer, or my sensors would have alerted me earlier. He'd wanted to protect us, to protect me.

Visions of my dying mom assaulted me, shattered my frantic thoughts into a kaleidoscope of chaos. All of them, threatening to tear my heart right out of my chest. Mom had died in a pool of blood, and now Hunter was bleeding.

Because of me.

A motion caught my attention, and I glanced up. I saw Jensen stepping toward me, the knife still gleaming in his hand. Blood drops marred its shiny silver surface.

I saw the knife, and all of my thoughts streamlined into one, simple purpose.

He would pay. He would pay, now.

FIFTEEN

In the next heartbeat, I lunged. Before Jensen could even look up, my foot whipped out, catching him the chest. He crashed into a stainless steel skillet that dangled from a shiny hook, sending the metal pan clattering to the tile floor, narrowly missing Hunter's head. I started forward, but Jensen was already straightening, gathering himself. And then he was airborne.

I lurched back, but the kitchen was too tiny to avoid him. We collided, with his brawny hands grasping for my neck, and hit the pantry as one. My head exploded against wood with a deafening thud, but nothing could deter me, could quell the enraged thunder of my faux pulse. This man had hurt Hunter, and I would take him down.

His feet scrabbled for purchase on the tile floor, and I

waited, let him get his balance. I waited while his hands circled my throat and tightened. While he lifted his head, his eyes bright with victory. He thought he'd won.

No. Way.

My lip curled and with fierce eagerness, I lifted my hands and pried his from my throat, like they were a child's. Then, I jammed my knee hard into his gut, and as he started to double over, head-butted him. But I saw something, just before my knee connected. I saw Jensen's victory expression morph into wide eyes, numb lips. He looked like he'd spotted a ghost, and as he fell to the floor, he mouthed a name.

"Sarah."

A sharp twist; a flicker of memory that vanished the instant it appeared. Then, I shoved past him. I had no time for that now. Not when Hunter could be bleeding to death all over the kitchen floor.

I yanked a clean-looking dishtowel off the counter before dropping to my knees by Hunter's side. I pressed the fabric to his shoulder. The blood seeped through the thin material almost immediately, warm and wet and oh my god, Hunter was bleeding out, just like my mom, and nothing I could do would save him. . . .

A knot formed in my throat, practically swelling it shut, while ice splintered in my chest, sending tiny shards stabbing into my heart. This couldn't be happening. Not again. But it was. It was. It—

Body scan: Initiated.

My robotic voice interrupted, and I latched on to it like a parachute on a crashing plane. Too much emotion, when I needed logic. Logic could help me save him. Emotion would only help me cry while he died.

A glimmering 3-D replica of Hunter appeared, midair. Green letters flashed a constant stream of information:

Tearing to epidermal and dermal layers: Consistent with knife wound.

Muscles: Medial and anterior deltoid, severed from origin. Surgical repair required for maximal function.

Brachial artery: Nicked.

Critical blood loss: Possible.

Disorientation: Possible.

Shock: Possible.

Vital signs: Stable.

Heart rate slightly high: 100 bpm.

Conflicting thoughts bombarded me in a dizzying torrent.

Hunter's vitals are good—he might be okay.

But he could bleed to death.

Just like Mom.

No. NO.

I heard a scuffling on the floor behind me, followed by a low groan. I craned my head and watched Jensen stumble to his feet and grab for the counter to keep his shaky balance. He had picked up the knife, but when I met his eyes, his face drained of color again. The knife slipped from his hand and clattered to the floor. His nostrils flared, his eyes widened, and he stood motionless.

Once again, his lips moved, but nothing came out.

Holding his wide-eyed gaze with mine, I pushed to my feet. A spark burst through the fear, and I stoked the flame, urged it into a full-fledged fire. Anything to keep my worry over Hunter at bay. I shot toward him while he stared, stared, stared, continuing to mouth the name like the very sight of me had snatched his vocal cords and rendered him mute.

Sarah.

I covered the distance between us swiftly as an image of my face swam before me, only with brown eyes. Just like in the photo hanging on the fridge. Again, a tingle of perception pushed around the edges of my consciousness.

Sarah. I'd heard her name before Mom had ever uttered it, I knew I had.

More visions flashed, one after another, creating a disjointed video in my head. Waves. A sandy beach. A woman's laugh. Then, a sensation of overwhelming heat. Smoke, clogging my lungs. Pain.

I doubled over, hands going to my throat, gasping for breath. Air. My lungs burned like fire. I needed air.

Overhead, I swear I heard something crack. A man's voice, calling my name.

"Sarah!"

Memory banks compromised, defragment.

Image recall.

I blinked, and just like that, *poof!* Everything disappeared, completely. Like the scenes had never existed in the first place. No sand. No laughter. No fire. I was in a kitchen, still clutching my throat, staring as a tear-streaked man—Jensen—lifted a hesitant hand toward me, as if to touch my cheek.

And on the floor, to my right, was Hunter. His blood splashed across the white tile floor.

My gaze returned to Jensen, and deep inside me, something dangerous burst free.

Engage?

Human loss: Acceptable.

The sound that escaped my mouth was low and guttural.

Surprise yanked him upright, snapping him out of his semicatatonic state. But I was already on him. I shoved him hard in the chest. He staggered back into the cupboards and I followed, pinning him in place when my hands shot out to wrap around his throat.

Target: Immobilized.

Eliminate target?

My hands clamped down. Squeezing against rising resistance.

His strangled gurgle made me pause. I relaxed my grip, just enough for him to wheeze air into his trachea, and put my mouth right next to his ear.

"Listen to me," I whispered, anger still pouring through my limbs, my head, in a smoldering, lavalike concoction. This man had hurt Hunter. This man was involved with the Vita Obscura.

This man was another Holland.

I willed my hands not to clench in response at the thought of Holland's name, while Jensen writhed against me, gasping for air.

Control. I had to retain control.

"You will fix Hunter's arm, and you'll do it now. If you don't, I'll squeeze the life right out of you . . . and enjoy every second of it."

And in that moment, I meant it. Jensen was going to help me save Hunter. He would help me . . . or he would die, too.

With one final, hard squeeze, I relaxed my grasp completely. Jensen was already nodding his head. He tried to respond but wheezed again, then barked a weak cough. Five seconds, that's all I gave him to regain his breath. Then I picked up the gun on the floor and shoved it in my back waistband. As angry and homicidal as I was feeling, for some reason, I couldn't bring myself to aim it at Jensen.

Not that it would have done any good.

Ammo inventory: Last bullet fired.

So all I could do was order Jensen, through gritted teeth, to "Fix. His. Arm."

"Okay," he finally managed. "I'll help."

I staggered back a step, recognition tingling along my skin like electricity. That voice. It was raspy from the number I'd done on his throat, but even so, the tone, the cadence, the deep pitch—I'd heard them all before. Many, many times. Because that same voice had played, over and over again, in my memories. That voice had soothed childhood injuries, cheered at Phillies' games, laughed at the beach.

That voice matched the face, exactly—the face that belonged to my "dad."

He straightened and turned to stride to a cabinet. "But I'll have to do it here. We can't take him to a hospital. It'd be far too risky—for you," he added. His hands shook while he gathered some clean cloths and a bottle of alcohol. "The rest of my supplies are in the garage."

He shoved the items he held toward me. "Hold these, and I'll pick him up—"

"No!" I whirled and squatted beside Hunter. His eyelashes fluttered open to reveal pain-glazed eyes, and his moan made me sick to my stomach. "Mi—?" he started, but I was already shaking my head, gently touching my finger to his lips. They were uncharacteristically pale—and chilled to the touch.

"Shhhh, save your strength."

"I'm s-sorry. He surprised me and I . . . drew the gun."

Then Hunter shuddered, gasped, and went completely still in my arms.

"Hunter?" I cried as panic surged through me.

"He's just passed out," Jensen said calmly.

Even though I could read Hunter's vitals in a split second and figure that out for myself, I was so filled with rage that my capabilities seemed completely insignificant and useless. I stood and faced Jensen. "If he dies—" I started, fury wrenching my throat closed.

"He won't. This way." Shaking his head slightly, with a tiny, strange, bittersweet smile on his lips as if in disbelief, Jensen walked down the stairs, toward the lower level, surprisingly quiet on his feet for such a tall man. I followed as he turned left, past another den and a bathroom, all decorated in that same minimalist style. We walked into a large laundry room, toward a door with an electrical box next to it. He yanked it open and led us into the garage.

As I entered, I realized that the three-car space held no cars, but tons and tons of equipment and boxes. A military-issue ATV sat in the corner, right next to a black Honda motorcycle. A network of three computers hummed on three interlocking desks. Towering shelves dominated the left side of the wall. Colorful bins were tucked away inside, most of them labeled. FLASHLIGHTS. CAMPING. ELECTRONICS. EMERGENCY. Two larger radios, assorted speakers, and walkie-talkies nestled among them. On the bottom shelf, tucked away in a corner, were four folded sets of camos, three sets of worn, military-issued combat boots beside them.

Hooks up near the front door sagged under an assortment of backpacks, sleeping bags, scanners, climbing gear, and other paraphernalia. The layout bothered me. Nothing was flush against the walls. Even the hooks were on a freestanding rack. Everything was a good seven inches away from touching the walls, and the lack of logic burrowed under my skin.

I tried to tune in, opened my mind and listened with my android sensors. A very faint hum replied, but nothing else.

I gave up and turned back to Hunter, my stomach knotting at his pallor. If Jensen wanted to plan for the apocalypse, that was his business. So long as he could fix Hunter.

Jensen paused in the process of clearing off a long, sturdy worktable. He followed my gaze. "I like to be prepared," he said curtly, obviously noting my inspection. He finished moving a power saw and thumped the table. "Put him down here."

I settled him as gently as I could onto the cold, hard surface. He lay as still as death.

"Here we go." Jensen plunked a medium-sized box labeled FIELD FIRST AID on the edge of the computer table and popped off the lid. After pulling out a giant bandage—Tegaderm—two large sterile gauze pads, and some stretchy elastic wrap, he produced a syringe and a small vial. His sure hands worked the needle into the bottle while I shot to my feet. If he thought I was just going to sit there and smile pretty while he jabbed Hunter with some foul-looking crap, he was dead wrong.

I shoved my body between him and Hunter. "Don't even think about it," I snapped. "No way I'm letting you poison him."

Jensen ignored my command and continued to fill the syringe.

"I'm warning you—"

"Oh, give me a break," Jensen said. His tone was mild but his cheeks flushed red, and somehow I just knew that he was this close to losing his temper. "We've already established that you can kick my ass all over this garage, and then shoot me when you're done. Now back up so I can help your friend."

I stood my ground, acting like the gun was loaded when in fact it was utterly useless.

"And you expect me to trust you?"

His brown eyes drilled into mine, like he was seeking something—or someone. "I learned to ditch my expectations a long time ago," he finally said.

A total nonanswer that made me grit my teeth in frustration.

"Did Mom really used to be friends with you? And if so—what was she thinking?"

That got a bigger reaction. I watched his hand stiffen on the syringe and squeeze it until his knuckles turned white.

I was afraid the entire thing would explode and douse me with mystery fluid. He drew in an audible, shaky breath. "I've asked myself that same question thousands of times. Now, hold out your hand."

"What?"

His syringe hand flicked impatiently toward me. "Your hand, hold it out," he barked.

Some long-buried instinct urged me to obey, to the point that my traitorous hand even twitched in his direction. I recovered and in a fit of childish rebellion, shoved the offending appendage behind my back. Super mature. I might as well have stuck my tongue out while I was at it.

But instead of looking pissed off, Jensen just cast his eyes toward the ceiling, as if seeking divine intervention. Then he snapped his fingers and gestured them in a way that clearly meant *quit being a pain in the butt and give me your hand already.*

"Just as stubborn as ever. Look, you have a device, under the index finger of your left hand. If I dribble a drop of the liquid from this vial, you'll be able to detect what the chemical components are. Then you'll know I'm not trying to poison your friend there—I'm trying to save him from a lot of pain."

Barely startled by his revelation, I extended my hand toward him. It wasn't like special features hadn't popped up out of nowhere before.

"If this is some kind of trick . . . ," I warned, and Jensen nodded.

"Yeah, I've got it. You'll choke me and feel good about it. I'm going to have to have a talk with Nicole about how she's been teaching you. Looks like you need to cut back on the violent cartoons."

I winced at the mention of Mom. Sympathy, unwanted as it might be. This man from Mom's past clearly had no idea that she was gone. He'd never get a chance to talk to her about violent cartoons or me or anything, ever again. Neither of us would.

His callused fingers gripped mine, firm but gentle . . . and I was instantly transported back. To memories, of him holding my hand crossing a street, helping me with a baseball mitt. Ghostly memories bringing with them a sense of love, of belonging . . . something that I practically ached for.

But what was real? And what was programmed? Had I finally found someone who could tell me the truth? And maybe truth went beyond words, sometimes. Maybe truth could reside in something as simple as a touch. Because while words could lie, surely a true connection was harder to fabricate.

He flipped my hand, palm up.

Pulling back the skin on my index finger with one hand, he lowered the syringe with the other. As we watched, a tiny drop bubbled to the end of the needle. He touched it to the underside of my nail. A thin, barely visible line emerged in my nail bed, allowing the medicine to seep inside.

Warmth blossomed in my finger, then my hand, before traveling up my arm in that all-too-familiar electric surge. A blink later, red words glowed in front of me, accompanied by a smooth, digitized voice. My voice, only the robot version.

Chemical components: Ketamine.

Uses: Analgesia, anesthetic.

Safe for human ingestion.

Common side effects: Hallucinations, elevated blood pressure, bronchodilation, delirium, dizziness.

All of that info, in the blink of an eye. From one tiny drop of solution under my nail.

I realized that Jensen still grasped my hand. Gripped my fingers tightly, just this side of a true squeeze, as if he couldn't bear to let me go. And once again he stared at my face, drinking in every detail, his expression rotating between wonder and maybe even hope. And then, an odd twitch of his lips. Indicating . . . disgust?

Screw him.

I yanked my hand away and he averted his gaze. "Do it, already," I snapped.

His face whipped up, brows lowered, lips parted. For an instant, I braced myself, getting this weird sensation that I was about to be reprimanded like a child. Instead he shook his head and flipped me a half-assed salute. Then, he turned his back, cleaned a spot on Hunter's good arm, right over the bulk of his bicep, and inserted the needle into his skin.

Hunter's upper body flinched. His eyes shot open suddenly. "Sorry," I said, grabbing his free hand with mine. He looked so frail, lying there with his blood seeping away.

He rolled his head toward me and attempted a weak smile. "S'okay. Can't have you thinking I'm a big wimp."

"How can you possibly believe . . ." I glanced away, closed my eyes. Fumbling for the strength not to cry. "Never. I'd never think that."

Jensen hovered near Hunter's injured shoulder, pressing a clean towel to the wound. "That should kick in within a minute or so. Afterward, your . . . boyfriend should be feeling pretty good. Groggy, but good."

"Are you sure we should wait?" I asked, desperate for reassurance even though my sensors assured me he was stable.

Heart rate: 82 bpm.

Other vital signs: Stable.

Blood loss: Slowed.

Full recovery probable.

"Yes, unless you want to hear him scream when I stitch him up."

My gaze flew to Hunter. He frowned, but squeezed my hand encouragingly. "*I'm sorry*," he mouthed.

All this, and he still was trying to apologize. For something that wasn't really his fault.

"Just rest," I murmured.

"Ask your dad why he's so knife happy," he said, his words already starting to slur. Behind me, I heard something smack the floor, but I didn't turn around, desperately hoping that Jensen wouldn't give anything away. I clung to Hunter's hand and waited, urged him to fall asleep. He was out less than a minute later, his breathing slow and steady.

I felt a presence behind me. "He's ready."

Jensen appeared in my line of vision. He dropped the first aid box, then paused, his hands curled around the edges of the table, white-knuckled. He kept his gaze cast downward, at Hunter, but when he spoke, his words were slow and tense. "You told him I was your dad?"

His voice cracked on *dad*. Everything about his posture screamed imminent explosion, like the sliver of control he grasped was about to slide free, but the way he said *dad* . . . it was like grief and hope and disbelief and terror, all rolled into one.

"I had to tell him something to explain why I needed to find you." God, even to my own ears, the excuse sounded awful, weak. Selfish. "He doesn't know . . ."

The way Jensen's face crumpled, even briefly—I could only describe as anguished. For one horror-struck moment, I was sure he would burst into tears. He bowed his head.

But when he straightened, he'd regained his composure.

He cleared his throat. "He doesn't know what you are." That was all he said, before he returned to the box and, over the next few minutes, busied himself by tending to Hunter's wounds. Soon the garage was filled with the pungent reek of Betadine and the crinkle of gauze pads being opened. He swiped the wound with the dark liquid, then carefully wiped the excess away. So far, so good, I thought, until I saw him withdraw a needle.

He glanced up at me when I scooted closer. "Hate to stitch it because of the infection risk, but I'm afraid of the skin tearing more."

With precision that seemed at odds with his large hands, he carefully threaded the needle and sewed up the wound, his tiny stitches almost seamstress perfect.

Odd, his precision and neatness, given his appearance. Here the man looked like he barely remembered to shower, and if he owned a hairbrush I would have been stunned. His jaw was grizzled with an emerging beard, but it was darker on one side than the other. Like he'd forgotten to shave half of his face. And yet the house, his possessions—everything was so tidy.

It occurred to me, then, that this was a man who had either been on his own way too long, or one who no longer cared about himself at all.

"He'll still have a scar, but it won't be nearly as bad."

After assuring myself that Hunter was fine, I let go of his hand. With the anger pulsing through my body, I was afraid I might inadvertently squeeze too hard. Really, what I wanted to squeeze was Jensen's neck again. If I didn't need him—

"Relax, he's going to be fine." Jensen's voice penetrated my haze, but his words had the opposite effect of soothing me.

"You could have killed him!"

"Yes, I could have—if I'd been trying. But I wasn't," he said, curtly. Then he sighed, wiping a towel across his brow. "That probably sounds harsh. Look, I don't take kindly to strangers breaking into my home and pulling guns on me. Priority one is *survival.* That's what's kept me safe. You should have thought of that before you brought a civilian into this."

"I'm a civilian," I whispered.

He leaned over to toss the towel into a basket on the floor, but I still caught the sorrow that flickered across his features. "No, you're not." He replaced the unused supplies in the box and turned, resting his hips against the computer table, crossing his arms until his biceps bulged from under his short sleeves. "Now, do you want to keep wasting time with the blame game, or tell me what you came here for?"

I wanted to hold on to the anger, I really did. But as I stared into his weather-beaten face, that wave of familiarity enveloped me again.

Was it possible to ever know the truth, when even your memories were lies?

The anger drained, leaving behind a string of questions, and a weary hope that maybe, once I had all the answers, the promise of a real life would quit hovering just outside of my grasp, quit being this imaginary thing that I dreamed of but could never really touch.

"Who are you?" I asked.

Then I braced myself for the answer.

SIXTEEN

Stiff legs carried Jensen two steps to a swivel chair, which he dropped into with a thud. His eyes roved over my features while his mouth shifted into a humorless smile.

"You really don't know, do you?"

Then he cocked his head in a way that triggered an echo inside my head, a ghost of the past. Except that ghost only existed in my implanted memories, and this was a real man.

Who had a picture of my mom and me—or was it Sarah?

"No, I don't."

He rubbed his bare ring finger and exhaled loudly. "Right. Well, grab one of those camping chairs and take a seat then—this might take a while."

I skirted the table to grab a chair, then paused, stopping

to brush a strand of hair that dangled over Hunter's eye. His chest lifted and lowered with ease now, and his bandage didn't show any new bleeding, but what if—

"I told you, he'll be fine."

I shouldn't trust Jensen—no, I didn't trust him. Still, something in the quiet confidence of his voice propelled me to approach. With trepidation, I lowered myself into an empty chair. He rested his hands on his knees and leaned forward. As I waited for him to speak, my memory whirred.

Dad, leaning forward toward the TV in our townhouse. "C'mon—strike him out!"

The Dad from my past and Jensen superimposed, until the two images blended into one. Disconcerted, I covered my eyes while evicting the old image from my head. No. I needed to focus, and this wasn't helping.

"I was serving time in the army when Nicole Laurent was first recruited. Right away there was a buzz about her. She had a medical and computer science background—was a prodigy. God, she was young back then," he added, his gaze now sliding beyond me, into a past that only he could see. "I'd been assigned to the special division your mom was part of—that's how we met."

I watched him, riveted. Finally. I was finally going to hear the whole story. Learn about Mom's past—*my* past. "And you two were a couple?" I prodded.

"Yes. Nicole and I were together, for many years . . ." He

coughed and looked down at the ground. "Until we had a difference of opinion. One that we just couldn't get past."

He paused again, and it was all I could do not to shake him. I uncurled my toes, told myself to be patient. I'd been waiting for answers for a long time now. A few more minutes wouldn't hurt me.

"So I took a dishonorable discharge and got the hell out of there. Months later, this guy knocks on my door in the middle of the night. He's been watching me, keeping track of my workout schedule. He tells me he's with a company called the Vita Obscura, and they'd like to hire me away from my crap job. Great pay, great hours—all I'd have to do is share a little classified info—no big deal."

His exhalation was a sharp rattle while he shoved his hands into his pockets. "Of course, I told him to screw off. Why would I risk a cold, dark military prison just for the sake of a few bucks?"

"So what changed your mind?" I asked, enrapt.

His lip curled, and suddenly, I knew what he was going to say before he said it.

"Holland."

Holland. Of course. Why did it not surprise me that he was at the root of everything bad?

"A woman came to see me next—Quinn. The head of the Vita Obscura. She told me things—suggested things—I knew Holland was an egotistical bastard, but I never believed that he would be so cruel, that he could—" He pressed a fist to his mouth and sagged into the chair, his eyes squeezed shut.

I reached over to comfort him before I even realized what I was doing. Startled, I snatched my hand away. This made no sense. I didn't know this man, not really. But for some reason, confusion blurred the edges of my logic, dampened my certainty. There was no denying it; the sight of his distress triggered a wave of sympathy inside me. I wanted to soothe his pain.

Ridiculous. He'd hurt Hunter, I reminded myself grimly, so why did I feel this compassion for him?

When I saw a tear trickle a wet path down his scruffy cheek, my heart twisted again. I'd experienced firsthand Holland's brand of pain. "So, you went to work for the Vita Obscura?" I prodded, when he remained speechless a minute later.

"Yes. Quinn said it was the only way to keep *you* safe."

The way he said *you* was like a blessing and a curse, both reverent and repulsed. It made no sense.

"Quinn said all they wanted to do was figure out your technology, without hurt—damaging you at all. She also sold me on my suspicions about Holland, and I saw red. I wanted revenge. She promised—well, never mind what she promised."

He kicked the desk leg, then had to let the resulting clang

die before he continued. "They were lying. I was leery, of course, so I did a little snooping. I hacked into their computer, read one of their emails. They had no plans to keep you safe at all. So I snuck away."

The photograph flashed before my eyes—Mom, Jensen, and the girl who looked just like me.

"The photograph on the fridge, the one of you, Mom, and a girl who looks like me. Who is she? An earlier version of me?"

He made a choking sound, deep in his throat. When he met my eyes, his own were haunted. "The girl in the photo is Sarah, but she's not an earlier version, not in the way that you mean. She was human."

Real? The girl in the photo was real? The truth seemed to hinge on the mystery of a girl named Sarah. A girl who looked just like me—a girl who inspired profound emotion, in both my mom and this man who had once masqueraded for a short while as my dad.

"Who is Sarah?" I whispered, as a horrible suspicion took root and sprouted, embedding my body in a mass of thorny doubts. My fake heart pounded, then slowed.

"Sarah was my daughter. Mine and Nicole's."

His voice was rough and raw, like the answer had been ripped from somewhere deep inside him.

Thump. Thump.

Thump.

I staggered to my feet. Terror. Need. Terror. They fought for supremacy as I groped for the courage to ask another question. Daughter. That girl who looked exactly like me was their daughter. Human. Blood and bones and all the things that made someone real. But if Mom had a real daughter out there, why had she been hiding out with me?

But I knew. After all, Jensen didn't say "is" my daughter. He said *was*. "Where is she now?"

"She's dead." A shuddering exhale, and then, "You, the rest of the Milas—you were all made in her image."

Thump.

My pseudo heart froze in place with a painful shudder. A bubble of hysteria rose in my throat, choking me, drenching my tongue with a bitterness I'd never experienced before. But maybe Sarah had.

Nicole Laurent/Daily. Closer to being my mom than I'd ever realized. And yet further, too. Because, once upon a time, the woman I'd thought of as Mom had a real daughter. But she'd died and somehow, someway, Mom had re-created a machine in her image.

Or more precisely, she'd created *me*. In that crazy, overwhelming instant, I felt a terrible, hateful jealousy. I was jealous of a dead girl—the human version that I'd so longed to be.

I bolted out of the chair. "What—what kind of people would do that? I can't believe Mom would be so cold—"

His hand shot out to grab my wrist. "Don't talk about Nicole that way," he growled.

I yanked my arm free. "Oh, I'm sorry, that's right—Nicole. Not Mom. Not Dad. Silly me—I'm just the freakish machine you two created to look like a dead girl!"

"Goddamn—" He smashed his fist into the table, causing the computer and everything on it to jump. So the opposite of Mom. Her voice had barely ever risen, and taking her anger out on inanimate objects? Not likely.

So the opposite of Mom . . . but so like me. A creature of my emotions, though I hoped to remedy that.

I bit my lip, to keep it from trembling. Or maybe it wasn't really going to tremble, but just felt that way—an emotional programming system gone haywire.

His cheeks lost some of their reddish hue. "You don't understand. We thought we were doing the right thing."

"And now?"

Painful silence, which told me all I needed to know. A mistake. A billion-dollar mistake, that's what the man who was almost—but not quite—my dad thought. And I shouldn't care, but I did. The rejection crushed me until I wanted to collapse in a ruined heap.

"You're not a complete machine. Not all of you."

"What do you mean?" But I was afraid I knew.

"Sarah was a very special girl. She was brilliant, not just normal brilliance, but brilliant in a unique way. Almost like a savant, but not, because she didn't have any of the disorders that sometimes accompany that. Because of our positions, and because of what she was, we had people clamoring to study her. To keep her out of the limelight, we agreed to do it ourselves."

He hesitated, then continued. He clutched his thighs, as if bracing himself. "When she died, unexpectedly in a fire from smoke inhalation, we recovered her body. The MILA project had always called for human brain tissue, and we just . . . knew."

"I don't—I don't—" I tried to speak, but couldn't force my tongue to function.

"They used parts of Sarah's brain in all three versions of you."

I sat there, stunned, unable to move and unable to feel anything beyond my own fake pulse, enveloping me with staccato accusation.

All three versions.

Subject died.

Fire.

Three.

No! I shrieked. Or thought I did. It must have been silent, because no sound erupted from my throat. I bowed my head into my hands, trying to shut out everything I'd just heard. But I couldn't. I could no more forget than I could summon Mom from the dead. A piece of Sarah's brain, inside my head. A piece of Sarah's brain, in Three.

Not sisters, like Three had claimed. But part of the same whole.

Three's head, melting until it was nothing. With part of Sarah inside.

Inconceivably horrifying, and yet, based on the sadness pulling at Jensen's features, incontrovertible. Finally, I had the truth I'd been so desperately seeking. But living with it—how, how?

Sarah. Sarah. *Sarah.*

The memory rushed me. *Waves crashing, Dad's rumbling laugh. Mom and Dad, twirling in the sand. A seagull crying. Feeling warm, so warm, and then suddenly, smothered.*

Trapped inside my bedroom, the doorknob hot to the touch. Escaping out a window, gasping for fresh air, relief flooding me—then spotting Mom and Dad's car, in the driveway.

Memory banks compromised . . . defragment.

The words pulsed into my head, trying to obliterate the images. *No. Mine.*

With a surge of energy, I grabbed them, crushed the words into a fine powder, shoved them away. No. They would not steal this from me. I grasped for the images, a fist clutching my throat when I couldn't find them at first. Then, in a shadowy pathway, I found them hidden in the darkness, and gently coaxed them out.

A desperate scramble over the roof, fighting my way back into the house. Falling, falling, down to the first floor. Dad's face, there in the flames. His voice, calling for me.

"Sarah!"

"Dad?" I whispered, just before the pain struck, burning red hot through my skin. Then . . . nothing.

I opened my eyes, and the images faded. But there, before me, sat Jensen. "The truth is complicated," he said softly. "But I can tell you this—Nicole never regretted a thing. Not when it came to you."

Tears burned in my eyes, and in my heart, a bittersweet ache. Mom hadn't regretted my existence. Deep down, I'd known that all along.

What I hadn't known was that inside me, I housed a piece of a girl I'd never met. A girl who'd been stolen from this world far too quickly.

A girl who had been Mom's true daughter.

I traced my fingers over my scalp, through my hair. As though maybe I could find the parts of Sarah that lay underneath.

I wasn't fully a machine, but I also wasn't fully human.

I was something in between. A hybrid.

Bitterness sucked me down into a deep, dark abyss. I'd just been coming to accept myself as an android, and now . . . after all this, I really was some kind of freak.

I gave us both time to gather ourselves before asking a question that had bubbled to the surface. "Do I remind you of Sarah? I mean, apart from how I look?"

He flinched, like just her name held a power over him. Such a large man, so strong, and yet so easily wounded. He was turning out to be nothing like Holland at all.

"Why don't you ask Nicole?"

An agonizing lurch in my chest; a sharp ache beneath my ribs. My pseudo heart, about to burst from sorrow. He didn't know. He was looking at me, those expectant brown eyes from my memories demanding an answer, and he didn't know.

"Don't you watch the news?" I said, trying to buy myself some time.

His eyes narrowed. "Usually, but I've been busy with a . . . project. What is it? Is it Holland? Did he catch her?"

I braced my hands on my thighs and drew in a deep, shaky breath. There was no easy way to say this. There was nothing easy about this at all.

I forced myself to meet his eyes. "She's dead," I said, simply.

For an instant, the expressionless mask remained in place on Jensen's face, and I wondered if I'd somehow miscalculated. Maybe he didn't care about Mom at all—maybe I'd been projecting. Or hoping.

But then it cracked—no, exploded—shattered by a whirlwind of emotions. Wide eyes and parted lips, followed by his entire body sagging. As if someone had sucked every bit of energy from him. He turned away, ducking his head, his hand covering his eyes. Then, I saw his shoulders shake.

I felt helpless—even more so because his sadness spurred my own. Reminded me that Mom was gone. Forever.

Watching him felt a little too invasive, so I turned to check on Hunter. His chest rose and fell in a steady, easy pattern, and while the bandage showed a few signs of seepage, overall it remained clean.

I turned back to check on Jensen. His body had stilled and he'd dropped his hand. "What happened?" he whispered, unashamed tears streaming down his face.

And so I told him the whole story. The ranch in Clearwater, the V.O. attack, our escape to Canada—and our subsequent capture. Holland's compound, the tests, Lucas helping us escape. And finally, haltingly, Mom getting shot—bleeding out before I could do a damn thing to help her.

After I finished, a strange sense of relief poured through me. Like by finally spewing all the details to someone, I'd relieved a toxic pressure I hadn't known was building. But when I looked up at Jensen, that pleasant sensation abruptly fled. Because all signs of grief had been stripped from his face and his mouth had taken on a grim twist.

I prepared myself for a verbal attack, but all he said was, "I need to get some antibiotics for Hunter from the house."

And then he spun and covered the short path to the garage door with long strides.

Alarmed, I stared after him for a moment, debating whether or not I should follow. Just in case.

Then I heard a faint voice behind me.

"Mila?"

I whirled—in time to watch Hunter open his eyes.

SEVENTEEN

"Hunter? Are you feeling okay?" I rushed to his side and clasped his hand in mine. My other hand went to his cheek. Pale, but still warm, and grazed with just the slightest hint of stubble.

"Mmmm," he mumbled, but at least now his blue eyes were open. Well, more at half-mast, and even that appeared to be a struggle. He only managed to hold them open for a few seconds at a time, before they'd dip shut again.

"Shhh, it's okay. Just go back to sleep," I soothed, stroking my fingers down his cheek.

His eyes stayed shut this time, and his breathing once again deepened, which made it easier for me to relax. So I jumped when his hand shot out and grabbed my arm.

"Got to tell you something . . ."

I waited, buzzing with anticipation, but it was like the words zapped all of his strength. His grip weakened, his fingers slid. For a second, I was certain his arm would crash back to the table, and I made a move to grab it. But his hand tightened and caught hold of my sleeve. He opened his eyes, really opened them this time, so I was bombarded with a full dose of that faded blue.

For someone so sleepy just a moment ago, his gaze was oddly intent.

"When I wake up, less run away together, kay?" he slurred. "Jus you an me."

My phantom pulse leaped. Underneath it all, Hunter couldn't deny his feelings.

But then I realized that his mind was foggy, from the anesthetic. I just stood there, speechless, trying to stamp out the hope that was steadily rising with each passing second. There was no way he meant it, I warned myself. He couldn't. Not after everything that had happened.

Then I felt an insistent pressure on my arm. "Hey, I asked a quession," he said. Frown lines appeared on his forehead, like my failure to snap out an affirmative answer was causing him massive amounts of stress.

"Maybe we should talk about this later—"

He gave a violent shake of his head and immediately groaned.

I winced. "Sorry! I'm so sorry—I didn't mean—"

He held up his hand and I let the sentence die. I waited

until he recovered. Then, smiling ever so faintly, he placed his hand on my face and gently cupped my cheek. "The two of us, together. Okay?"

And then his lips touched mine, and all I could think of was him.

Warmth. Joy. A feeling of pure bliss, like every single part of my body was alive and aware. Like I was suddenly comprised of millions more nerve cells than before. His kiss took me beyond the garage, and for those few tiny moments, we were connected in a way that I'd never experienced before. His heartbeat, his scent, his body heat—they all wrapped around me, enveloping me in a sense of belonging.

So, this was what it felt like to truly be alive.

I pulled away, reluctantly, realizing that he was still groggy from the drugs. All the fight had drained out of me, leaving only contentment behind.

"Okay," I agreed. And somehow, just the act of agreeing freed the chains that had caged the hope inside me. Reminding myself that hallucinations were one of the side effects of the drugs couldn't catch the hope either.

A faint smile curved his amazing lips, even as the rest of his body went slack. His fingers slipped from my arm, and I gently captured his hand and laid it across his chest. But even as the drug dragged him under, the faint smile lingered, and somewhere, deep inside, my all-too-human android heart responded.

He was in and out for the next ten minutes and by the

time he'd freed himself from the drug's influence, Jensen still hadn't returned. I decided he must've gotten sidetracked, because how hard was it to find antibiotics in a house as barren and neat as his?

Unease flickered through me.

Track subject?

I stood. "I'll be right back."

I'd only taken four steps toward the door that led into the house when the garage plunged into darkness.

"What's going on?" Hunter asked, sounding curious rather than concerned. Not me. I'd started spinning in a slow circle.

Night vision activated.

No human threat detected.

For once, the lack of a discernible threat did little to soothe my growing fear. A loud metallic click yanked my attention to the door.

Neither did that.

"Jensen!" I yelled. Where was he? I hadn't picked up on any threats while waiting for him to return, but what if I'd been so involved with Hunter that I'd missed something? When my hand found the doorknob, the damn thing wouldn't budge.

The fear that had been a slow trickle until now turned full blast. That click had been someone locking the door. Hunter and I were trapped in here.

I cursed under my breath, but apparently not low enough.

"You okay?" Hunter asked.

"Fine. The door's just sticking," I lied. No need to alarm him yet. My hand tightened on the knob, and I pushed, harder and harder, with every bit of strength I had. With growing shock, I realized the knob wasn't going to give. It didn't budge, not even a little.

Keeping as quiet as possible, I planted my hands shoulder-width apart on the door and pushed. But the second my skin touched the surface, I knew. This door wasn't made from wood, and it wasn't some flimsy sheet metal. This was an industrial-strength monster, the kind they probably used in bank vaults.

Counterpressure: 1105 lbs. per square inch.

I finally had to concede defeat. For a second I let my forehead fall forward and rest against the chilly, slick surface of my nemesis. This was not your typical homeowner's garage. Which I guess made sense, since Jensen wasn't your typical homeowner.

I clenched my teeth. Then again, I wasn't your typical houseguest, and there was no way I was letting a simple door defeat me—metal or not. I flexed my hands. I'd rip that thing right off the hinges if I had to. But before I could try again, a flash of red light flickered, once, twice. Then, red lines pulsed into existence between me and the door, accompanied by an increase in the soft hum. The one I'd picked up on earlier. I craned my head back, and what I saw wasn't comforting. Not at all. The lines extended from the ceiling all the way down to the floor.

As I watched, the light emitting from them brightened and faded, in a strange, coordinated rhythm. Almost like they had a heartbeat all their own. They *pulsed.* The hum also ebbed and waned, like a solitary bee flitting from flower to flower. The hum of electricity.

Laser beams.

What the . . . ?

I took a step back to get a better feel for whatever was going on, and got another gut punch of dread. The beams didn't cover just the door, or the surrounding wall. I spun slowly. They covered the entire perimeter of the garage. Just a centimeter or so from the walls.

Now I knew the reason for the odd spacing issues. All the better to imprison Hunter and me in a glowing red cage.

"Mila? What are those for?"

I hesitated, partly because I wasn't one hundred percent sure what was going on yet. But mostly because the theory I did have was beyond disturbing. Amid the fear circulating an icy-cold river through my system, I approached the lasers. I stopped less than six inches from the beams, taking a moment to watch the barest flicker of their light. I lifted my hand, slowly, slowly.

Warning: High voltage.

Damage likely.

I froze, my hand hovering midair. An electric fence. Jensen had the entire garage wired with some kind of high-tech electric fence.

I turned a slow pirouette, but just as I suspected, there was no escape.

"Mila?" Hunter again, more anxious now.

"It's okay. Just don't move." I turned back to the door. Fear pricked along my skin. My android sensors had never been wrong before, but it didn't matter. I had to try.

I extended my index finger, reaching toward a cloud of shimmering red.

My flesh made contact . . . and then the room exploded into a haze of static.

The shock knocked my legs right out from under me and propelled me back, one, three, five feet. I made a frantic grab for the table on the way down, but it couldn't hold me. As my back slammed the hard floor, the table tipped, pelting me with a barrage of vials, bandages, and ointments. My ears rang, and the world moved around me in staticky, jerky waves.

Disjointed commands burst through my head: *Override lock. Upload. Project.*

And then my hands collapsed to my sides, and my thoughts were no longer my own—my brain, completely derailed. Robotic voice. Taking. Control.

Systems check:

Impact: 500 volts, damage possible.

Checking internal functions.

Checking data processing.

Checking memory.

A red light.

Blink. Blink. Blink.

From somewhere in the distance, I heard Hunter's voice, heard a clatter as something hit the ground. "Mila? Mila?"

Panic. Mine, or his?

Blink. Blink. Blink.

I tried to free my thoughts from the systems check, but every . . .

Checking internal transistors.

. . . time I pried my brain free, the . . .

Checking living tissue.

Oxygen levels low. Increase uptake.

My chest expanded and deflated, rapidly. A machine, breathing for me.

Part of me wanted to fight; but acceptance won out. The android part knew what it was doing, and I had to let it help. I had Hunter's life at stake.

Finally, a slowing in the streams of red commands, the contraction of my lungs.

Oxygen levels: Acceptable.

And just like that, I slipped back into my own mind.

What the hell had that been about? It wasn't the first time I'd frozen up, but it was definitely the worst. All of that malfunctioning, all of the weird memory fragments . . . something was wrong inside me. I could feel it.

A warm hand grasped my shoulders. I opened my eyes to see Hunter kneeling over me, pale and tight-lipped, his bad arm dangling awkwardly. But his eyes were wild, his movements choppy and frantic. "Mila? Mila!"

"Don't worry, I'm okay," I managed, but the words came out all wrong. No, not the words—my voice.

My hand flew to my mouth, as if I could take back the deep, impersonal, digitized sound emitting from my throat. The same sound that echoed through the garage.

Not my voice at all. A robot's voice.

Hunter's hand went slack. His lips moved, but the only thing I heard was a sharp hiss of air between his teeth. Finally, he said, "I don't understand . . ."

And then he did the thing I'd always feared, from the moment I'd learned what I truly was. The entire reason I'd lied from the start.

In angry disbelief, Hunter backed away from me, one, two, three steps. Like I was something too terrible to touch.

"Hunter," I started, only to stop when he flinched at the wrongness of my voice.

I closed my eyes, balled my fists. What the hell was happening? Had the electricity fried something inside me?

There had to be a way to reset, surely. I couldn't live with this masculine, robotic noise spewing forth every time I opened my mouth.

Voice software: Systems check?

The words blinked, at the ready.

Yes.

Running scan . . . systems check complete. Restore original voice?

My chest heaved in relief.

Yes.

A slight vibration in my throat; a tightening sensation just under my chin.

Restoration complete.

Too late, though. I knew that as soon as I registered Hunter's horrified expression.

"What are you?" he whispered.

Inch by inch, I raised my eyes, until they connected with his. When I'd pictured this moment in the past, I'd always finessed my way to the ultimate reveal, circling the reality in hopes of slowly breaking Hunter in. That way, I'd figured, maybe he'd be less likely to be repulsed.

But not now. I would apologize for lying, but I couldn't bring myself to apologize for what I was.

Even if that meant Hunter never looked at me with acceptance and longing again. If I couldn't be true to myself, then I was worthless to anyone else, anyway. I looked him right in the eye, and with a steady voice, finally stopped lying.

"I'm an android."

If my heart hadn't been knotting itself into a painful ball, the expression on his face would have been comical.

"An android?" he repeated, with a slight lilt. Like maybe he'd misunderstood.

I nodded.

"You're joking. Right?" In his voice I heard hope, doubt, and fear. I watched as his mind whirled, undoubtedly playing back the parts of our journey that, up to this point, hadn't really made much sense.

The way I'd overpowered Grady and Ashleigh. The ease we'd had breaking into this very house. My driving without headlights. And, I saw the second he realized—my arm.

With his attention firmly focused on my arm, he backed up another step. "It's not possible." But I heard the lack of conviction in his voice. I'm sure he wanted his words to be true. But wanting didn't affect reality. I could tell him that.

I tilted my head to the side, pulling back my earlobe hard. We might as well get this over with. "Look," I said, exposing the hidden USB port.

He stepped closer, gingerly, leaning forward to take a peek. His gasp twisted the pain deeper.

"How . . . when . . . ?" One finger reached out as if to touch, then he recoiled before contact was made.

Another twist. But I managed a brave smile. "It's a long

story. But I can give you the short version. Here, come sit down."

He immediately retracted another step. "I'm fine right here."

"Hunter, please," I said, forcing the hurt from my voice and trying to sound soothing. "You need to sit—"

"Don't talk to me like I'm a child! And don't you get it? I don't want to be near you. Not now!"

His words slashed like razors, but I pushed that aside because in his weakened state, his vehemence made him stumble. I darted forward as he regained his balance. He held up his hand.

"Don't. Don't touch me." A beat and then, "Please."

Soft and pleading, and coated with a world of hurt. My heart bled for Hunter and for me. And for this unbridgeable chasm between us.

This was the way I'd always known it would end. Inevitable, from the first moment I discovered what I really was. And, despite coming to terms with my own otherness, I didn't blame Hunter. After all, it had taken me a long time to get here.

I turned away from him. No longer able to bear the repulsed expression on his face.

"This doesn't change anything. We've still got to find a way out."

Hunter's strangled gasp punched me straight in the gut.

"Doesn't change anything? Are you out of your mind? It changes everything. *Everything!*"

I whirled back, concerned that he was overexerting himself. Sure enough, his legs trembled, and his forehead beaded with sweat. But his eyes glittered with a dark, feverish anger.

It felt awful, knowing I brought out the worst in him. But I couldn't back down. "Why? Because I'm different than you? Trust me, I'm not as different as you might imagine. I think. I feel. I want."

"Don't try to turn this around on me! That's bullshit, and you know it."

I winced.

"And it's not because you're different. Even though we're not talking you're-from-out-of-town-and-like-to-eat-with-your-toes different here and more like this-makes-me-wonder-if-I've-been-sniffing-glue different. It's not," he insisted, when I shot him a skeptical look. "Not just that anyway. It's because you've been lying to me from the start. About everything."

I had no comeback for that. I mean, I could argue that I hadn't known from the start, either, but what was the point?

I stared at the floor, my eyes swimming with tears.

"Can you name even one thing you've been honest about? One part of your life where you told me the truth? Or how about just telling me something that's true right now?" His voice was soft now, resigned.

I lifted my head bravely, even as the tears slid down my cheeks. A million thoughts poured through my head. *You're amazing. No one has ever made me feel this alive.* But what finally came out was pure. Simple. And unfortunately, far too late.

"I love you."

For a moment, the hard shell of his expression cracked, and I caught a glimpse of the old Hunter beneath. The vulnerable, open, easy boy I'd fallen for. His lashes fluttered down, and he sighed. But then the stranger's mask slipped back on. His eyes were guarded, before he presented me with his back. Not even acknowledging what I'd said. "You were right—we need to focus on finding a way out."

Unable to bear his rejection, my phantom heart cracked, shattered, burst. I stared at his rigid shoulders and decided we needed a plan. Because the faster we escaped Jensen's garage, the faster I could get away from Hunter.

At this precise moment, the idea of being stuck with him in a confined space was more terrifying than a thousand Hollands.

I walked the perimeter of the room. If even one of the lasers had a weakness, maybe we could force our way out.

"What are you doing?" Hunter asked, as he eased himself back onto the table. His face held an unnatural pallor that worried me.

"Inspecting the lasers to see if there's a chink in the system."

Keeping a respectful distance this time, I started at the one closest to the door and worked my way clockwise around the room.

500 volts.

500 volts.

500 volts.

"You can tell? Just by looking at them?"

"I can sense the voltage."

Silence, so I resumed my inspection. Two hundred and twenty-two stops later, I was back in the center of the room. Whatever tiny bit of hope I'd been clinging to regarding a flaw in the system had long since disappeared. All the beams were functional, and they were way too close together to even attempt to squeeze through. I'd pulled a ladder into the middle of the room and pounded on the ceiling, but it was every bit as solid as the door.

It was like Hunter and I had been locked away in a glowing, metal tomb.

In frustration, I picked up the nearest object—Jensen's keyboard—and chucked it at the lights with all my might.

Sparks exploded like fireworks. Without thinking, I dove for Hunter and threw myself on top of him, protecting his body with my own. Lightning streaks of red flashed overhead. I had hoped that maybe the power would dim somehow, but the red poles glowed as brightly as ever.

I became aware of Hunter's stiff body beneath mine, and scrambled back. "Sorry, I was trying to . . ." I scooted away, blowing a stray piece of hair out of my eyes. No sense explaining.

"I know what you were trying to do," he said, in a hard-to-decipher tone. A pause. "So basically, we're stuck inside a giant booby-trapped garage, in a prison made out of . . . of . . . lights? Who the hell is this guy, anyway? Since obviously he's not your father."

He wasn't and yet . . . he kind of was. "He's former military. Part of the original project to create me. Then he left and fell in with another group who wanted to steal me from the government, and ultimately left them too."

He pondered that. "So what you're saying is, he's some kind of whacked-out loner?"

Yeah. That about summed him up.

"What does he want with us?"

This one was simple enough to answer. "I don't know."

What I did know was that none of the possibilities were good.

"Jesus," he muttered. He forgot about his injury and shoved both hands into his hair, then yelped and grabbed at his shoulder. He chewed his lower lip, suddenly thoughtful. "This other group who wants to steal you—is that the Vita Obscura?"

I nodded absently before realizing my mistake. Too late.

His eyes narrowed, and his chest rose and fell. "You thought I was part of a group that was trying to steal you? And then what?"

I opened my mouth, closed it, clenched my hands together and opened them again. No sense in lying now. "They want to take me apart and assess my technology. Strip me and sell off the most valuable pieces."

I watched his jaw muscles work, beneath his skin. Teeth clenching and unclenching. "And that . . . GPS thing you found? That's one of theirs?"

I nodded. "Mom and I found one when they were chasing us before."

A curt nod, that was all. I had no idea what he was thinking. Maybe it was better that way.

"You never trusted me at all, did you?" A hint of sadness. Of resignation.

"That's not true," I whispered. "I just didn't really trust myself." No response, so I said, "You should sit down, try to get some rest."

"You think I can just lie down and sleep? Now?"

I hadn't said that sleeping would be easy, not after all the shocks he had had. But that didn't mean he shouldn't try. If we were going to escape, he needed to be as rested as possible. And even then—

A shrill buzzing sounded.

I frowned, shook my head. Thinking it might just be internal.

"Is everything okay?" Hunter asked, with a slight frown. If I didn't know better, I'd say he was worried. But that was just me being hopeful.

"Do you hear that?" I asked, while at the same time, my prompt flashed:

Hearing function: Maximum levels.

The buzzing rose, higher and higher, drowning out everything but the insistent drone. Around us, the red light beams of our prison pulsed brighter.

"Hunter?" I whispered, hands over my ears, watching the lights with growing suspicion.

"I see it."

The buzzing subsided and a rumble sounded from overhead. It felt like the entire garage shuddered. Then a whir, coming from the direction of the automatic door.

"Get up!" No time to worry over his sensibilities now. I reached down, preparing to yell if necessary, but to my surprise he clasped my outstretched hand and allowed me to pull him to his feet. As he gained his balance, the red lights flashed off.

I steadied him, then took a step forward, ready to act as a shield, while beneath the door, a strip of dim light formed.

"Get ready. The garage door is opening."

Hunter moved up and wrapped his hand around mine. I

fought not to be undone by the relief and comfort I felt by his presence. I glanced over at him. His features were set in a determined mask.

The door continued to rise at an ominously slow pace, revealing a pair of narrow black boots with just a hint of a heel. A woman's feet.

More ground was revealed, showing more feet in the background—four pairs. But not all soldier's boots, as I'd been expecting. Boots, navy blue high-tops, white-and-yellow track shoes, black basketball shoes. No uniformity.

I allowed myself a moment of hope. Maybe this wasn't as bad as I thought. Maybe Jensen had called people to help. Because so far, this didn't have the feel of an organized army.

Weapons scan:

A flicker in the red words. And then:

Information lost.

I shook my head again to clear it. Perhaps there was some interference? But I was distracted by the garage door continuing its grinding climb, revealing more of the scene on the driveway.

Night vision. Activated.

The shadows brightened into recognizable shapes for just an instant, long enough for me to make out Jensen's SUV a few feet away, and beyond it, a white van, at the far end of the driveway.

Night vision lost.

Human threat dete–

Information lost.

My hand tightened on Hunter's. I tried to remain focused, despite the panic clawing its way into my heart. There were five of them, and I had no idea if they were armed. Maybe I could engage them by myself—but with Hunter to protect . . .

Although he'd rejected me, I could never reject him.

I shifted my attention back to the woman in front. She stood the closest, so the automatic outdoor lighting was enough to inspect her. Black pants. Black shirt, under which I could detect the faint outline of a vest. Kevlar? Finally, the door rose high enough to reveal a round face with familiar cheekbones. She had short blond hair, wide-set eyes.

Faded blue eyes. A variation of which I'd seen a hundred times before . . .

Beside me, Hunter's startled intake of breath confirmed my suspicions.

"Mom?"

EIGHTEEN

A man of average height with broad shoulders stepped out of the shadows into the light. Overall, there was nothing particularly memorable about his appearance. Faintly receding brown hair, oval-shaped face. Neither slim nor obese. Attractive in a plain way. The kind of man you'd see and never think of twice.

Only, I recognized him, too.

"Peyton?" Hunter's stunned exclamation confirmed it.

The man was Peyton Lowe. Hunter's stepfather.

Once Hunter's initial shock faded, he released my hand, his relief evident. "I can't tell you how happy I am to see you guys. How did you know where we were?" He half turned to me. "Mila, that's my mom, Sophia, and my stepdad, Peyton."

Sophia gave me a hesitant smile, while Peyton nodded. I gazed at the pair of them, taking in more details. Sophia wore little makeup, and though her good posture suggested confidence, the way she shifted her weight from side to side meant she was a little antsy. That fit with the ragged skin next to her nails, which suggested a nervous biting habit.

Peyton, on the other hand, stood easily, with a quiet confidence that hinted at capability under pressure.

I searched with my android sensors for any hint of weapons.

Nothing but static. Still jammed. Or, possibly some residual damage from Jensen's booby trap. Speaking of . . . where was he?

I eyed Peyton over the top of Hunter's head, taking in the outline of Kevlar under his shirt. Hunter's parents, showing up here just when we needed them, decked out in Kevlar? Suspicion whispered down my spine.

"What are we waiting for? Let's get the hell out of here, before that crazy guy gets back." Hunter tugged at my wrist, but I refused to budge. He might not have asked the right questions yet, but I had. And the answers I'd come up with weren't promising. Not for me.

"Come on, Mila," Hunter said, frowning.

I shook my head, my gut slowly sinking as, when Peyton took an easy step forward, I made out a telltale silver instrument, sticking out of his pocket. As my eyes zeroed in on that small, rectangular device, my body twitched. I remembered the feeling of being shocked into flat-lining all too vividly.

"Ask him again how they knew to come here," I said. Softly. Staring right at Peyton.

Peyton sighed before giving the faintest of nods, acknowledging my challenge with a hint of admiration glinting in his eyes. Clearly he appreciated my brazenness. "Move away from her, Hunter," he ordered.

"What's going on?" Hunter said, his gaze switching from me to Peyton.

I turned my head to gauge his expression, to see if somehow, this was an elaborate act. If I'd been right before, about Hunter's role in all this. But no. Genuine confusion creased his brow, and his eyes were guileless. Besides, why would he bother to lie at this point? This was checkmate, and I was the losing player.

The perplexed furrow in his brow deepened. "How *did* you guys know to come here? I thought you were away on business? Did the police find out somehow and call you?"

I wondered how long it would take Hunter to puzzle out the truth. I couldn't be certain until they confirmed it, but I had a pretty good idea. My hands trembled, and I crossed my arms to hide them. Please, please, let me be wrong.

Just then, the wall that'd stopped me from using my android senses faltered. In the blink of an eye, I scanned the people in the driveway. Behind Hunter's mom and slightly to the left were two males.

First male threat:

Suggested age range: 23–28.

Height: 5 ft. 10 in.

Approximate weight range: 149–155 lbs.

Ethnicity: Hispanic.

Distinguishing features: 1 mm. symmetrical black mole, left cheekbone.

Second male threat:

Suggested age range: 38–42.

Height: 5 ft. 9 in.

Approximate weight range: 185–192 lbs.

Ethnicity: Caucasian.

Distinguishing features: None.

And then I felt a faint fluttering in my mind, like someone was thumbing through pages of memories.

Scanning internal database.

Match found.

In a burst of color, a different image of the second man appeared, standing in the doorway, in a workman's disguise. Short, burly, wearing a navy hat. Then, the wall snapped back into place.

I'd seen enough, though. He was the man who'd tried to break into our motel room, back when Mom and I were on the run, and also the man whose fingerprint was on the GPS device on Hunter's Jeep. Apparently my computer brain had the ability to store images and recall them on command. Did that mean everyone I'd ever met was lurking somewhere inside my mind?

The man glared at me, and I recalled another fact—he was also the guy whose partner I'd stabbed in the brachial plexus with a hair dryer and threatened to torture for information. A man who definitely held a grudge, based on the way his dark eyes burned through me. His fingers stroked the Taser, almost lovingly.

I'd also scanned the other two. They all wore a mishmash of clothing and of the five, I could only tell that two of them were armed. But both of them had weapons of choice for dealing with runaway androids.

Tasers.

Based on the eclectic dressing choices, this group had nothing to do with Holland. And I could only think of one other group who'd know to have a Taser at the ready.

Peyton's watch made a sudden noise, and he looked down, frowning. "Like I said, we can discuss all of that later."

He didn't look like a bad guy. Just an everyday businessman, or banker, or high-school teacher. I glanced at Hunter. A father. Not that you could always tell by looking, of course. But I didn't see cruelty in the lines of his face, the curve of his lips, the depths of his eyes. Just a quiet confidence; a belief in his ability to get things done.

Peyton stepped forward, and I took a matching step back. Hunter cringed a little.

"Look, Hunter, there's a lot to explain," Peyton said. Though he spoke to Hunter, his shrewd eyes never left me. His limbs held coiled tension, but he wasn't stressed. Just ready. Whoever this man was, he was no ordinary businessman. Cruel or not, he was far too comfortable in this role. "Later. Right now, we need to get you kids into that van and out of here, before it's too late."

"No." The rejection shot out of me before I could stop it. "You need to answer his questions first."

Sophia shook her head, her worried gaze darting over her shoulder. She appeared steady and calm, but I noticed that her hands kept flitting toward her mouth before balling at her sides. Trying to fight off the urge to chew. And, every so often, she'd continue her side-to-side sway as she shifted her weight from foot to foot. For whatever reason, she wasn't as at ease in all this as her husband was. If Peyton was the calm, self-assured businessman, then she was the harried, overworked, underconfident housewife. "Once we're in a safe location, we can tell you everything."

Hunter looked from them to me and back again. I watched realization dawn. "Are you telling me—you guys work for the government, too?" His accusatory question was for his parents, but I was the one who answered.

"No. They work for the Vita Obscura."

Hunter mouthed the words after me, "*Vita Obscura*." He scowled. "Not that again." He turned back to his parents. "Tell her how crazy that is. Tell her," he repeated, when neither of them spoke at first. "Tell her you know nothing about this Vita Obscura."

Sophia's tired eyes met Peyton's. He gave her a swift nod, once again demonstrating that he was the one in charge. She smoothed her hands on her pants and sighed. "Actually, she's right. We are with the V.O."

The news clearly didn't sink in at first, because Hunter just stood there, looking expectant. Several seconds ticked by before realization hit. Hunter visibly recoiled. "No," he said, shaking his head. "No. That can't be true."

The look he threw at me was a cocktail of pain—guilt and horror—and my stomach clenched for him. For both of us.

"Look, it's not what you think—"

"Stop!" He threw his hand out. "Stop. *I* don't even know what I think yet, so I know damn well you don't."

"Hunter!" Peyton snapped, his muscular body going rigid with tension. "Don't speak to your mother like that."

"Sorry," Hunter responded reflexively. Then he laughed, but the sound was harsh. "Seriously? You just told me that you're part of some secret, illegal espionage group, but you're worried that I said *damn*? Unbelievable." His fists bunched at his sides, and his eyes closed. I watched him battle for control, his chest rising and falling rapidly.

"Here's what I think," he said, when he could finally speak. "I think you're telling me you're part of an organization that's been hunting Mila down and trying to kidnap her. I think you've been lying to me, all this time, about where you've been going. Business trips? Jesus." He shoved his hands in his pockets, forgetting about his injured arm, and flinched.

Maternal concern twisted Sophia's face. Her hands fluttered helplessly as she stepped forward. "Hunter, are you okay?"

He laughed again—a raw, humorless bark. "Am I okay?" he mused, like he was contemplating the weather. "What do you think? I just . . . first Mila, and now you. This can't be happening. This can't be my life."

He dragged his good hand through his hair, then stopped abruptly. "Oh my god," he said, with dawning horror as more puzzle pieces clicked together. "You're the ones who told me to be nice to the girl I saw at Dairy Queen. To make a new friend. You knew, didn't you? Even then, you were setting me up. Lying. Have you been tracking me this whole time? Tracking *us*? I know this was probably Peyton's thing, but Mom, how could you?"

That last was a little boy's plea, one that broke my heart. A plea that dredged up memories. My mom, finally telling me the truth, and the aching despair I'd felt, knowing she'd lied. Hunter had been there for me. Had helped ease the pain a little.

"How could you lie to me, after everything that happened with Dad?"

He was shouting now, so I reached out to touch his arm. Hoping to give him even a tiny measure of the comfort he'd given me. "Hunter, try to calm down."

A brief hesitation, an indrawn breath. For a moment, I thought I'd gotten through.

Then, he snatched his arm away and whirled on me. "Calm down? How can I calm down? Of course, it's probably easy for you to say. It's not like you were telling me the truth all along either."

His words said one thing, but his eyes another. They were frantic. With his back to his parents, he mouthed, "*Get ready to run.*"

I froze, stunned into silence, and something flickered across his face. Pain. Regret, maybe. But then he turned away, striding toward an opening in the driveway. As he walked, only one thing went through my mind.

After everything I'd put him through, he was still trying to help me.

My eyes stung with unshed tears, but I willed them away. He was right. If I wanted a fighting chance of escaping, I had to do it now.

"I'm getting the hell out of here. I need time to think."

The man from the motel room moved to block his path, and Hunter practically snarled. "Back off."

"Riggs, step aside," Hunter's stepfather said.

"I don't need you to speak on my behalf," Hunter yelled, turning to face Peyton. "I don't need you to speak at all. Don't think I don't know that you got her into this. I trusted you!"

"Hunter, now is not the time—" Peyton started, but after a meaningful glance over his shoulder at me, Hunter whirled, his shoulder bumping Riggs.

Now.

I broke into a run, but as I flew forward, I caught a glimmer of motion from Riggs as his expression soured. Everyone else's eyes were on Hunter, so no one else watched his hand go to his Taser.

Leave him, the logical part of my brain demanded. This was my only shot.

My heart rebelled.

As Riggs lifted the Taser and took aim at Hunter, I shifted course.

"Get down," I yelled desperately, when Riggs fumbled for the switch.

Sophia screamed, "Stop!" but she wasn't close enough to help. I dove for Hunter at the same time Riggs flicked the switch, knocking him to safety just before the Taser discharged. It sizzled across the driveway harmlessly.

Voltage: 1100.

Shock trapped my feet in place. Eleven hundred volts? That Taser was set for me. If it had hit Hunter . . .

A yank on my arm made me stumble forward. "Mila, run!" Hunter hissed. I allowed him to pull me forward and we headed toward the driveway.

Peyton's angry shout sounded as he rounded on Riggs, but I didn't pay attention. Our feet pounded the asphalt. All the while, all I could think was, *Please don't let them hurt Hunter. Please.*

"The van!" he whispered, pointing at the stationary vehicle at the end of the driveway.

For the first time, hope rose in my throat. Maybe we did have a chance, after all. If we could get inside the van, with just a little head start . . .

"No Tasers!" Sophia yelled from behind us. "It's too risky!"

If my sensors weren't jammed and only allowing some information to trickle in, I would have known about the two men with ample warning. Instead, my first inkling was when one jumped out from behind the car. He grabbed at my arm, tearing me from Hunter's grip and catching me completely off guard.

Hunter stumbled, going down on one knee, while the man jerked me off balance.

I recovered before he could make a second move. I broke

the guard's grip on my elbow with one fluid motion, before using that momentum to crank his arm into a painfully awkward position. My right foot whipped out and slammed into his right knee.

Impact: 720 lbs. per square inch.

The measurement flickered in front of me at the exact same time he grunted in pain. The next moment, he was on the ground, clutching his injured knee soundlessly.

Another man rushed Hunter from the side. I intercepted, hit him with a hard uppercut to the kidney. I feinted closer to follow up, only to feel someone closing in from behind. I dropped low and whirled, sweeping the third man's feet out from under him. As he fell back I followed, diving onto him and slamming his head into the ground.

After one moan he was silent.

"This is ridiculous! Surrender now, before one of you gets hurt! Riggs, what the hell are you doing? Call off your men!"

Peyton's command rang out, but no one heeded his words. It all made sense now. Riggs hated me, and he was spurring on the attack. He wanted us to get hurt.

He owed me.

Harsh fingers tangled in my hair, yanked me away. I flew back, and a brawny arm curled around my neck. Without a second thought, I rocked back on my heels, then thrust all my weight over and down. He flipped over my head, pulling me with him. He landed back first on the hard ground, with me on the top, his arm slackening on impact. I flipped over, rose, and slammed my heel into his groin. Blanching, he curled into a fetal position.

I raced back to Hunter, who had squared off with the guy who'd stood next to Riggs. Hunter's right eye was already starting to swell shut. The man reared back to deliver another blow.

I leaned to the side and lifted my leg high, striking the ball of my foot hard into his lower back.

Impact: 1000 lbs. per square inch.

Even through my shoe, I felt vertebrae yielding, the unnatural crack piercing the air. The guard crumpled like a puppet without strings.

I grabbed Hunter's wrist. "Come on!"

The van, it was so close.

We closed in on the driver's door, our legs pumping hard. Then, a flutter of motion, as another man exploded out of the back—with a gun, fully extended.

"Get in the van!" I yelled, shoving Hunter toward the driver's door as I plowed straight ahead. Right for our attacker.

His eyes widened when I was still three steps away, narrowed at two. I saw his finger twitch on the trigger at one, heard the slight snick of the bullet releasing from the silenced chamber. I veered to the left, a blur just barely grazing my arm. Then I batted the gun away before diving headfirst into his chest.

He crashed backward and I somersaulted over him, regaining my feet and his gun, but now facing the wrong way.

"No guns! No guns!" Peyton shouted, but he'd lost all control of the situation. "Back off of him!"

Hunter.

I whirled, already in stride. Hunter fumbled for the door handle with one hand and frantically urged me on with the other. He yanked open the door and stepped back, making room for me to dive in first.

"Mila!" he yelled.

A man grabbed him from behind and yanked him backward, wrapping one burly arm around Hunter's throat.

"Hunter!" I screamed, desperately propelling myself toward him.

Just in time to watch Hunter's eyes bulge, watch his hands claw at the arm to no avail. To watch the guard use his free hand to press something against Hunter's neck.

Just in time to watch his mouth form one final "Mila?"—just in time to catch him as his body convulsed and his legs buckled beneath him.

"Noooooo!"

As my arms reached for him, I heard a loud zap, saw a bright crackle of light. And then a powerful electrical fire surged up my spine. Current blazed through my body: hot, hot, sizzling.

My thoughts jerked, jerked, disrupted by the same static that bristled through my ears.

Taser was my final coherent thought, before I————

————————————————————

————————————————————

————————————————————

————————————————

NINETEEN

A familiar buzzing filled my head in short, disjointed bursts. Buzz. Buzz. Buzz. Followed by a head-smashing bump.

"Sorry about that," I thought I heard an unfamiliar woman's voice say. But it came from far, far away and was distorted, like the words had to travel through a long, narrow tunnel to reach me.

More buzzing. Then distorted images, flashing by in broken pieces. A horse's hoof. A patch of green, green grass. Twirling on a beach. A white floor, marred by a swath of steel chains and the pungent scent of bleach. The inside of a car, with brightly colored candies in a tiny little cubby. Fans shrieking at a baseball game, as the Phillies batter smacked the ball. The acrid smell of smoke. A body. Collapsing.

Faded blue eyes . . .

Faded blue eyes . . .

Faded . . .

Hunter.

With a gasp like I'd been holding my breath underwater for far too long and I'd finally broken the surface, my own eyes flipped open, only to stare directly at a pair of spotless brown boots with three-inch stiletto heels and two, no, three silver buckles on the side encasing smallish feet. Long, long legs crossed at the knee, a navy blue skirt, with a high slit on the left side. A matching, fitted blazer, blanketed by a mass of auburn hair. An oval face with high, defined cheekbones, full lips, and thickly lashed blue eyes framed by delicately arched auburn brows.

The full lips curved into a welcoming smile and the body leaned toward me, encompassing me in some kind of spicy vanilla scent. "Hello, Mila." Then, she shook her head, a soft laugh echoing through the room. "Wow, you probably have no idea how long I've been waiting to say that. I'm so glad you're finally here."

I blinked up at her upside-down face, my mind still a little cloudy. Here? Where was here? Sensations kicked in, and I realized the soft, squishy material beneath me was leather. I was stretched out on a brown leather couch, while the smiling woman lounged next to me in a matching chair.

With more effort than I should have needed, I jerked

myself up into a sitting position.

Her forehead wrinkled, and she reached out to stabilize my arm, throwing her hands up in silent platitude when I leaned away from her touch.

"Easy," she said. "I just wanted to make sure you were okay. You took in quite a bit of juice. That absolutely was not meant to happen." A scowl tightened her lips.

Juice?

Voltage. *Taser.*

It was all coming back.

"Anyway, you should relax for a bit. Let your body recover. Can I get you anything?"

She rested her elbows on her skirt and leaned closer as if concerned, engulfing me in another waft of vanilla.

"Who are you?" I tried to say, in lieu of a request. But my voice was somehow locked up. All that came out was a grunt-like sound. *"Hoo."*

Her blue eyes widened. "Oh. Right. Nice going, Quinn—in all the excitement, you forgot to introduce yourself. Quinn Taylor, founder of the Vita Obscura."

Quinn . . . this woman was *the* Quinn? The founder of the V.O., the organization that had terrified my mom so much, and even had Holland crazy with anxiety? In all the time I'd tried to visualize who might be the mastermind of the faceless organization after us, I'd never once pictured someone like this. For one, she was so pretty. Petite. She looked more suited to a boardroom or a magazine cover than the leader of an underground criminal organization. I mean, I knew better than to underestimate people based on looks, but still.

For two, she seemed so . . . *sincere.*

Something niggled at the back of my head. Something was wrong. The details of the fight in the driveway flew through my head, and my body went rigid with remembered dread.

"Where's . . . Hunter?" I managed. This time, the words came out, but in that too low, too robotic voice from the garage. The one I hated more than anything.

Quinn frowned. "Has that happened before?"

I scowled. "Hunter?" I demanded, in the same robotic tone.

"Hmmm. It's probably just a side effect of the Taser, or other electrical insults, like too much current. It should wear off in a few seconds. But if it ever persists, let me know, and I'll see what I can do. I can tell that must be upsetting for you. As far as Hunter goes, he's safe, with his parents."

My relief over his safety was short-lived. Hunter's parents. I'd forgotten, until just now. How was he coping, knowing that they'd used him? How was he coping in general? The choke hold . . .

I didn't speak, but my eyes must have expressed my worries.

"He's fine, I promise. You can even see him soon, if you like."

I nodded, then bit my lip. Of course I wanted to see him, more than anything. I just wasn't sure he'd say the same thing about me. He might have been willing to help me escape, but that had to be guilt guiding his actions.

He'd made it very clear that he wanted nothing to do with me.

At the thought, a hollow formed in my heart.

I cleared my throat, hoping that my voice would work this time. "His parents," I started carefully. Relief flowed through me when my voice once again sounded familiar. "They work for you?"

"Yes, though mainly his stepfather. They were instrumental in helping to locate you and bring you in, thanks to Hunter."

I winced, and she sighed. "I swear, nothing is quite as bad as it might seem right now. I know you must think we're the devil, but I hope to prove otherwise. Well, except for Riggs. But don't worry. He's being dealt with." For a moment, her mouth hardened, and her voice lost its musical cadence. In that moment, I caught a glimmer of something menacing. "Do you mind . . . ?" she said, reaching out for me again.

I didn't want to say yes, but I also didn't want to piss her off. Not until I had some kind of idea what game she was playing at here. She seemed sincere, but all of Mom's warnings flew through my head, telling me to exercise extreme caution.

I gave a brief, jerky nod, and she cradled my hand in her own. Warm. Her palms were warm. Her expression lit up, and I felt her body release a tiny sigh. "Amazing. Simply amazing."

Now that she was closer, I could see that she wasn't as young as I'd first thought. Tiny crow's feet fanned from her skin. Her grip tightened; her eyes glowed with intensity. Suddenly uncomfortable, I yanked my hand away, then worried I'd offended her. I wasn't exactly in a bargaining position at the moment.

To my surprise, she apologized. "There I go again, getting ahead of myself. I'm sure you must be incredibly confused about me and my group. Speaking of which, I'm being a terrible host."

She rose, smoothing her skirt down her slim legs, and motioned me to follow her toward the door. "Let me show you around and introduce you to my crew, so you can settle in before we get down to business. I think you're going to like it here."

I stood slowly. Warily. The whole hostess act didn't fit with anything I knew about the V.O. Not the men who'd tried to grab Mom and me back at the motel, or the fight that had broken out at Jensen's house.

"I think what I'd like is to know where I am."

My GPS wasn't functioning yet, or else I would have figured it out for myself.

"You'll know. When the time is right," Quinn replied, her eyes soft, not elusive. "Trust me. It's for your own protection that some things are a mystery right now. I don't want anything to happen to you."

This made no sense. *She* made no sense. I should be plotting my escape, I knew that. But shell shock must have taken a toll, because all I could do for now was follow behind her, and wonder what the hell was going on. In my defense, the more information I had, the better. And it was clear that Quinn was full of information.

Besides, I consoled myself—I couldn't do anything until I saw that Hunter was safe, with my own eyes.

She laughed suddenly, tapping herself lightly on the head with two pink-tipped fingers. "You must think I'm nutty. I should have apologized immediately for the way you were brought in. Way too chaotic, but it was partly because one of my tech guys had intercepted a message that Holland had a trace on you. We think he may have managed to disable your stealth mode, somehow. Probably when you were connecting to the internet."

Three, at the bus stop. The weird wormhole sensation in my head. Suddenly, it was all making sense. It was possible that I'd led Holland and Three right to me.

An image of Three's body melting to nothing under the semi flashed through my mind, accompanied by the scent of burning flesh and hair. I shivered and shoved the memory away.

Quinn paused in the doorway. "Mila, I know this is going to sound crazy, but we have a mutual enemy. General Holland." Just like that, all traces of softness vanished again. Her stiff posture and jutting chin radiated aggression. Beneath that pretty, sunny exterior, I suspected something explosive lurked. Like dynamite disguised beneath a carefully applied layer of paint and glitter. "And I think it's long past time we made him pay."

Even if I doubted everything else, there was no doubting that Quinn despised General Holland. Possibly as much as I did. But why?

A quick shake of auburn hair, and she was walking again. "Enough of that for now. Let me introduce you to the rest of the group."

I followed, slowly, mentally ticking through everything I knew about the V.O. And how none of it so far was tracking. I had to be missing something. Somewhere, along the way, a trap would surely be sprung. Maybe allaying my suspicions was all part of the plan, somehow.

And yet . . . as I watched Quinn's hair swish while we walked, I realized I did believe one thing. Quinn was genuinely happy to have me here, whatever the reason. The first person who'd ever known what I truly was, and welcomed me anyway.

Still. That didn't mean I trusted her.

From somewhere down near the end of the long hall, I could just make out noises. A clank. A spurt of laughter. A sudden shout, followed by muffled voices.

Quinn groaned. "Children, children," she said, but her tone brimmed with amused tolerance. "You'll find that we work hard here, but we play just as hard."

I had to admit, my curiosity was piqued.

With her efficient, long strides, she led me down the corridor. White walls, synthetic fiber on the floor. The hallway curved slowly, until we approached a set of open doors. The sounds emitted from inside the room grew louder: voices, laughter, the staccato, rapid-fire *ping ping ping* of a recorded gun. Pool balls, clinking together.

Against my will, hope fluttered in my chest. Would I find Hunter in there? Part of me wanted to see him again, and part of me lived in terror, of how he would treat me now that he knew everything.

Now that he knew what I was.

Before we could enter the doorway, footsteps thudded down the hall, back from the way we came. We both turned, to see Jensen striding toward us.

I tensed, my stomach twisting at the sight of him. Here,

in the V.O.'s hideout. There went any last sliver of hope that he wasn't working with them again. As obvious as his involvement might have seemed back at his house, the fact that he'd disappeared before Quinn arrived left me with a tiny reservoir of doubt. But now that reservoir dried up, refilled instead with the certainty of his betrayal.

His gaze swept over me, from head to toe. Seemingly satisfied with whatever he saw, he nodded at Quinn. "She okay?"

"She's fine, which you can see for yourself."

He grunted, and I gritted my teeth. "*She* is right here, and can even form sentences of her own." I paused, then added, "She's also wondering how you can live with yourself, knowing what a traitor you've been to Mom's memory."

The satisfaction I felt when he flinched was fleeting. "I'll be in the gym if you need me."

Quinn flashed her white teeth. "Working out some issues, Daniel?"

He stared her down for a moment, not saying a word. Then, with a scowl, he turned and strode away.

"Well. That was interesting, don't you think?" Quinn mused.

I watched his retreat, and despite myself, couldn't help but feel a knife twist in my chest.

Not your dad, I reminded myself. Sarah's.

Raised voices preceded a door flying open on the other

side of the hallway. And just like that, Hunter appeared.

My eyes greedily drank him in, checking for any injuries, any bruises. The knot I hadn't even known was in my stomach loosened. He really was okay. Hunter was okay.

Our eyes met, and it was like all of the trauma of the past two days just fell away. Something crackled between us, making my breath catch. He swallowed, hard, while need tore through me, aching and pure, and I hoped against all logic that whatever he said would offer a sliver of a chance.

"We aren't finished here—" Sophia's face appeared in the doorway. When she saw us, her voice quieted, though her smile was forced. She nodded politely, then tugged on Hunter's good arm. "Come on."

With one last, searching look at me, Hunter turned and disappeared back inside. The click of the door signaled my heart to resume pumping.

I was aware of Quinn studying me, so I ducked my head to hide my face.

"Love sucks, doesn't it?" is what she finally said, before guiding me toward the common room.

Was I really that obvious?

Threat detected: 11 humans in a 30-ft. radius.

My scan kicked in, itemizing heights and weights and distinguishing characteristics, in less than two seconds. Quinn announced, "Look who's here."

All eleven people stopped what they were doing, and

chatter cut off like a cord sliced with a knife. Silence reigned for an initial, uncomfortable moment, and I saw various emotions flit across faces. I braced myself for rejection.

Several people clumped around a worn pool table that had seen better days, while others were looking up from where they slumped on the couch, playing video games. Another group sat around an overturned box, playing a card game involving matches. I wasn't sure why I was so surprised. I guess in the back of my head, I'd been expecting something sterile, like Holland's compound. In comparison, this place was actually . . . homey.

Excited murmurs, lots of exchanged glances. And most of them, young. Not the hardened mercenaries I was expecting, though many of them did look a little rough around the edges. None of them were the men in the driveway from Jensen's place, either.

I was surprised to see overstuffed couches and love seats, a small kitchen in the corner with a microwave and full-sized refrigerator, and on the counter, a restaurant-style soft drink dispenser. A foosball table sat next to a pool table. Two fifty-five-inch-screen TVs dominated the room. In the far corner, three young adults sat in front of computer monitors, busily tapping away.

"So, these are my people," she said, spreading her arms wide.

The boy closest to us chewed his sandwich and raised

his fist. "Free technology!" he said, through a mouthful of crumbs. The others nearby heard, and repeated the words. "Free technology!" soon rumbled through the room.

I frowned. Free technology? The question must have shown on my face, because Quinn responded. "Not what you were expecting? Don't worry—money is important to our quality of life. But we try to only gain it from big business and the government, and to subsidize our bigger goal—to share technology with the masses. Information should be free—a right, not a privilege."

A few scattered cheers.

Quinn straightened then, folding her arms. Her clear voice carried. "Don't get too excited yet. I'm sure you heard about the tracer—I'm going to be needing some answers as to why we didn't see that coming," she said, turning to glare at the boys in front of the computer monitors.

"None of our alarms were tripped," said a brunette girl with glasses.

"Well, find out why! Jared, Teek, I want updates, as soon as possible. We need to get this back under control. And everyone, break time is almost over."

Something in her pocket buzzed, and she grabbed a phone. She frowned at the screen before turning to me. "I need to go check on this—then I'll be back to bring you up to speed. Dixon, can you stick with Mila for now?"

The fidgety boy of Asian heritage dropped his cards and

pushed away from the table with an easy smile. "Sure." Quinn patted my shoulder, then turned and exited the room, leaving a trail of vanilla behind her.

"Welcome to Club Quinn," he said, bouncing on the balls of his feet. "So, you're really an android with feelings? What's that like?"

His question was bold, but full of curiosity, nothing else. It probably shouldn't have felt so weird, but it floored me. No one had ever asked before. Not even Mom.

I hadn't really meant to respond to any of them—but I couldn't resist. It felt good to be out in the open for a change. Not having to hide who I was from the world. "Normal, freakish, both at the same time?"

Dixon's slow smile revealed a crooked front tooth. "You'll fit in just fine here, then. We're overflowing with freaks," he said, but he didn't sound concerned. No, he made *freak* seem like an attribute.

Not sure what to say, I followed him over to the table, surprised by the sudden lifting of tension from my shoulders.

A boy with buzzed blond hair, rangy-lean muscles showing beneath a tank top, and a match between his teeth, waited until he saw Quinn exit the room before pushing up from the card table. "That really her?" he said, giving me a once-over. "'Cuz she don't look like all that."

"What did you expect her to look like, Leo?" the

stringy-haired guy next to him said. "One of the girls from those magazines you hide in your sleeping bag?" He snickered, but Leo just shrugged.

"Dude, they make a chick from scratch, least they can do is add a little . . ." His hands shaped two oversized semicircles near his chest. "No offense," he added.

Stringy-haired boy gave this half snicker while beside me, Dixon jiggled his leg. "Shut it, Leo." Then to me, he whispered, "Sorry."

Stringy-hair said, "Dude, I'd shut up if I were you. I think you're pissing her off."

Leo shrugged. "My apologies. If it helps, I talk to all the girls like that."

Wow. Okay. "I'm not sure if that makes it better or worse," I answered, though if I were being entirely honest, I'd admit that being treated like every other girl under the circumstances felt surprisingly good.

Leo twirled the match with his teeth, his chapped lips curling into a slightly feral smile. "Yeah? Good. I like to keep people guessing."

Okay, then. Maybe I'd just avoid this one.

An oversized bear of a man with red curls pushed to his feet, blocking Leo's path. He appeared at least five years older than the blond, and must have outweighed him by a good thirty pounds. "You've got the manners of a gutter rat," he said, rolling his words in a lilting burr. Scottish.

He turned his back and extended his hand to me. "Excuse these brutes—they don't get out from behind their monitors enough. I'm Samuel, the civilized one in this rat hole."

I eyed the beefy hand, my gaze traveling back up to catch a wide mouth that looked meant for smiling and a broad walnut of a nose. Pale skin and deep brown eyes, alight with humor.

"Mila," I said, taking his hand. He shook it gently before releasing, and that gesture seemed to act like a balm to any of my remaining nerves.

I could like this guy, I thought. And maybe that meant—I could like it *here*.

A tall blond girl, who'd been silent the entire time, scooted her chair to make room for the one Samuel had pulled up for me.

"I'll just watch," I said, relaxing into the seat. It was so difficult to fathom how their acceptance could be real, but I didn't believe they were pretending.

Even though no one so far had accepted me for what I was. Ever. Not even Hunter.

Fresh pain lashed at me, and I wrapped my arms around my waist.

My admission that I didn't know how to play degenerated into a chorus of surprise, and conflicting instructions on how to win at poker.

"Always go for the better hand."

"Don't listen to him—do you see how small his stash of matches is? If the electricity goes out, he's totally fu—"

"Poker's a sport for wee girly men anyway—no offense to the ladies," Samuel interjected.

Someone groaned. "Oh, here we go again. Talking about how real men throw trees for fun."

Leo scowled, clearly not wanting to hear that. He leaned closer to the blond girl and grabbed a piece of her hair. "Hey, Abby, maybe you'll finally change your mind tonight and let me—argh!"

As quick as a snake, she'd grabbed his free hand, while her other hand shoved the matchstick under his fingernail. Hard.

He jumped to his feet and shook his hand, cursing. "Jesus, Abby, what the hell is wrong with you? I was only messing around."

Abby caught my eye and flashed me a quick grin, an action which softened the bony planes of her face. I returned her smile. I was pretty sure I could like this girl. Dixon cracked his knuckles. "As you can see, most of us can take care of ourselves. Side effect of living on the streets. Before Quinn found us, of course."

"How did she find you?"

He shrugged. "Some of us, through state testing. She hacks the system, finds the high scorers who lack the economic means to do the college thing. Or sometimes, just through the hacking community. Sooner or later, we tend to get in a bit of trouble. Samuel, over there, she rescued from jail time. She cleans us up—well, all except for Russo," he said. The stringy-haired guy flipped a card at him in response. "And then, gives us access to technology and sets us loose. A hacker's dream life."

"So, you basically . . . do what?"

He shrugged. "Steal shit."

Abby, who hadn't said a word until then, popped her head up. "Not just to steal it, though. To share it. We steal technology from the rich so the poor can benefit, too."

I had a billion more questions, but just then, Quinn strolled back into the room. She spotted me and waved me over. I rose reluctantly, a little annoyed at being separated from the others so soon, while she clapped her hands. "Everyone, make sure you continue following through on uploading that last feed. And remember—keep watching Holland's movements. Don't screw anything up—I want monitors going twenty-four-seven, email accounts scrutinized. Samuel, Teek—the video equipment—you've got that under way?"

"On it," Samuel said, saluting. Teek simply grunted from his post at the computer.

She gave a satisfied nod. "Perfect."

The space filled with the sounds of chairs being pushed back, people rising to their feet.

"Dixon, I need you and Abby to take Mila to the equipment room and get her prepared."

Equipment room.

Prepared.

Visions of Holland's lab, his reprogramming machine, assaulted me. Never, ever again.

I backed away, assessing the room for the nearest weapon. "I'm not prepping for anything," I said, backing away.

Samuel guffawed and patted my arm. "Down, tiger. Quinn just wants to make sure your stealth mode is on, so we can keep the military out of your pretty little head. Though it's not so pretty right now, with the way you're glaring at me like you'd just as soon gnaw on my skull."

Abby snorted. "It's those pretty ones you've got to watch out for, Samuel. They're always the skull gnawers."

Their easy camaraderie soothed some of my tension away. "That's all you're doing?" I said, looking directly at Quinn.

"I'll walk you through every step, if you like," she said, holding my gaze steadily. Not even a hint of rancor at my suspicions showed. Either she was good—very good—or she really did want me to feel comfortable.

Both thoughts were equally disconcerting, in entirely different ways.

I couldn't detect even the slightest hint of a lie, not from any of them. And according to Quinn, I did need to have my stealth reenabled. Otherwise, the second I left here,

Holland would track me down.

If I ever left here. With a pang, I realized—I didn't really have any pressing places to go at the moment. At one time, I'd thought maybe Hunter . . .

My gaze flickered toward the hall, to where Hunter had disappeared through a door. I wondered where he'd gone. If that one last look, across a noisy hallway, was the last time I'd ever see his face.

Claws dug into my heart and tore it into raw, aching strips. No. I couldn't think about that now. Not when I had to focus. "This way," Dixon said, jiggling his hands in his pockets. He flashed his charming, crooked-toothed smile, whirling and practically jogging from the room. Abby and I trailed him.

We followed the narrow hall down a semicircle before Dixon led us through a set of doors. We passed three other people, scampering the other way. In so much of a hurry, they barely spared us a glance.

"So, you ready?" Dixon said.

I shrugged, then stopped short when we entered the room. It wasn't small, but it felt cramped—maybe because it was overstuffed with things. And for some reason, the scent of stale sweat lingered. Like maybe at one time it'd been used as an additional locker room.

The synthetic carpet frayed in spots, showing a faint trail leading to the door. When I stepped inside, my feet crunched the stiff fibers, feeling the uneven wear. A dozen monitors sprawled along the wall. Video surveillance, I realized, of all different locations. Each monitor switched to a new area every five seconds.

I couldn't suppress the feeling that I was on display.

"They're mainly programmed with pictures of the individuals we're hunting down," Dixon said, his voice animated again. "They alert us in the main computer room when there's a match. It's basically all human-free."

I started to turn away, but an image on one of the screens caught my eye.

Riggs.

Dixon followed my gaze, blanched, then fumbled for a remote on the table. That monitor powered off.

"Sorry," he muttered. "You just . . . Quinn's great and all, but you don't want to cross her."

I frowned. It was just a picture of him, nothing more. And I couldn't blame Quinn for being mad. Riggs had broken orders and tried to Taser Hunter.

I returned to inspecting the room, taking in the oversized tables spread out across the floor. Machines in different stages of dismantlement sat on top of them—everything from hard drives to a huge satellite disc to some monstrosity I couldn't even identify. Every shade of silver and gray under the sun, but with an unexpected burst of color here and there, from a wire or a plastic casing. It looked more like a junk heap than a laboratory, but even so, I felt a chill.

Machines. Any one of those could just as easily be me.

I pictured Three's melting head and flinched at an unexpected stab of loss. I averted my eyes, hoping to force the feeling away.

"All high-tech stuff we've snaked from some bigwig who thinks his security is badass," Dixon said, pride evident in his voice as he trailed his fingers here and there, touching everything. "Quinn and a few of the engineers work on those as time permits. They figure out the technology, copy and improve it, then share it with the world at a fraction of the original cost. Or often, we release it for free. Anything we can get from the military is an added bonus. Believe it or not, we've got a wide range of beliefs here, but we're pretty much all united on the antiwar front. And if there's one thing that history's proven, time and time again, it's that military research, if left in the government's hands, always ends in lost lives."

"So, you really do just sit around all day and steal?"

Abby, a silent companion up to this point, finally spoke. "It's not stealing if it's information that everyone can benefit from," she said, in husky-soft voice. "Everyone deserves access to technology—not just the rich."

Dixon grinned. "Abby there is an idealist, god help us all."

Abby stuck her tongue out while I asked, "And what are you?"

Dixon rubbed his chin, as if debating. "Me? I'm a whatever-it-takes-to-get-my-hands-on-the-good-stuff-ologist."

"Bullshit," Abby fake coughed. Then she grinned. "He just doesn't like exposing his softer side, that's all."

"Whatever," he said, but I could tell from the way he looked away and smiled that he was secretly pleased.

A small but growing patch of warmth opened up, somewhere deep inside me, followed by a wave of longing. I'd never had this before, what they had. Even being included on the periphery felt nice.

I thought about what Dixon had said, about the military. About antiwar ideals and saving lives. Maybe I could help these people. Maybe I could find a place here, helping prevent future Hollands.

The warm patch in my chest grew and grew until it blossomed into something more tangible: hope.

"Over here," he said, pointing at a nook tucked into the far corner of the room. As I looked, my android functions kicked in, and I scanned the room at record pace.

Off-white curtains, plastic, attached to a metal bar by 38 thin rings.

Computer monitor, 18 in. diameter.

Square table, 10 in. across, stacked with five rectangular cases, all stainless steel.

And in the middle of it all, a reclining cot, adorned with

a black and rose cushion. Hovering above that was a strange metal helmet—only with holes and wires everywhere. I edged forward, uncertainty giving way to stony resolve. I sat down, then twisted until I was lying on my back, legs propped up, head on the built-in headrest.

The click-click of Quinn's heels preceded her into the doorway. She smoothed an errant strand of auburn hair off her face. "So are we almost ready to start?"

Jensen poked his head into the doorway. Quinn waved him in. "You going to watch?" she asked.

He gave me a cursory glance and grimaced. "No, thanks. Let me know when you're done."

Another pinch, sharper than the last, at his rejection.

Stupid, I berated. *I didn't need him.*

As I glanced around, once again marveling at how different things were here than I'd expected, I realized something had been niggling at the back of my head. In Holland's compound, they'd given me some files, before my second test. One included reports on a man named Trenton Blaine, who, according to the file, was the founder of the V.O. The other contained a photo of a younger man thought to be a mole for the group. Granted, the photo had been blurry, but still. None of the people I'd seen so far were even close to matching, and I'd had yet to hear anyone refer to another member as Trenton. Besides, every bit of information pointed to Quinn running the group.

"Who's Trenton Blaine?" I asked.

Her head jerked to the side and her blue eyes widened. "Where did you hear that name?" she demanded.

"Holland. He gave me some files when he captured me."

She waited, shoulders tense, as if for me to tell her more. When I didn't offer up further information—there wasn't much to tell—she relaxed her guard. "That's a pseudonym for a man who works for us sometimes, but he rarely stays at the compound. He has a family. We mainly just recruit him for special jobs." She flicked an imaginary piece of lint from her suit. "You never saw a photo?"

"They didn't have one. So, he's not the founding member?"

Quinn laughed then—a full-bodied, rich laugh that filled the room. "No. That's just what I want Holland to believe. It's pretty much cake, given that he thinks women aren't smart enough to run things."

"All the stuff I read at Holland's compound? Even the Agent Orange? That's all bogus?"

She shrugged. "Having your father die of military-inflicted chemicals sounds like a legitimate reason for a gripe, right?"

"What about the mole?"

Quinn busied herself with the monitor, shook her head. "Fictional. A wild goose chase, to keep Holland distracted."

That struck me as odd, but ingenious. If Holland knew

the group existed, why not give him a false lead to chase down? Then, all his resources would be sent that way, while Quinn could continue operating without disruption.

She hit a button on my recliner, and it rose, slowly and smoothly, until I was almost upright. Then, she grabbed the dangling helmet and pulled it down. "Okay, let's begin."

TWENTY

The helmet swallowed my head, flooded me with the scent of copper and steel, encasing my skull in a sleek, chilly prison. Slow, deep breaths helped relax my ready-to-bolt muscles. "What are you doing now?"

She adjusted the fit of the helmet. Then, she pulled down the mass of wires that dangled beside it. After reaching into a silver box and extracting a pack of long, thin needles, she began attaching a wire to one, and then pushing it into my scalp.

I braced for pain, but of course, felt none. The very limited pain sensation I'd been programmed with rarely surfaced. All I felt was a foreign presence invading my skull.

"First, we need to locate your tracking mechanism. Once we find it, I can fry it—permanently."

See? Nothing to fear, and everything to gain. Still, my pulse pounded. This was too reminiscent of another lab.

The sound of someone clearing his throat interrupted us. Quinn craned her head over her shoulder. "Oh, good, you're here."

I couldn't see who was approaching, but I heard the heavy scrape of footsteps ripple across the carpet.

A face appeared in front of me, topped with red curls. Samuel.

I relaxed a little. For some reason, the oversized Scotsman put me at ease.

"Samuel is an expert in all things AV and GPS, so he's going to help me make some adjustments here. I bet . . ." She broke off, fiddling with the helmet until it was adjusted just so, then backed away to the keyboard on the tiny table. "Samuel, take a peek?"

The redhead gave me a jaunty salute, before peering at the monitor, whistling an off-key tune under his breath.

"Nope, not there. *There*," he said, pointing.

"Got it! Hang on—" Quinn hit a few keys. The helmet started to warm up, smothering my scalp with a dry heat. A thin vibration, like that of a tuning fork, buzzed through my ears.

"Ah, ah—keep facing straight ahead," she warned, when I made a motion to turn toward the monitor she watched like a hawk. I caught a glimpse of pink-tipped fingers flying over the keys, and the tip of her tongue protruding between her teeth, before Samuel's snap got my attention.

"Look this way. I'm sure you've never seen such a fine hunk o' a Scottish specimen before, have ya, lass?" he said, executing a slow turn while his voice dipped into an exaggerated brogue. When he faced me again, he winked. "There you go. You're doing perfect."

Quinn swore under her breath, but a moment later, she clapped her hands. "Aha, just what I thought—no, they didn't make your video feed live, but I think it can still be done. Samuel?"

"I know it'll be hard to keep your eyes off my stunning physique, but you keep looking straight ahead!" Another wink, and he ambled his considerable girth over to Quinn.

I lay there, waiting, listening to them mutter to each other, occasionally argue. And always, the constant tapping of fingers.

Finally, Quinn's voice rang out, triumphant. "I think we've got it. In three . . ." Her fingers flew faster. "Two . . . one."

"And you're offline," she said, but continued to poke around.

"Hmmm . . . okay. No, no . . . damn," she muttered, humming in between words.

"What is it?"

A pause. "Oh, nothing, really. Just some parameters that

we can alter later, if need be. But we'll discuss that another time," she said when I stiffened.

"Well, that's it for now. Hang tight while I disconnect everything . . ." A minute or so passed, filled with her on-and-off humming. Suddenly, I was free. "You can sit up now."

That was it? She'd done exactly what she'd said, and that was all? No attempts to tap further into my head? To copy my data? To reprogram me or terminate me, or cut me up and sell me for scrap?

"You don't have to look so surprised," she teased, watching my expression. On a more serious note, she added, "Look, I know you have no reason to trust me yet, but we'll get there. I think it's time to finish our talk now."

I waved good-bye to Dixon and Abby, then followed Quinn back into the hallway. She led me to a room I'd yet to visit, a little way down on the left.

From what I could gather, we were in her office; only it was less office, more mini-lounge. The walls were adorned with monitors, four tall by four wide, and she had an Ikea-style desk. Four computers hummed on top. In the corner was a freestanding shelving unit, holding snacks and a fancy espresso maker. A mini-fridge squatted next to it. Besides the monitors, the walls were bare, except for a single framed photo.

Her and Holland, what must have been years ago. Sitting

at an outdoor table on a patio somewhere. They weren't embracing, but the way their heads tilted toward each other suggested intimacy. His face, still unwrinkled then, swam before me, and rage churned, reaching out with inky black hands and holding my body hostage to its grip.

She followed my gaze and nodded with grim satisfaction. "I knew we'd agree on this."

"How do you know him?" I asked.

Her lips parted, but before she could answer, a familiar voice boomed from the door.

"She knows him because they were in the military together. She's the one who actually came up with the initial plan to create you."

Dad. *Dad.*

I shook off the knee-jerk response. Not Dad. Jensen. No, wait. *Daniel Lusk.* I might as well start calling him by his real name, like Quinn.

His words sank in, and I bolted upright. "What?"

He strode into the room and made himself comfortable on the couch. "Were you going to call me, or just conveniently forget?" he said mildly, but his wary posture was anything but mild.

Quinn just laughed, and the musical trill floated through the room. "So suspicious!" she said, also mildly. But there was steel laced underneath. Then, noting my surprised expression, she continued. "I know it's a lot to take in, but he's right. I am the one who came up with the plan that brought you into existence. Amazing, huh?"

Amazing, insane, terrible, and wonderful. Lonely. Futile. In the end, not enough words existed to encompass the emotions her declaration aroused. I swallowed, my mind reeling, bombarded with questions, unsure of which one to voice first. Nowhere along the way had any of this come up—not from Mom, not from Holland. Not even Jensen. Would there ever be a time when I'd stop being surprised by the past? A time when finally, I knew all there was to know about me and my creation?

Right now, the truth seemed nebulous at best. A never-ending journey where, just when I thought I'd finally struggled my way to the end, the pathway took a sharp turn, once again plunging me into darkness.

She sighed. "Let's see—since it sounds like Daniel didn't fill you in, I'm sure you want to be brought up to speed on all the details."

She leaned back, a faraway look in her eyes. "I came up with the concept of using a high-tech teenage android as an antiterrorist unit. I spent years researching, putting together the proposal, explaining why it would work. Who would suspect an American teenage girl of being a spy? You were to be my life's greatest accomplishment. I was going to prove my contemporaries wrong, that a woman really could achieve greatness in the military. I shared it all with

Holland. Even then, still craving male approval. Only . . ."

Her voice had risen over the last few words. She paused, removed her fingers from the furrows she'd formed in the couch, and began smoothing them out. "Only, he stole it. Holland took my years of sweat and blood and passed my work off as his own."

"How?"

She laughed then, harshly. "The usual way. We were together. I trusted him," she said.

Simple words, but ones that made my head spin. I glanced at the photo again, at their tilted heads. "Together? You mean—"

"We were lovers. I was young and stupid, and yes, starry-eyed when someone with his rank gave me the time of day. Our relationship was forbidden, of course it was. And he made damn sure to keep it completely secret. So I had nothing, nothing, to fall back on when I threatened to expose him. He'd taken care to erase anything that could link us together outside of work. He laughed at me—called me a stupid girl. He told me there was no way anyone would take my word over his—a lowly woman, contesting the powerful general—and you know what? He was right. My biggest creation, gone—all because I'd trusted unwisely."

I couldn't help but feel a pang of sympathy, an answering outrage, on her behalf. Holland. He destroyed everything he touched.

Daniel cleared his throat, kicking his leg restlessly against the sofa. "Tell her what happened next."

She scowled at him. "I was getting to that. After that happened, I was too humiliated—too irate—to stay in the military any longer. I felt trapped, like I had no one to turn to for support, and I hated that feeling. I entered the military to feel more powerful, not weaker, and I wanted that power back. Plus, perhaps it's petty, but I wanted revenge. He deserves it, on so many fronts," she said, her crystal-blue gaze capturing mine.

Yes. Yes, he did.

"So I formed the Vita Obscura. It doesn't just focus on military technology, of course, but the more I can steal from them—and especially Holland—the happier I am. Steal from the rich, and get richer ourselves. I recruited the best hackers and engineers, along with a few of the best con men around—they come in handy when I need to finesse information from someone. But the one thing I always knew I wanted back was you."

She spread her arms wide and smiled, showing even, white teeth. "Welcome home, Mila. You're finally right where you belong."

Rebellion. That was my first instinct. Mom certainly didn't think I belonged here. She'd done everything in her power to keep me away.

But then again, had Mom really ever accepted me, fully?

Or had she been fantasizing about a lost daughter?

"You were always so brave, Sarah."

Was it possible I was more Sarah than Mila? I remembered Mom being surprised by some of my memories, as though they weren't exactly what she'd programmed. I looked at Daniel. "Am I like Sarah?"

His boot hit the floor. "It doesn't matter," he muttered, after a lengthy pause. "You aren't her." Then, almost like he was talking to himself, he added, "You're her spitting image, though. When I first saw you, it was like Nicole brought you back to life."

Three times. Mom had brought Sarah back to life three times. And now, two of those three versions were dead, and any parts of Sarah, lost along with them.

Grief hit me out of nowhere, and I choked on a breath. Part of me, gone forever.

"You're okay," Jensen murmured, as though soothing a baby. Was he talking to me?

A whisper of a memory. His face, only younger, as my small hand clasped his much larger one while getting onto the tallest Ferris wheel I'd ever seen.

Him saying, "It's going to be okay," as he ruffled my hair.

And my younger, high-pitched voice, demanding, "Promise?"

"You said something similar when we rode the Ferris wheel," I said.

I watched as his throat spasmed; his mouth opened, but nothing came out. He stood abruptly and turned away, but not before I recognized the pain of loss in his eyes, felt an answering twist of my own heart. Mom. Three. Both gone forever, because of me.

"Are the memories normal?" he asked gruffly, his back still to us.

"What's normal?" Quinn said. "We're talking cutting-edge science, prototypes. There is no normal. Only what is."

"The problem is, Holland didn't make all of your features as effective as I could have—of course not. The original research wasn't his, and he had to rely on the scientist who came after me to follow my notes."

The scientist who came after. I looked at Jensen, my heart twisting. "That would be Mom."

"Nicole and me, yes. We worked from Quinn's notes and diagrams."

"But my grandmother taught me to always leave one critical ingredient out of a recipe you were sharing with someone, so the food was never as good as yours," Quinn said. "So you're not completely as I envisioned you. For the final steps, I'll need access to your brain center."

My brain center? At my stunned silence, she held up her hands. "Don't panic. It's all entirely up to you. For upgrades. I can upgrade your functionality, give you abilities you never had before. New defense systems. I can even help you overcome your emotions, if you choose. Think about it. No more pain, no more sorrow. Ever. I saw the way you looked at Hunter, back in the hall. That has to hurt," she said gently. "Your mom." I flinched. "Daniel. You deserve better. You didn't choose this life, and you don't deserve to suffer for it."

For a moment, temptation tugged at me, urging me to consider her proposition. No more pain. No more ache when I thought of Mom. No heart-crushing cascade of devastation when Hunter turned his back on me for good, as he inevitably would.

But, then who would I be? A version of Three? Hadn't that been what I'd yearned for, these past few days? Maybe ultimately, it would be for the best.

Something buried in the depths of my pseudo human heart rebelled. That was a coward's way out. Besides, I was just starting to feel accepted for the first time. Maybe life here would be bearable, good even . . . with my emotions intact.

Quinn must have read my decision on my face, because she sighed. "Well, just think about it, okay? It's your choice. There's no rush."

"Thank you," I said.

Daniel was staring at us again, his expression enigmatic. He opened his mouth as if to say something to me, then thought the better of it.

"Now, let me show you to the sleeping area. I've put you in with the rest of the gang—I hope that's okay?"

Unease brushed across my skin like a chilly breeze, but I nodded gamely. Even though everyone had been accepting so far, I was worried how they'd feel about a machine in their midst overnight. But then I pushed the anxiety away, determined not to succumb to that defeatist mind-set. This could be a brand new start, and I'd be stupid not to grab it with both hands.

She led us to a double door at the end of a tiny hall, which opened into a large, gym-like space. Completely empty except for cots clumped across the floor, in two separate groups. Each cot had a navy blue sleeping bag and a matching pillow, while duffel bags were tucked underneath.

Samuel, Dixon, and Abby were already in the room. "Well, look who's gracing us with her presence," Samuel said, in his booming voice. His grin told me he was teasing.

"Oh, man, I'm sorry, Mila. The only empty bunk is next to Abby's, and she snores like a freaking bulldozer."

"Shut up," Abby said, punching him in the arm.

Dixon paused midlaugh, eyes widening in an arrested expression. "Hey, do you even need to sleep?"

Before I could stiffen, Abby yelled, "Dixon!" She pulled her fist back to punch him again, but he darted away.

"What? No offense, Mila. I was just thinking how cool it would be if you didn't have to—think of all the practical jokes you could pull in the middle of the night."

He winked, and just like that, I felt included again. Crazy how something so small could be so reassuring.

Samuel groaned, sitting on his cot and pulling off his shoes. "She's not going to think of that regardless, because she's not five, you arse."

Abby pinched her nose and backed away. "Oh my god, could your feet reek any more?" She scooted over to me and patted a cot that looked freshly made. "Here's where you're sleeping—let me show you where we change."

I bit back a smile at their ridiculousness as I looked down at my stale clothes. "I, uh, don't think I have anything to change into."

"Oh, I loaned you a pair of sweats and a T-shirt—I figure we're close enough in size. They're under your cot."

I reached down and sure enough, there was a bag, holding a few items. I grabbed the makeshift pajamas from inside and clutched them tightly. Sharing her clothes, like I was any other girl. Her thoughtfulness ignited a wave of emotion and made my eyes burn.

"Thanks," I said, trying to swipe at my eyes without anyone noticing.

"Oh, Jesus. Not another crybaby like Abby. I tell you, that wee girl might be tough, but she cries whenever she sees a kitten. It's pathetic," Samuel joked.

"I'll show you pathetic," Abby shrieked, pulling off her

shoe and lobbing it at his head. He ducked, his laughter booming through the room.

"Ignore them, Mila. They can't help it if they're an inferior species. Men," she said, shaking her head.

As I followed her to the bathroom, I allowed another spark of hope to bloom, deep in my chest.

Welcome home, Mila, Quinn had said.

The spark fanned into a larger flame, and a newfound optimism lightened my footsteps. Maybe, just maybe, she'd been right.

When we came back, the room had filled up. I got a few curious glances, but mostly smiles. "Glad you made it here," said a brunette with the cot on the other side of mine.

I smiled.

After lounging back on my pillow, listening to Abby grouse about boys for the next fifteen minutes, the call came. "Lights out!"

"Five, four, three, two, one . . . ," Samuel counted, and on target, the room plunged into darkness.

Someone screamed, and I shot up.

Room scan: Activated.

But then the laughter that followed told me this was a regular occurrence.

Practical jokes. Right. That might take a little getting used to.

It took me a while for my sleeping algorithms to kick in,

but it wasn't because of all the sounds—the breathing, the tossing and turning, the creaking of cots. Well, maybe it was. But instead of finding the noises bothersome, I found them comforting. They reminded me that here, in this room, there were people who didn't find my very existence repulsive. They reminded me that I could have some sort of real life.

I rolled onto my side, the growing flood of warmth only slightly dampened by a bittersweet chill. For the first time, without Hunter, I didn't feel alone.

The next morning, I woke up, soft snores and heavy breathing alerting me that most everyone was still asleep. I slid from my cot and edged my way to the bathroom to change.

When I returned, the hall was restless with slow risers and whispers. Then, like a cannonball blast from nowhere came Samuel's deep boom of a voice. "WAKE UP, YOU LAZY BASTARDS!"

An instant later, the lights all turned on. The room burst to life with groans, threats, and good-natured insults.

"You survive your first night okay?" Abby asked, still snuggling into her sleeping bag and rubbing her eyes.

"Looks that way."

I followed her to breakfast, in the lounge room, where food was out buffet-style.

"Dude, I bet you could eat, like, a thousand sausages a

day and never put on any weight," Dixon said to me, stuffing his face with eggs.

Abby rolled her eyes. "And that's different from you how?"

"Good point," he said, after shoveling in another mouthful.

I smiled as I listened to their silly banter, and again, the sharp longing tugged at me. I let myself fantasize. I could be part of this. Or maybe I was grasping at straws, because the alternative was too grim to bear. Without Mom, without Hunter, I had no plans beyond here. Beyond now.

Somehow, my life had boiled down to this: without the Vita Obscura, I had nowhere to go.

Near the end of breakfast, Quinn sauntered into the room, looking trim and fresh in a pair of black riding pants and a fitted green sweater. She wore the same boots as yesterday. "Mila, can I talk to you for a moment?"

When we got to the hall, I noticed she had a duffel bag in her hands. My duffel bag.

She sighed. "I'm sorry to bother you when you're still settling in, but we're going to need to put you in your own room."

I took the bag she offered numbly. "Why?"

"I'm afraid that a couple of the crew complained about the sleeping arrangements. Don't worry, I'm sure it's just temporary, until they get to know you better. But we do some important work here, believe it or not, and I can't have them rattled. I'm sorry."

"What did they say?" The newfound thrill I'd felt, just this morning, punctured like a balloon, leaving behind an empty ache.

"Just that they were a little uncomfortable, for the time being."

I read between the lines. They weren't uncomfortable—I *made* them uncomfortable, with my otherness. So much for the acceptance.

Her hand fell on my shoulder. "I'm sure it's only a matter of time . . . and hey, you'll get a private room out of it. Everyone will be jealous, trust me."

"Can I ask who?"

She cleared her throat, looked at the floor. "I probably shouldn't tell you this, but I guess there's not any harm. Samuel was one of them."

Samuel. The person I'd felt so at ease with. That made it even worse.

But as she led me to my new bunk, I wanted to tell her I didn't want them to be jealous. I didn't want a private room.

All I wanted was someone, somewhere, to accept me for who I was.

Well, I supposed there was still one person. And that person was Quinn.

After she dropped me off, I curled up in the smallish

but cozy room, too upset to emerge and face everyone. It actually had a single bed with a comforter versus a cot, and a dresser, and a tiny nightstand. It was probably a closet at one time, converted into a makeshift bedroom. But I would gladly trade all of those things.

I lay down on the bed, stared at the ceiling, and mourned.

It must have been an hour before I heard his footsteps in the hall. Easy, familiar. But with a pace that faltered as they neared my doorway.

The sound of his approach alone was enough to make my pulse quicken to a thready thump-thump-thump beat. My heart, it would never care how much percent machine I was, or that it was manufactured in a lab. My heart craved, needed, felt. It begged for another chance with this boy. It insisted on feeling one hundred percent human.

On the other side of the door, the footsteps hesitated. I imagined him pressing his forehead against the wood, contemplating turning back. Hating me, yet maybe somewhere inside, there remained a glimmer of hope for us. A spark that wouldn't die, despite everything.

My hands curled into fists as I stared at the door and willed him to open it. And even though I'd steeled myself time and time again for the revulsion on his face, my heart, my stupid, needful, aching yet mechanical heart, clutched at a tiny speck of light. Maybe, just maybe, the fact that I was partly human would mean something to him. That look he'd given me in the hall, the brief words. He hadn't ignored me, or curled his lip, or looked right through me. I'd seen something flicker in his blue eyes. Emotion. Not hate, not anger. Something else.

If he could feel something, there was a chance for us.

But he had to make the first move. I'd promised myself that I would respect his wishes, even if that meant we never talked again. Never touched. Never laughed, or rode a Ferris wheel, never shared Slurpees or walked on the beach. Never kissed.

I rose on unsteady feet, took a halting step toward the door, then cursed my weakness. Waiting, waiting, waiting . . .

A soft knock finally sounded, and the sigh that escaped my lips was half sob, half laugh.

"Mila? It's Hunter."

His voice was soft, a little hoarser than usual. Raw. The sound formed a noose around my chest and tightened, bunching every bit of longing and need together, until I thought I might implode.

"Come in."

The door slowly pushed open, and there he was.

Even though I'd seen him briefly earlier, the sight of him there, in my doorway, all floppy hair and hesitant smile and anxious fingertips, drumming his thigh, made my entire body shudder.

He carefully edged inside, his usual confidence nowhere

to be found. His lips parted, like he wanted to speak, but no words came. But it was his eyes I watched with complete fascination. His eyes that made my heart begin to rev, slowly at first, but with an ever-increasing frequency. A pumping, beating, bursting beacon of hope.

Because his eyes, they weren't full of disgust, or fear, or even anger. No, in the depths of his faded blue eyes, I saw a longing that was echoed deep in my core. Or, if I were being poetic—my soul.

My feet demanded that I run to him; my arms wanted nothing more than to fly around him and never let him go. But it was always me, running to him. Always me, foisting myself on others—all except for Quinn. I couldn't force the choice this time. He had to come to me, freely.

Like I'd willed it so, he started to move toward me, his eyes locked with mine. Everything else in the room felt like it froze, like the world ceased to exist except for the two of us. One step closer, two. He was only a few paces away now, and then he paused.

Noooo!

The word rebounded in my head, so loud, I was surprised he couldn't hear it.

I braced myself for the rejection I knew had to follow.

"Maybe we could just start over. Hi, I'm Hunter Lowe. My parents are crazy people who take part in secret underground technology-stealing, and use me as their unwitting dupe to get info. Oh, and don't forget—I like really crappy TV."

He smirked, lifted a brow, and gave me a pointed look.

It was hard at first. Even now, knowing that he knew, that everything was out in the open once and for all, it was so incredibly, heartbreakingly, painfully hard to get the first words out. But once I started, the tightness in my chest eased. Like each word I spoke released a tiny bit of pressure, until nothing remained but freedom.

"Hi, I'm Mila, and I'm an android. I was made in a lab, but even though I'm mostly machine, I feel like a real person." The freedom was invigorating, so I continued. "I'm still figuring out who and what I am, how I work, what I need. Most of the time, I'm confused. But I do know one thing for sure. When I told you I loved you, I wasn't lying. You, Hunter Lowe, are the best thing in this crazy, messed-up life of mine. When I'm with you, I feel alive."

He reached out, and with one gentle finger, traced a line down my cheek. Then, both hands were gingerly cupping my face, and his smile was pure sunlight. "It's nice to meet you, Mila."

"How are you holding up?" I asked him. I knew all too well what he must be going through, and to be honest, he seemed to be handling things way better than I ever did.

"I think I'm in shock." His hands slipped away from my face and grasped my hands. "It's like I'm living in some kind of alternate reality, or like I'm watching myself from outside my body. I guess I don't quite know how to explain it."

"You don't need to," I said.

"I just want to pretend like this isn't happening. Like all of this is a dream and when I wake up, we'll be back in Virginia Beach."

We. I wasn't sure if I'd ever hear him say that word again.

Suddenly, a woman's voice called out from the hall. "Hunter! Peyton needs you."

Startled, his hands fell away from mine and he half-turned toward his mom, who continued her approach. "Can he wait a few minutes?"

She smiled easily. "I'm afraid not."

He turned back to me, and his smile, his wonderful lop-sided, off-kilter smile, reappeared. "Sorry. We'll talk more later."

"Okay."

He strode toward the door. "You coming?" he said, when he reached his mom.

"In a few. Quinn wanted me to pass on a few things to Mila first."

She walked into my room, and I hastily straightened my rumpled shirt, nerves aflutter. A silly, insignificant thing, I knew, but this was Hunter's mom, and even though I knew her to be the kind of person who would manipulate and con her own child, I still wanted to make the best impression possible. I'd sort of already blown the whole totally-normal-girl thing by virtue of being an android and all, so I had to try to make up with brownie points wherever I could.

"Would you like to sit down?" I said, darting over to pull out a chair. Her hand on my shoulder stilled me.

"Why don't we both sit down here?"

I lowered myself gingerly to the bed next to her and waited while she did the same.

"Are you settling in okay?" She fidgeted on the edge of the bed, her gaze darting toward the door.

I shrugged. I noticed a lightness in my shoulders, my posture, as if a massive burden had just been lifted. Hunter and I might have a long way to go to reclaim our fledgling relationship, but at least the potential was there.

"Better than expected, all things considered."

Her smile reminded me of Hunter's: slightly off-kilter, but full of genuine warmth. "Good, I'm glad." She patted me on the shoulder before returning her hands to her lap. She inhaled and the smile fled.

I frowned. "What's wrong? Does Quinn have bad news?"

The hands in her lap clenched tightly. "Actually, I'm afraid I do. Mila, I wanted to get you alone because I wanted to talk to you about Hunter. Has he told you anything about his past?"

"You mean, about his real dad?"

She nodded. "So you know. Good. I think that will make what I have to say easier." She smiled again, but this time, her eyes were sad. "Mila, I see how you feel about Hunter, and how he feels about you."

She paused, and I sat quietly, trying to pretend like my stomach hadn't just flipped with joy. How he felt about me? Did that mean he still felt the same way?

She gave a harsh sigh and appeared to square her shoulders. As if prepping herself for something. "I see it, and it just can't go on."

My stomach crashed hard. "What do you mean?"

She averted her gaze. "I think you know what I mean. Hunter's been through a lot. His dad, who's a horrible human being; adjusting to a stepdad; then this, which I'm sure he sees as another betrayal. He deserves a chance at a normal life, a happy life. He might seem strong to you, but I've seen the wounds his father left on him. They run deep."

I curled my fingers into the bedding, my throat tightening. "But I would never hurt him—"

"Not on purpose, I'm sure," she interjected. "But haven't you already hurt him, by lying?"

One strike to my heart.

"What about his arm?"

Two.

"Didn't you put him in danger, by not telling him the truth?"

A stab, right in the middle.

"Maybe we weren't a threat, but General Holland certainly is."

Skewered.

I opened my mouth to protest, but there were no words. No defenses. Even though some of what she was saying was pretty hypocritical.

"Look, I know this must be hard for you, and I'm sorry to be the one to deliver the news. But deep down, surely you understand. He deserves a girl he can really love, someone more . . . like him. Someone who doesn't bring turmoil to his life, like his father did. If you really care for my son, I'm asking you, please . . . let him go."

As she spoke, it was like her eyes begged me to forgive her. But there was nothing to forgive. Nothing except the truth.

And the truth, as I'd come to learn, didn't care how it made you feel. The truth could be brutal.

No, no arguments from me, because deep down, I did understand. Deep down, I knew she was right.

Hadn't I been telling myself the very same thing, all along?

I'd known involving Hunter was selfish. I'd known I'd risked his safety. I'd known that we shouldn't be together.

But I'd wanted so, so badly for the logic to disappear. To just surrender to my emotions so I could revel in the way he made me *feel*.

I bowed my head. I'd been making choices all along, but none of them were based on truth. The truth was, I was bad for Hunter. The truth was, I had to let him go. But not before I asked her an important question.

"Why did you?" I said simply.

Her right eyebrow raised in a high arch. "Why what?"

"If Quinn wanted me so badly, why didn't you just take me as soon as you figured out I was at the Dairy Queen? Why did you encourage Hunter to get to know me?" I noticed how her face stiffened with each elaboration, but I kept going, hoping that she'd set the record straight although I was making her squirm. "I just . . . don't understand any of it."

"We were just following the directive," she said, coolly.

"What does that mean?"

"I wish I could tell you. Hunter, too. He asked me all the same questions." I felt a hand curl around my shoulder and squeeze. "Quinn's the only person who can give you that information."

The bed creaked as she stood, and I heard her footsteps retreat to the door.

Without lifting my head, I called out flatly. "Did she even really need anything?"

"Yes," she said softly. "She wanted me to tell you that Daniel is gone."

That pulled my head up. "Gone? Gone where?"

She gave a flutter of her hands. "He left. She said he told her that being near you was just too hard, given . . . well, you know."

I didn't respond. I just bowed my head back into my hands and let the pain wash over me. I hadn't admitted to myself until this very moment that I'd held out hope for rekindling some kind of relationship with Daniel. Stupid, I knew that. He'd never see me as a daughter, just like Hunter would never see me as a girlfriend. Because everyone could see clearly what I never could, until this very moment. I wasn't human, and I never would be. And the human parts I did have? They were useless. No, worse than useless. Damaging. Everyone I cared about or who cared about me got hurt in the end. Mom. Lucas. Hunter. And now Daniel.

But where did that leave me? What did I have left? Besides pain—this terrible, gaping, ragged-edged pain?

My breaths came in short, aching gasps as I grappled for something, anything, to dull the agony. I wished I could just suck out all this pain and bury it in a hole somewhere. All of my hope, gone. I'd been fooling myself all along. No one would ever accept me as I was. No one would ever love me for me.

I punched the bed, over and over again, until the mattress

was nothing but a mass of holes. What a waste all of this was. So much feeling, amounting to nothing. If only I could channel it into something productive.

If only I could keep my heart from feeling like it was being shredded, strip by strip.

Then I remembered. Quinn. She had relief for me. She had a purpose. A cause. All I had to do was undergo her upgrades, and then Holland, the person who'd sent me down this rabbit hole of despair, who caused everyone around him to suffer without remorse, would pay. If I was selfish, then he was a supreme narcissist of the first order.

If I couldn't have Hunter or a real human life, then my feelings were worthless anyway. A painful, haunting reminder of everything I couldn't have. How could I possibly think of anything when I could swear my heart was cracking, cracking, cracking, into a million tiny fissures that would eventually crumble into dust? How could I think logically when my entire being felt like it might splinter in two?

My emotions, I couldn't function with them. Couldn't breathe, couldn't think.

Quinn had been right, all along. My emotions had to go.

"I think you're making a very wise decision. I'm so proud of you," Quinn said, as she readied me on the table an hour later. "Your emotional reactions are crippling, and there's no need for that. This way you can focus on Holland. You won't feel the guilt over Nicole's death."

Not just Mom's death. Three's, too. A part of me I hadn't known about, until it was too late.

Both of those things, my fault.

No. Holland's fault.

As I sat there, my initial misgivings gave way to a deeper, primal urge. A growing thirst, to claim whatever knowledge Quinn had to bestow. Ultimately, upgrades meant power, and power meant a better chance at punishing Holland.

I would allow Quinn to vacuum out my feelings—my despair, my pain—and gladly. They hurt. They hurt so incredibly much. And in their place, I would take Holland. His reputation, his life, everything he had. It was no more than he deserved.

"Are you ready?"

Upgrades. Improved functionality. Emotional control.

Lessening the pain.

Though I knew I should keep my guard up, I felt myself being dragged under her spell. I raised glazed eyes and nodded my assent.

"Ready," I answered.

Ready for the new, improved Mila. Ready to stop hurting, once and for all.

Hunter's face flashed through my mind, igniting a deep yearning. I curled my toes. Yearning never amounted to anything good. It led to pain and disappointment, destruction and death.

The only thing I wanted to yearn for anymore was revenge.

I tucked my hands into my lap, tucking away any last misgivings at the same time. I wasn't Sarah. There was nothing here to save.

"Quinn? We ready?"

Samuel appeared, looking a little worse for wear. His shirt was rumpled, and red lines zagged in the whites of his eyes.

"Yep. Perfect timing."

He paused a couple of feet from the table. "Are we . . . are you sure about this?" he asked. The question seemed directed at Quinn, but he was staring at me.

Slowly, deliberately, Quinn pushed to her full height. Despite her small stature, her posture suggested fangs coiled beneath the pretty exterior, just waiting to strike. Obviously, she didn't like being questioned by her subordinates. "We are both completely sure, thank you, Samuel," she said. A sharpness cut the pleasantness of her words.

He ignored her, though, and continued to stare directly at me. He lifted a red brow, as if prodding for an answer. I didn't understand why he would care. Not after how he'd had my sleeping arrangements changed. I guess maybe I didn't make him uncomfortable here, in the lab. "Yes."

His shoulders slouched a little, before he straightened. "Fine. Let's get this going," he said, suddenly all business.

Quinn watched him as he fiddled with instruments, before sighing. "This is going to work out for the best. For all of us. If Holland thought I'd just step aside and look pretty and take what he dished out, he misjudged me by a mile."

"That's your personal vendetta," Samuel muttered almost inaudibly under his breath.

Quinn's breath caught, and her expression turned stormy. I thought she'd say something, but she surprised me by glancing at me and letting it go.

"All right, then. Let's get these upgrades in."

Upgrades. Once again the word rolled through my head, and deep inside me, a hunger awakened. Once upon a time, any mention of android functions would have sent shame coursing through my manufactured veins. Now, all I felt was strength.

My mind wandered off as they got to work. I heard Quinn talking, off and on. Telling me how Holland had actually contacted her to see if she could help with his missing "project," as he called me. Telling me we were going to expose him for the fool he was, and get him where it hurt via public humiliation. Telling me not to worry, that everything would be okay. Telling me that I wouldn't have to endure emotional pain again.

Maybe in the end, we'd both be satisfied.

At the very least, I wouldn't be hurting.

"Okay, part one has been taken care of. Now, on to the next. Time to change your emotional settings."

Emotional settings. I thought of Hunter, of Mom, and triggered a cascade of pain.

I was ready to embrace the numbness.

"We're not turning your emotions off, mind you, just containing them with a new microchip. Building a high threshold for all of the emotions that might hinder or hurt you."

Abby's teeth flashed as she chewed on her lip. "What's the point of this?" She'd joined in partway through the procedure.

Quinn didn't spare her a glance. "She's suffering, that's the point. Do you think that's helpful, or even necessary?"

"But you're saving some of her emotions?" Abby asked.

"Oh yes. Anger. And hate. Those two emotions will give her the fuel she needs to carry out this task."

As I listened to her words, I wondered—was what she was saying possible? Could she somehow press a few buttons, implant a switch, and then, bam! My pain would go away? Did I definitely want this, assuming it was going to work? Should I want this?

I thought of Mom. Of Sarah. Of the part of me I'd killed. A fist grabbed my heart, squeezed the life out of it, and I concluded yes. I'd give anything to make it all go away.

Quinn's gaze was watchful, almost like she could see the conflict going on inside me. "Don't worry," she said. "We'll best Holland at his own game. Succeed where he failed. Don't you think it's time he paid, for what he did to your mom?"

Not only Mom, but the way he'd pitted me against Three, against myself. And suddenly, it *was* all too much to bear. Watching as Mom died. Watching as Three—Sarah—melted into oblivion.

There was Jensen and Mom, memories I could feel but never touch. And then there were the memories I could touch but wished I'd never seen. Blood. Death. There was me, wasting my precious time with Mom by acting surly.

There was even a girl I didn't know but whose life was forever entwined with mine. Together, they clamored inside of me, making me feel, hurt, yearn, and bleed, and yet I didn't have real blood, and suddenly it wasn't okay, it was too much, with overwhelming tides of despair, dragging me under, gripping my ankles and pulling me down until I had no hope of surfacing again.

Too much.

I wanted it gone. I wanted all of it gone. The idea that for once, I could banish these feelings that dragged me down into a sinkhole of despair, sounded like my salvation. I was an android, and now my human ties had been severed. I didn't want the emotions to remind me of what I had lost. Of how much that loss crushed me.

Sarah. The name whispered through my head, as if chastising my choice, and I wavered. Part of me was human, after all. Part of Three had been human. And I'd killed her.

My hands clenched.

Quinn frowned. "Think of Holland. Or revenge. Of how very much you hate him."

The emotions flared readily, the second I summoned Holland's face. I hated him, with every fiber of my being.

"Good. Perfect. Now, sit very still," Quinn said. She shifted a few needles, this time near the back of my skull, and went back to her computer. I heard clicking, and then felt something warm and hard pulsate through my head, concentrated just on one tiny area. An electrical buzz followed, wrapping netlike until it encircled that entire portion of my brain.

Quinn fiddled with the buttons as the net tightened. Other members of the group came and went, all except for Abby. She stayed by my side, twirling a wisp of blond hair around her finger, her eyes steady. Occasionally, she'd frown, but mostly she just sat and watched. Silently.

Finally, Quinn must have been satisfied with the data on her screen, because she stretched her arms and stood. "I think it's all in place. Mila, how do you feel about losing your mom?"

I felt the niggling of something, a momentary pang. But it was like something was pressing it back, keeping it dormant, until nothing remained but a pleasant numbness.

Somewhere, some tiny voice whispered in my head, telling me to fight this sudden onslaught of apathy. But any time I tried, it was like I hit a ceiling, like my emotions banged against cage doors until they dissipated. And once the calmness descended, I wondered—why fight that? Why fight something that made me more in control, more logical?

"Fine," I said, easily. I detected no trace of turmoil.

"Wonderful. This is going to work out so well. Now I just need to run a scan and we'll be all set for the next one."

She detached a handheld scanner, akin to the ones I saw used at the airport, and started running it up and down my limbs. She paused over my abdominal area, a perplexed wrinkle above her nose. "Samuel . . . ?"

"Yeah, got it." Silence for a moment as he withdrew the needles from my scalp, and then, "Can you move that a little to the right?"

She complied. "What is it?"

"Come over and take a look." His voice sounded grim.

"Is everything okay?"

More silence. Finally, Quinn spoke. "Fine. Everything's fine. Just a glitch with the system. Now, on to the next one."

I heard Samuel shuffle his oversized feet. "I don't know—" he started, but Quinn cut him off.

"I do. We still have the last upgrade, and then we'll be good to go."

"Next upgrade?"

"Hop up and let's go," she said, ignoring my question. I did as she asked, following her out of the room and into the next door down. A tiny space, this one. And bare, except for a steel cupboard. Samuel followed, and as I took a seat on the low table, his brow wrinkled.

"You sure about this?" he said in a low voice, eyes never leaving my face.

Quinn withdrew some kind of thick dressing-gown-like garment and pulled it over her head. It was padded and stiff. Like a shield of some kind.

"Don't worry, everything will be fine." Then, she reached into her pocket and plunked a headset on top of her head, adjusting it until she gave a satisfied grunt.

But it was clear that Samuel wasn't sure everything would be fine.

"Hang on, Mila, we're going to put you in sleep mode for this one," she said.

She opened the steel cabinet, plucked a different helmet from inside. This one was solid, thick. After settling it on my head, she connected it via a wire to something inside the cabinet. All of a sudden, I felt something push at my skull, forcing its way in, building intense pressure inside. And then, I felt an intrusion burrowing into my mind.

Sleep.

A snapshot of the room appeared before me. Then, all of a sudden, it was like I'd drifted off to a different level of consciousness. I could see the room, see Quinn and Samuel, but couldn't comprehend anything. It was like I was just there, in a dormant state. A hibernating bear, waiting for the first signs of spring to erupt so I could erupt as well.

TWENTY-ONE

Reboot.

I came to on the couch in Quinn's lounge. As awareness returned, I noticed that something seemed off with my body. I felt heavier, somehow. Weighted. And in the back of my mind lurked a foreign presence. Hidden, but seething with untapped power.

That should have worried me, but . . . nothing. No pinch, no twist of anxiety. Everything felt smooth, serene. I pushed myself into a sitting position and rose to my feet. Movement, coordination—my body appeared to be working just fine.

Walking around the room, I cataloged everything. All was as it had been before, except for one thing: the photo of Quinn and Holland was missing.

Heat flared in my gut, and my hands clenched. No anxiety, but apparently rage was still in my emotional repertoire. *Holland.*

A click sounded. I looked up, in time to watch the door open and watch Hunter walk in.

My body tensed for the pain, for the choking, stabbing sensation of loving someone you couldn't ever have. I braced myself against the sweep of joy that always rushed me at the sight of him.

Instead, I felt empty. Serene. Looking at him was like looking at a stranger.

I looked at Hunter's face, and I felt . . . nothing.

Not even relief.

"Quinn told me you underwent some kind of serious procedure. Are you okay?"

He crossed the room to stand before me, and then, after a hesitation, he muttered "screw it" and pulled me into a tight, one-armed hug.

I felt the weight of his arms, the pressure of his chest against mine. I could smell his scent of soap and sandalwood, and his breath, stirring my hair. I experienced all of those sensations and yet, deep inside me, there was no tug at my heart. No jab. There was just a pleasant emptiness. A true void.

I didn't lift my arms up to return the embrace. Why bother?

I just waited for him to finish.

Finally, he dropped his hands and stepped back, frowning. He narrowed his eyes, and I noticed their color. Light blue with a hint of gray, I thought clinically. Rarer than the majority of eye colors, but nothing unusual.

I remembered how staring into his eyes had once filled me with a sweet pleasure, but I couldn't recall the actual sensation of it. And while I understood the word *pleasure*, I didn't *feel* it. It seemed odd. Why would staring into eyes bring about any reaction other than noting pigmentation and percentages?

"What's wrong?" he asked, his gaze sweeping over me.

I shook my head. "Nothing." For once, it was finally true.

He studied me intently, as if searching my face for a sign. His feet scuffed the floor. He seemed agitated.

Odd.

"Are you mad because of my mom and stepdad? I swear, I had no idea about their real lives." His shoulders slumped. "Look, you have every right to hate me. You were right. I mean, I might not have been part of that group, but my parents . . . at first, they wouldn't tell me a thing, but I finally got some information out of them. They'd set everything up from the start. You were the reason we moved to Clearwater. When I told Peyton about spotting you at the Dairy Queen, he knew who I was talking about because they were there to try to get you back. But then they decided that it would be better to let me get close to you. To study you. They didn't know why your mom had stolen you. So, technically I was spying for them. Even though I didn't know it. And I'm sorry. I'm so incredibly sorry."

He reached out to touch my arm, and I let him. His fingers on my skin were cool. Light. They evoked nothing but a sensation of mild pressure.

"It doesn't matter," I said. My voice sounded even, empty. Almost robotic in tone, and yet it was a girl's voice, not the grating digitized sound I heard right after I got zapped.

"Is . . . is something wrong?" he asked, moving nearer.

I thought about it objectively, then shrugged. "No. Not that I'm aware of."

He dropped his hand to drum his fingers against his thigh. A nervous tic, I remembered. I made him nervous. Peculiar.

"Look, I know I reacted poorly to your news in the garage, and I'm sorry. But you have to understand what a shock that was for me. Sure, I knew you were different, but how could I ever possibly guess that you . . ." He trailed off, so I helped him by filling in.

"Were an android?"

"Exactly."

I shrugged again, unfazed. "Like I said, it doesn't matter anymore."

He cursed under his breath. "It does matter," he said, his eyes searing into mine. "Just because you're not what I expected doesn't mean all of my feelings just turned off. I was mad before, hurt that you lied, and yes, a little scared by everything, but I've had time to calm down. And what I realize is that . . . I still care about you, Mila. I'm not going to lie and say I know what that means, but I thought you should know."

He stood there, seeming to be waiting for me to respond. Something pinged at the back of my head, like I should have reacted to his speech. Felt . . . something other than mild uninterest.

He took a deep breath, then cradled my face between his hands. "We were going to run away together, remember?"

I remembered, but what I couldn't recall was why I'd ever thought that was a good idea. Me, running away with a human boy, to do . . . what, exactly? Ludicrous.

My heart remained gratifyingly steady.

"I'm afraid that plan is no longer going to work. It's extremely illogical."

Surprise widened his eyes, before his hands fells away. "What did they do to you?" he asked.

"Quinn upgraded me," I said simply.

His gaze skimmed my body, like maybe he could see them externally. "What kind of upgrades?"

My programming told me to smile, so I did. "She

removed my troublesome emotions, so I could be more efficient."

"She . . ." He trailed off, nostrils flaring. "You're joking, right? This is all some kind of practical joke."

"No," I said. "I don't find jokes amusing anymore."

Finally, whatever he saw, or didn't see, in my eyes must have convinced him, because he started shaking his head. "No. No, no, no." I watched him clinically as he expressed agitation by fisting his hands and pacing.

"How could you let her do that? You were fine—no, great—just the way you were!"

I blinked. "Your recollection of the past is faulty. You didn't like me once you discovered I was an android," I pointed out, to be helpful.

"I was wrong. And you're wrong, too. I'll prove it."

Then he crossed the distance between us, and his lips landed on mine with a fierce intensity. I allowed the kiss. I felt the sweep of his tongue, the heat of his mouth. The warmth of his skin against mine. Where before my body had wanted to curl and expand, where I had been aware of sensations throughout my body, now I felt—

—a memory triggered, of the first time Hunter kissed me. Something beat its wings inside that tiny block of my brain. Inside my chest, I felt my heart try to accelerate, buck against the tethers that held it steady. Pushing, harder and harder. The restraints tightened, and the rhythm subsided back to normal.

I left the sliver of sorrow behind. Painful feelings were unnecessary complications, and Quinn was right.

I felt nothing, and I was better off that way. To be fair, the warmth of his skin probably would be nice, had I been cold. But since cold didn't really affect me . . .

I was just stepping back to disentangle myself from his embrace when I heard the familiar drawl.

His drawl.

"What we are doing here today—"

I shoved Hunter aside and twisted around to face the monitors. Holland's broad, wrinkled face was reflected in each one as he explained the MILA project. The previous void inside me was now filled with a rush of hot, bitter concoction, desperate to erupt.

My hands fisted as I imagined his throat beneath them.

"Bastard!" I growled through clenched teeth.

My anger was palpable, liberating. At the moment, I had one purpose, and one purpose only.

I was going to destroy him.

"Excellent," Quinn announced.

I spun around to see her standing in the doorway, looking victorious. She smiled. "You passed my little test. The unnecessary emotions are gone, but rage remains."

"What did you do to her?" Hunter asked.

"I made her into what we needed her to be—a more efficient weapon."

Hunter sucked in an audible breath, and his focus

switched to me. "You . . . no. You can't . . . that's wrong! What about Mila?"

Quinn came over to drape a hand on my shoulder. "What about Mila? Don't you think she's better off now? What did she really have to care about, Hunter? You? A boy who abandoned her when he found out the truth? A dead mother, who's not even her true flesh and blood, not really? A father who can't stand the sight of her? I did her a favor."

"Don't pretend you did any of this to help her," he spat out, and she laughed.

"Okay, fine. Have it your way. I did it because we need her like this. We need to make Holland pay, and the upheaval that's going to cause will give us the perfect opportunity to steal more technology from SMART Ops. Ultimately, sacrificing Mila's emotions is just a tiny price to pay."

"It's not your choice to make!"

"Ah, but you see? I didn't make the choice. Mila did. She had to, or else the enhancements might not have worked. Her brain is too complex to adjust emotionally if she'd been fighting it."

Quinn squeezed my shoulder, then barked an order to someone out in the hall. "Teek, come take Hunter away now. Make sure they're all situated for the final test."

Teek came inside, brandishing a gun. Hunter, his eyes on me, slowly raised his hands in the air. "Don't let them do this to you, Mila. Please." His voice was incredibly soft. Pleading.

The sight of the gun aimed at his head made something in mine twinge in an unpleasant way. A different gun, a different person. Mom. The pain bucked harder against the restraints this time, and for an instant, I felt a pang. It was gone so fast, I wondered if I'd imagined it. Something about its absence seemed wrong, but I couldn't put my finger on why. The numbness flooded me again, and I succumbed to its seductive embrace.

Teek motioned with the gun and Hunter exited the room.

What a silly comment was my thought as he walked away. Clearly the procedure had already been performed.

"Where's Daniel?"

She watched me carefully. "Daniel is here, but he's . . . incapacitated at the moment. We need him to run the final test, to ensure your emotional upgrades are working perfectly."

"You lied?" I said. A tiny spark flared, but it died quickly. The truth was, I didn't really care about Daniel, so her lying about him didn't impact me one way or the other.

"For your own good," she said. "To make sure we could better reach our ultimate goal." She nodded at the monitors, where Holland's face was frozen, front and center.

The familiar rage filled me, and I nodded curtly. That was acceptable.

We waited for Teek to radio and let us know they were ready. He did a few minutes later, so I followed Quinn to a doorway that led to a room I'd yet to investigate.

At first, all I saw was an empty room. But as we passed through the narrow entrance, the space widened and revealed what was inside.

Or rather, I was inside.

Surprise slammed my chest, catching me off guard, but subdued quickly as it hit the boundaries of my chip. On the far left side sat four chairs, positioned neatly in a row. And in those chairs were four people. Not just Daniel, as I'd expected, but Sophia and Peyton.

And Hunter.

None of them uttered a word at my appearance, and for good reason. All four of them were gagged, their wrists and ankles bound with thin but sturdy-looking twine.

Perplexed, I frowned at Quinn. "What's this all about?"

Quinn waited for the door to close behind us before strolling casually over to a barren counter. On top rested one metal box. The clasps snapped when she opened it, and the next moment, she withdrew a gun. All traces of amusement had faded from her face, and for the first time in a while, her expression tightened into serious lines.

After staring at the gun for several long beats, she walked back over to stand before me. "This is the final test, Mila. We need to know that the chip works, under all conditions. As it turns out, all of these people know too much, and we need to restrict our liabilities. So it's a win-win situation."

A win-win situation? "I'm sorry, I'm still not following."

With the utmost care, she placed the gun in my palm, gently pressing on my fingers until they curled around it. "It's simple, really. You'll see soon enough. Teek, can we get the live feed going?"

Teek sat behind a work desk, his fingers flying away. "Three, two, one . . . we're live."

Quinn looked up at the monitor on the far wall. The picture burst to life, showing me with the gun, Quinn, and the four prisoners.

Teek must have activated the video camera. But I still didn't know why.

"Now, can you pull Holland up, on the other monitor?"

"Almost there . . . here we go!"

The monitor to the left flickered, and then suddenly, Holland's face appeared.

He scratched his head and scowled into the screen. "I can't see anything. What's going on, Quinn?"

The fire kindled in my core. Not a video this time. Live feed.

Live.

A snarl rose in my throat, vicious and fierce.

"Can you hear me?" Quinn asked.

Holland frowned. "I can hear you, but I can't see a damn thing. I don't know why the hell we had to do this, anyway. Can't you just use a phone like a normal person?"

"Now?" Teek asked.

Quinn nodded once.

I knew the exact moment Holland saw me, because he half-rose, his square jaw going slack. "*Son of a bitch*," he mouthed. "You found her! How did you—wait, tell me that later. Why the hell isn't she locked down? Get her restrained, and I'll—"

"You'll sit your ass back in your chair and listen to something besides your own voice for a change," Quinn said.

Holland's throat spasmed, and his cheeks turned a blotchy, angry red. But wisely, he sank back into his chair.

"What are you playing at?" he whispered. His eagle eyes were trained on me.

The beast inside me bucked, twisted, rose in a blistering inferno. Every cell in my body was aware that just a few feet away, on that video screen, sat the person I loathed most in the world.

My fists tightened, my legs tensed to pounce. Seeing him so close made all the dark feelings pound my skull, summoned the bitter need to squeeze every bit of life from his sadistic body. Watch him bleed out the way Mom had.

"I'm not playing at anything," Quinn said. She strolled over to me, rested one manicured hand on my shoulder. "I'm showing you up. For the record, we're recording every detail of this transaction. Ah, not so fast. If you sign off, the events will still happen as planned, but instead of giving you options, I'll be forced to release a video of your epic failure to all of your superiors. To the DOJ. To the entire country, actually. The damage will be done, even if you don't stick around to see it. At least if you stay tuned, I'll give you a choice."

Beneath the surface in my head, something powerful coiled, biding its time. Eager to be unleashed.

I would rain destruction down upon Holland's head, and I would enjoy it. I would fill this empty hole inside me with his pain for once. His suffering.

Holland stood by, shoulders back, trying to appear impassive. "You schedule some kind of freak show?" he said to Quinn, but I noticed that his teeth clenched down on the gum he'd been chewing, and he was scratching his palm with his index finger. An obsessive, repetitive motion.

"This man is General Holland, with the U.S. military," she started, staring right into the camera.

"He's been trying to hide something from the American people, and I think it's time they knew the truth. This man not only created a multimillion-dollar weapon in robotic science, he let it escape, putting all of you in danger. Then he tried to cover up the escape—you know why? Because he cares more about saving his own ass than he does about anything else."

Holland sat motionless, shoulders back. But his cheeks were pooling with blood again, flushing a bright red.

"This girl, right here?" Her fingers dug into my shoulder. "She might look like a normal teen girl, but she's not. She's dangerous. A weapon. An experiment in robot science. Mila, show the camera your USB port."

The video camera whirred as Teek typed in the command for a close-up.

"Now for a demonstration on exactly how out of control the general is with his expensive piece of equipment. Mila, show him the gun."

I lifted the gun high, let Holland inspect it.

"Now, this is the part that I love the most. General Holland isn't just an out-of-control egomaniac, he's also a common thief. He stole this project from me, years ago. My ideas, my research. He created this android, the MILA 2.0, to have emotions. But he and his team messed it up. They gave her too many, made her feel too much. She escaped once, and when he got her back, he realized his mistake and tried to rectify it. He couldn't, of course. So, I've fixed what he couldn't. I took all of the emotions that were hindering Mila out, and in doing so, made her the efficient weapon that General Holland here couldn't create. We're going to demonstrate that now. Teek, pan in on the prisoners."

The camera swept over the four bound and gagged hostages, and Holland swore.

"What the . . . ?'"

"So, here's what's going to happen," Quinn continued,

ignoring him completely. "Mila is going to execute the prisoners, as a little demonstration of my success. Of course, you can keep that from happening at any time by giving me the access codes to the intel accounts."

Execute the prisoners. Why did that sound so very wrong? At the same time something dark twisted inside me, I watched a bead of sweat trickle down Holland's craggy face. The sight of him squirming created a power surge, deep within my core. For once, I was in control.

"Jesus," he breathed. "You're the Vita Obscura."

She tossed her hair and laughed, putting her hands together for three slow claps. "Ah, he finally sees. I knew you'd figure it out eventually."

"Extortion, Quinn? That's what you've resorted to? You know I can't give you those codes."

She shrugged, a dainty motion. "Then I guess they'll all die, and I'll be forced to release this footage. Kiss your career—really, your entire life—good-bye."

Another trickle of sweat joined the first. "You'll never do it. It'd mean signing your own death sentence."

Her eyes glittered, and her smile bared her teeth. "Then I'll die happy, knowing I took you down with me. I'm willing to take that risk. I have followers who will continue on in my name, freeing technology and bringing it to the people. Stopping megalomaniacs like you from acquiring power."

Conviction rang in her voice, and her chin remained up.

This was no bluff, I thought clinically. Even from whatever distance away and through a TV screen, Holland could see that.

Quinn left my side to stand in front of the prisoners. "Now, who goes first?" she said, her gaze inspecting them one by one. "I think we'll start with someone easy, to give you time to warm up. Peyton," she announced, reaching down to pull the gag from his mouth. "Any last words?"

He turned his head to look at Sophia, who had tears leaking down her cheeks, and then Hunter, who stared ahead stoically.

Another ping in my head, this one stronger. The restraints subdued it immediately.

"I'm sorry," Peyton rasped. "Hunter, you were right. I shouldn't have gotten any of you into this."

I watched the tableau, felt another burst of emotion, of absolute wrongness. My skin went frigid, before the sensation was zapped into oblivion. Then . . . blissful emptiness. My gaze swept over to Daniel, who met my eyes unblinkingly. He didn't look frightened or alarmed. He looked . . . sad. And even though it probably wasn't true, I had a feeling his sadness wasn't for him, but me.

I blinked and shook my head. What an odd thought.

"Mila, if there's any of you left . . . I'm sorry I made such a huge mistake. Please, don't do this. Not in front of my family."

A pretty speech. I could admire the honesty.

Quinn nodded at me, encouraging me to proceed. "You know what needs to be done," she said softly.

My fingers tightened on the gun and released the safety. A pretty speech, but for me, a wasted one. Across the way, I saw Samuel wince and turn his head.

Hunter came to life then, thrashing against his restraints. His words were stifled by the gag, though. In the subdued part of my brain, a voice tried to cry out. This was wrong. So very wrong. But I couldn't feel why, and without emotion, I couldn't fight it.

Something screamed from a deep, buried place, urging me to break free of whatever shackles Quinn had used to tie me down. But every time sympathy or guilt surged, to provide me with incentive, it receded just as quickly.

I felt like I should care, like I was missing a key component here.

"This is what happens when the government can't control its technology, and won't share with the people. They get in over their heads. They create a danger for all of us. We're going to show you exactly how dangerous they really are."

Her voice swept across the room, growing louder and louder in her fervor. Her hands reached out, as if beckoning to the masses to join her.

"The government is failing you. The military is failing

you. If I could steal this weapon so easily, don't you think our enemies could? We need to make the government quit making decisions on our behalves, and quit trying to control all the technology. Technology should be free."

She inhaled, then said, "Sometimes, to make a point, we have to make sacrifices. Mila, please aim the gun at Peyton."

Without concern, my fingers gripped the gun tightly. My hand raised the weapon upward, in a slow and steady arc, until the barrel pointed right at the center of Peyton's forehead. The air was heavy with fear and sweat, and beneath the gag, I could hear a low, muffled whimper from Sophia.

"Quinn, this is insane! You've proved your point. We'll take you back—I'll even acknowledge your role in the research. Let's talk about this," Holland bellowed, but Quinn ignored him.

I ignored him, too. Because I was pointing a gun at someone's head, and instead of feeling terrified, or sad, or any of those awful, draining things, an electric-like energy surged through my limbs. Power. Right now, I had it. And I wasn't about to give it up.

"Last chance. Holland, do you want to give me the codes?"

Silence on his end.

Quinn sighed. "I'm sorry, Peyton. Hopefully you find it comforting knowing that your death will help further the cause."

Peyton swallowed, and closed his eyes.

"Fire."

Without emotions to hold me back, it was a simple thing. Cake. I simply squeezed the trigger, and sent the bullet flying. A small red circle bloomed in the middle of Peyton's forehead, before his entire body jerked back against the chair. A moment later, he slumped, while somewhere behind me a girl shrieked.

I stared at him, and something dark writhed around inside me. Something was wrong here, I could sense it. But the feeling kept getting subverted under the barrier in my mind. Security, holding everything in check.

"Oh my god. Oh my god, oh my god," someone repeated between sobs. Abby. Then came the sound of shoes, hitting the floor fast. Racing away.

"Holy shit, Quinn! That gun wasn't supposed to be loaded! What did you do?" The roar of protest came from Samuel.

"Change of plans," she said. "Did you really think Holland would be impressed by a pretend show of force? Please. Like I said, sacrifices have to be made sometimes to reach the final goal."

"Not like that," Samuel whispered, his horror-struck gaze bound to Peyton's limp form.

"Yes, just like that," she snapped. "Whatever it takes. You can't be a revolutionary if you aren't willing to have losses. Grow up, Samuel."

Silence ticked by, broken only by Sophia's moans. Nearby, Hunter stared straight ahead, at nothing. Almost as if he'd shut down.

My pulse continued to beat at its normal pace.

"If this is what growing up is all about, I'm done here." With that, Samuel turned and walked, his footsteps heavy.

"Don't even think about coming back with a weapon, Samuel. I've got guards stationed outside," Quinn yelled after him. Silence greeted her.

"Now, on to the next." She stalled in front of Hunter for a bit, then turned to Daniel instead. "Daniel next, I think. We'll save the hardest for last."

She removed his gag. "How about you? Any last words for your makeshift daughter? How poetic, really. That a part of Sarah will be responsible for ending your life. After all, you and Nicole were responsible for creating hers . . . and Mila's."

I listened without interest, waiting for her to finish so I could get on with it.

Daniel didn't rise to Quinn's bait, instead focusing directly on me. "Mila, I made a mistake in turning you over to Quinn. Your mom would hate me right now for this . . . and she'd be right. She was always right." He paused, cleared his throat. "I'm sorry I didn't listen to her. No matter what happens, I want you to know—you are my daughter. I tried to reject that, because it hurt too damn much, but it's the truth."

His words resonated in me. I knew all about trying to reject hurt. I couldn't blame him.

"Listen, you need to fight it off. Sarah, if you're in there—please. Fight this. You're better than this. You've done a terrible thing, but if you carry her plan out entirely . . . there's no coming back from that. Do you hear me? You will never make it back with your soul intact."

I wanted to fight, but I couldn't. There was nothing left inside to give me the desire.

"I don't have a soul," I said. Again, a little tug at my heart, one that quickly subsided.

"Not true! If people have souls, then so do you. Mila? Mila, I hope you can hear me."

At first, I thought the voice was a figment of my imagination. Like I'd finally cracked . . . or I was just dreaming it into existence. But then I heard it again. A deep voice. A familiar male one.

Lucas? I formed the question mentally.

We don't have much time. I'm going to help you break free of this chip. Just . . . give me a second. In the back of my brain, where Quinn had poked with her needles, where the insert was, I felt something moving. Probing. A new presence.

"Quinn, there's a very special place in hell for you—right along with Holland," Daniel said, giving up.

She shook her head impatiently. "You don't understand. You never were a true believer. You go into revolution knowing that people will die. That's just how it works. You should die content, knowing you've furthered the cause. But you're just a coward, like most of them."

"This chip in your head, it's controlling everything. Your movements, your emotions. I'm trying, but you need to help. You need to feel to fight this."

How? How did I fight it? And . . . maybe I didn't want to. I didn't really want Daniel to die, but maybe . . . maybe it was easier than the alternative. At least when I shot him, it wouldn't hurt me inside.

And, to be honest, I didn't really want him to not die, either. My hand lifted, almost as if of its own accord.

Think of something powerful. Something—someone—that moves you. Your mom?

A drum pounded, in that spot in the back of my head. Harder. And harder. Mom.

The drumbeat grew stronger, throbbing against the constraints. The constraints held, but under the constant onslaught, I felt the tiniest bit of give.

Good, but that's not enough. Push harder. Think of the things that caused you to feel the happiest. Or the saddest. Whatever you do, just try to feel.

Mom, telling me to live with her last breath.

Hunter's lips, pressed to mine.

The beach, twirling with my parents, with the man standing before me. The man who I was threatening with a gun. Kicking water at Hunter, racing for the waves.

Rejection. Betrayal. Anguish.

Joy. Love. Belonging.

Hunter, asking me to run away with him . . .

This time, the pressure exploded, and a thin fissure raced through the confinement. Beneath the demanding swell of my caged emotions, begging to break free, I felt the barrier crack.

"Holland, are you ready to concede yet?"

Silence from the monitor.

That's it. I've almost got it—whatever you're doing, it's working. Don't stop. Good or bad, just keep it powerful.

His words awakened a startling realization. Not just love—pain. Not just joy—fear. In order to have the good, you had to also take the bad, because without the lows, the highs wouldn't, couldn't, exist. All emotions were crucial to living. All of them.

Wisps of Mom's blond hair, matted with blood. "I don't regret any of this."

In the fire, panicking, searching for Mom and Dad in a black curtain of smoke.

Joy. Love. Belonging.

"Okay, then. Mila, fire."

The pressure skyrocketed and the restraints splintered, just as my index finger twitched on the trigger. I saw Daniel's eyes flutter closed, his mouth droop with sorrow. Waiting for the bullet to strike.

No!

My heart froze, and terror clawed down my spine. I was going to be too late.

Mom. Hunter. *Love.*

Got it! Lucas exclaimed.

Security breach detected, flashed the red warning in my head.

Just as my finger pulled the trigger.

TWENTY-TWO

A split-second rush of static in my head, like the roar of a river. An instant rise in pressure. Then, release, as the chip exploded.

I jerked my hand to the side, away from Daniel. The bullet whizzed past his ear.

It wasn't until the feelings surged into the void, flooding me with a chaos of emotion, that I realized how much I'd missed them.

"How the—" Quinn began. She shook her head angrily. "Never mind. Auto-shutdown, activate."

It took a second to dawn on me what was happening, and that second cost me. By the time I understood, it was too late to fight the incoming command.

Auto-shutdown commencing.

Just before it happened, I thought I heard Lucas. *Mila? Are you okay?* But it was so faint—almost like a buzz. Then the buzzing grew, louder and louder . . . until a peaceful silence took it all away.

I was walking by the water, cotton candy sticky on my lips. My mom's hand ruffled my hair, which was thick with the salty scent of the sea. "Someone's going to need a bath tonight," she teased.

I whirled to stick out my tongue, and thrust my pink-sugared hands forward as if to grab hers.

She squealed and tried to run, but my dad grabbed her from behind, laughing. "Get her, Sarah. You know how she loves to be sticky."

I giggled as Mom tried to free her hands, but was distracted by someone yelling. A boy. He wasn't yelling my name, but it seemed . . . familiar.

"Mila! Mila, can you hear me? Wake up!"

I turned back to Mom and Dad, but they were already fading. The voice grew more insistent. "Mila!"

Panic crackled through me. I wanted my parents! Who was this person, and why had he taken them away?

Mom? Dad? I tried to shout . . . but nothing came. My parents' faces faded, faded, merged into one new face, a boy's. It looked familiar somehow, at home on the slowly disappearing boardwalk. Light blue eyes . . .

The scene vanished, leaving behind a searing heat.

Why was it so hot?

I opened my eyes . . . to a harsh glare. The sun. But way too bright for Virginia Beach.

My shoulder . . . it ached.

Then I saw a face, a boy's—but not the one from my memory. Everything came rushing back. I didn't have a mom and dad. I wasn't Sarah.

Except for one tiny piece of me.

"Lucas?" I tried, but the voice that I summoned sounded all wrong. Mine, but not mine. My human voice was gone, replaced by the dispassionate, robotic version that spoke in my head. My android voice.

Horror swam through my limbs, flooded my mouth. I flinched, or thought I did, but I felt . . . nothing. No movement at all. I tried to turn my head; it wouldn't budge. Frantically, I attempted to wiggle my fingers and toes. Nothing. It was as if they were no longer under my control.

The last events came rushing back, and with it, a crushing pain in my shoulder. Oh, god. Quinn. Hunter. The things I'd said to him, when my emotions were contained. Holland . . . wait. Holland's face was the last thing I remembered seeing. Was that when Quinn shorted me? But why? And what had happened to everyone else?

My body stiffened, as if bracing for a blow. Why couldn't I remember? The clutch of dread in my chest grew stronger, but I forced myself to remain calm. Patient. Just because I felt apprehensive about my memory lapse didn't mean anything terrible had happened. The information would return. I just needed a few minutes to recover from the shock.

Despite my sound reasoning, a shudder wracked my body.

There would be ample time later. Every single day.

"What . . . why can't I move?" I said. Or at least, the smooth, digital version of my voice spoke.

Lucas shook his head. "Too many reboots in too short a time. It's just going to take longer to get everything up and running. But don't worry," he said, hastily, "we will. I won't leave you like this."

I stared into his hazel eyes and saw nothing but determination. Confidence. No trace that he was lying. Lucas really believed he could fix me, and I believed in him. I studied him as best as I could. When I'd last seen him, he'd been bleeding, passed out. He looked none the worse for wear.

"This . . . has happened before. Without reboots. I've frozen up, for no reason. Called up memory fragments . . . of my mom. Of before."

His head jerked up. "Before? You mean . . . before you were an android?"

At my nod, his eyes widened. *Wow*, he mouthed. He stared off into the distance for a moment, as if concentrating. "We'll get to the bottom of this," he finally said.

He leaned over my neck, holding some gadget that made a series of clicks. I saw his sandy hair, all mussed and lopsided as usual, and felt the first stirrings of genuine warmth I'd felt since . . .

Hunter's face flashed through my mind, but his features were all contorted. A chill swept across my skin. Was the image real, or imagined? I shook off the image, determined to focus on the present. On what little I did know.

Lucas had rescued me, and for now, that had to be enough. I just hoped my memory would return. Soon.

Speaking of . . . "How did you get me away from Quinn and her men?"

Lucas's head shot up, his eyes round with surprise. "Get you . . . ? Mila, I didn't get you away. I mean, I was able to activate your tracer, and was on my way out to help . . . but then you moved. It took me two days to get to you, but I did."

"Moved?"

Sweat drops balled on his forehead, and he reached up to wipe them away. His hand slid to his cheek, then his jaw, which he rubbed while gazing out into the distance. "I found you here. In the middle of the desert," he said, sweeping his other arm wide. "They just . . . dumped you."

Dumped you. Like an old TV that had stopped working.

But Lucas sounded less disgusted over their behavior than concerned.

He returned to his device, to the clicking. As I waited, a heavy weight settled in my chest. Something was off. Lucas was usually more irreverent, more awkward. Right now, he was neither of those things—just deadly serious.

"What's wrong?" I asked. He flinched, and I knew I was right. He was hiding something. Maybe he was holding a grudge. He had plenty of reasons. "Holland didn't find out about you helping us, did he?" My voice remained robotic, but rose in volume, which somehow managed to convey my rising concern. "Are you okay? Are you—"

"What? No!" Lucas said, looking alarmed at first. Then his expression softened, and he gazed down at me with an odd tenderness. "I'm fine, I promise."

When he was satisfied I'd accepted his reassurance, he reached out, his hand hovering just above my cheek. "There's, uh, hair. On your face. Do you mind . . . ?"

Now there was the awkward boy I remembered. "Go ahead."

Gently, he pushed the strand back, tucked it behind my ear. His eyes were wary, uncertain.

"What is it?"

He sighed, glanced down at the device. "It's just . . . I don't get it. I don't understand why they'd just . . . leave you out here. I'm trying to make sure they didn't alter you in any way, or, I don't know . . . steal something. That's what I'm checking on right now."

He went back to the device, moving down my arms and legs.

"Quinn messed with my circuitry. She could have done anything."

"This will pick up anything unusual, but I still don't understand why she would leave you out here. You were her vision."

"Maybe she got pissed because we bypassed her emotion chip."

He smiled. "Yeah, you didn't turn out to be what they expected. But still it's odd."

He grew so quiet that I got antsy. "Anything?" I asked.

"Everything seems to check out so far. Now, I'm just going to insert this card into your neck port. I sort of . . . borrowed it from the lab before I left. It will run a systems check, make sure I didn't miss anything. After that, we should have a better idea of when you'll be able to move again."

Systems check. Systems check. That reminded me—a lot of weird things had happened since I'd last seen Lucas. Maybe he had some kind of explanation.

I opened my mouth, but he was already brushing the hair away from my ear, exposing my port. The same one he'd introduced me to, back at the compound.

"This shouldn't hurt at all," he said, lifting the card, which was attached to the device in his hand by a thin cord. "You ready?" The skin around his eyes crinkled with worry, and I managed a tiny smile.

"Yes. Thank you. Thank you for everything. Without you . . ."

He shook his head. "But there is no without me, so there's no sense in thinking about it." His free hand went to his collar, rolling it in a way that had grown familiar to me, even in our brief time together. He was anxious about something.

"What?"

"It's just . . . hang on." Oh so gently, he inserted the card into my neck. A tentative smile formed on his lips, which grew in magnitude, lending a softness to his usually angular face. He gazed down at me, and though his eyes were pretty with their green and gold flecks, it was his inner beauty that lighted them. "It's going to sound really lame, but I'm just so glad—"

Inside my neck, a spark of awareness, a surge of electricity. A sunburst of hot pain. I jerked, my face twisting, and I couldn't help but cry out, just a little.

"Mila, what the . . . what's wrong?"

Through hazy eyes, I watched Lucas punch frantically at buttons as the heat surged into my fingers, my toes. Screamed through my brain like someone had lit every last neuron on fire.

Dimly, I realized that it shouldn't hurt. The underlying sensations were exactly what I'd experienced every other time a card or USB or any type of digital device had been plugged into one of my ports. So why the pain now?

"Jesus. Hang on, I'm going to figure this out. I just . . . wow, look at that. I can't even . . . but that's a good thing . . ."

Suddenly, my arms twitched, and with a heavy, sweeping rush of energy, I could move them again. And my head. And legs.

"Hey, I can move." I frowned, feeling a strange sensation on my abdomen. I lifted my shirt partway, revealing a long incision. "Looks like someone tried to steal a kidney—bet they were disappointed," I joked.

But I shut up when I saw Lucas's face. Despite the last words he'd uttered, the color had drained from his cheeks, leaving him paler than usual, and his hands trembled. His mouth opened and closed, his throat clenched as he swallowed, then his mouth opened again.

"No. No, no, that can't be . . . damn it!" Lucas's words were choppy, choked.

In my head, a red light flashed.

Systems Check: Complete.

Functional.

But despite that seemingly good news, Lucas bowed his head before me. And then he shocked me by completely abandoning his usual calm and collected self by viciously slamming the device to the ground. Sand flew up, the tiny particles spraying like water.

I pushed to a kneel and reached for his shoulder, feeling his sharp flinch as my fingers landed. But he didn't pull away. Instead, he took an audibly deep breath and forced his head up.

And his incredible, sweet, compassionate eyes glittered with moisture.

"Just tell me," I whispered, as sharp talons of dread dug into my back.

"I . . . ," he started, shuddered, then tried again. "Do you want the good news, or the bad news first?"

"Good news." If only because he looked like he could use some.

He drew in a deep breath. "So, you remember that body scan we did, back in D.C.?"

At my sigh of impatience—did he think I could possibly forget?—he continued. "Well, things have changed since then."

"What things?"

"The good news . . . the good news is that some of your live cells appear to be regenerating."

Regenerating. Which meant—

"That explains the newfound pain. You're becoming more human."

More. Human. Everything I'd ever wanted . . . coming true. It felt like too much to believe and yet, deep inside me, a spark fired to life.

But I couldn't let it flare too brightly yet. "And the bad?" Though surely, surely it couldn't compare to the good. Lucas had to be overreacting—

"Well, Holland must have rigged the scan, too. He wanted to hide something."

He paused, closed his eyes—as if drawing strength. When he opened them again, he reached forward, taking my shoulders in his hands.

"I know why the V.O. ditched you. Holland . . . Holland hid a bomb inside you."

Around us, there was nothing—just mounds of sand and the whisper of the intermittent breeze, and in the distance, a few stray cacti. Lucas was talking, but for once, I couldn't focus. All I could see were Quinn's and Samuel's faces, frowning at something that showed up on my abdominal scan. All I could hear was that one word, beating a terrifying drum in my soul.

Bomb. Bomb.

Bomb.

"There's more. The V.O. must have primed it, somehow. The slightest provocation could set it off now."

I could feel a heart that wasn't really there, a pulse that didn't really exist. But somewhere, inside my body, an actual bomb ticked away, and I couldn't feel that.

"How long?" I whispered, not wanting to know and needing to know, all at the same time. "How long do I have, once it's set to go off?"

Lucas looked at me helplessly. "Two hours."

Two hours.

Lucas grabbed my hand, and I clung to it, fighting back the mounting despair. All this time, I'd been searching for the truth, when really, I should have known.

The most important truths were the truths I held inside me. Other truths could be manipulated, distorted. In some cases, even memories lied.

But the truth in my heart was pure. Real. And right now, it was telling me one thing.

I didn't want to die.

ACKNOWLEDGMENTS

This book was only made possible through the attention and care of many, many others. (In other words: HELP, I needed it!) Thanks so much to all of the wonderful folks at Harper, from copy editors to cover designers to media specialists—your enthusiasm for this series never goes unappreciated. Thanks to my editors and agent—I never would have made it through the hair-pulling sequel process without you. Thanks to my family for their support, even during such a challenging year—I love you. Thanks to the bloggers and readers out there, and the other YA writers—you all make our community great.

Finally, a special thanks to my friends, both writers and nonwriters. This past year has been challenging in ways I never would have imagined, and your support, strength, and compassion is what pulled me through. Thank you for being there when I needed you.